The Abduction of
Rosalind Thorne

Darcie Wilde is also the author of:

**The Rosalind Thorne Mysteries /
The Useful Woman Mysteries**

The Abduction of Rosalind Thorne

The Matter of the Secret Bride

The Secret of the Lady's Maid

The Secret of the Lost Pearls

A Counterfeit Suitor

A Lady Compromised

And Dangerous to Know

A Purely Private Matter

A Useful Woman

The Young Queen Victoria Mysteries

The Heir

The Abduction of Rosalind Thorne

Darcie Wilde

KENSINGTON
PUBLISHING CORP.

kensingtonbooks.com

KENSINGTON BOOKS are published by

Kensington Publishing Corp.
900 Third Avenue
New York, NY 10022

All Kensington titles, imprints, and distributed lines are available at special quantity discounts for bulk purchases for sales promotion, premiums, fund-raising, educational, or institutional use. Special book excerpts or customized printings can also be created to fit specific needs. For details, write or phone the office of the Kensington Special Sales Manager: Attn. Special Sales Department, Kensington Publishing Corp., 900 Third Avenue, New York, NY 10022. Phone: 1-800-221-2647.

Library of Congress Control Number: 2026935111

KENSINGTON and the K with book logo Reg. U.S. Pat. & TM. Off.

ISBN: 978-1-4967-5066-2
First Kensington Hardcover Edition: July 2026

ISBN: 978-1-4967-5067-9 (e-book)

10 9 8 7 6 5 4 3 2 1

Printed in the United States of America

The authorized representative in the EU for product safety and compliance is eucomply OU, Parnu mnt 139b-14, Apt 123
Tallinn, Berlin 11317, hello@eucompliancepartner.com

The Abduction of
Rosalind Thorne

PROLOGUE

Two Friends Out for a Stroll

*"What! Would I be turned back from doing a
thing that I had determined to do, and that I
knew to be right, by the airs and interference of
such a person, or of any person I may say? No, I
have no idea of being so easily persuaded."*

Jane Austen, *Persuasion*

Nathanial Spence stood idly at the edge of the market and
watched a man in an immaculately cut green coat attempt to sell a brown mare to a fool.

Normally he would have referred to such a horse as
"chestnut" or "bay," depending on the shade of its coat. This
horse, however, had been so thoroughly dyed—probably
with a mix of goose grease and boot blacking on a curry
comb—it was impossible to discern its true color. Even the
mane had been dyed. The dealer should be thanking his stars
that the rain had decided to hold off today, otherwise his purported thoroughbred would have more stripes than a zebra.

". . . sired from the line of Sir William Mulligan of County
Kildare," the dealer was saying. "Being a gentleman of the
turf, you'll have heard of him, certainly?"

The fool—a lean, pockmarked man with bushy whiskers and a bulbous nose—nodded his head sagely.

The dealer smiled. "Sir William's horses have won more prizes across Ireland than any other breeder. But he's been reluctant to begin selling in England. National prejudice, y'see. Doesn't believe the English know horseflesh. It's fallen to me to convince him otherwise. So, I can only sell to the *most* discerning gentlemen. That's why I've made no announcements in the papers. Now, our mutual friend assures me—"

It was an old fraud, probably one of the oldest, and the dealer was playing it well. Although Spence was absorbed in the patter, he still heard the man who came puffing up behind him.

"You're late, Mr. Wallace," Spence grumbled.

"My apologies, Mr. Spence." Wallace stepped up beside Spence. The day was relatively cool, but Wallace's face was still shiny with perspiration. "I was talking with a client. He wanted some additional reassurances, and I could not appear hurried."

The fool in front of them was pulling out his billfold. The dealer was writing up a bill of sale.

"Friend of yours?" Spence jerked his chin toward the dealer. "He's got your patter down."

"And he's welcome to it," Wallace replied. "It's a good scheme in a pinch, but frankly, it's exhausting, and far too dependent on the vagaries of the weather and the horse for my liking. Shall we walk?"

Spence nodded and strolled away. The bustle of the market enveloped the two men. Hawkers at their stalls and barrows bellowed to the shifting crowds. Everything was for sale—from chickens to cheeses, guns to goats. Summer had settled in and the warmth of the day was spreading, along with the miasma that came of so many people and animals packed together so closely.

Wallace fell into step beside him, silent except for his usual puffing. Wallace was tall, but stout. The slightest bit of effort seemed to leave him short of breath and turned his pink face bright red. This, however, was an asset to their mutual business. People assumed a stout, red-faced man must either be jolly or slightly foolish. Wallace could appear to be both at the drop of a hat.

Spence, on the other hand, would never fool anyone into thinking he was anything but what he was—someone who had spent his life working hard and living rough. His face was craggy and burnt brown by the sun. His shoulders were broad, and his hands were formed for hard labor, or fist-fights. His coat and shirt were plain stuff, and his breeches and boots were both work stained.

"Is there any news?" Spence kept his tone casual. "Were you able to talk to Sylvia?"

"I was," answered Wallace. "She says things are continuing smoothly with the family. Oh, and I've got a missive from your lady love here." He pulled the sealed letter from his coat pocket and handed it over.

"Thanks." Spence tucked the note into his pocket. He'd read it later, when Wallace wasn't looking over his shoulder.

"You're looking a bit pale, Mr. Spence," said Wallace. "Are you troubled about something?"

"As it happens, I am, Mr. Wallace," Spence drawled.

"What could possibly be worrying you? Mrs. Lynn assures me our principal remains fully invested and perfectly amenable to all our plans. Your own diligent efforts have helped us secure some excellent investment—"

Which was just about enough. Spence stopped in his tracks and swung round to face Wallace.

"I'll tell you what's worrying me, Mr. Wallace." He turned the name into a sneer and had the grim satisfaction of watching the stout man's confident smile falter. "What's worrying me is that it's my future you're gambling with."

"But it's not a gamble," said Wallace. "It never has been. The plan—"

"I know about the plan," growled Spence. "You've told me all about your almighty plan—"

"Our plan, Mr. Spence," said Wallace softly. "It was you who sought me out."

Which was true, and Spence could not deny it, although he was starting to wish he could.

"Never mind that," he snapped. "This time, I'm going to tell you something—" Spence emphasized this with a poke into the other man's chest. "And you're going to listen!"

"Of course, of course!" cried Wallace. "When have I ever failed to listen?" He spread his hands. "Only let us step to the side, Mr. Spence."

They'd moved past the market now, and the walk had cleared. Passersby strolled along, enjoying the sunshine, most of them deeply involved in their own affairs. But one or two were hesitating, taking a minute to glance toward the two men who looked like they might be starting to quarrel.

Spence hauled hard on his temper. On their left, a short alley led to a courtyard. Mr. Wallace stepped into the shadows between the buildings and pretended to be fussing with his gloves. Spence came to stand beside him.

"What we're doing is depending on Sir Anthony to be a blind fool." Spence folded his arms behind his back, hiding the fact that he was clenching both fists. "Well and good. The man's never been anything else. But his girls are not fools, and neither is his nibs, the duke. They know something's up."

"Of course they do," said Wallace breezily. "How could they not? As you say, they're not fools. But the daughters have all been raised to defer to their father, and his nibs, as you dub him, has to be careful not to offend the man he hopes will soon become his father-in-law. We are not dependent on them not becoming suspicious. But *what* do they suspect?" Wallace spread his hands. "Nothing close to the truth. We know that. So, they worry and run in circles and in the meantime we proceed unhindered." He beamed. "All that matters to us is what Sir Anthony thinks, and he thinks that in a fortnight he will be an extremely wealthy man."

"And what if he changes his mind?" Spence stared moodily at the street. Carriages and vans rattled past. Ladies dressed in their lightest muslin and carrying pastel-colored parasols walked by in twos and threes.

Wallace frowned. "But why should he? Who is going to change it for him?"

Spence faced the stout man. "Have you ever heard of a woman named Rosalind Thorne?"

CHAPTER 1

—In Preparation

June 1822
London

> . . . *she was ashamed of herself, quite ashamed of*
> *being so nervous, so overcome by such a trifle;*
> *but so it was.*

Jane Austen, *Persuasion*

"Are you certain you don't want me to stay?" asked Alice, for the third time.

Rosalind smiled at her friend. "I'm positive."

The two women stood together in front of the long mirror in Rosalind's boudoir. Rosalind had just taken delivery of three new gowns from her modiste, as well as two new bonnets with matching pelisses in the latest styles. It was a luxury that would have been unthinkable to her a few years ago.

The dress she wore currently was a deep forest green, trimmed with blond lace. In recent years, the mode had declared that a woman's dress should be a relatively plain, straight sheath with a high waist and square neckline. But slowly, that fashion was being replaced by a lower waist, fuller skirts, puffed sleeves, and a higher ruffled collar. Rosalind found herself admitting that the new style looked rather well on her. Rosalind was a tall woman with a heavy fall of dark gold hair and deep blue eyes. Now that she was in her middle twenties—a time society considered "mature," especially for an unmarried woman—she was permitted to put aside pastels and dress in the bolder colors that better suited her complexion. The newer, more fitted bodice was also more flattering to her figure, which might best be described as *queenly.*

In addition to Rosalind's own reflection, the mirror also showed Alice hovering behind her, looking unusually anxious. Tiny, quick, dark Alice Littlefield had been Rosalind's best friend and confidante since they met at school. Alice could face the worst of storms and remain cheerfully defiant. To see her so worried about an afternoon luncheon made Rosalind smile.

"It's only natural you should be nervous," Alice was saying. "I would be nervous."

"It seems to me we've had this conversation before." Rosalind turned away from the mirror to her dressing table.

"A variation on it," said Alice. "When you were getting ready to go to Cassell House over the business with Helen Corbyn. Which ended with what was *supposed* to be your final break with Devon."

Rosalind sighed as she leaned forward to pin an enamel brooch in the center of her collar. "Devon and I did not break. We parted as good friends."

"And now he's back," said Alice.

"Did you expect him to vanish?"

"Of course not. However, I never expected your former fiancé to bring *his* new fiancée to your house for lunch."

Rosalind suppressed a sigh. "Devon was never my fiancé."

"But he wanted to be, and you wanted it as well."

Rosalind was silent for a moment. Alice was right. Rosalind was a daughter of the baronet, Sir Reginald Thorne. While such a position came with many advantages and privileges, they were all contingent on adhering to a long list of expectations. Rosalind was to advance her family's interests. She was to keep their secrets and be the outward face of their inviolate respectability. She was never to engage in any type of employment in exchange for money.

Most importantly, however, she must marry a man of equal or higher rank as soon as that became feasible.

When she was a young woman, it seemed to Rosalind that she would easily accomplish each item on this list. Her education might be piecemeal due to abrupt shifts in her father's whims and financial status, but it thoroughly covered those accomplishments suited to a gently bred young lady, such as music and modern languages. She'd made her debut at Almack's and entered into the social season on a firm footing. She'd attracted the attention of Devon Winterbourne, the younger son of the Duke of Casselmaine. There had been difficulties, but Rosalind had believed that they would eventually marry, and that she would settle into a peaceful domestic existence managing a household, raising children, and taking her place in society as a hostess.

Then, it all went wrong.

Her father's debts, and his crimes, destroyed the family fortunes. He fled in the middle of the night, taking Rosalind's older sister Charlotte with him. Rosalind and her mother were left alone in the ruin.

Strain and scandal broke her mother's mind, and then her health. Rosalind was taken in by her godmother. In that good lady's house, she learned that her only hope of survival, respectability, and marriage was to make herself useful to the ladies of other families among the gentility.

To everyone's surprise, Rosalind proved to have a gift for organization, and for comprehending who made the wheels of the world turn. She took her time to cultivate all manner of relationships in furtherance of her various aims—whether it was to organize a grand ball at the height of the season or acquire two tickets to a particularly popular theatrical performance.

Eventually, Rosalind's status as one of society's "useful women" expanded from helping her various ladies with guest lists and charity balls to solving more consequential dilemmas that might even include blackmail, or murder.

What had been a series of private favors turned into a mode of living, and then into a business. Discreet gifts of money became a schedule of fees drawn up by her man of business. A coterie of wealthy and independent women invested in her enterprise and now expected a share of its profits in return. Rosalind's name and her accomplishments were reported in the newspapers. Her activities were discussed—and debated—in drawing rooms.

For most of her life, Rosalind had been taught that such a state of affairs would only leave her wretched and degraded. No respectable woman would agree to know her. And yet, here Rosalind stood in her comfortably furnished boudoir, in the pleasant house to which she held the lease. She was in charge of a full staff of servants. Her bank account was sound enough that she had recently been able to suggest to her man of business that some of the profits should be invested in the shares. Her desk was piled high with requests for help from women across Great Britain.

Even her relationship with Alice had changed. Alice had gone from being her housemate and staunchest friend to her official assistant, and the recipient of a salary that Rosalind paid to her quarterly.

This difference between what she'd always been taught and what she had experienced was a contradiction. It was confusing. And Alice was correct. It had indeed taken Rosalind a long time to accept it and she had indulged in much self-doubt and many vacillations along the way. Even though she had sought these changes, she had also hung back, afraid to leave the shelter provided by society's rules.

Especially when it came to her choice of husbands.

"What is it that really worries you, Alice?" asked Rosalind.

Alice frowned. "I don't know, exactly. It took you so long to get . . . comfortable with what you've become. With *who* you've become. I've been afraid . . . well, regret is a powerful thing."

"I do not regret Devon," said Rosalind firmly.

"But how do you feel about the Duke of Casselmaine?" asked Alice.

And there, at least by some measures, was the real question.

By the rules of society, Rosalind's rank must follow her husband's. A duke's wife became a duchess, but a baker's wife—no matter what her status had been previously—became a baker.

When Rosalind had met Devon Winterbourne, he was the younger brother. It was Hugo Winterbourne who stood to inherit the title and the estate of Casselmaine. But the profligate Hugo had died suddenly, and Devon had come into the title. Unfortunately, this happened at the same time that Rosalind's family was breaking apart and her world—and her prospects—were collapsing.

She and Devon did not see each other for years after that. When a combination of fortune and misfortune brought them together again, Rosalind found her circumstances, and her feelings, had changed beyond recall. Instead of becoming part of one of the oldest and most highly placed families in England, Rosalind had become engaged to one Mr. Adam Harkness.

Adam was formerly a principle officer of the famed Bow

Street Police Station, and a solid son of London's working classes. Rosalind loved him with a depth she'd never expected to feel for anyone, and his devotion took her breath away.

Rosalind turned around and pressed Alice's hand.

"I never loved the Duke of Casselmaine, not even when I was given the chance." This was nothing less than the truth, but it felt like both a relief and a bit of a surprise to say it out loud.

Alice's own smile was wry. "This is a ridiculous conversation, isn't it?"

"No," replied Rosalind firmly. "I'm grateful for your concern, truly. Especially when so much is set to change. However, it is time for you to be on your way. You cannot keep Mr. Colburn waiting."

Alice Littlefield had once earned her living as a gossip writer for the twice-weekly paper the *London Chronicle*, but more recently, her first three-volume novel had been published by the famed, and very shrewd, Henry Colburn. The reviews had been good, and Mr. Colburn described the sales as "most promising." He was now anxious to hear about the progress of Alice's new endeavor, and to this end had invited her to luncheon with himself and Mrs. Colburn.

"Very well," said Alice. "But I could—"

Now Rosalind laughed. "Let me face down the demons of my past. I promise you I shall not weaken."

"I would give a great deal to see Casselmaine's face when he learns you called him a demon."

Rosalind returned her best "headmistress" frown. "Go, Alice."

Alice threw up her hands. "I'm going! I'm going!"

Suiting actions to words, Alice gathered her gloves, her notebook, and her reticule from the various places they had been strewn about the room. She kissed Rosalind's cheek and took herself off downstairs. Rosalind stayed where she was until she heard Alice's cheery, and very probably cheeky, farewell to the footman, Mortimer. Then, she heard the door to the street close.

Rosalind turned back to her reflection. The dress was lovely. The whole of her appearance was entirely correct. Her emotions . . .

She was not nervous, not really. She did not find herself filled with sorrow, regret, jealousy, or any of the other petty and maudlin feelings that were supposed to come when reuniting with a lost love. But neither was she calm. Her heart was beating too quickly; she could not bring herself to sit down. She paced from the window to the mirror, and back again.

Just as she was turning to pace back to the window, the door opened and Laurel, the upstairs maid, entered.

"If you please, Miss Thorne, his grace the Duke of Casselmaine and Miss Kinsdale have arrived."

Rosalind laid her hand against her stomach, as if that would calm its unaccountable tremblings.

"Thank you, Laurel. Tell them I shall be down directly."

Laurel took her leave and Rosalind faced herself in the mirror once more.

"What is it I'm afraid of?" she asked her reflection. Because she was afraid. She had not wanted to admit it—not to Alice, not to herself—but it was true. Because there was one question she had not let herself, or Alice, ask.

What if I can't like her? What then?

Rosalind looked into her own eyes for a long moment. "Well, I won't know if I'm hiding in here."

With that, Rosalind drew her shoulders back and lifted her chin. She turned and opened the door. It was time to face her past, and her future.

CHAPTER 2

Making New Acquaintances

*Still, however, she had the sensation of there being
something more than immediately appeared . . .*

Jane Austen, *Persuasion*

Once, Rosalind and Devon Winterbourne had danced
furtively around the London ballrooms, treading on
each other's toes and laughing about it. Now, as Lord Casselmaine, he stood gracefully to meet her as she entered the sitting room.

"Lord Casselmaine." Rosalind presented her hand to Devon
so he could bow over it. "How very good of you to accept
my invitation."

Devon Winterbourne, Duke of Casselmaine, had always
been handsome. When Rosalind had first met him, he had
been a tall youth with an easy laugh, intelligent blue eyes,
and a sweep of black hair. As he grew into his position, his
title, and himself, he transformed into a strong man with a
comfortable presence that could turn commanding when he
needed it to. He had managed to keep the kindness and the
humor of that youth, however, and Rosalind admired him
for it.

"Delighted that you should have us, Miss Thorne." Devon straightened and turned to the woman beside him. "May I introduce you to my fiancée, Miss Clara Kinsdale?"

Rosalind turned to greet Miss Kinsdale, and her first thought was *striking*.

Clara Kinsdale was tall. Even Rosalind had to lift her chin slightly to look her in the eye. She was willowy, with long arms and sloping shoulders. Her eyes were an arresting emerald green and her hair a rich auburn. Her whole air was one of capability and intelligence, but Rosalind also glimpsed a trace of humor underneath it all. Her dress was a fresh muslin sprigged with green and lavender, and fashioned after the latest mode, and she wore it well.

Rosalind smiled, and—given all her earlier dithering and imagined fears—it was easier than she had expected.

"I am delighted to meet you, Miss Kinsdale." Rosalind dipped a curtsy in greeting and received Miss Kinsdale's in return. "Thank you so much for coming. Won't you please sit down?" she said to them both. "Luncheon will be ready shortly."

Claire, who worked as Rosalind's housekeeper and also did the offices of a parlor maid, arrived with the tea tray. Any potentially awkward initial silence was alleviated by the ceremony of pouring out, inquiring as to whether Miss Kinsdale took milk or lemon (milk). Did she care for sugar (just one please)? And please do try one of the ginger biscuits, which were Mrs. Singh's specialty.

Devon took his tea as he ever did, without milk but with two sugars, and showed no hesitation in helping himself to a biscuit.

According to the ceremonies of parlor etiquette, now was the time for the light conversation to begin. Miss Kinsdale stepped up at once to face this particular challenge.

"What a lovely home you have, Miss Thorne."

"Thank you," replied Rosalind. "We have been very comfortable here. I understand you're residing in Bath, Miss Kinsdale?" This detail had been included in Devon's letter, although it was one of only a few.

"Yes. We removed there for my father's health." Miss Kinsdale spoke the words smoothly. However, Rosalind's long experience with drawing room manners told her there was a great deal waiting underneath that simple phrase. "As I'm sure Casselmaine has told you, our family property is near to his."

"I trust your journey to London was uneventful?" continued Rosalind, which was a remark that either party could answer.

"Very pleasant," said Devon. "The roads were quite dry for the time of year."

And so it went, back and forth. They took turns with their remarks on the roads, the fine summer weather, the commonplace difficulties of coaching inns. Miss Kinsdale kept up her end with practiced ease. She had clearly been raised to the ways of parlors and politesse, just as Rosalind had been.

For the most part, Devon seemed content to hold back and let Rosalind and Miss Kinsdale have the greater share of this initial conversation. Rosalind remained aware of him, however. She noted how his attention flickered about the room, taking in the furnishings, the books, the draperies. He was looking to see if she was as easy and comfortable as she seemed. He was wondering, she knew, if all was indeed right with her.

Rosalind found herself warmed by this sign of his continued care, but also slightly piqued. Before she had time to examine this emotion, Claire returned and announced that luncheon was served.

"Will Mr. Harkness be joining us?" asked Devon as they went through to the dining room.

"He sends his regrets," said Rosalind. "He has been detained on business."

In fact, Adam was tracking down a vengeful former employee of the printer who published the famous *Boyle's Court and Country Guide*. Mrs. Boyle was a widow who had taken over her husband's business. She had come to Rosalind in a state of anger and alarm. Someone had been calling on prominent persons and telling them that if they wished to be listed in the guide's future editions, they would need to pay for the privilege. The man then collected their money and vanished.

"Fortunately, the fellow also seems to lack imagination," Adam had told Rosalind yesterday. "He's using the guide itself, and soliciting his victims one street at a time, in alphabetical order."

Adam hoped to catch up with this orderly miscreant before suppertime.

Because they had no knowledge of Miss Kinsdale's personal tastes, Mrs. Singh had prepared a highly traditional summer luncheon. There was a green salad and lobster and mayonnaise, which was followed by lamb cutlets in white sauce and new potatoes dressed with lemon and parsley. A strawberry and rhubarb tart stood on the sideboard for their dessert.

Thankfully, Miss Kinsdale was not one of those fashionable women who felt it necessary to display a dainty appetite. She let herself be helped to some of everything and even took seconds of the lobster and the salad. All in all, Rosalind found herself very satisfied with Devon's choice.

As if your permission was needed, she scolded herself.

And yet she knew in some obscure way that it was. In the same way, some corner of herself wanted Devon to approve of Adam. It was not logical, but it was nonetheless real.

"Oh, Miss Thorne, I called on Mrs. Percival Short the other morning," Miss Kinsdale remarked as Devon helped her to more potatoes. "She sends her regards."

"I did not know you were acquainted with Mrs. Short," said Rosalind. "Tell me, how is her sister? And the new baby?"

With that, the conversation broadened to common acquaintances and their families. By now, the three of them had relaxed enough to begin including stories of past amusements and favorite, well-worn bits of gossip. At the same time, Rosalind felt worry begin to tap at the back of her mind. Something simmered beneath the surface of this conversation. As the meal progressed, Devon's glances toward Miss Kinsdale changed from admiring to anticipating, and even anxious. Miss Kinsdale was responding to his meaningful looks with tiny, fleeting frowns.

Rosalind told herself to be patient, but it was not easy.

At last, the tart was finished and they all adjourned again to the parlor. Claire brought fresh tea and Rosalind once again handed round the cups. As she poured her own tea, Rosalind decided it was time to take matters in hand. She turned to Devon.

"Was there something particular you wanted to talk about, Casselmaine?"

Devon laughed. "Good lord, have we been that obvious?"

"I'm afraid so, yes." Rosalind smiled. "Perhaps, Miss Kinsdale, you would do me the favor of letting me know what this is about?"

"Oh dear." Miss Kinsdale blushed ever so slightly. "I'm sorry. Casselmaine did tell me I should be direct, but I couldn't bring myself to do it."

"Manners can be very hard to set aside," said Rosalind, thinking of all her recent past and her struggle to accept it. "But there is something, isn't there?"

"There is." Miss Kinsdale stopped, shook her head at some inner thought, and began again. "I must confess, Miss Thorne, I asked Casselmaine to introduce us. You see, I find I am very much in need of your help."

CHAPTER 3

Family Matters

*She would have liked to know how he felt as to a
meeting. Perhaps indifferent, if indifference could
exist under such circumstances.*

Jane Austen, *Persuasion*

Rosalind felt her brows arch. She resisted slipping a glance toward Devon. "Of course, I'd be glad to help in any way I can. What has happened, Miss Kinsdale?"

Rosalind found herself hoping that it was a matter of introductions, or guest lists, or being unable to find some particular item needed for the engagement celebration. A second glance, however, showed how Miss Kinsdale's demeanor had changed. The poised, polite woman had become uncertain, and a little angry. Whatever troubled her, it was nothing so trivial as her guest list.

Devon nodded encouragingly to Miss Kinsdale. Rosalind had the distinct feeling that if she had not been there to see it, he would have taken his fiancée's hand.

"It is regarding my father," said Miss Kinsdale. She set down her teacup and knotted her fingers together. Rosalind recognized the gesture. Miss Kinsdale was fighting to maintain that disinterested demeanor that all gently reared young women were taught they must display when in company.

"I don't know how much you know about my circumstances, Miss Thorne," Miss Kinsdale said. "The Kinsdales are country people, not known for much except a love of horses. In the past, our family raised some notable thoroughbreds. But my father . . . he is not a careful manager of his own resources."

"I understand," said Rosalind. She did. This was an extremely common story. Law and custom granted fathers, husbands, and brothers complete charge of a family's finances. However, not all men were educated or equipped to manage such responsibility. The results could range from dispiriting to disastrous.

"The income from rents, stud fees, and the sale of our brood mares has not been enough to make up for the estate's expenditures in recent years." Miss Kinsdale paused and took another swallow of tea.

"I imagine your father gambles on his horses as well," said Rosalind.

"His, and others. He believes himself to be an infallible judge of horseflesh, and people."

Again, Rosalind nodded. Pride was another very common element in these stories.

When Miss Kinsdale spoke again, her voice was little more than a whisper. "I am being very blunt, I know. A daughter should be more discreet about her father's faults."

"That is what we're always taught," said Rosalind. However bad circumstances became, mothers, daughters, and most especially wives were expected to maintain a decorous silence regarding their circumstances in order to preserve the family reputation. "But there comes a time when plain speaking is all that is left to us."

The tiniest smile flickered across Miss Kinsdale's features. "Casselmaine said you would understand."

But he clearly did not tell you why. Rosalind felt a small rush of relief. She was not sure where that reaction came from, because it seemed to indicate she had somehow doubted Devon would keep her secrets.

I and my conscience will need to have some conversation after this.

But that was for later.

"So, we have sold our stock, even our saddle horses." Miss Kinsdale glanced at Devon. Her hand moved slightly, as if she wanted to reach out to clasp his, but remembered at the last minute that they were in company. "Finally, we rented the house to Admiral Robert Walsingham. Our family—that is myself, my father, and my two sisters—removed to Bath. The idea was that we could live there with greater economy." She met Devon's eyes briefly, and her blush returned.

Devon smiled gently. "What Miss Kinsdale isn't saying is that she also wanted to avoid me."

"He, however, was not interested in being avoided, " put in Miss Kinsdale.

"—And so I followed her to Bath," Devon continued. "And made myself perfectly at home on her doorstep."

"I'd tried to refuse him, you see," said Miss Kinsdale. "He'd asked me to marry him and then everything collapsed, and I couldn't—"

"—but I determined I was not going to repeat past mistakes," said Devon quietly.

Rosalind found she had to drop her gaze to the sugar bowl at this. Thankfully, Miss Kinsdale did not seem to notice.

"So, I found myself being very much courted," Miss Kinsdale said. "And, well, I confess I became entirely wrapped up in trying to decide what I should do about it. As a result, I didn't pay sufficient attention to what was happening with my family. No, don't worry," she added quickly to Devon. "I'm not blaming myself." Obviously, this had been a subject of much discussion between them. "It is simply the truth. I wasn't paying attention. It was Cynthia who first realized that something was amiss."

"Cynthia is Clara's younger sister," Devon supplied. "The oldest is Elizabeth."

"And the latest trouble began with Elizabeth." Miss Kinsdale frowned again. "Or at least, she was the door by which trouble managed to enter. You see, shortly before we came to Bath, Elizabeth became acquainted with a young widow named Mrs. Sylvia Lynn. Mrs. Lynn is a lovely woman with engaging manners and claims an acquaintance with some of the best people in the district. All of this recommended her to my father as a suitable companion for Elizabeth, indeed, for all of us, once we did move to Bath." Miss Kinsdale's tone remained bland, but Rosalind could see the spark of anger in her eyes. "It was through Mrs. Lynn's frequent visits with my sister and her inclusion in our family parties that my father became acquainted with her."

Rosalind felt she now understood, at least in part, where this story was leading.

"After I told my family that I'd accepted Casselmaine's proposal, Cynthia came to me and said she was afraid that Mrs. Lynn was visiting us as much to spend time with Father as with Elizabeth. Elizabeth was delighted. But Cynthia was worried."

"Why?" asked Rosalind.

"Bath widows have a certain . . . reputation."

"As fortune hunters?" suggested Rosalind.

"Yes," said Miss Kinsdale. "And the connection had grown . . . much closer of late."

Meaning her father was most likely conducting a romantic affair with Mrs. Lynn.

"Obviously, we have nothing of our own that would attract a fortune hunter," Miss Kinsdale went on. "And anyone who bothered to ask would easily find that out. But my being engaged to Casselmaine changes matters."

Rosalind nodded. Since Devon had assumed the title, he'd worked hard to restore the family's fortune.

"What is it that made you suspect Mrs. Lynn's intentions?" asked Rosalind. "Aside from the timing of this closer connection?"

Miss Kinsdale considered this. Rosalind waited. Devon felt the strain, she knew. He wanted to explain; he wanted to direct the situation; he wanted to support and protect Miss Kinsdale, but he also knew the best way to do these things was to let her speak for herself.

This was the Devon Rosalind had always known, and she was glad to see him here and now.

"To be honest, what raises the most concern is that the gossip is so inconsistent," said Miss Kinsdale finally. "When it became clear that my father was developing a regard for Mrs. Lynn, Cynthia and I began asking our Bath acquaintance about her. And the stories we heard back . . . they clashed. Everyone agrees that she was widowed, and that her previous husband had been a London financier who had left her with a modest fortune. As she had no plans to marry again—at least not immediately—she'd decided her money would go further in Bath."

"Elizabeth told us this much," put in Devon. "And I've heard some of it from Mrs. Lynn myself."

"But beyond that . . ." Miss Kinsdale made a helpless gesture. "We have heard alternately that her family is Irish but her mother raised her in London. However, we've also heard that her family is from Manchester and made their money from the new cotton mills, but sold their interests and moved down to London."

"There's also a story that her father was a diplomat who profited from his posting in Paris and then returned to set up his establishment in London," put in Devon.

"Oh, yes," said Miss Kinsdale wearily. "I'd forgotten that one." She shook her head again. "But when it comes down to it, no one can agree on what they've heard, and no one can remember having met her or her family in London, or Paris, or Manchester, or anywhere else."

Rosalind could well understand why these inconsistencies would worry Miss Kinsdale. London's *haut ton* was a small, gossiping world. Its hostesses' sharp eyes and busy tongues could quickly lay bare the story—and the secrets—of any new arrival. Since Bath was smaller, the talk and news spread even faster.

"Gossip, of course, breeds inconsistency and rumor," said Rosalind. "But I am surprised that no one can remember knowing her, or her family. Do you know the name of her late husband? Or the financial firm where he was employed?"

Devon and Miss Kinsdale looked at each other. Neither, it seemed, had an answer.

"Did you ask Louisa?" Louisa was Devon's cousin. She had married an ambitious banker and the pair were now very much rising stars in the social circles of the financial world. "With her husband's connections throughout the City, he may have heard of the man."

"We did ask," said Devon. "But he could not recall anyone who answered what little description we had."

"I imagine, Miss Kinsdale, that you've spoken with your father?" Rosalind asked.

"I have, but of course he will not listen," she replied. "And Elizabeth remains entirely on Mrs. Lynn's side." She stopped. "I love my family, Miss Thorne, but since my mother died, we seem to have lost our sense of direction." She stopped again. "Please, if I'm being ridiculous, tell me straightaway. Casselmaine says your . . . occupation is helping women and their families with private matters, and that you may be relied upon absolutely."

"Casselmaine is very kind," said Rosalind. "And yes, I have been able to help other families with this sort of inquiry." Usually, it came in the form of nervous parents fretting over a child's unexpected suitor. Once upon a time, a family might be able to use their own personal connections to ferret out the truth. But travel across the country—and even from the Continent—was becoming faster and more frequent, which meant the social world was being stretched by the arrival of all sorts of new families. These families came with plenty of money, but without connections to established London society. That made reliable information regarding their sons, and their daughters, more difficult to come by.

For Rosalind, this meant more families who came asking if she could look into the backgrounds of such persons and determine that they were in fact who they claimed to be.

"I wish I didn't have to ask this," said Devon. "But there's a certain urgency—"

Rosalind nodded her understanding. "When are you planning to be married?"

"In the fall," said Miss Kinsdale. "We were hoping to celebrate our engagement in Bath and then be married from Cassell House."

Which only contributed to the urgency. It was already June and any such ball would need to be held by late July or early August, when travel was still easy, and before families began returning to London in preparation for the social season.

Rosalind was silent for a moment, considering her list of current commitments. She was busy, but there was nothing that she could not set aside, at least for a little while.

"I can begin by making some inquiries among my acquaintance," she told them. "Tell me, Miss Kinsdale, do you know Mrs. Lynn's given name?"

"Westerford," she answered. "Sylvia Westerford."

"Thank you. Since we do not have a great deal of time, I would suggest that I also go to Bath. That way, I can speak with Mrs. Lynn directly, which might give us a better indication of how to proceed."

"Oh, thank you, Miss Thorne!" cried Miss Kinsdale. "This is exactly what I was hoping for."

But while Miss Kinsdale declared her relief, Devon was

looking at Rosalind oddly. Rosalind met his gaze and was rewarded by a blush, and the unusual sight of Devon Winterbourne, Duke of Casselmaine, fumbling for words.

"Thank you for agreeing to come to us on such short notice. We're returning to Bath almost immediately."

"Then I will begin inquiries today," said Rosalind. "And I will write to you about further arrangements first thing tomorrow morning, if you will leave me your direction?"

Miss Kinsdale gave Rosalind her card, and they began the ceremonies of saying a polite farewell. Through it all, Devon was still looking at her with that same odd expression.

They all rose, and Rosalind opened the door to conduct them into the foyer, but at that same moment, Mortimer opened the front door and Adam stepped in. He saw Miss Kinsdale and Devon at once, drew himself up, and removed his high-crowned hat.

"Mr. Harkness," said Rosalind. "I was not expecting you so soon. May I introduce Miss Clara Kinsdale?"

"Your servant, Miss Kinsdale." Adam bowed, his usual polite, businesslike gesture.

"How do you do, sir?" she replied.

"And you remember his grace, of course?" Rosalind went on.

"Mr. Harkness." Devon bowed.

"Your grace." Adam bowed.

The men met each other's gazes. Neither one betrayed any sort of belligerence, but it was a measuring look on both sides. Rosalind found herself with the urge to laugh, but she did not know where it came from.

Claire arrived carrying Devon's and Miss Kinsdale's outer things. They dressed. Farewells were said, and the pair took their leave.

Rosalind opened her mouth to ask how Adam's business had gone, but as Mortimer closed the door, Adam hesitated. He stared at the door, as if he suspected it of something.

"What is it?" asked Rosalind.

Adam did not answer. Instead, he turned on his heel and retreated to the parlor. Rosalind blinked in surprise at Mortimer, who simply shrugged. In his opinion there was no understanding the ways of a former Bow Street officer.

Rosalind hurried into the parlor. Adam stood by the windows, staring intently across the street. As she started forward, he held up his hand to stop her, and then gestured that she should come stand directly behind him.

Rosalind followed the line his gesture indicated, skirting the walls rather than crossing the center of the room.

"What is it?"

"We're being watched." Adam pointed across the street. Rosalind followed the direction of his gaze.

He was right.

CHAPTER 4

The Sudden Arrival

"Only give me a hearing. You will soon be able to judge of the general credit due, by listening to some particulars which you can yourself immediately contradict or confirm."

Jane Austen, *Persuasion*

It was easy to see what attracted Adam's attention. Across the street, in the narrow alley between the park and her opposite neighbor's garden wall, stood a furtive young woman. She wore a white day dress and an enormous straw bonnet and clutched her reticule in both hands as she stared fixedly at their house. As Rosalind and Adam watched, she peered in both directions, cautious as a mouse who fears the cat is lurking around the corner. Then, just like the mouse, she scurried across the street.

Rosalind did not bother to ring for Mortimer. She ran to the front door herself and pulled it open. The young woman threw herself across the threshold.

Rosalind closed the door and the young woman turned to face her. This unexpected guest was small and slender. Her pink and white skin had the pallor that came when one has been strictly scolded about the dangers of allowing the sun to fall on her face. Her eyes were wide and brown, and her hair, where it showed under her bonnet, was a gleaming chestnut color.

"Are you Miss Thorne?" Her voice quavered.

"I am," replied Rosalind.

"I'm so sorry for making such a . . . a strange scene, only I must speak with you immediately."

"It's quite all right. You are entirely welcome here."

"Thank you, oh, thank you!"

Adam must have rung for Claire. The maid strode into the foyer, ready to take the young woman's things, but their visitor clutched her pelisse and shook her head so hard she nearly dislodged her poorly pinned bonnet. "No, no, I mustn't stay. I can't."

"But you will come and sit down?" said Rosalind. "We cannot talk standing here."

"Oh, I can't, I mustn't, I mustn't be seen here. . . ."

"There is no one to see except myself and Mr. Harkness. Please." Rosalind stepped aside with a gesture of invitation.

The young woman bit her lip, practically vibrating in her distress.

"Yes, all right," she said at last. Rosalind gave Claire a glance and mouthed "a fresh cup." Claire nodded and moved smoothly to deliver the request to the kitchen while Rosalind led the young woman into the parlor.

"May I present Mr. Adam Harkness?" said Rosalind to their visitor.

Adam stood beside the hearth. He bowed to their visitor but did not move forward. He had, of course, sized up the situation and understood that the close proximity of a strange man might further upset their skittish visitor. He had also drawn the drapes, which left the room dim, and a little stuffy, but the young woman saw this, and she wilted a little with evident relief.

"Mr. Harkness, this is Miss . . ." Rosalind hesitated.

"I . . . my name is Mary Smith," their visitor said.

It almost certainly was not, but Rosalind decided now was not the time to point this out.

"Please, won't you sit down?"

Miss Smith sat gingerly in the proffered chair. Rosalind then took her usual place on the settee. Adam kept to his corner, but she saw his eyes narrow, watching Miss Smith carefully.

"How can we help you, Miss Smith?" Rosalind asked.

"Oh, it's not me. That is—I mean, have, has, have you, you did, I saw—but . . ." Miss Smith blushed furiously and dropped her gaze to her gloved hands. "You have spoken with Clara Kinsdale today, haven't you? Just now, I mean."

"I'm sorry, Miss Smith," said Rosalind. "I cannot possibly discuss who has visited me."

"But I *saw* her, and him and . . ." Miss Smith gulped air. Rosalind glanced at Adam. He arched one brow.

Claire entered bringing a small tray bearing a new teapot and fresh cups. All discussion paused until Rosalind poured out a cup for Miss Smith and held it out for her. Miss Smith took the cup into her gloved hands and drank a huge gulp with all appearance of gratitude.

Rosalind watched her visitor. She noted the other woman's arms and her throat and the shape of her face as she lowered the cup and visibly struggled to compose herself. There was something in her appearance and her soft, girlish voice that was not right. Adam had seen it. Now Rosalind found herself cataloguing its details.

"I'm sorry," Miss Smith said again. "I'm better now. Truly. Of course you can't say who you've seen. It's only that if Miss Kinsdale was here to see you about Sylvia Westerford— Sylvia Lynn, I mean. Mrs. Lynn—" She broke off again and leaned anxiously forward, clutching her cup so hard that for a moment Rosalind was afraid she might break it.

"Did Miss Kinsdale ask you to find out about her?" she

blurted out. "Because you mustn't, Miss Thorne! You must let her be!"

"Is she in danger?" Adam spoke quietly, but Miss Smith jumped. Her tea sloshed. She had probably forgotten he was there. Adam had a particular skill of fading into the shadows when he wished.

"She is," declared Miss Smith. "Not anything bad, I mean, anything that might involve the law, but she's in danger of being exposed, and well, that would be disastrous."

"Exposed?" Rosalind asked gently. "Is she accused of something?"

Miss Smith swallowed. She took another drink of tea. This time she set the cup down on its saucer and stared at it for a long moment.

When she did speak, it wasn't an answer.

"She just wants to live quietly, you see. To have a home and some stability. But she, well, she does have secrets in her past, but they're not bad, not really. But the daughters—the Kinsdale daughters I mean—they think she must have done *something* bad. They think she must be a fraud or a fortune hunter, and she isn't. Not really. You must believe me!"

Rosalind sat back and let the jumble of words settle into silence. Miss Smith ducked her head. The wide bonnet helped hide her expression.

"How is it you know Mrs. Lynn?" asked Rosalind.

"I'm her secret." Miss Smith turned her face a little further away, as if to hide shame or tears. "I'm her daughter."

Rosalind straightened, just a little. Adam folded his hands behind his back. Miss Smith looked toward the door, and then the curtained windows, as if she was afraid someone might leap out from behind the drapes and shout, "I knew it!"

"I see," said Rosalind. "In that case, perhaps we should begin again. Will you tell me your name?"

Their visitor blushed and twisted her fingers. "My name really is Smith," she said. "Sophia Smith."

"And where do you live, Miss Smith?" Rosalind asked.

"I'm at school," she said, but then stopped. "But you cannot possibly need to know that. Or anything about me. I only came to beg you to leave my mother alone. Please. You are supposed to be such a clever woman. You must see that I'm telling you the truth. Mama only wants to make a home, so that I can come live with her. If the Kinsdales find out about me before she tells them properly, she'll have to run away again and then I'll never . . ." She stopped and took deep, shuddering breath.

Rosalind nodded and exchanged a solemn glance with Adam. They both understood the problem. Not every gentlewoman who found herself in financial straits was as fortunate as Rosalind and Alice had been. Only a very few could find a way to make any sort of living, let alone a good one. Without family to take them in, most ladies' hopes depended entirely on finding a husband. Such women were decried as fortune hunters by those very same forces and persons who made it impossible for them to take up any occupation or profession of their own.

But if a woman had a child out of wedlock, her chance of finding a husband of any standing at all was reduced to almost nothing. The most common answer to this dilemma was to hide the child.

Miss Smith's story was very old, and very familiar. It was also neatly calculated to engage Rosalind's sympathy.

"But you are in touch with your mother?" Rosalind asked.

"She sends letters sometimes," said Miss Smith. "Through a friend. He's Mama's man of business, but I think he's also my uncle. He makes sure my expenses are taken care of and brings me letters from Mama sometimes. It was he who warned me that someone might come looking for me, and I mustn't talk to them because they were trying to find Mama."

"Did the letter tell you to come here?" asked Adam.

"No," replied Miss Smith. "But after that letter, I had one directly from Mama. She told me Miss Kinsdale and her fiancé were coming to London, and that they'd been growing suspicious of her. And, well, I'd made up my mind to go and speak to her myself."

"So it was coincidence that you arrived here just after Miss Kinsdale and his grace?" said Adam.

Fear flickered behind Miss Smith's eyes, and Rosalind could have sworn it was genuine. "No, it wasn't, not really. I'd . . . found out that Miss Kinsdale was staying with friends, you see. But when I got there, she was out. I spoke with one of the maids, and she told me Miss Kinsdale was coming here. Everyone knows that one goes to Miss Thorne to find things out. So it wasn't difficult to guess that Miss Kinsdale was going to ask you about Mama. So, I thought I would come here and talk to you instead."

"How did you come?" asked Adam. "There was no carriage in the street."

Miss Smith took up her teacup again, took a swallow and stared into the dregs, clearly trying to decide how much to say.

"Before I . . . before now, I traveled a great deal with Mama. Hiring a cab is not beyond me. And I have a little pin money."

"I see," murmured Rosalind.

Miss Smith glanced toward the door. "I should go. I'll be missed." Miss Smith blinked rapidly, her eyes wide and shining. "Please, Miss Thorne, Mr. Harkness. Just let Miss Kinsdale know there's nothing to worry about. Beg her to give Mama a chance to tell the family about me in her own time. That cannot be so much to ask, can it?"

Before Rosalind could answer this, she heard the sound of the front door banging open.

"Hullo!" came a cheery call from the foyer. It was Alice returning from her own luncheon with Mr. Colburn. "Oh, Mortimer, thank you, you can take those to my writing room. . . ."

Miss Smith shot to her feet, her cup still in her hand. "I've stayed too long."

"Please, sit down," said Rosalind. "It's only—"

But Miss Smith didn't let Rosalind finish. She rushed out of the room, pushing right past Alice, pressing her teacup into the other woman's hands as she did, and barging out the front door straight past a very startled Mortimer.

"I'll go," said Adam at once, and he took off after her, not even pausing to collect his hat.

Alice stared after Adam even though the door had shut. She looked at the cup in her hands, and then at Rosalind.

"Well," she said. "Did anything happen while I was away?"

CHAPTER 5

The Nature of the Business

"... that she is a clever, insinuating, handsome woman, poor and plausible ..."

Jane Austen, *Persuasion*

Adam returned an hour later, unusually chagrined. He came into the parlor where Rosalind and Alice were waiting, with the drapes now opened, and a fresh pot of tea between them.

"I do not know who our Miss Smith may be, but she is not a schoolgirl, at least not an ordinary one." He settled onto the sofa. Rosalind handed him a cup of tea and he nodded his thanks. "She gave me the slip with embarrassing thoroughness before we'd gotten to the high street. I'm only glad Goutier and Tauton weren't there to see it." He raised his cup in salute to Alice and drank. "Did Rosalind tell you what happened?"

"She did." Alice had taken her preferred spot on the window seat and was sipping her own tea. "I'm beginning to wish I'd refused Mr. Colburn's invitation. It seems that all the truly interesting conversation was happening here."

"Certainly something was happening." Adam was plainly

annoyed with himself at having lost his quarry. "Who is this Mrs. Lynn our young woman says is her mother?"

"I first heard about her today from Miss Clara Kinsdale, Devon's fiancée," said Rosalind. "Miss Clara says Mrs. Lynn is a Bath widow who has attached herself to the Kinsdale family. Miss Clara and one of her sisters, Cynthia, are afraid that Mrs. Lynn plans to marry their father in order to take advantage of the fact that a wealthy duke is about to become part of their family."

"What of the third sister?"

"The third sister is Elizabeth. According to Miss Clara, Elizabeth is in favor of the match, or at least the association. Mrs. Lynn was her friend before becoming closely acquainted with the rest of the family."

Adam looked toward the window, taking in the details of the street outside. The neighborhood was beginning to show all its afternoon busyness with maids and ladies finishing the day's errands, while the carriages of doctors and bankers filled the streets so their owners could return home to change before dinner.

"It is very interesting that Miss Smith made her appearance as soon as Casselmaine and Miss Kinsdale were out the door," Adam said.

"Especially since she said it was Miss Kinsdale she wanted to speak to," said Rosalind. "If that was the case, why didn't she approach Miss Kinsdale as she left? Or come to the door while she was still here? Why wait and tell her secrets to a stranger?"

"I was wondering the same thing," said Adam.

"Perhaps she didn't want to say anything in front of Devon," suggested Alice.

"But she knows where Miss Kinsdale is staying," Rosalind pointed out. "She told us that herself. Why not simply wait for her to come home? Or even follow her home and speak to her once Devon left? Why involve us?"

"Unless it was us, or you, at least, that she wanted to throw off the scent," concluded Adam.

"Well, schoolgirls are not all saints, or even innocents," said Alice. "As you and I know, Rosalind."

"She was not a schoolgirl," said Adam and Rosalind together.

Alice threw back her head and laughed. "Well! Since you both say it, it must be true. How could you tell?"

"Because she was not as young as she was pretending to be, for one thing," said Rosalind.

"You noticed?" Adam reached for the teapot again and filled his own cup.

"Her throat," said Rosalind. "The line of her throat was that of a grown woman, not a girl. She would have done better to affect a high collar."

"And her figure," said Adam.

Rosalind quirked a brow.

Adam dropped his gaze, in lieu of a blush. "She'd bound herself to appear . . . less developed than she is. And she did not take off her gloves."

"Yes, I saw that as well." A lady did not eat or drink with her gloves on. But hands were an excellent indicator of age and social class. A woman who wished to pass herself off as a gently bred lady (or girl) could not afford to show a chapped or calloused hand.

"So if she was not the schoolgirl she claimed to be, who was she?" asked Alice. "Could she really have been Mrs. Lynn's daughter?"

"At this point, there is no knowing," said Rosalind. "But if she is not, why is she trying to help this Mrs. Lynn?"

"And is she still watching this house?" said Adam quietly. "Or having it watched?"

Rosalind did not let herself glance toward the street, but it was difficult.

"Well, to me it all seems a great deal of trouble to go through to attach oneself to a man of no fortune," announced Alice. "I mean, a duke in the family is a lovely thing, but there's no guarantee that Casselmaine will be interested in supporting this profligate Sir Anthony indefinitely."

"And Miss Kinsdale is of age, I believe," said Rosalind. "So she does not need her father's permission to marry, nor does there necessarily need to be any contracts or settlements." She paused. "Casselmaine would not cut his in-laws if he had any other choice, but neither would he permit Sir Anthony to become a danger to the family's stability." Devon had already seen what a careless man could do to even the largest fortune. "And he certainly would not risk his reputation by allowing Sir Anthony to trade on his title, or expectations."

They all sat in silence for a moment, each of them turning over this information in their own minds.

"We know this Miss Smith is lying," said Adam. "The question is, is she working with Mrs. Lynn or against her?"

Rosalind considered. "Yes. I thought the story of an illegitimate daughter was meant to engage sympathy, but it could also be a simple way to create enough of a scandal so that the Kinsdales would decide to drop Mrs. Lynn."

"But *why?*" said Alice again. "It was quite the risk to take."

"It is," said Adam. "Usually, that means that for someone, the stakes are very high," he added.

"I think," said Rosalind, "we need to get to Bath as soon as possible."

"Good," said Alice. "I'll pack, and I'll write to—"

"I'm sorry, Alice, I will need you to stay in London for the time being."

"You'd go to Bath without your trusted assistant?" Alice sounded both shocked and wounded.

"I'll have Adam," Rosalind reminded her.

Alice frowned. "I thought Adam was looking for that fellow who was defrauding Mrs. Boyle."

"Found him this afternoon," Adam told her.

"That was fast," remarked Alice.

"I caught up with him in Chapel Street," he told them. "His name is Leeland, by the by, and he was very sulky about the whole business. But in the end, I took him back to Mrs. Boyle and he turned over the day's takings and promised not to do it again." There was no question of arrest or charges. What Mr. Leeland had been doing was not, strictly speaking, illegal. Mrs. Boyle could take him to civil court for blackening her good name, but women's suits were less likely to succeed on such grounds, so this was the best available outcome.

"Well," huffed Alice. "I trust that if I am to be excluded from this little expedition to Bath, I hope you have a good reason."

"I do," said Rosalind. "I need someone here who can work with Sanderson Faulks, and your brother George."

Adam nodded. "I agree. Whatever her aims may be, we should keep apprised of Miss Smith's whereabouts."

"But if she's working with Mrs. Lynn, and watching the house, she's sure to send word to Bath as soon as she sees you leave," Alice pointed out. "Won't that tip your hand?"

"It will," said Rosalind. "Therefore, we must make sure Miss Smith does not know we've gone."

CHAPTER 6

A Meeting of Minds

*"Yes, yes we will have a snug walk together, and I
have something to tell you as we go along."*

Jane Austen, *Persuasion*

"Such a crowd," remarked Mrs. Lynn to Sir Anthony Kinsdale as they entered the Pump Rooms. "So many new faces!"

"And so few worth looking at." Sir Anthony smiled at his own quip. Mrs. Lynn allowed herself a pretty roll of her eyes that might have been agreement, or a moment of shared amusement with Elizabeth, who walked along with them.

The Pump Rooms were a peculiar Bath institution—a grand building created so that the *haut ton* could drink the spa's healthful waters in comfort, and at the same time see and be seen against a graceful backdrop. To manage this, the rooms had been designed as a sort of indoor park. Guests strolled about with each other, admired the view from the soaring windows, and, of course, engaged in all manner of gossip. Flirtations were carried out. Private plans were concluded, and notes furtively passed between young lovers. The fact that the rooms allowed for the mixing of all conditions and classes of persons was routinely decried by those who valued exclusivity, and yet all of fashionable Bath came anyway.

It was early afternoon and the rooms were full almost to bursting with fashionables, spa patients, and those who came to gawk at both. Therefore, the arrival of Sir Anthony Kinsdale, his eldest daughter, and her pretty companion caused rather less of a stir than that gentleman may have wished. Nonetheless, he walked with a great swinging of his stick, reflective of his general desire to take up as much room as possible. Mrs. Lynn, who rested her hand lightly on his arm, recognized this particular tendency and had carefully fluffed out her skirts to their maximum extent.

Elizabeth Kinsdale walked a pace behind the companionable couple but did not regard either of them. Her gaze swept furtively over the crowd, searching for someone or something, but trying not to show it.

Sir Anthony knew no such hesitation. He scrutinized all the persons they passed, looking for particular acquaintances, or persons with whom he wished to become acquainted. He nodded his head this way and that, or sketched a lazy swoop in the air with his stick to indicate that he had in fact seen some such person. If the reaction to these eloquent gestures was a puzzled glance, Sir Anthony did not deign to notice. He understood that appearance was the thing. Therefore, he would appear to be a grand and much regarded man.

"It is a great a pity Cynthia could not be with us today," said Mrs. Lynn in an effort to spur conversation.

"Oh, my dear." Sir Anthony's lazy drawl, like his restless stick, was an affectation. The world understood that even the speech of a truly fashionable gentleman should never be hurried. "You know Cynthia does not care for society. She is better off at home where no one will see her frowns."

"Still." Mrs. Lynn sighed. "It cannot be good for a girl of her age to be so much alone. I should warn you, Sir Anthony, I mean to set myself to drawing her out."

"There is no need to concern yourself over Cynthia. She will hardly thank you for it," said Sir Anthony. "Now, there is Lord Harringdon." The stick swept toward a portly gentleman in a flamboyant silver and blue waistcoat. "I'm afraid I must go and speak with him. I'm sure I can rely on you ladies to keep each other company?" Without waiting for an answer, Sir Anthony slipped his arm from under Mrs. Lynn's hand and sauntered toward the unsuspecting Lord Harringdon.

Mrs. Lynn stepped back so she now stood beside Elizabeth, who had not yet left off searching the crowd.

"What do you suppose Sir Anthony wishes to speak about with Lord Harringdon?" she asked. Then, she leaned in close to the younger woman and said more softly, "I don't think your beau's here yet."

"Oh." Despite this depressing news, Elizabeth managed to keep her expression tolerably still. She even made herself turn her attention toward her father, who by now had pinned his quarry in a corner. "Lord Harringdon is a sporting gentleman," said Elizabeth. "I expect Father is talking about the races."

Part of the reason that the Pump Rooms were so full was the rapid approach of Race Week. The town, and its famed racecourse at Lansdown, were readying themselves for a week of thoroughbred racing. The annual event drew great crowds of people from across Great Britain, indeed, across the Continent, all come to watch, to bet, and to buy.

"A sporting gentleman, you say?" murmured Mrs. Lynn, craning her neck to get a better look at Lord Harringdon. "Is he someone we should invite to the card party, do you think?"

Elizabeth considered. "He might be interested," she said. "I'm told he has bet large sums on other races."

"Well, then, I shall speak to Sir Anthony and make sure he

has issued the invitation." Mrs. Lynn squeezed Elizabeth's arm. "Do you spy anyone else who might be helpful to our general enterprise?"

"Are you sure we need anyone else?" murmured Elizabeth. "I worry we are too large for safety as it is. What if people start talking?"

Mrs. Lynn laid her hand on her friend's arm. "It will be all right, Elizabeth."

"Will it?" asked Elizabeth sharply.

"Trust a woman who has some experience of the world. I understand that right now is an anxious time, but it will pass. And as for the size of the thing, the bigger the better."

"Well, if it falls apart, I suppose we can still rely on Clara and her good Lord Casselmaine to save us all." Elizabeth pulled a face.

"Stop that," Mrs. Lynn said. "You mustn't be frowning when your father returns. He will exile you as he does Cynthia, and then how will you contrive to meet your beau?"

Elizabeth looked abashed for a moment, but then managed to regain control of her features.

"Much better." Mrs. Lynn squeezed her arm. The latest gaggle of visitors streamed through the main doorway, causing the crowds to stir and reform themselves. Mrs. Lynn noted two faces in particular among the new arrivals.

"Oh, look, Elizabeth, is that not your friend Miss Summerscale?"

Elizabeth's face brightened at once. "It is. Mrs. Lynn, will you mind very much if I go speak to her?"

"Not at all," said Mrs. Lynn breezily. "In fact, I spy one of my own friends." She nodded toward the tall, stout man with the pink face who was writing his name carefully in the visitors' book.

"A male acquaintance?" breathed Elizabeth with mock horror. "Why, Mrs. Lynn!"

"Shh, you little terror." Mrs. Lynn nudged Elizabeth playfully with her shoulder. "You will have Sir Anthony turning me out into the street."

The two women shared a brief giggle. Then, Elizabeth turned and hurried to catch up to her acquaintance. Miss Summerscale was a rather gawky young woman who, Mrs. Lynn happened to know, fancied herself a social rebel. This made her glad to help Elizabeth slip her father's (admittedly very loose) nets.

Once Mrs. Lynn saw that Elizabeth and Miss Summerscale were safely engaged in conversation, she looked toward Sir Anthony. He and Lord Harringdon were now talking with a third gentleman, which was a most welcome development. Satisfied she was not needed or too closely observed, she set about making her way toward the pink-faced gentleman. He had finished laboring over his signature and now moved toward the windows. The movement seemed to cost him some effort, because a sheen of perspiration now covered his brow. He pulled a large handkerchief from his pocket with which to mop his face.

He saw her approaching through the crowd and beamed broadly.

"Mrs. Lynn. How delightful." He bowed. "I had heard you were in Bath."

"Mr. Wallace." She made her curtsy. "How do you do?"

"Very well, very well, thank you."

"And your friend, Mr. Spence. How is he?"

Wallace chuckled ruefully and tucked his handkerchief away. "Dissatisfied as always, but I think not more than is usual for him."

"Is he here?"

"Out in the gardens, I believe. You know his penchant for the delights of fresh air." They smiled sagely at each other. "Do I find you alone?"

"No, no." Mrs. Lynn waved casually toward the room. "I am here with Sir Anthony and his eldest daughter, but both are engaged at the moment."

Wallace nodded. "Well, I trust Sir Anthony will not think it improper for you to take a turn with me?"

"I am sure he will not mind in the least, as you are such an old friend of my family."

Mr. Wallace offered Mrs. Lynn his arm. Together, they joined the procession of fashionables walking in a large, lazy circle about the room's perimeter. Their various conversations made a constant noise, much like the rush of a river. Everyone was so busy with their own affairs and gossip, and no one wasted a moment attending to what this new couple might have to say.

"Have the middle Kinsdale girl and her duke returned from London yet?" inquired Mr. Wallace.

"They have," replied Mrs. Lynn calmly. "She's been breezing about the house, making a great show of being contentedly involved in her engagement preparations. Honestly, she should take acting lessons from her sister." She lifted her gaze to the broad doorways just in time to see Elizabeth stroll out with her friend beside her.

"Syl," said Wallace suddenly. "I've been thinking we should consider closing shop early."

Sylvia bit down hard on her initial startled exclamation. "Whatever for?" she asked, making sure that the tone held a casual laugh, in case anyone was listening. It was true that a crowded room was one of the safest places for one to engage in private conversation, but one must still exercise discretion.

"One of our fish is getting suspicious," replied Wallace softly.

"If you mean Miss Clara, it is all in hand."

"What do you mean? You must know that she and her duke meant to visit this Rosalind Thorne woman?"

"Of course I knew, and they did."

That startled him. His arm tensed. "How do you know what they did?"

"I sent Sophia after them."

"What!" he cried.

"Hush, Wallace!" She dug her fingers into his arm. "You'll have people looking."

Wallace dropped his voice to a polite murmur, but his tone lost none of its urgency, or its outrage. "You sent Sophia on an errand without saying anything to me!"

"What, and have you tell Spence? He would have raised a hue and cry and tried to forbid it, and we would have had to argue with him, and that would take up time that we do not have."

Wallace glanced away, unable to deny her assertion.

"And what, exactly, was your plan when you decided to haul Sophia away from her post?" he murmured.

"To delay Miss Thorne's arrival, of course. Sophie gave out that she's my illegitimate daughter, and that this is the dread secret I am harboring, and begged her to please give me time to tell Sir Anthony the truth in my own way."

"You think Miss Thorne will believe her?"

Sylvia shrugged. "She might, especially given the gossip circling the Kinsdale girls. But to tell you the truth, I'm hoping she won't believe it."

The force it took to hold back his immediate exclamation turned Wallace's pink face an alarming shade of red. "Then why . . . ?"

"Because if Sophie's done her job properly, Miss Thorne is even now taxing her imagination for ways to try to hunt her down. After all, whoever Sophia may be, she must know some vital secret that she and I are trying to protect. Otherwise why would she appear so suddenly to make such a dramatic claim? And if Miss Thorne is chasing Sophie about London, she can't be here causing trouble."

Wallace stared at her, his look slowly changing from disbe-lief to admiration.

"I never should have doubted you, Syl."

"No, you shouldn't." She beamed at him. "Be patient, Wal-lace. We only need to delay Miss Thorne for another se'en night, and we'll all have everything our hearts could desire. Now," she said, firmly changing the subject. "Tell me how things are on your end. How goes the betting talk locally?"

"Very much as we would hope," answered Wallace. "Sir Anthony's helping us at every turn." He nodded toward the corner where Sir Anthony was still in confidential conversa-tion with Lord Harringdon and the other gentleman.

"I was sure that he would," Mrs. Lynn murmured, at the same time another, unwelcome worry stirred. This one, she could not successfully keep out of her expression.

"What is it, Syl?" asked Wallace. "And don't tell me noth-ing. You haven't gone soft on the mark, have you?"

"Never," said Mrs. Lynn firmly. But she saw she must give him some answer. "It's the girls. They're going to be crushed when this is over."

"Pfft." Wallace waved this away. "The duke will take care of them. They've nothing to fear."

"It's not always about money, Wallace."

"So I've heard." He touched her elbow. "You'll keep to your part in this, won't you?"

"When have I ever not?"

"First time for everything, isn't there?"

Her brow knitted. "And what's that supposed to mean?"

"It means that I'm frightened, Syl," said Wallace. "If we don't pull this thing off, there will be some very angry people looking for us and not all of them are gentlemen."

Sylvia fell silent, her mind racing. She thought of the money, of course, and Sir Anthony and all his daughters, and the famous Miss Thorne, who might soon be swooping down on them like a witch out of legend to work her evil deeds.

She thought about Elizabeth's concern that their little enterprise had grown too large for safety, and found herself wondering if the girl might be sensing something that she herself had missed.

If that was the case, though, what could be done? It was already too late to change course.

Wasn't it?

CHAPTER 7

Upon Arrival

*These were thoughts, with their attendant visions,
which occupied and flurried her too much to leave
her any power of observation.*

Jane Austen, *Persuasion*

"Well now!" Mr. Leigh, the landlord of the Green Briar Inn, placed the step beneath the carriage and held up his broad, calloused hand to help Rosalind down. "Good morning, Miss Thorne. Or I suppose I should be saying Mrs. Rutherford, shouldn't I?" Leigh gave Rosalind a heavy wink and a grin as he used Rosalind's *nom de voyage*. "We've been expecting you an hour since. Welcome to Bath!"

Adam dismounted his horse and came to Rosalind's side. At the same time, Laurel, their maid, climbed down from the box and immediately began to give orders to the inn's porters about the luggage.

The Green Briar stood on the edge of Bath's oldest quarter. It was a U-shaped building with a deep cobbled yard and open balconies on the second floor. When the weather was good, trestle tables and benches filled the courtyard. Rosalind had heard that once upon a time, traveling players had performed in that yard, and that the landlord was in the habit of telling his guests that one such troop contained a promising young playwright named William Shakespeare.

"Hush now, Leigh!" The landlady bustled up to the carriage, drying her hands on her starched apron. "She's traveling quiet like!"

Mrs. Leigh was a wiry, dark woman with a sharp nose and a chin to match. Her gaze was as shrewd as it was lively. Rosalind could feel her taking in the dress and details of her new guests with an exactness that would have done credit to any London hostess.

"Oh, get away with you, woman!" her husband cried cheerfully. "There's none to hear. Now then, Mr. H . . . Rutherford is it?" Leigh clapped Adam's hand in friendly greeting. "You're both welcome! Ah, now there you are, Mrs. Kendricks! Here is your—" Leigh broke off because his wife was glowering at him, and pulled a face. "—Mrs. Rutherford come to stay."

The woman who emerged from the inn was plainly related to Mrs. Leigh. Indeed, they were almost twins. Mrs. Kendricks was also a thin, dark woman. She also had the same severe eyes and narrow hands that Mrs. Leigh possessed.

It had been years since Rosalind had last seen her.

Mrs. Kendricks had kept house for Rosalind's family. When her father deserted them, Mrs. Kendricks stayed. When her mother died, and even Rosalind was forced to move out of her godparent's house, Mrs. Kendricks had come with her. She'd even—albeit reluctantly—assisted in the first of the inquiries that had confirmed Rosalind as a useful woman to know if one was attempting to avoid scandal, or worse.

They had finally parted ways when Rosalind turned down Devon's proposal of marriage once and for all. With that act, Rosalind had decided to walk toward the very uncertain future that held her independence, and her relationship with

Adam Harkness. This time, Mrs. Kendricks chose not to follow her. As a woman who had already worked through years of little or no pay, she had to consider her own future. So, when her sister in Bath offered her a place helping to run their inn, Mrs. Kendricks decided she would accept.

Rosalind missed her but did not in any way blame her. Rosalind had, after all, rejected both security and societal expectations for the slenderest of reasons. Also, it was generally expected that an employer would provide their closest servants with a pension, or legacy. Rosalind could promise Mrs. Kendricks neither. At the time, she couldn't even have promised to keep a roof over their heads.

Now, Rosalind met Mrs. Kendricks's searching gaze, and was aware of being very nervous, as if she'd been called into the headmistress's office.

"It is good to see you again, ma'am, sir." Mrs. Kendricks dropped a brief curtsy.

"Mrs. Kendricks," said Adam. "You are looking very well." He bowed.

"Thank you, sir," she replied stiffly.

Mrs. Leigh was looking curiously from Adam to Mrs. Kendricks. "Well, now, I was just about to show Mrs. Rutherford up to her rooms."

"Oh, you needn't bother, Mrs. Leigh," said Mrs. Kendricks. "I'll do that. If you'll come with me, ma'am?"

"I'll follow with the trunks, ma'am," said Laurel to Rosalind.

Miss Thorne thanked her and started after Mrs. Kendricks, leaving Adam to pay off the driver and make arrangements for the return of the extra horse they'd hired.

Once Rosalind had agreed to help Miss Kinsdale, it had taken three full days to organize their travel plans to Bath. To begin with, Rosalind found herself with over two dozen letters to write. First, she wrote to Clara Kinsdale to affirm that she would be traveling to Bath as soon as possible to look into matters there. Then, it was necessary to arrange lodgings, because Rosalind and Adam might need a freedom of movement that they would not find if they stayed either with the Kinsdales or Devon. After that, Rosalind wrote to her sister, Charlotte, and to her friend, Sanderson Faulks, requesting their help with various matters. After that, she wrote to her patronesses and her current clients, clarifying the state of all their affairs. She informed them that while she was away, Miss Alice Littlefield would be supervising all current matters and making sure they were proceeding as expected.

Alice, in turn, spoke to her brother George, as well as her particular friend, Amelia McGowan. She let them know she would be managing Rosalind's business for the next fortnight or so, and that she would be grateful if they would call on her at Orchard Street, preferably during the days when anyone who might be paying attention could see them, and thus be led to believe that Miss Thorne remained at home to visitors.

After that, there were letters to write to various friends and acquaintances to try to find out if anyone might have known a financier named Lynn who had married a Miss Sylvia Westerford. In particular, Rosalind wrote to Devon's cousin, Louisa. While Devon and Miss Kinsdale said she had been unable to help them, it was possible that time and consideration might have unearthed something from her, or her husband's memory. Replies were to be directed to the Green Briar Inn in care of one Mrs. A. Rutherford.

Adam, for his part, had requested permission from Sir David Royce—the coroner for London and Westminster whom he served as an assistant—to take leave. Once this was granted, he arranged to hire a carriage and horses for the journey. He also engaged a driver—who, for a relatively modest additional fee—was willing to drive the carriage to Clements Circulating Library on the day of their departure. There, the driver met with a gentleman dressed in a plain buff coat and tall hat, who was accompanied by a lady in a straw bonnet and light blue pelisse, and that lady's maid. He then drove these persons to Orchard Street, where he let them out.

Roughly half an hour later, he returned to the same house. A man in a plain buff coat and tall hat, accompanied by a lady in a straw bonnet and light blue pelisse, emerged, followed by the lady's maid. The whole party climbed into the carriage and drove away.

Shortly after that, anyone who was watching the house would have seen another lady, in a much lighter bonnet and a green coat, going to and fro on various errands about the neighborhood, accompanied by her petite, dark-haired friend. Had they stopped to gossip with the neighbors, they would most certainly have been told that the taller lady was the notorious Miss Rosalind Thorne, and the other was her friend Alice Littlefield, and they were doubtlessly up to some of those inscrutable "doings" that the lady seemed continually involved in.

"And here we are, ma'am." Mrs. Kendricks opened the door to Rosalind's room. It was small but scrupulously clean, and while the bed was narrow, it was comfortably made up with thick quilts and snow-white pillows. The wardrobe, table, chairs, and washstand all looked to be in good repair. There was even a window out onto the courtyard.

"The parlor's at the end of the hall," Mrs. Kendricks said. "I'll have the girl bring up tea and there's fresh bread and a good stew on the fire now if you're hungry."

"Thank you, Mrs. Kendricks. That will be lovely."

Mrs. Kendricks met her gaze. Rosalind found she was holding her breath.

"You look well," said Mrs. Kendricks.

"Thank you," said Rosalind. "I am well."

"Truly?" A world of meaning filled that single word.

Rosalind nodded. "And vastly content. But how are you?"

"Run off my feet daily," Mrs. Kendricks answered, and they both laughed a little. "But the work is good and there's the children, and my sister. I am glad to be with my family, and I find I quite like being part of building a good living to pass onto the young ones. Not that I regret my time in service, of course. . . ."

"Of course not," said Rosalind promptly. "I am glad you've found yourself a good place here. I know you've always preferred a busy house."

"That I have." Mrs. Kendricks smoothed her skirts needlessly. "Well, I had best let you settle in. There's some letters for you on the table, and a card came just this morning."

"Thank you. And, Mrs. Kendricks?"

"Yes, miss? Ma'am?" she quickly corrected herself.

"Would you spare a kind word for Mr. Harkness?" asked Rosalind. "He's afraid you don't like him."

Mrs. Kendricks lifted her chin, but Rosalind did not miss the sparkle in her eye. "I dare say, that since you look well, and are, as you say, vastly content, I can bring myself to extend some Christian charity to the man."

"Thank you, Mrs. Kendricks," said Rosalind solemnly. "You set my mind quite at ease."

"Not at all, ma'am. Ring if you need anything."

The door opened then, and Laurel arrived ahead of a strapping young man bearing Rosalind's trunk on his shoulders. Mrs. Kendricks slipped away, and Rosalind and Laurel began the business of unpacking her things and putting the room in order.

At the same time, Rosalind found herself with the melancholy awareness that at least for now, she would not be saving room for Adam.

The journey to Bath had been a strange interlude for Rosalind. She and Adam had decided that they would travel incognito, and for simplicity's sake, give their names as Mr. and Mrs. Rutherford.

To have a wedding trip, however brief, before the wedding was scandalous in the extreme. At one time, Rosalind would have turned away from even the suggestion that she would do such a thing. Even now, if it was discovered she had traveled incognito in Adam's company, Rosalind might come to regret it. For this moment, though, she found herself enjoying an unexpected sense of discovery.

It was her first time playing through the day-to-day details involved in an intimate partnership, and she was pleased to find that there were a number of practical advantages to the arrangement. Rosalind was, of course, perfectly capable of giving instructions at a coaching inn. But as Mrs. Rutherford, she could give instructions to the landlord while Adam, as Mr. Rutherford, dealt with the grooms and arranged for the change of horses. Then, while Mrs. Rutherford gave orders for their dinner and dickered over the cost of candles and fresh linens, Mr. Rutherford saw their bags ferried up to the room for Laurel to unpack.

At first, Rosalind thought Laurel might be an awkward presence for the journey. It was necessary for Rosalind to have a maid with her, otherwise no one would believe her to be a lady of any standing whatsoever. Laurel, however, proved herself to be a very easy companion. She declared that since it was her first time leaving London, she was determined to view as much of the country as she could, and coaxed their driver to allow her to sit up on the box with him. This left the interior of the carriage entirely to Rosalind and Adam. Although, sometimes, when they slowed for some obstacle or to pass another carriage, Laurel's careless laughter floated down from the box and they found themselves looking at each other with raised brows.

"Should you say something to her?" asked Adam.

"She's above twenty," said Rosalind. "And she's been in service much of her life, which means she's hardly a sheltered girl. Her sister runs a boardinghouse, and looks after their ailing mother, and they depend on Laurel's support, so I do not think she will risk too much on a light flirtation."

"Well, then, perhaps we should follow her example?" Adam took her hand and pressed his lips to her fingers. "Have I told you, Mrs. Rutherford, how very lovely you look today?"

"Mr. Rutherford, you are incorrigible."

"Entirely, Mrs. Rutherford."

If their two days of travel were filled with tiny discoveries, the night was a haven of ease—beginning with the fact that they could enter the same room without creating suspicious looks. There was no need for Adam to wait until the household had gone to bed so he could sneak in to meet her, and he did not have to leave before dawn. Rosalind could fall asleep beside him, knowing that she would wake in the morning and see him there—rumpled and stubbled and yet somehow handsome beyond her wildest imaginings. She could relish the moment when he yelped and laughed because she had pressed her cold feet against his, or when she yelped and started because he rolled over and threw his arm around her waist.

At the last post inn before Bath, they stopped once more. There, Adam hired a horse, so that he could ride into town as the proper escort of an unmarried lady. The change left Rosalind feeling more bereft than she expected, and she found herself musing over the details of her trousseau with unusual sentiment, and wondering if there might be money enough for at least a short honeymoon.

There will be time enough for all that, Rosalind told herself sternly. *For now, there is work to do, for both of us.*

CHAPTER 8

The Lay of the Land

*". . . you tell me nothing which does not accord
with what I have known, or could imagine."*

Jane Austen, *Persuasion*

Adam was unsurprised to find that the Green Briar was an orderly and cheerful place. He knew Mrs. Kendricks well enough to be certain that she wouldn't be connected to any establishment that wasn't immaculate. The yard was swept, and all the buildings seemed to be in good trim. The men all seemed to be brothers or cousins of the Leighs, and they clearly knew their business when it came to the horses. Adam soon had his box stowed in his room at the end of the hall, next to the private parlor. He heard Rosalind's and Laurel's voices coming out of her room as he passed, and considered knocking on the door, but decided against it.

Let her have this moment to settle in. She needs it.

Once he'd unpacked his belongings, Adam took himself downstairs to get the lay of the land. He knew he wouldn't sleep easily tonight if he hadn't gone over the property at least once, especially since Rosalind was with him. He wasn't a nervous man, but he was cautious. Rosalind's inquiries, and his own, had brought trouble to their doorsteps more than once. He wasn't about to wait for an emergency to find out where the inn's exits and entrances were.

He'd just finished his circle around the outside and was coming back into the yard when he ran into Mr. Leigh.

"Now then, Mr. Rutherford." Leigh added a wink as he spoke the name. "All squared away?"

"You've a fine house here, Mr. Leigh," said Adam.

"Well, I do thank you. Mrs. Kendricks, she'd a deal to do with it. A right slovenly lot we were when she came to us, but she had us all whipped into shape inside a month." This last at least, Adam could readily believe.

"It's a hot day, Mr. Leigh," he ventured. "I'd be glad to share a drink with you, if you've the time?"

Leigh grinned. "I was just saying to myself that a drop would be most welcome. After you, sir."

The public room looked out onto the courtyard. The windows were open, letting in the fresh breeze but also the smells of hay and city summers. Sir Anthony brought down two pewter pots from the hooks above the bar and filled them both from a crockery jug.

"There now." He set a pot in front of Adam. "You try that and tell me if it's not the best you've ever tasted."

The ale was excellent, and Adam said so. Leigh's grin broadened.

"That's Mrs. Leigh's doing. She brews it and won't tell anyone her secret. Founding the family fortune she is."

Adam raised his pint. "To Mrs. Leigh's very good health."

"And to the health of Mrs. Rutherford," Leigh returned, raising his own. "Mrs. Kendricks says you're here to do with the races."

"The races?" said Adam surprised.

"Well, you're here about the Kinsdales, so it's got to be some'at to do with the races."

"I know Sir Anthony breeds horses," said Adam. "But I

hadn't heard that he was running any this year." In fact, from what Rosalind had told him, there weren't any left to run.

Leigh was giving Adam a sideways glance, as if deciding how much to say.

Adam leaned over the bar. "Mr. Leigh, this business, it's personal for my wife." As he called Rosalind his wife out loud, his heart thudded once, hard. "There's an old friend of hers who could be hurt if things go badly for the family, and she wants to prevent that. If you know anything that might be helpful . . ."

Leigh glanced toward the door. "Well, all I can rightly say is this friend, whoever they may be, should think long and hard before putting their money on Kinsdale's Pride."

Adam raised his brow, and waited.

"Now, I don't know if you're a betting man yourself," Leigh went on. "But the races here attract all sorts. The men who have horses in the running come early, if they can. Gives the horses time to rest from the journey, get fed, work with the trainers and the riders. Get fighting fit, as it were. Some of the lads from the stables and the trainers come here when they've a night off, and I can't help but hear some of the talk."

Adam gestured gently with his pint pot, indicating that no one could help hearing the things said right in front of them.

"Now, you know and I know that when it comes to a race, the real money's not coming from the prize, is it? The real money's in the betting."

Adam nodded. This was true everywhere.

"So, from what I hear, this Sir Anthony, he's got some sort of reputation for breeding horses, or at least his family did some time back. But what they're saying is that this year he's brought in a skinny nag . . . the lads were having a right laugh over it. Bag of bones, they say. Couldn't outrun a drunken snail. But Sir Anthony, he keeps bringing these sporting types out to the stables. Paid off at least one of the men to get him to say nice things about the horse. Even got his ladyfriend batting her eyes at them and all—"

"Ladyfriend?" said Adam casually.

"You know how it is." Leigh gave Adam another one of his heavy, knowing winks.

Adam did indeed. He finished his pint and laid a couple of coins down on the bar. "Thank you for the drink, and thank Mrs. Leigh," he said. "If it happens you hear anyone talking about the Kinsdale horse, you might let me know, if it's no trouble?"

The coins were gone before Adam could blink. "I can't see it being any trouble, sir, you being friends with my wife's sister and all."

Adam took his leave of the landlord. He went back out into the courtyard. The sound of children's laughter rang out and a flock of the youngest Leighs raced screeching across the yard, followed by Mrs. Kendricks flapping her apron at them.

"Away! Away with all of you!" she cried, but when she saw Adam, she drew up short.

"Good afternoon, Mrs. Kendricks." Adam tried to keep his tone conversational, but he was conscious of more than a little wariness. Mrs. Kendricks did not exactly blame him for Rosalind's failure to accept Devon Winterbourne's proposal, but she didn't entirely absolve him either.

"Good afternoon, sir." Mrs. Kendricks smoothed her apron down. "Little urchins," she added fondly. "I found them in the larder, rooting through the apple barrel. It seems one of them has done something to the window latch."

"Children can be very enterprising in that way. My siblings and I were in constant trouble with our mother." *And a good number of the neighbors.*

Mrs. Kendricks's expression said she could readily believe that. "I trust you've found everything satisfactory with your room?"

"Indeed I have, thank you."

"If you were looking for Miss . . . Mrs. Rutherford, I believe you'll find her in the parlor."

"Thank you, Mrs. Kendricks."

"Mr. . . . Rutherford?"

"Yes, Mrs. Kendricks?"

She drew herself up very straight and met his gaze. "I have not yet had the chance to congratulate you on your forthcoming marriage. I wish you very happy."

Adam bowed. "Thank you, Mrs. Kendricks."

She nodded, smoothed her apron with a brisk gesture, and marched straight back into the inn.

Adam felt himself smile, and went to find Rosalind.

As Mrs. Kendricks predicted, Rosalind was in the private parlor at the end of the hall. She sat at a table by the window, with several letters spread out in front of her. She looked up as he entered and smiled in welcome. Adam's heart performed a complicated maneuver—something between a flip and a tight squeeze, and he knew he'd best get used to it, because it was the inevitable result of seeing Rosalind light up when she knew he was there.

"I was just about to come looking for you," she said, as he took the chair opposite her. "We've an invitation from Sir Anthony Kinsdale for tomorrow." She held up the card. "'There's to be an evening of supper and cards with a, quote, few select friends, end quote. Devon's also written." She held up one of the letters. "He says he'll be there, and has offered to send his carriage for us at seven. He thinks it advisable to impress upon Sir Anthony that we are his special guests."

"This means evening dress, doesn't it?" said Adam.

"I'm afraid so."

Until he'd met Rosalind, Adam had never worn evening dress, let alone owned its components. It was actually their friend Sanderson Faulks who took him aside and told him that his wedding present to Rosalind would be to make sure that Adam was properly outfitted to escort her to (almost) any sort of event. He'd taken Adam to his tailor and during a session that he sincerely hoped none of his former Bow Street colleagues ever found out about, Adam had been measured for a suit of clothes that he (reluctantly) admitted would prove useful to own, but that he mostly tried to ignore.

Rosalind was watching him. "Is everything all right?"

"Except for the evening dress, it's all as it should be," he answered. "But I did have a word with Leigh and he had some interesting things to say about Sir Anthony Kinsdale."

"Did he?"

Adam nodded. "It may be that Mrs. Lynn isn't after access to Casselmaine's fortune after all, or at least that might not be what drew her to this family."

"You think she might not be a fortune hunter?"

"It's more a question of which fortune she's hunting. We knew the Kinsdale family has a reputation in racing circles."

"Yes, and Clara said they were forced to sell all their horses."

"But it seems they kept one," Adam told her. "And Sir Anthony has entered it in the sweepstakes at Lansdown. The men who work at the stables don't think much of its chances."

"Ah. That might explain why Clara didn't like to mention it. But what has this to do with Mrs. Lynn?"

"Where there's racing, there's betting," said Adam. "And where's there's betting, there's cheating."

Rosalind considered this. "Well, if this is about a horse rather than simply access to ready money, it would explain a question I've had."

"What question is that?"

"The timing of Mrs. Lynn's entry into the Kinsdale family circle," said Rosalind. "From Clara's account, Mrs. Lynn became attached to Elizabeth before the Kinsdales moved to Bath. That was while Clara's relationship with Devon was still in a state of considerable uncertainty. What hardened fortune hunter would spend time on a relationship when the fortune might still fall through? Unless she'd planned to try to snare Devon for herself, but that doesn't seem to be the case."

"And if she thought she could facilitate matters, she would attach herself to Clara rather than Elizabeth," said Adam.

"But you think she's attached herself to a bad horse instead?"

"It's not as outrageous as it first appears," said Adam. "There's plenty of people who can be convinced to believe in a long shot, if someone tells them a good enough story."

Rosalind nodded. She'd certainly seen that for herself.

"Well," she murmured. "One thing we can say is that this will surely be a most interesting card party."

CHAPTER 9

A Second Meeting

*. . . she said all that was reasonable and proper on
the business . . .*

Jane Austen, *Persuasion*

"Thank you so much for coming, Miss Smith." Alice
ushered the woman calling herself Miss Sophia Smith
into the parlor. Tea was waiting, along with a plate of Alice's
favorite muffins, and dishes of fresh butter and jam. "I am
Alice Littlefield, Miss Thorne's private secretary. Won't you
sit down?" She gestured to the chair she had positioned
across the tea table from the sofa.

"Thank you."

Alice poured out a fresh cup of tea, surreptitiously eyeing
her guest as she did. Miss Smith was much as Rosalind had
described her—a mature woman dressed to make herself appear younger. She wore a simple white dress with a modest,
square neckline and trimmed with pink ribbons. Her dark
hair had been braided and coiled into a simple knot at the
back of her head. She kept her eyes downcast and her hands
neatly folded.

Really, it's an excellent performance.

"How do you take your tea?" Alice asked.

"Just milk, if you please," replied Miss Smith. "Will Miss Thorne will be us soon?"

"I'm so sorry." Alice passed the cup. "Miss Thorne is not free at present. Lady Jersey had requested a confidential meeting, which is something she simply could not ignore. I'm sure you understand." Alice held out the plate of muffins.

"Oh, yes, of course." Miss Smith selected a muffin and set it on her plate. "Only . . . I thought, well, with the advertisement in the paper . . ."

Rosalind had left her sister Charlotte and Alice with the responsibility of making sure it looked like Rosalind was still at home in Orchard Street. But she'd also left them the job of finding this young woman who had made such a deliberate scene, then vanished, and gave every sign of not wishing to be found again. Alice and Charlotte had talked the matter over and both agreed this was one time when the direct approach was probably best.

"It will also have the advantage of making it look like no one here suspects there is any deception at work," Charlotte had said, and Alice agreed.

So, Alice had sent her brother, George, who wrote for the *London Chronicle,* out to place personal notices in several of the most widely read newspapers. The notice read:

> *Will Miss S. Smith please return for tea this Tuesday? She will then hear something to her advantage regarding her personal business.*

After that, there had been nothing to do but wait, and hope Miss Sophia Smith read the correct papers.

"I'm sorry if you feel you were invited under any false pretenses," Alice told Miss Smith. Although, of course, that was exactly what happened. However, since Miss Smith's arrival was also under false pretenses, Alice didn't feel the least bit guilty. "You may be sure, however, that I am acting in accordance with Miss Thorne's instructions." This much was perfectly true.

"Oh. Yes. I didn't mean to imply . . . And Mr. Harkness? Will he be here?"

Alice smiled sympathetically. "Miss Smith, your visit the other day caused some small upset, and if what you have already said is true, there must be some changes in what had previously been settled plans."

Miss Smith's chin quivered and her eyes widened. "You don't . . . you don't believe me?"

Oh, bravo! Alice put her cup down and reached out to take Miss Smith's hand.

"Oh, Miss Smith, please, please forgive me!" Alice cried. "But you must understand, I find myself in a delicate position." Alice drew back, and dropped her gaze for good measure. "You see, as part of my work for Miss Thorne, I am responsible for making sure that her affairs remain in good order. As her reputation has increased, some ladies, and not a few gentlemen, have begun seeking her out under genuinely false pretenses"—*If I ever used such a phrase in a manuscript, Mr. Colburn would stab his quill right through the paper!*—"and when they do, they tend to present rather remarkable stories. You understand, I'm sure?"

Miss Smith's gaze didn't waver. "Oh, yes. People can be so deceitful."

Alice smiled, as if grateful to be understood. "So, it is my responsibility to make sure those who arrive without appointments, but *with* stories, are, in fact, who they say they are."

"Oh, yes, of course!" said Miss Smith earnestly. "I do see that."

"I'm glad. Because you'll understand then that since you ended your visit so suddenly when you were last here—without even leaving a card!—we were entirely perplexed as to how we would find you. The advertisement was the only way we could think of."

"I'm sorry to have put you through the trouble. I should have thought." Miss Smith blinked rapidly, as if holding back tears of self-recrimination. Alice mentally saluted her. She really was very good at this. "But I was so worried about Mama, and then about being found out. They're very strict at my school, you see."

"And perhaps you did not think Miss Thorne would want to speak with you again?" suggested Alice. It was as close as she planned to get to a real question, but she also very much wanted to see what Miss Smith would say.

"Oh, no," said Miss Smith breathlessly. "I felt sure she would. I had in fact, planned to come back." *That's a nice touch*, thought Alice. "I ask you to understand, Miss Little-field, when you have been forced to keep so much of yourself secret, it becomes very difficult to be fully honest, even when one knows one should."

Alice returned her most benevolent smile. "I do understand, and I know that we can quickly clear everything up. Then, Miss Thorne will be able to assure Miss Kinsdale that all is right. That, in turn, will allow Mrs. Lynn to tell the family everything they need to know in her own time."

"Are you sure?"

"I am. I've known Miss Thorne for a long time, and I promise you, she always does her best to help those ladies who are navigating thorny personal issues." Now was not the time to go into the fact that the one thing that Rosalind abhorred above secrets was being lied to.

And this particular lie, as embodied by Miss Smith, was becoming more elaborate by the minute.

"Now," said Alice briskly. "Do you have a card?"

"Oh, no," said Miss Smith. "They don't let us have our own at school."

"Well, that's understandable. Which school is it?" Alice reached for her pencil and notebook.

"Lady Norfolk's Select Finishing Academy for Young Ladies," replied Miss Smith. "In Bolton Street."

Alice wrote this down. "Excellent. Now all that's needed is for me to call on the headmistress and confirm your enrollment. Once that's done, I will be able to assure Miss Thorne as to the veracity of your story, and she will know how best to act."

She fully expected Miss Smith to beg her not to go anywhere near the school in Bolton Street (if there was one). But the young woman surprised her.

"I do see that you would have to call at the school. All I ask is that you not say who you are. I don't . . . I'd never ask anyone to lie, but if the headmistress knew that I'd slipped out, and to where, I'd be in terrible trouble! I might even be expelled!"

"I do understand," Alice assured her. "I shall say only that I am looking into schools for my niece and that your mother recommended Lady Norfolk's. Would that do?"

"Ye . . . es," said Miss Smith slowly. "That should do very well. Thank you for understanding, Miss Littlefield. And . . . and please let Miss Thorne know I'm sorry to have caused any trouble."

"That's quite all right, my dear." Alice patted Miss Smith's hand again. "It's perfectly natural, considering the circumstances. Now." She glanced at the clock. "I have another appointment and I'm sure you must be getting back to your school. Shall I have Mortimer arrange for a cab?"

"That would be very kind. Thank you."

"Not at all." Alice beamed. "You've been through so much. I know Miss Thorne will want to help you and your mother however she can."

Miss Smith's smile was filled with relief and gratitude, and was, Alice felt sure, just as false as her own.

A few short minutes later, Alice stood on the front step as Mortimer helped Miss Smith into the cab he'd fetched for her. She watched with a glow of contentment as the young lady was driven away.

That contentment turned just a little bit fierce as, less than a minute later, a second cab drove up the street. When this new vehicle passed the house, its curtains opened to reveal an (to Alice's eyes) adorable ginger-haired woman, who waved enthusiastically.

Alice blew her a kiss and grinned. She grinned again as the cab passed, and she was treated to the most unusual sight of a long-legged man in a worn coat and trousers perched on the cab's luggage rack. This unusual choice of seat meant that he would be next to invisible to anyone looking at the cab from the front. He would also be able to slip off, unseen, as soon as the cab stopped.

The man, who happened to be Alice's brother George, touched his hat brim to Alice. Alice curtsied briefly in response.

Mortimer observed all this with a level of stoicism that verged on boredom. "Anything else, miss?"

"Not at present, thank you," replied Alice.

Alice took herself back inside the house and into the parlor. "That sounded like it went well."

Mrs. Charlotte Black, Rosalind's older sister, was seated at the tea table, spreading a muffin with butter and jam.

"I hope so." Alice poured herself out some fresh tea. "But Miss Smith was far too prepared for my liking."

"Yes, she's definitely a canny one." Charlotte took a healthy bite of muffin. She was with child again, she'd informed Alice, and the result was a greatly increased appetite. "I admit, I'm surprised she didn't balk when you said you'd call on the headmistress of that school."

"So am I, a little."

"You don't think she's actually enrolled?"

"Good lord, no. I think somebody's bribed the headmistress."

"Yes, I would tend to agree." Before her marriage, Charlotte had had what could charitably be described as a colorful career. It included some years as a successful courtesan, and some others as a courier and spy for the crown. These experiences gave her an astonishing breadth of insight. "I also expect she'll stop her cab at some random point, and insist to the driver she can't risk being seen arriving at the school in such a fashion."

"We can trust Amelia and George to be ready for that."

"I have every confidence." Charlotte finished her muffin and wiped her fingers delicately. "What will you do now?"

"Write to Rosalind," said Alice promptly. "She'll want to know we've unearthed the mysterious Miss Smith and shall soon take full possession every one of her secrets."

Charlotte's brow furrowed. "Let us just hope that in the process she doesn't take full possession of ours."

CHAPTER 10

All Manner of Arrivals

". . . that she is a clever, insinuating, handsome woman, poor and plausible . . ."

Jane Austen, *Persuasion*

There were very few things in the world that made Adam Harkness grumble. One of those, however, was evening dress.

However much Rosalind might assure him that he looked stunningly handsome in white silk breeches and a black coat—especially when paired with a simple blue waistcoat—he would only pull a face and tug at his sleeves.

"I'm sure I'd be much more use talking to Leigh and the grooms," he said.

They met in the Green Briar's private parlor. Rosalind wore one of her new gowns—a deep blue creation trimmed with silk brocade and sapphire ribbons. A light cap with a small white feather covered her hair, an affectation that conveyed her status as a married woman.

"I'm afraid I cannot possibly go without you," Rosalind told him. "You are my disguise."

Adam arched his brows.

"Rosalind Thorne is famously unmarried," she reminded him. "The best mask I can wear is that of a married woman. But to do that convincingly, I am afraid I must be able to display a living husband." She brushed at his coat's shoulders.

Adam sighed dramatically and lifted his chin. Rosalind smiled, and reached up to perform that most wifely of duties—she retied his cravat.

"I love you," said Adam, more to the ceiling than to her.

"And I love you," said Rosalind. "Now more than ever. And you look devastatingly handsome."

"I look like I've been trussed up for market."

"You most certainly do not! I tie a very simple and stylish cravat."

"I most heartily beg your pardon. I did not mean to fault your skills." He held out his arm. "Shall we?"

Devon's carriage arrived promptly at seven. He had evidently decided to put his rank on full display. Not only did the carriage have gilded trimming and the ducal crest on the door, it was accompanied by a large number of attendants in livery to carry torches, manage the horses, place the steps, and help both Rosalind and Adam inside where Devon waited for them. Laurel, who was accompanying them, took her preferred seat on the box, once again saying that if she was going to be traveling, she wanted to see as much as possible.

As the doors were closed, Rosalind, Adam, and Devon all wished each other good evening and Devon ordered the driver to touch up the horses.

"We are most honored, your grace," Rosalind said lightly as the carriage started forward.

"Yes, I know, it's a bit much." Devon gestured to indicate all the outriders and link boys surrounding the grand vehicle. "But I need to put on a show for tonight. In fact, if I'm being honest, I am making blatant use of you both."

"Oh, really?" Rosalind did her best to put on an indignant frown, and almost managed it.

Devon returned a sheepish grin. "I'm afraid so. You see, since the Kinsdales arrived in Bath, Sir Anthony has been hosting these card parties. Clara, though, has been insistent that I keep away from them. The fact that I need to be on hand to introduce you to the family is my excuse to barge in and see the situation for myself."

"You're worried about something?" Adam asked him.

"Very much," said Devon. "I've seen rather too much of what 'a little card party' can turn into." He stopped, pensive, and his gloved hands shifted uneasily on the walking stick he seldom carried.

"However, it may be that I'm too suspicious," he went on, in the tone of one trying to convince themselves. "Bath has its own social divides, and some people consider themselves above mixing in the assembly rooms. That makes entertaining privately a mark of consequence, which would be very much in keeping with Sir Anthony's character, and careless nature."

"But just in case, you hope to frighten him into better behavior?" asked Rosalind lightly, but her question was serious, and Devon took it so.

"Yes," he answered flatly. "And, frankly, to make it that much harder to ignore whatever questions you end up asking, *and* whatever you discover about Mrs. Lynn." He paused, and then said softly, "I love Clara, and we will be married unless she decides to refuse me. But I can't ignore the fact that it would be much better for both of us if she could start her career as Duchess of Casselmaine without the extra weight of scandal pressing on us both."

Adam and Rosalind shared a long look of understanding.

"We'll do what we can," she said.

Devon inclined his head. "That's all I ask."

*   *   *

Rosalind had not spent much time in Bath. She and Charlotte had visited several times when their mother decided to take the waters, and, incidentally, find opportunities to meet families who were "worth knowing" on a more intimate footing than London's rigid rules afforded. As a girl, Rosalind had very little appreciation of how hard their mother worked to contrive acquaintance and influence. Father was a valued dinner guest wherever he was known, but it was Mother who made sure he was known.

She did remember that Bath was a place of contrasts. The busy city was nestled in quiet green hills with a tranquil river winding through them. The half-timbered buildings that had looked out over the cobbled streets since the days of Queen Elizabeth were hemmed in on all sides by classically styled public buildings and modern terraced housing, with the great sweep of the Royal Crescent presiding over them all.

The direction given on the invitation was for the King's Circus, an unusual series of town houses that curved around a central drive. Three streets radiated between the blocks of houses like spokes from a wheel. The Kinsdales' home was on the end of one of these blocks, which made it one of the larger homes in the Circus.

As soon as Devon's people helped them from the coach, footmen in indigo and silver livery emerged to usher them all through the modest-looking front door. But the front door, it seemed, was all that was modest about the dwelling.

"Oh," said Rosalind as the maid removed her cloak and bonnet.

"Well," added Adam.

"Yes," agreed Devon.

The interior of the house was nothing short of opulent. Whoever had been responsible for its decoration had obviously been deeply affected by the previous decade's mania for all things Russian. The entrance hall was hung with amber silk

and flanked by columns of pink marble with gilded finials. A
red carpet led from the door all the way up the long, straight
staircase to the first floor.

Two footmen in full livery, as well as a cluster of maids,
stood ready to help Rosalind, Adam, and Devon with their
things, while yet another footman bowed to them all. "Your
grace, sir, ma'am, Sir Anthony has requested you join him
and the family in the salon. If you will follow me, please?"

The interior of the house followed the plan of the entrance
hall with red and black pillars, marble everywhere it might
be managed, and gilding on all the finials and scrollwork.
The salon to which they were shown was done in shades of
vibrant turquoise. Peacock feathers accented the flower arrangements in the brass and cloisonné vases. The footman opened
the door and announced them, and all the salon's occupants
turned toward them.

It was Clara who came forward at once and they all exchanged their reverences.

"Good evening, your grace. Mrs. Rutherford, Mr. Rutherford, how very good of you to come. Please, allow me to introduce you to my family."

She led them forward to where an aging man in an old-
fashioned (and very bright) brocade coat stood with a small
cluster of women. Rosalind was hard pressed not to cast a
glance at Adam to say, *you see how things could have been
worse?*

"Your grace!" The man—surely Sir Anthony—cried. "How
very good of you to lend your presence to our humble gathering!" He bowed in a great, theatrical sweep, complete with
an extended leg.

Sir Anthony was a tall man. His hair had gone quite gray,
although a few streaks of auburn remained. His coat was
rose pink and silver, with a cravat tied in the elaborate "water-
fall" style spilling down his shirt front. A gold quizzing glass
hung from a chain about his neck. As far as Rosalind could

tell, the only concession he made to current tastes was in forgoing lace cuffs to trail from his coat sleeves.

"Father?" said Clara to him. "May I introduce Mr. Adam Rutherford and Mrs. Rutherford. Mrs. Rutherford, Mr. Rutherford, my father, Sir Anthony Kinsdale."

"Delighted, ma'am, delighted, sir. Yes, delighted." Sir Anthony favored them both with his sweeping bow, but his voice had turned bland, almost bored. Adam's smile tightened the tiniest bit, and his eyes narrowed. Rosalind felt sure that Sir Anthony's characteristics were all being catalogued for analysis, and that analysis would be accurate, but far from flattering. She herself noted that good living had filled out a paunch beneath Sir Anthony's silk waistcoat and left him with a saggy chin and rheumy eyes, all of which rendered his performance of the manners of a sophisticated bon vivant from some bygone day more than a little awkward.

If he was aware of any particular scrutiny however, Sir Anthony gave no sign. "Do allow me to present my oldest daughter, Elizabeth, and her sister, Cynthia."

Elizabeth, the oldest of the Kinsdale sisters, was a match for Clara in terms of her sweep of auburn hair, green eyes, and pale skin. But Elizabeth was thinner than Clara, her face sharper, and the expression in her dramatic eyes was altogether harder, as if she were constantly looking for flaws and fabrications.

Cynthia, however, was shorter and rounder than either Elizabeth or Clara, and where they possessed auburn hair, hers was a plain brown. But the differences did not end there. Cynthia wore the air of someone who had been looked down on both literally and figuratively. Elizabeth might give the impression she was looking about for flaws. Cynthia, however, was waiting for criticism.

Rosalind wondered at all of this, and at the fact that Elizabeth was introduced as "my oldest daughter" while Cynthia was "her sister."

"And this"—Sir Anthony now drew himself back as if making way for royalty—"is Mrs. Sylvia Lynn."

"Oh, heavens, Sir Anthony!" Mrs. Lynn laughed. "With so much pomp, you'll make the Rutherfords quite afraid of me." She beamed at them all and made her curtsy. "How do you do? It is lovely to see you again, your grace. Mrs. Rutherford, Mr. Rutherford, I am delighted to meet you."

That voice, thought Rosalind, would be her chief attractant. It was low and sylvan and very smooth. Mrs. Lynn was a mature woman, and a bit taller than average, though not as tall as Rosalind. A pretty little cap crowned her dark hair, signifying her widowed status. She had a plump figure and a vivacious air. Her peach-colored gown with its single row of ruffles and net sleeves was in the latest mode, and exhibited all the tasteful restraint that Sir Anthony lacked.

Rosalind found herself searching Mrs. Lynn's countenance for resemblances to Miss Smith, but could not make up her mind if she really saw them.

"Do make yourselves comfortable," Mrs. Lynn continued. "You'll take some sherry?" She didn't wait for an answer but instead went straight to the sideboard and began filling glasses from a crystal decanter. Now that the necessary introductions had been made, it was very clear that she was the one who would perform the hostess's duties for this occasion. Rosalind looked to the Kinsdale sisters to note their reactions to this: Elizabeth appeared indifferent, and Clara a trifle embarrassed. Cynthia, however, very much looked as though she wanted to be elsewhere.

On the surface, Mrs. Lynn appeared to notice none of this. Rosalind, however, watched her eyes. In contrast to her appearance of insouciance, Mrs. Lynn's gaze was sharp. She took in all the people, how they stood, and what their deportment said of them, and all this while she was pouring out the sherry and handing around the glasses.

We shall have to be very careful, thought Rosalind as she accepted her sherry.

It was Elizabeth, however, who opened the conversation, and she did so with what Rosalind could only interpret as a challenge.

"Mrs. Rutherford, Casselmaine was just telling us that you've known his family for quite some time," said Elizabeth. "How odd it is that we have not crossed paths before."

Clara drew a little closer to Devon, and Rosalind had the suspicion she might be holding her breath. However, Rosalind had expected this question and she and Adam had between them planned their answer.

"Her grace the duchess met my family in London during the season," she said. "It was the year I made my debut, as it happens."

"Oh, yes," said Clara brightly. "I think Casselmaine told me you danced?"

Devon laughed. "If one can call it dancing, but that was my fault," he added quickly. "I'd shot up six inches that summer and barely knew where my feet were."

"You are too generous," said Rosalind. "I was so unnerved by finding myself the center of so much attention that I could barely remember my own name, let alone how to manage a country dance." This much was quite true, whatever might have come afterward. "Shortly after that my father received a posting in Paris, but Lady Casselmaine and my mother kept up a regular correspondence."

There was some risk in this declaration. While Rosalind spoke good French, neither she nor Adam had ever been to Paris. But no one had a chance to quiz them any further. All conversation was cut off by the sound of a door slamming and men's voices shouting, followed by the rapid clomp of boots as someone ran up the stairs.

The ladies froze. Sir Anthony jumped back. Devon and Adam—seemingly acting on the same thought—both moved to put themselves between the door and the assembled company.

The door flew open and a tall, broad man in a naval uniform coat stormed into the room. He had fading yellow hair and a face that had been bronzed and battered by sun and wind. One of the Kinsdales' many footmen trailed behind him.

"I'm sorry, Sir Anthony, I tried to stop—"

"I'll have a word with you, sir," snapped the naval man.

"Admiral Walsingham!" Clara stepped around Devon. "What brings you here?"

"Your father brings me here, Miss Clara," Admiral Walsingham announced. "Your father who means to throw my wife and myself out of our home!"

CHAPTER 11

A Confrontation

It was a struggle between propriety and vanity;
but vanity got the better . . .

Jane Austen, *Persuasion*

"It is not your home, sir," drawled Sir Anthony. His face had gone pale, but his tone remained as it had been—bland and a little bored. He did not, however, make any move to step closer to Admiral Walsingham. Instead, he raised his quizzing glass, as if it could act as a shield between himself and the intruder. "It is my house—nay, it is my ancestral home—which I was persuaded to lend to you, and that much against my better judgment. Now, by your conduct, I see that I was right to hesitate."

"What is it you are suggesting, sir?" demanded the admiral.

"That you have violated the terms of our agreement, sir," replied Sir Anthony. "In a most underhanded and ungentlemanly fashion. I was assured—repeatedly assured—that you and your wife were childless. And yet what do I hear now?" Sir Anthony drew himself up with self-righteous dignity. "There's a boy—a most rambunctious and uncontrollable boy—running riot over my grounds and wrecking heaven knows what sort of havoc in the house that has been home to the Kinsdale line for generations!"

In her dealings with the *haut ton*, Rosalind had witnessed many well-bred people taking offense over entirely trivial matters. This, however, was beyond anything in her experience. Sir Anthony's declaration was so aggrieved, but stated offense so small, Rosalind found it hard not to gape at him.

"That boy is my nephew, sir," said the admiral. "And—"

"And the house is *my* house," interrupted Sir Anthony.

The admiral set his jaw. "I was warned," he growled. "I was told Sir Anthony is vain, he is capricious. He has unending pride in his family but no care of his reputation, never mind that of his daughters. I was warned to have no dealings with him because he is a fool!"

Adam was holding himself very still. Rosalind recognized that particular alertness in him. He was watching the admiral, watching Sir Anthony, watching Devon, waiting to see which of the men would move first, and getting ready for whatever they might do.

Sir Anthony's pale face flushed red. "You, sir!" he cried, his voice high and thin with anger, and not a little fear. "You may remove yourself, your wife, and whatever urchins you have brought with you, back to Liverpool or Plymouth or wherever it is the navy skulks about these days."

"I shall remove you to a court of law!" bellowed the admiral. "I have been to the stables, sir, I know the game you're playing! You should be ashamed, sir!"

Stables?

But any reply Sir Anthony meant to make was interrupted by a peal of laughter.

"Oh dear!" Mrs. Lynn cried. "Oh, I am sorry." She pressed a flowing silk kerchief against her cheeks, and her eyes. "But truly, there is nothing more amusing than two gentlemen quarreling before dinner, do you not find, Mrs. Rutherford?"

She winked at Rosalind. "Especially when it is over some silly misunderstanding."

The admiral drew himself up even taller. Mrs. Lynn did not seem to notice this at all. Rather, she glided forward, slipping neatly past both Adam and Devon. "Now, Admiral Walsingham, you will understand you have arrived at a most awkward moment." She laid her hand delicately on the admiral's blue sleeve. "I am sure that was entirely unintentional. The navy, after all, is famed for its punctuality, and its foresight. But under the circumstances, you will, I'm sure, accept Sir Anthony's apology for not being able to attend to your business immediately; which I know would be his preference as well as yours!" She beamed at Sir Anthony. That gentleman looked quite ready to give his opinion on the matter, but she did not leave him room to speak. "I also know that you will be happy to accept Sir Anthony's promise that his man of affairs will wait on you first thing tomorrow—" She stopped, pressing her kerchief against her mouth with an air of pretty confusion "Oh! I should not say such a thing to a naval man! Your idea of 'first thing' is sure to be quite different from that of us lazy landlubbers!" She laughed again. "Shall we say ten o'clock, Sir Anthony?" She turned to him briefly, and then turned back to the admiral, just exactly as if she had received a response. "Yes. Ten o'clock. Matters may be fully explained then. I'm certain it will be discovered that Admiral Walsingham's dear nephew is only visiting, and that it was his urgent concern that there should be no misapprehensions between you that brought him here this evening. Naturally, had you two gentlemen been able to behave as you ought, we would have learned that his only desire was to promise he would stand the cost of any trifling damage the precocious child might inflict during his brief stay. Is that not the case, Admiral?" She blinked up at him.

Now Rosalind saw the resemblance to Miss Smith clearly. One of them had very obviously learned that expression of lovely innocence from the other.

But the admiral was not looking at Mrs. Lynn. He was looking past Devon's shoulder, at herself, and the Kinsdale sisters who had all clustered closely together. But exactly what he was looking for, or what he saw, Rosalind could not tell.

Despite this, Admiral Walsingham seemed to have heard, and understood Mrs. Lynn's words.

"Yes," he said curtly. "Yes, that was it."

Mrs. Lynn laughed again. "I must say, Admiral, a note would have done just as well, but I know that none of us can fault the navy for taking direct action to set matters right!" She beamed up at him. "You will, I hope, give my best regards to Mrs. Walsingham. Is she in town with you?"

"No, she stayed behind. I had no wish to expose her to this . . . unpleasant business, or to the fact that when we agreed to take Kinsdale House, we were misled as to the conditions, and the reasons."

Sir Anthony flushed more deeply and was ready to make a fresh angry retort, but once again Mrs. Lynn gave him no time.

"Well, perhaps you will be so good as to carry a letter to her from me? I will send it by Sir Anthony's man tomorrow."

It was an exquisitely discreet dismissal, and delivered as lightly as the rest of Mrs. Lynn's remarks. But something had changed. There was something brittle under the words. Rosalind watched the admiral consider whether to take further exception to this off-hand treatment, but instead, he squared his shoulders, and bowed.

"Your servant, ma'am," he said. But then he looked over her head, again, toward the knot of silent, disconcerted Kinsdales. "Sir Anthony, I look forward to meeting with your man. But I promise you, I will not spare him my opinion, nor will I conceal what I have learned. Neither am I afraid to stand up in a court of law in defense of my rights. A man who cries so loudly over his possessions and yet takes so little care of his reputation—or that of his family—sir, is not one who deserves any consideration."

He bowed again to the full company, and took his leave. The footman hurried after him, possibly to make sure he really did leave the house.

"Insufferable man!" Sir Anthony puffed out his chest. "Does he have any idea whom he is addressing? I have condescended to allow him the use of the Kinsdales' ancestral home, and this is how I am spoken to!"

"Why, Sir Anthony!" cried Mrs. Lynn. "I am surprised at you! To allow yourself to become so agitated over such a trifle! Come, sir." She turned to the sideboard and poured out a fresh glass of the sherry. "I must insist that you take this glass and calm yourself. Otherwise you will be unable to greet our guests this evening with that *esprit* they all expect from Sir Anthony Kinsdale." She handed him the sherry with the air of a nurse giving a child their medicine, and Sir Anthony drank it much in that manner.

"There!" Mrs. Lynn took the glass and set it aside. "Now, we shall have no more unpleasantness. I banish it all entirely." She waved her hands in a grand gesture. "Look, here is Perkins to tell us supper is ready. Lord Casselmaine, will you kindly escort Mrs. Rutherford in? Mr. Rutherford, will you please escort Clara?" The rules of the dining room declared that husbands and wives did not walk in together, and Mrs. Lynn seemed prepared to take advantage of this. "Sir Anthony, you have no objection to my arm, I hope?" She threaded her arm through his. "Thank you."

It was an extraordinary display of social expertise. Rosalind had seldom seen anything like it. She was taking Devon's arm, but her gaze shifted to Adam.

That was very neatly done. His expression told her.

Most impressive. Rosalind let her eyes flicker to signal her agreement. She wondered if Adam noticed what Mrs. Lynn had not done.

Mrs. Lynn had managed to reassure both men, and smooth over the disagreement about the house, and the child. She had not, however, said one word about the admiral's mention of the stables, or that he felt sure Sir Anthony was playing some game.

Where there's betting, there's cheating, Adam had said.

As Devon led her into the baroque dining room, Rosalind found herself noting the expressions of Clara and her sisters. Clara looked resigned. Elizabeth frowned, clearly concerned, and possibly a little afraid.

But it was Cynthia who truly drew Rosalind's attention. Her face had gone dead white and her eyes were entirely stunned. Indeed, the youngest Kinsdale sister looked as if she'd been dealt a severe and most unexpected blow.

CHAPTER 12

The Cook

"The day has produced some effects however; has had some consequences which must be considered as the very reverse of frightful."

Jane Austen, *Persuasion*

"Do you do a lot of this then?" Amelia asked George. She was currently sitting with Alice's tall, slender brother in a hired cab watching the front entrance of a new-ish terraced house in a quiet, tidy London neighborhood. They'd kept the curtains almost entirely closed, and the windows up to avoid being seen, or overheard. Unfortunately, one result of these precautions was that the tiny space was also mostly airless.

"A lot of sitting in cabs on sweltering summer evenings?" replied George. "Not as such."

"I meant skulking about in front of private residences."

"Not as much since I got married, but as a bachelor, I skulked with the best of 'em."

"Odd, Alice never mentioned it."

"Weeelll," George drawled. "It's not the sort of thing a chap talks about with his sister, really."

Amelia grinned. She liked George. She'd been worried about how Alice's brother would regard her, considering the nature of her relationship with Alice. But George had taken their situation in stride.

"Alice has every right to keep company how and with whom she chooses," he had said. "And if anyone wants to argue the point, I recommend they take it up with Alice. I also recommend they alert their appointed heirs beforehand."

But as much as Amelia liked him, and respected the skills he'd picked up in his years as a newspaperman, she was beginning to feel her patience wearing the tiniest bit thin. It had been several hours since they had seen Miss Smith (or whoever she really was) disappear into the pretty row house across the way. Since then the only sign of life from the house had been one of the servants going out with a basket to do a bit of late shopping.

"So, the plan is that we wait here until Miss Whoever-shemightbe comes out again?" asked Amelia.

"It is," replied George.

Amelia tapped her fingers restlessly against the carriage door handle. "What if I had a different idea?"

George cocked his head toward her. "That would depend on what it was."

Amelia leaned forward. "How are you at playing a drunken layabout?"

Amelia stood on the street, consulting a little notebook and squinting at the house numbers, as if looking for a particular address. Out of the corner of her eye, she could see the woman they'd watched leave Miss Smith's house stumping up the street, her basket full to bursting with vegetables and parcels wrapped in brown paper.

George was there as well. But he was hanging off the area railing of the house next door, and singing.

"There were three drunken maidens!" George sang, or, rather, slurred. "Come from the Isle of Wight!"

As she passed George, the cook, as Amelia guessed she was, turned up her nose and quickened her step. George lurched into her wake.

"An' they drank from Saturday morning!" he bawled. "Nor stopped for Saturday night!"

The cook hurried forward, and George broke into a staggering run to keep up. "When Saturday night came in, me boys, they would not then . . . !"

Amelia drew aside, but in the wrong direction. She collided with the cook, and then George crashed into them both. The cook shrieked and staggered. Her basket slipped off her arm, and the contents scattered all across the cobbles.

George roared with laughter. Amelia grabbed the basket.

"Get away with you!" She swung the basket at his head. "Souse! Roistering sot! Shame on you! Making trouble for honest women!"

"Hey! Hey! Stop tha'!" George drawled, but he also snatched the basket out of her hand and, dangling it high over her head, he half ran, half staggered off in the other direction.

"Oooo! Men!" cried Amelia, but she quickly turned back to the cook. "Are you all right?"

The woman was puffing and holding her sides. "Just about. Young rowdy! He's lucky I didn't get my hands on him, is all I have to say."

"Here, let me help you with those things." Amelia bent down and started gathering up packages. Soon, she had her arms full, and the woman was leading her down the stairs and through the door to the kitchen of Miss Smith's row house.

"Put those down there, would you?" The woman indicated the broad work counter that ran down the center of the room. "Thank you so much, Miss . . . ?"

"McGowan. Amelia McGowan."

"Maggie Stokes," the woman introduced herself. "I'm cook here, as I'm sure you've sorted out by now. Will you take a cup of tea by way of thank you? There's just time. Herself"—she jerked her chin toward the ceiling, indicating the young woman upstairs—"will be wanting supper early, as she's going out tonight, and the girl's got a bad tooth and gone to get it pulled, so I've no help at all today. Still, mustn't grumble."

Amelia settled herself on a stool, and worked hard to suppress her grin. Like most people who declared one "mustn't grumble," Mrs. Stokes did, in fact, grumble at length and was glad enough to have someone listen while she did.

She grumbled about the rudeness of young men as she picked over her packages, carrots, potatoes, swedes, and runner beans. She grumbled about the prices at the market and the impossibility of finding anything truly fresh these days at the poulterers, about the general uselessness of all "girls" and not a few of the men, who worked on the staff with her, which left her to do all manner of chores that she wouldn't have had to in a better managed house.

She also poured out a mug of tea so black it could have been coffee and pushed it toward Amelia.

"Is your lady the particular type?" Amelia blew on the tea to cool it. "Or is it that hard to find good help?"

This (as intended) set off a fresh round of grumbles. This time mostly about how "too many" was "too proud" to even think of taking up a position in the household of a single woman, and that just because she *was* a single woman. You might believe that beggars would think twice about being such choosers, times being what they were, but no, they just declared that their reputations would be spoiled and they would rather be out on the cobbles than do honest work in an honest house.

Mrs. Stokes further declared that she minded her own

business, and as long as her wages were paid on time, she was grateful for a place. Times were never good for a woman getting on in years, and one had to think of the future.

"Is it that hard then?" prompted Amelia. "I've never been in service with a single lady." Which was a lie, as she'd been in service with Miss Thorne, at least for a little while, but Mrs. Stokes didn't need to know that.

"Much less trouble than a bachelor establishment if you ask me," said Mrs. Stokes. "Much more regular habits and much less riot. If she takes herself off like she does tonight, it just leaves me more time to do my work and have things all nice and ready for the morning, and I needn't worry about her bringing a whole party back with her at last minute and turning the household on its head. Now, I'll say that Michaels— she's the lady's maid—she's got more reason to grumble than some, but between you and me, Miss McGowan, she's as much a gadabout as Miss herself, and so they suit each other perfectly well. To my way of thinking, Michaels should count herself lucky to have this place. She might find herself in a mischief in some other house." She nodded her head several times to emphasize that point.

"Where do they go?" asked Amelia, leaning forward, as if she was eager for the gossip. "The theater? Almack's?"

"Phew! As if one of those snobs would let a lady on her own through their doors! And that just for the crime of *being* on her own." Mrs. Stokes sniffed. "No. It's Barron's tonight, I heard Michaels say. And Olmstead's afterward and then a late supper at Rule's."

Barron's and Olmstead's were both gaming clubs, Amelia knew, and Rule's was a restaurant, one that didn't normally admit women at all.

Mrs. Stokes insistence that this was a respectable house was suddenly looking a bit questionable. But Amelia kept that observation to herself and finished her tea. While she did, Mrs. Stokes moved about the kitchen, putting things away and continuing with her long list of things she felt she mustn't grumble about.

"Well, I should be getting on," Amelia said when her mug was empty. "Thanks ever so much for the tea, and good luck with the supper tonight."

"Good luck to you, my girl, and if you're ever in need of a good place for yourself, you come see Mrs. Stokes. I'm sure we can find something for you."

Amelia hesitated for a single heartbeat. "You mean that, Mrs. Stokes?"

Mrs. Stokes looked hard at her. "You have experience?"

"I do. I been upstairs maid and lady's maid. I can make a light, clean and mend, and do hair."

"Where last?"

"Mrs. Charlotte Black," she said promptly. "Only the family's moving abroad, and I ain't going to no foreign parts."

"Good girl," said Mrs. Stokes. She drummed her fingers on the counter. "All right. You come with me."

"Where have you been!" cried George when Amelia climbed back into the cab.

"Getting a job in Miss Smith's establishment," she replied. The sight of George's jaw dropping was positively heartwarming.

"As far as anyone in the household knows, I'm on my way home to get my kit and I'm to be back at seven tomorrow morning. Oh, and Miss Smith herself is going to be at Barron's tonight," said Amelia.

"You're positively amazing."

"I know," replied Amelia calmly, and George laughed.

"You said Barron's?" George pulled out his memorandum book and made a note. "That's quite the destination for someone who's still supposed to be in the schoolroom."

"And quite the schoolgirl to have a whole establishment of her own, even if they are a little lax about checking up with references." Amelia let him help her into the carriage. "Seems to me we might want to send word to Sanderson Faulks. He's a member at Barron's, isn't he?"

"Faulks is a member everywhere," said George. "It's what makes him such a useful fellow to know." He tucked his book away. "Let's see if we can track him down, shall we?"

CHAPTER 13

The Dinner

*. . . longed for the power of representing to them
all what they were about, and of pointing out
some of the evils they were exposing themselves to.*

Jane Austen, *Persuasion*

It was possible that Rosalind had endured less comfortable
meals. At the moment, however, she was having difficulty
recalling when that might have been.

The food was plentiful and elaborately dressed, but for all
its garnish, the soup was watery, and the fish was perhaps a
trifle older than it should have been. The joint was tough, the
sauces were more flour and water than stock and wine, and
the seasoning on the greens was paltry, if it was there at all.

The staff was like the meal—plentiful but not evidencing
any particular quality or skill. The footmen who waited the
table did so stiffly. Their expressions were not merely the
blank mask of the professional servant, but actively bored.
They were not engaged with their work, Rosalind thought.
They were simply going through the required motions, and
waiting for the meal, and the day, to be over.

The diners were arranged in the conventional fashion—by

rank, sex, and age. Devon had been seated at the foot of the table while Sir Anthony presided at its head. The ladies, and Adam, were spaced between them. No effort, it seemed, had been made to bring in other guests who might "balance" the table, which contributed to the awkwardness of the meal.

It was Mrs. Lynn who kept up at least some semblance of conversation during this uneasy supper. She managed mostly by remarking on this person or that in such a way that would allow Sir Anthony to deliver some pronouncement about them. These, Rosalind could not help noticing, were generally unfavorable. While this tactic worked to keep Sir Anthony amused, it did nothing to relax the general company, much less soothe the anger blossoming behind Cynthia's silence.

At last—perhaps realizing that she had best attend to the mood of the rest of the table—Mrs. Lynn turned to Devon.

"Lord Casselmaine, you have not told us anything of your recent trip to London." Her eyes shone with a bright mischief. "I am dying to know if you found time to see the famous Miss Rosalind Thorne. A little bird tells me you know each other quite well."

Years spent in drawing rooms had given Rosalind a great deal of practice in the art of concealing her reaction to any statement, and she was grateful for it now. Otherwise she might have paused in scraping her fork through the thick gravy that accompanied the joint, or even blushed.

"The *famous* Miss Thorne?" cried Sir Anthony. "Infamous I would have thought."

"Her family and mine know each other," said Devon coolly. "I have met her on a number of occasions."

"On a number of occasions." Mrs. Lynn drew the words out, indicating that she had heard rather more from the aforementioned little bird. "But come, now! Everyone knows you two are fast friends! You must tell us, what is she like? A woman who can ferret out the secrets of the highest in the land . . . how I long to know her!"

Clara had colored a little. Rosalind felt her breath hitch the tiniest amount.

Elizabeth attempted a laugh. "Well, I for one hope she does not turn her gimlet eyes to us here in Bath. I am not sure our society could bear the scrutiny!"

"But how would we know if she did?" Mrs. Lynn's tone turned arch. "They say she is quite capable of disguising herself as all sorts of persons. Why, it is nearly race week, the town is full, and all manner of scandalous persons are flocking to Bath! She might already be among us!"

"You must not talk such nonsense, my dear Mrs. Lynn," said Sir Anthony. "Were she to come among us, we should know this Miss Thorne upon first sight, no matter how she was disguised."

"Would we indeed, sir?" inquired Rosalind. Adam raised both brows, and took a sip of wine. Devon suddenly seemed to find the greens left on his plate quite fascinating. Clara, on the other hand, busied herself by slicing her beef into minute ribbons.

"Yes, yes, of course," Sir Anthony said. "Such a woman must inevitably be coarsened by her association with so many rough and inferior types. Writers! Newspapermen! Bow Street Runners!"

Rosalind had to drop her gaze to her own plate. If she looked at Adam a moment longer she would lose all countenance.

"No, no," Sir Anthony continued. "We would know her at once by her weathered face. Her eyes must lack any true brilliancy, but instead be filled with native cunning! To say nothing of the state of her hands—which must be entirely stained and ruined by the grubbing about she surely must do. I defer to the delicacy of my current company and decline to refer to the stout, graceless figure that such a woman must possess."

Devon opened his mouth. Rosalind shot him a sharp look of warning. He closed it again.

"And yet, I understand she is received by Lady Jersey herself," Mrs. Lynn remarked.

Sir Anthony shrugged. "Lady Jersey may find her useful, and may even bestow upon her some condescension or false flattery. However, you can be certain that Lady Jersey withholds from this Thorne creature that true meeting of mind and manners which must occur among women of superior birth and breeding."

There, at least, his guess came close to the truth. Regardless, Rosalind felt it was past time to change the subject.

She smiled. "Well, however Miss Thorne may be spending her evening, I daresay she is not talking about us."

Mrs. Lynn laughed. "Oh, you are surely right, Mrs. Rutherford!"

"But what do you think might bring Miss Thorne to Bath?" Adam asked Mrs. Lynn. "Has there been some grave scandal?"

Rosalind bit down on her tongue. What was Adam doing, allowing this line of conversation to continue?

Mrs. Lynn laughed. "Oh, you must not mind me, Mr. Rutherford. I say all sorts of nonsense, mostly to hear myself talk." Her smile was pretty and vacuous, and did not reach her eyes. "As a matter of fact, I happen to know that Miss Thorne is ensconced in London."

"And how do you know that?" asked Elizabeth. There was a tense expectation underlying her question. "Have you set some sort of spy on her?"

Mrs. Lynn laughed again. "Good gracious, Elizabeth, how very melodramatic of you! No, I have no spy, but I do have the London papers. Miss Thorne lists her at home days in the social columns. They are Tuesdays and Thursdays, by the by. If she had left London, she would have noted that she would *not* be at home those days. There." Mrs. Lynn raised her wineglass to herself and her conclusions.

Elizabeth applauded and Mrs. Lynn bowed her head in acknowledgment. Rosalind noted the relief in Elizabeth's eyes.

But why would Elizabeth be the one worried about Miss Thorne?

The brief silence allowed Adam to pick a fresh topic for conversation.

"I understand, Sir Anthony, you have a horse entered in the sweepstakes at Lansdown?"

"Are you a sporting man, Mr. Rutherford?" Sir Anthony inquired.

"I have an interest in the turf," replied Adam mildly.

"Well, then, you will be *interested* to know that I shall be fielding not just a horse, but the winning horse." Sir Anthony smiled with a feigned self-deprecation. "You may not be aware of the reputation of the Kinsdale stables, but the bloodline of our horses is unmatched. I have of late been holding back my participation in the races. The breeding and training of thoroughbreds requires the greatest patience, as well as a superior understanding of horseflesh. But this year the Kinsdale line will return to the turf. Make no mistake, sir, Kinsdale's Pride will take the purse at the Somersetshire Sweepstakes, and that will be only the beginning."

"Of what?" breathed Cynthia.

Sir Anthony turned to her, clearly irritated. "What is that you say, Cynthia?"

Clara winced. A moment later, so did Cynthia, probably because of a sisterly kick to her ankle. But she did not take the hint. Instead, Cynthia drew herself up and looked her father directly in the eye.

"I asked, the beginning of what? The final ruin and humiliation of our family?"

"My dear—" began Mrs. Lynn.

Cynthia did not seem to hear her. "And is that humiliation to be with or without our bankruptcy?"

"Cynthia," said Sir Anthony sternly. "You will cease this unbecoming behavior immediately!"

"I will not!" Cynthia shot to her feet. "Why should I? You have ruined us! You have listened to this woman"—she stabbed her finger at Mrs. Lynn—"and put the last of our money on that ridiculous horse that will probably drop dead before it reaches the post! And if that was not enough, you have just demeaned and insulted the man who is our one remaining source of income! Over *nothing*!" Her voice rose to a shout. "And it was all in front of Casselmaine, who is probably now wondering what he's gotten himself into, *and* trying to decide if we can scrape together the money to sue him for breach of promise if he decides to abandon Clara!"

"That is quite enough," drawled Sir Anthony. "If you are unable to conduct yourself as befits a young woman of your breeding, you may leave the table this instant."

"Or what?" demanded Cynthia. "What else can you do to me?" She swept her hands out, indicating both her sisters. "To any of us?"

"I can order you from my house," said Sir Anthony coldly. "Indeed, I begin to wonder if I should have done before now."

Rosalind waited for Mrs. Lynn to interrupt with her laughter and her bright teasing, but even she seemed struck by the chill in Sir Anthony's words.

"Cynthia, you'd better go," whispered Clara.

"And there will be no need for you to attend the party this evening," said Sir Anthony.

Cynthia stared at them all. "Yes, of course I should be the one who leaves. The fault is entirely mine for speaking the truth. Well, at least I am excused from another outrageous gathering, and that is something." Cynthia grabbed up her skirts and shoved her way past the chairs and out of the room.

The silence she left behind was deafening.

"I do apologize for my daughter, Casselmaine, Mr. Rutherford, Mrs. Rutherford." Sir Anthony's voice was dry and drawling as it had been when he was commenting on his horse. "I cannot think what has gotten into her of late. She was always such a meek little thing as a girl. Do you think, Mrs. Lynn, that she should be advised to take the waters?"

"I think she needs a little quiet," said Mrs. Lynn, but Rosalind could not help but notice the tinge of worry in her bright voice. "Clearly, she has become overwrought, and who can blame her? There has been so much excitement, what with Clara's upcoming engagement, and the races, and all the new society we have been introduced to of late. What a good thought you had, dear Sir Anthony, to excuse her from the card party tonight. After a night of rest, I'm sure she will be as right as rain. Now." Mrs. Lynn stood and beamed at the company. "I think it is time for we ladies to withdraw."

There was nothing to do then but for Rosalind to get to her feet and follow along.

CHAPTER 14

Some Cards with Friends

*It was but a card party, it was but a mixture of
those who had never met before, and those who
met too often; a commonplace business, too nu-
merous for intimacy, too small for variety . . .*

Jane Austen, *Persuasion*

Thinking on it afterward, Rosalind could only describe the
time she spent over coffee with the ladies of the Kinsdale
House as brittle.

It was not, however, subdued in any way. The greatest
shift in attitude came from Elizabeth. The contentious meal,
not to mention Cynthia's expulsion from the company,
seemed to have energized her. She joined Mrs. Lynn in insisting Clara describe her visits to London's warehouses, and
further requiring that she bring down the fabric swatches she
had picked out. These were then gone over with enthusiasm
and many sage pronouncements.

Clara herself was pale and piqued, and trying very hard to
hide it. Was she worried about Cynthia's exile? Or was it
something else? There was no way for Rosalind to ask. Elizabeth and Mrs. Lynn between them kept up such a steady
stream of talk that she could not get a word in edgewise.

By the time the footman entered to say that the first of the guests' carriages had arrived, Rosalind had begun to wonder if this was deliberate.

There was no formal ballroom in the house. There was, however, a series of airy rooms that led into one another and eventually opened out onto a pied-à-terre and the back garden. Tonight, the largest of these rooms had been filled with tables of various sizes, all covered in green baize. Here, the guests could settle themselves down for whatever game might interest them.

Elizabeth and Cynthia, along with Mrs. Lynn and Sir Anthony, stationed themselves at the entranceway to receive the guests. Rosalind took up a position near the threshold between the salon and the card room. She opened her fan, and pasted a small, interested smile on her face. Her plan was to watch as the arriving guests split into couples and knots and began to find their places for the evening.

Adam excused himself from a whispered conversation with Devon and came to stand beside her.

"This is going to be an interesting party," Adam murmured. Following his gaze to the gaming room, Rosalind saw that in addition to the usual packets of cards, and boards for cribbage, there were tables set up for some less well-regarded pastimes.

"Vingt-et-un," she remarked.

"And faro." Adam nodded toward the long table with the distinctive box positioned in the middle.

Faro was a highly popular gambling game that involved betting on which cards would be pulled from a spring-loaded box that was operated by a hand crank. It had a notorious reputation, and so many fortunes had been lost at the faro table that Parliament had passed several laws seeking to regulate its play. None of them had had any noticeable effect.

"I am counting twenty persons at the tables so far," Rosalind said.

"At least thirty more in the receiving line," said Adam. "I believe we were told this was to be a small party?"

Rosalind nodded, but she had no opportunity to say anything more. Devon had extricated himself from a party of enthusiastic gentlemen, half of whom appeared to be taking snuff as they spoke, and made his way to them.

"I am using you as a shield," he said to them. "Please keep me talking."

"At your service, sir," said Adam.

"Are you all right?" asked Rosalind.

But she could already see he was not. In fact, he looked positively grim. "I begin to understand why I've been kept away from these little card parties."

Rosalind nodded. Adam knew the story of Devon's past, and his antipathy toward gambling—especially by men who could not afford to lose.

Some instinct must have stirred in Clara Kinsdale, because she turned her head and met Devon's gaze. Even from where they stood, Rosalind could see the shame and remorse on her countenance.

"Go to her," said Rosalind. "She will think she's the one who's made you angry."

But he didn't move. Instead, Devon made a little gesture to Clara, as if he were lightly tossing something toward her. It must have meant something between them, because Clara smiled, and closed her hand, as if she were catching that same thing he threw. With that, she turned back to the receiving line and gave her attention to whatever it was her father and Mrs. Lynn were saying.

Devon watched her for a moment, smiling softly.

"You're the etiquette expert, Mrs. Rutherford," remarked Devon, his gaze still resting on Clara. "Would it be bad *ton* if I just bundled her into the carriage and drove hell-for-leather for Gretna Green?"

"I would not advise it," said Rosalind. "You did, after all, say you wanted to begin your married life without scandal."

"I may have changed my mind," Devon muttered.

"Understandable," said Adam. "But if you can hold your patience for another few hours, I think we'll be able to put any focus for scandal where it belongs."

"So soon?"

"I agree." Rosalind let her gaze rove around the room. She heard the slap of cards, and the rising tide of shouts, laughter, and curses. The receiving line was dissolving. Mrs. Lynn had taken Sir Anthony's arm to lead him on a circuit of the room. The couple paused every few feet to greet some gaudily dressed lady or red-faced gentleman. "This environment is made for letting secrets drop."

Devon was once again looking at her oddly. It was that same look she had noted when he sat in her parlor and listened to how she planned to proceed.

"Casselmaine," said Adam. "Let me ask you, have you seen this famous horse? Kinsdale's Pride?"

Devon's mouth twitched into a brief, mirthless smile. "I could hardly avoid it."

"Was Miss Cynthia's assessment accurate? Is it ready to drop dead at the post?"

"She exaggerated," said Devon. "But to my eye, not by much."

Adam was silent for a moment, taking this in. "Did you share your opinion with Sir Anthony? Perhaps try to dissuade him from racing the animal?"

"It hardly seemed worth the trouble," said Devon. "I thought it was simply one more concession to his vanity."

"How much has Mrs. Lynn encouraged this particular concession?" asked Rosalind.

"A great deal," said Devon. "But is it more than she encourages any of his other petty vices? I could not say for certain." He paused, turning over some thought in his mind. "That horse is like this house, like the coat he wears, and that quizzing glass. It's all part of his view of himself as an elevated and sophisticated man, and he will blame others if reality interferes with that view. Not too long ago, he dismissed his head groom without warning or reference. He'd been at a training run for Kinsdale's Pride and it didn't go well. He said the groom had been bribed by a rival breeder to poison the horse's feed."

"And was he?" asked Rosalind.

Devon stared at her, and when he saw she was serious, he blinked. "I don't know," he said. "I assumed not."

Adam and Rosalind exchanged a long look.

"You can't believe there was anything—" Devon stopped. "You do," he breathed. "You both do."

"I believe we don't know," said Adam. "But one thing we do know is that any conspiracy always involves more people than it appears on the surface, and has been in place longer than would seem possible."

"Conspiracy?" Devon barely remembered to keep his voice down. "Are you serious?"

"Look around," said Rosalind. "These are the people Mrs. Lynn names her friends. She has arranged for a place and time where they may all indulge a love of play for deep stakes. What if she's coaxing her friends to bet on more than cards?"

"So you think it's all to do with the *horse*?" hissed Devon.

Rosalind looked to Adam, and he nodded. "It's possible."

"I don't know whether to feel relieved or appalled," Devon muttered. "We asked you to find the truth about Mrs. Lynn but . . ." He shook his head.

"As Adam said, nothing's certain at this point," said Rosalind. "Casselmaine, if you will take my advice, you will go to Clara. She is going to be worried and need your reassurance. Let us work. We will have something more definite soon."

Again, that odd look. Now she felt she was beginning to understand it, and the result left a hollow feeling inside her.

But Devon bowed. "Thank you," he said, and left them.

He moved confidently through the rooms, artfully dodging attempts to engage him in conversation. He came up to Clara and bowed, and then took her hand. Clara looked up at him, and he smiled—not a small, polite smile, but a full, brilliant, thoroughly relieved smile. Rosalind imagined she could feel the warmth of it from across the room.

Something odd happened inside her, but she could not name what it was.

"Strange to see an old love so happy, isn't it?" murmured Adam beside her.

Rosalind felt herself begin to blush. "Does it show?"

"To me," murmured Adam. "And the feeling will ease itself. I promise."

"You speak from experience?"

Adam chuckled. "Rather a lot of it. I'm afraid before I met you I broke a lengthy string of hearts."

"Or a lengthy string of ladies broke yours?"

"A bit of both, perhaps," he admitted.

"You will please write out a complete list of the miscreants. I shall begin a vicious whispering campaign and ruin all their reputations."

Adam smiled, and reached out with two fingers to brush the back of her hand. Even through her glove, Rosalind felt her skin warming. She allowed herself to linger there, for no better purpose than to be beside him a bit longer.

As Rosalind and Adam watched, a set of chattering ladies moved from greeting the Kinsdales and Mrs. Lynn to a table set up for whist. A pair of gentlemen, already flushed with drink, seated themselves at the vignt-et-un table where one of the liveried footmen began to deal out the cards. From the eagerness of their expressions and the dexterity with which the cards were shuffled and dealt, Rosalind had the feeling that the play tonight would be very deep.

She let her gaze roam until she found Elizabeth Kinsdale. Elizabeth was still at the threshold of the salon. She was flushed with color and talking in a highly animated fashion with a cluster of gentlemen. She fluttered her fan in a show of enthusiasm.

But Elizabeth's attention was not on the men in front of her. It was on the case clock in the corner.

Rosalind felt her own eyes narrow.

"What is it you've seen?" murmured Adam.

"Elizabeth. She's waiting for someone, or for something."

"Any idea what it might be?"

"No. Not yet." She waved her own fan gently. "But I cannot help thinking of Admiral Walsingham, and Sir Anthony's expressed reason for ending the lease. What is it about a child that has him so disturbed?"

"Perhaps he was just looking for any excuse to remove his tenant. This one served."

"Yes, but again, why? It is clear he was very reluctant to rent the house, but he recognized the necessity of having some form of income. But now he has changed his mind. Why now? Before the race is run?"

"He's sure he's going to win," said Adam. "I have known some men to be that foolish."

"As have I. But again, I ask, why now? And why this excuse? What is it about a child in particular that so enrages him?"

Adam was silent.

"It may be nothing," she murmured, more to herself than to him.

"I'm sure it is not." He fell silent for a moment. "Well. I think I may try a hand of cards."

"An excellent idea," said Rosalind. There were few places so well suited to hear gossip than at the card table.

"And you?" he inquired.

"I believe it is time I gave some attention to the Misses Kinsdales." Rosalind snapped her fan shut. "And I believe I shall begin with Elizabeth."

CHAPTER 15

Party Manners

"There is always something offensive in the details of cunning. The maneuvers of selfishness and duplicity must ever be revolting, but I have heard nothing which really surprises me."

Jane Austen, *Persuasion*

Navigating a crowded party was a skill. Rosalind slipped casually between the knots of men and women, nodding politely when she happened to catch someone's eye. But for the most part Mrs. Lynn's gaudily dressed friends were deep in their own conversations. They talked and laughed with great energy. Unless she was much mistaken, they also kept up a steady stream of gossip about their fellow guests.

From the corner of her eye, Rosalind caught sight of Sir Anthony. He was holding forth to yet another group of gentlemen. The fact that this "card party" was more in the nature of a casino did not seem to have discommoded him at all. Rosalind was not surprised at his insouciance. His house was, after all, filled with guests. Mrs. Lynn had doubtlessly told him how many of these people who were now playing faro and vingt-et-un in his gilded salon were terribly important and influential. There was also the fact that from what she could hear, they paid him many pretty compliments.

It would be fairly easy to dismiss the whole party as just a harmless way to pass the time. The *haut ton* as a whole regarded gambling much the way it did strong drink. A man was expected to indulge in both wholeheartedly, and to stand the consequences with dignity. If he could not do so, he was regarded as less worthy in the eyes of his peers.

As with all things, the rules for women were different. A woman was never supposed to be seen to either drink or gamble to excess, but neither was she permitted to fully abstain. She must firmly control herself, and then aid and protect her male relations if their self-control failed.

The results of these twin expectations often brought women to Rosalind asking for help. Consequently, she had become rather more acquainted with the rules and customs of the gambling world than she had been previously.

"Mrs. Rutherford!" Mrs. Lynn glided into Rosalind's field of view, forcing Rosalind to turn and acknowledge her. "But you are all alone? How shocking!" Mrs. Lynn beamed. "It is, however, lucky for us both. I have been asked by Mrs. Collins to find us another player for our game of whist. You will oblige me, I'm sure?"

"I'm sorry, Mrs. Lynn," said Rosalind. "I must decline."

"Oh, don't be shy. Mrs. Collins is an excellent partner, and I am so unskilled, you are certain to take every trick."

Rosalind smiled. "I thank you for the invitation, but I do not play."

"Oh, tush. Everyone plays at least a little."

"Perhaps most people do. I do not."

Mrs. Lynn laid her fan across her bosom in a gesture of shock. "Do not tell me you are one of these Methodistical persons who frown upon innocent card games? I'm quite certain I saw Mr. Rutherford sit down for a congenial hand or two."

Rosalind smiled. "Perhaps Mr. Rutherford is a better player than I."

Mrs. Lynn's eyes narrowed. "I sense some mystery here. However, I shall not press you. Yet." She laughed. "But because of your stubborn refusal, I fear I must continue in my quest for a partner. Do enjoy your evening, Mrs. Rutherford." She patted Rosalind's hand in a friendly fashion and sailed away.

Rosalind stood back to let her pass, but when she looked up again, she saw Elizabeth Kinsdale was gone.

Well. She frowned to herself. *If that was a distraction, it was nicely done. I will have to be more careful.*

But now she was left with the question as to *why* Mrs. Lynn would want to keep her from reaching Elizabeth.

Rosalind strolled between the rooms, her gaze drifting across the gathering. Elizabeth, however, was nowhere to be seen.

Rosalind fluttered her fan and reached a decision. *Perhaps it is time to consider the obvious.*

Keeping her motions casual, she took herself through the French doors and out onto the pied-à-terre.

The back garden was a long, narrow space. It had been laid out with the same sort of taste as the interior of the house. Statuary—a promiscuous mingling of Greek and Roman styles—lined the brick walls. There was even what looked to be a folly toward the back. Rosalind suspected there was also a convenient door in the far wall, but the shadows were too thick for her to make out anything clearly.

Rosalind stepped to the side and drew back into the shadows between the house and a large stone urn. She waited quietly while her eyes adapted to the darkness.

There.

Now she saw movement among the deeper shadows. After a moment, she saw Elizabeth Kinsdale emerge, strolling toward the house as if nothing in the world were wrong.

Rosalind kept her gaze focused on the shadows behind Elizabeth.

There.

A silhouette waited in that deeper darkness. A man in a dark coat and a low-crowned hat, watched as Elizabeth returned to the party.

Rosalind held her breath.

Elizabeth passed her, walking back through the French doors without so much as flicking an eye in Rosalind's direction. The man stood where he was. Rosalind felt sure he was watching Elizabeth intently. She felt her throat tighten. Could he see her? What would he do?

But the man only faded deeper into the shadows. He moved cautiously but smoothly, like one used to the dark. If Rosalind had not been watching so closely, she would never have seen that back gate open, and close again.

Rosalind let out a long, soft breath. She stepped out of the shadows and turned to go back inside. Only to find herself face to face with Elizabeth.

CHAPTER 16

The Sisters

"Facts or opinions which are to pass through the hands of so many, to be misconceived by folly in one, and ignorance in another, can hardly have much truth left."

Jane Austen, *Persuasion*

Elizabeth stood on the threshold, all the light and noise of the party spilling out around her.

"Mrs. Rutherford." Her air of cheerful politeness that carried a diamond. "How are you enjoying your evening?"

"Very much," replied Rosalind. "Only, I find it rather close inside. One of the consequences of such a well-attended party, is it not?"

"Yes. Another is that it can be very difficult to speak in private."

Rosalind arched her brows.

Elizabeth laughed. "Oh, come, Mrs. Rutherford, let us not pretend. You saw me meeting a man in the garden."

"I did," replied Rosalind.

"And you are of course curious as to who it might be."

"I confess that I am."

Elizabeth laughed a little. But she also glanced over her shoulder. Rosalind could not tell what, or whom, she might be looking for, or indeed, if she found them. But Elizabeth stepped further out onto the pied-à-terre. Rosalind followed. Now they stood at the edge of the fall of light from the doorway—two casual acquaintances chatting and contemplating the shadowed statuary.

"Now I must ask for your discretion, Mrs. Rutherford." Rosalind's expression must have betrayed something, because Elizabeth laughed again. "Oh, no! It's not that! No. The man you saw is from the Lansdown stables, where we're keeping Kinsdale's Pride before the race." She dropped her voice yet lower, and the false cheerfulness fell away. "Since Father . . . well, the close care of an animal is not where his talents lie. So, I've asked the men to report to me whenever there's a change in her health. And you may understand, I cannot have Father thinking I am going behind his back—"

Rosalind nodded.

"So, discretion is needed. The man you saw leaving through the back gate is Caleb. Kinsdale's Pride has been off her feed and was showing signs of what might possibly be colic. However, he came to tell me that the draft she was given earlier seems to have done the trick and her appetite has returned."

"Well, that is excellent news," said Rosalind. "I'm sure you're much relieved."

"I am," said Elizabeth. "Mrs. Lynn tells me I worry far too much, and she's probably right. But when you've pinned every hope on one plan . . . it is difficult not to worry."

"I do understand," said Rosalind sincerely.

Elizabeth beamed, and in that instant, the expected party manners returned, drawing a veil over the young woman Rosalind had glimpsed so briefly.

"And now, you and I should return to the party before we are looked for. I trust the cards have been favorable for you?"

"I have not played," said Rosalind as they both strolled back into the heat and the light. Rosalind was not certain if the volume of noise had actually increased, or if her coming from the quiet of the garden made it seem that way. "I notice you do not seem to favor the tables either."

Elizabeth's smile at this was reflexive, and entirely bland. For a moment, Rosalind thought, she looked very like her father. Rosalind was aware of a mix of frustration and sadness. She felt she had almost glimpsed the truth of the young woman in front of her, but now Elizabeth retreated behind a veil of platitudes and clever talk.

"As you can imagine, Mrs. Rutherford, I have enough uncertainty in my life without adding games of chance." As if to emphasize this point, a burst of groans and laughter rose from one of the tables at that moment. Both Elizabeth and Rosalind turned to watch a young man delightedly raking in a large pile of tokens.

"I know what you're thinking." Elizabeth leaned in, holding up her fan to bring an air of confidentiality to their conversation. "It would not do at all in London, would it? Or even in our part of the country. But here in Bath things are much more free and easy. Personally, I am glad to have some life and color. Things were so quiet with us before we came here." The words flowed smoothly. Rosalind found herself wondering how many times Elizabeth had spoken them.

"I gather Mrs. Lynn arranges the guest list."

Elizabeth shrugged with one shoulder. "She knows so many people, it would be silly of us not to take advantage of her acquaintance."

"Was that how you came to know her? At a party?"

"Oh, no. It was the most absurd thing," replied Elizabeth. "A complete accident, if you must know. She was visiting a friend in our village. I had been making calls, and afterward decided to walk home, since the weather was so fine. I was passing through the market, and I heard a woman talking in a rather heated manner to a horse dealer. She was pointing out the defects in an animal that a friend of hers was planning to purchase. The friend, however, was dismissing all she said."

"This friend was a gentleman, I imagine?" put in Rosalind archly.

"Oh, naturally! Well, I don't know what imp took hold of me then, Mrs. Rutherford. It was most assuredly none of my business! But I stepped up to them both and said, "She is absolutely correct; what's more, the poor old beast's mane is very badly dyed." And I ran my hand down the mane—the creature was so dispirited it didn't even flick an eye toward me—and came away with black streaks all down my palm!" Elizabeth laughed at the recollection. "We'd gathered quite a crowd by then, and they all burst out in applause and catcalls and such noise! I took my leave as quickly as I could, because I really did think the dealer was about to meet with some violence from the mob! But before long, I heard someone calling after me. It was, of course, Mrs. Lynn. She thanked me for taking her part and insisted on purchasing me a new pair of gloves, and after that we went to the tearooms, and before the afternoon was over, we were fast friends."

"Was it their common love of horses that drew your father to her as well?" inquired Rosalind.

"That, and well"—she paused—"it is not the sort of thing one says, of course, but Father is one of those men who needs a woman's steadying influence. Since our mother died—" She stopped again. Rosalind waited. "—Well, he's been a bit lost. My sisters and I have tried to make up for it. At least, I tried," she amended, and Rosalind did not miss the bitterness under those words. It was the first genuine emotion she'd displayed since they had begun talking. "Clara has been too caught up in her own dramatics, and Cynthia, well, you saw my sister at dinner. She is either silent, or she's raging, and one can never be sure which way it will be from one moment to the next."

"She seems to feel she has cause for concern," said Rosalind. "Is she wrong?"

Elizabeth did not seem to hear the question. "If only she could see that she's not helping anything with her outbursts. Or her brooding. At least when Clara was worried she *did* something. . . ."

"You mean her engagement?"

Elizabeth turned fully toward her, her green eyes hard and assessing. "Do I shock you, Mrs. Rutherford? I'm sorry, I've become . . . well, jaded I suppose. But yes. Do not mistake me," she added quickly, remembering Rosalind was said to be a friend of Devon's family. "Clara truly cares for Casselmaine. But she wanted to wait. Not because of him, but because of everything our family has been through. That's always been Clara's problem. She doesn't trust herself, let alone any of us." These last words rippled with an old, cold anger. A moment later, however, Elizabeth seemed to realize she'd said too much. "But what must you think of me?" She forced her tone to become light and sunny. Now, she looked less like her father and more like Mrs. Lynn. "Spilling out my family troubles at a party, of all things! I'm so glad Sylvia—Mrs. Lynn, rather—did not hear me! She'd be teasing me for weeks! You won't say anything to her, will you?"

Rosalind made herself smile. "Your secret is safe with me."

"And now I must make the rounds." She sighed, her attention already drifting about the rooms. "You will excuse me, will you not?"

"Of course." Rosalind stood aside to let Elizabeth breeze past her into the card room, but she turned to watch where she went. Mrs. Lynn was also in the card room, at the faro table. She laughed and applauded along with the crowd of spectators as a fresh card was plucked from the box.

Elizabeth did not so much as nod at her friend. Instead, she made a beeline for the refreshment room. One heartbeat later, Mrs. Lynn left the faro table, and followed Elizabeth to the refreshments. They both stood facing the heavily laden table, but neither one of them helped themselves to anything. Elizabeth was talking. Mrs. Lynn was listening, and Rosalind, much to her frustration, could not discover any way to get closer to them both without being seen.

Rosalind turned away. She let herself drift into a quiet, or at least quieter, corner of the salon. She stood there for a while and thought about the evening. She thought about Admiral Walsingham, and his declaration that he knew what game Sir Anthony was playing and that he was not afraid to expose it. She thought about Cynthia in disgrace upstairs, and Elizabeth arranging meetings in the garden, possibly abetted by Mrs. Lynn.

She thought about the casino atmosphere all around them, and, most unusually for her, she found herself wondering once again about horses.

It was something of a relief to see Adam making his way toward her.

"I expected you to be a bit longer at your game," she remarked.

"So did I," said Adam. "Unfortunately, I don't have the ready money to join in most of the games the gentlemen are engaged in." His mouth tightened into a small, mirthless smile. "I did learn, however, that if I apply to a certain pair of gentlemen especially invited by Mrs. Lynn, I may obtain the requisite amount, by leaving my pledge to repay."

"Oh dear."

Adam nodded. "If I went to the magistrates now, I could make an excellent case that Sir Anthony should be arrested for running an illegal gaming house."

"Do you think he realizes?"

Adam's gaze swept the crowd. Sir Anthony was now standing with a little group of black-coated men who passed a snuff box back and forth between them.

"I think Mrs. Lynn will have deflected any concerns he might have had."

"I expect you are right."

"Several of the gentlemen did remark that the Kinsdale hospitality is much appreciated," Adam said. "And all the more so because it is widely understood there may not be many more evenings like this, especially once the sweepstakes are run."

"Given Cynthia's outburst at dinner, that's hardly surprising."

"Indeed. What did surprise me was that this sentiment wasn't universal."

"Oh?"

"Yes, there was an undercurrent of . . . something. Men at cards, some of them, will pretend to knowing more than they do, but there were some looks, some remarks. My lack of funds kept me from being able to stay in the game long enough to ferret out details, but something is going on."

"Something about the races?"

He nodded again, and dropped his voice even lower. "If I didn't already think there's some scheme centered around this poor horse of Sir Anthony's, I would now, and I think these parties, or at least some of the guests at these parties, play into it."

"I agree."

"Have you seen something?" Adam asked.

"An assignation in the garden, and a man who does not appear to be one of the party guests."

Adam's brows rose.

"And I believe that our hostess attempted to stop me from seeing Elizabeth leave."

Adam's brows inched higher.

"It was all easily explained however," she went on. "The person in question was one of the men from the stables, come to give her news regarding the horse's health. Apparently there was some concern about a colic developing."

Adam nodded. "That can be a very serious matter in a horse."

"So I am given to understand." Rosalind pursed her lips. "I think I should go visit Cynthia. She may be glad of someone to talk to who is not family."

"I think that would be a very good idea," said Adam. "I will try to have a few words with our host. And I think that tomorrow I will go speak with the admiral, before Sir Anthony's man of business arrives, if I can. I'd like to know exactly what he discovered when he visited the stables."

Rosalind nodded and folded her fan. She used the gesture to cover the touch of her hand on his arm. Adam smiled briefly, and they again went their separate ways.

CHAPTER 17

A Most Amusing Evening

*. . . she gave herself up to the demands of the
party, to the needful civilities of the moment . . .*

Jane Austen *Persuasion*

Barron's was one of a very particular type of London establishment. The usual gentleman's club existed to bring men of similar background together over at least a semblance of shared interest, such as horses, or clothes, or food. However, Barron's and its ilk existed to bring men together solely in order to separate them from their individual fortunes, however large or small those might be.

What kept Sanderson Faulks away from such places was less their dreary raison d'être and more their lack of imagination. They were, he found, tragically similar. The light was low to disguise any flaws in the room. Despite this, the gaming floors were kept bright with a great deal of gilding and a profusion of mirrors. There also tended to be a larger than usual number of paintings and statues that might be considered of a . . . stimulating nature to the majority of the gentlemen in attendance, and perhaps a few of the ladies.

Despite this, there could be a certain attraction in such

places. As much as he loved beautiful and precious objects, it was still the people, in all their glory, variety, and absurdity, that made any room interesting.

It was in the company of Rosalind and the Littlefields where Sanderson found a useful purpose for this combined love of people, beauty, and the absurd. This, in turn, had probably saved himself from succumbing to the all-to-common fate of becoming thoroughly jaded, not to mention more than a little absurd himself.

Now, for instance, he could make good use of his carte d'entrée into Barron's to discover more about the person George Littlefield had dubbed "the most mysterious Miss Smith."

She was quite easy to pick out, even in the crowded room. Amelia McGowan had described her with all the precision of an experienced servant. When one's living depended on the details of another person's body, one did naturally became very skilled at observation.

Sanderson watched Miss Smith from across the room. Even in the low lamplight, she shone like a beacon. She'd dressed herself to great advantage. In a place where the women favored ruby reds and sapphire blues, she was all in white silk and pink brilliantines. The effect was that of a child dressed up for a tea dance who'd somehow gotten left at the wrong address. Even her fan was white lace. She fluttered it, and her eyelids, expertly as she laughed with the gentlemen at the tables and coaxed them to place bets for her at the new roulette wheel.

Sanderson pursed his lips, and he waited.

One of the truths about a place like Barron's was that everyone was constantly in motion. Therefore, if one wished to be seen, all one really had to do was stand still. So, Sanderson lounged at the edge of the gaming floor, fully relaxed and ready for whatever, or whoever, might come his way. That someone proved to be an old friend.

"Faulks! My very dear fellow!"

"Mountrose." Sanderson nodded at the man who called his name. "I had no idea you were back in the country."

"Yes. It's the worst of the civil service. One never knows where one will be from this week to the next."

Gerald Mountrose was the younger son of a very old family. As with many old bloodlines, the fortunes had thinned out over the years, thanks in no small part to places like Barron's. This meant that a growing number of younger sons found themselves required to make their own way in the world. Sanderson had gravitated to the buying, selling, and critiquing of art. Mountrose had made the still unfashionable decision to do something potentially useful for the world, or at least the country, and joined the burgeoning diplomatic corps.

"We will have to have dinner," said Sanderson. "Come to my house tomorrow."

"I'd be delighted." Mountrose bowed. "But what brings you here? Not your usual haunt, I would have thought."

Sanderson shrugged. "Oh, I like to patrol the borders, see what's doing." He swung his walking stick idlly toward Miss Smith. "She's new."

"Eh?" Mountrose glance about. "Oh. The Wallace girl. Yes, she is rather."

"What's her line?"

Mountrose chuckled bitterly. "Nothing I'd recommend to any friend I wished to keep."

Sanderson let a smile flicker briefly across his face. At the roulette table, the crowd cheered, and Miss Smith bounced up and down on her toes. She also laid both her prettily gloved hands on the shoulder of the broad man nearest her. Sanderson and Mountrose watched as the man turned and poured a stream of coins into Miss Smith's open hands.

"She's the sort that makes herself the confidant of some likely gentleman," said Mountrose. "Then, she lets him know there's an opportunity she's been told about. It's a chance to make some real money, and get out of the life she's living, and so on. Only, poor innocent that she is, she doesn't know if she can trust the gentleman, and it's her whole savings. . . ."

"And her new confidential friend offers to look into the opportunity for her?" suggested Sanderson.

"Just so," agreed Mountrose. "And she thanks him profusely and gives him all the particulars. She even goes with him to meet the gentleman who is proposing this 'opportunity.' The next thing you know, he's sunk all his money into the scheme, whatever it may be this week."

Sanderson shook his head. The capacity of his fellow gentlemen to delude themselves when presented with a pretty face and fetching manners never ceased to amaze.

"Any word as to what the scheme is this week?"

"Sanderson, weren't you listening? You can't trust—"

"Oh, Mountrose, you know better. I never trust anyone. I'm simply curious."

Mountrose narrowed his eyes, indicating he did not entirely believe this statement. But Sanderson returned his suspicious gaze coolly, and in the end Mountrose just sighed.

"I could not say for certain, but I think it has something to do with the horses."

CHAPTER 18

A Cosy Chat

*She had a great deal to listen to; all the particulars
of past sad scenes, all the minutiae of distress
upon distress, which in former conversations had
been merely hinted at, were dwelt on now with a
natural indulgence.*

Jane Austen, *Persuasion*

Normally, the staff would have questions if a guest came to them asking for the family rooms. But the maids who were stationed at the edges of the receiving rooms did not seem to have any more interest in their work than the men serving at dinner had. Rosalind was pointed directly toward the stairs, and no one appeared to be the least bit curious as to why a guest should be deciding to roam about the house.

The decor on the second floor was much plainer than that on the main floor. There were very few pictures on the walls, and the corridor was only dimly lit by two lamps. Rosalind felt as if she had stepped backstage at the theater and could now see all the ropes and boards that held up the scenery.

There was only one corridor and it ran the length of the

house, ending in a back stairs. As directed, Rosalind went to the last door on the right and knocked. There was no answer. She knocked again.

This time the door opened. Cynthia stared back at her, shocked. Whatever she had been about to say, she swallowed it, rather painfully, Rosalind thought.

"I . . . oh . . . Mrs. Rutherford. I did not expect you."

"I came to see how you were doing," said Rosalind. "May I come in?"

Cynthia hesitated. "Well, yes. I suppose." She stepped aside to let Rosalind enter.

The private sitting room was plain, worn, and quiet. It was clearly shared by all three of the Kinsdale sisters and reflected their various tastes in leisure. A few books and poetry annuals were stacked on the tea table. A tapestry frame with a partially completed canvas stood by the window. There was also a table with a lit lamp, and three well-used portable writing desks. Through an open doorway, Rosalind could see a boudoir with three beds and as many dressing tables.

While Rosalind surveyed the apartment and waited for an invitation to sit down, Cynthia hurried to one of the writing desks and snatched the paper off it. Rosalind had the impression of a badly splotched page with a great deal of crossing out, before Cynthia shut it away.

"Will you sit down?" Cynthia said belatedly. "I'm sorry, I've nothing to offer you. . . ."

"Thank you, I don't need anything." Rosalind settled on the faded sofa by the hearth. "I just wanted to ask how you are."

Cynthia twisted her hands. "I will be much better if you can tell me that you've learned something useful about Mrs. Lynn."

"I know that you and your sister are right to be suspicious of her," said Rosalind. "Mr. Harkness and I both think that the story may be more complex than what is commonly known as fortune hunting."

"Yes, of course," murmured Cynthia. "Why should anything simple come to our doorstep?" She knotted her fists. "You must work quickly, Miss Thorne. You must. If you don't . . . with Father now saying he will end the admiral's lease . . ." She swallowed. "You understand, it is vital that Admiral Walsingham be allowed to keep Kinsdale House."

"Are your circumstances that difficult?"

Cynthia nodded rapidly, her jaw clenched as if she did not trust herself to speak. "I . . . We *need* him."

"How is it Admiral Walsingham came to be your father's tenant?" asked Rosalind. "Were they previously acquainted?"

To her surprise, Cynthia laughed. It was a harsh, unpleasant sound. "Oh, no. Father has a deep antipathy for naval men. He says they come from all sorts of undesirable classes and are filled with native cunning, and always sunburnt besides."

Rosalind thought of the nature of the gathering downstairs, and found her opinion of Sir Anthony lowering itself still further.

"As to how he came to be our tenant . . . it's something of a complicated story." Cynthia finally came to sit down on the sofa beside Rosalind. But she did not, Rosalind noted, meet her gaze. Instead, Cynthia's attention shifted restlessly from her own hands to the writing table and the curtained window, and then to the door. Round and round she shifted her gaze, as if trying to make sure everything remained as she left it.

"We actually—well, Clara, Elizabeth, and I—became acquainted with the admiral and his wife when our mother fell ill. Mother decided it would be better if we went to stay with a cousin of hers in Lyme." Cynthia paused. "I think she knew then she could not live, and wished to spare us. I wish she had not," she added softly. "But, of course, at the time we could not have known and because of that . . . well, I for one found our time away very pleasant. There was warmth at our cousin's house, and a kind of ease. I didn't feel like I always needed to be walking on tiptoe, or that there was constantly something that needed to be hushed up—" She giggled abruptly, a high-pitched manic sound. She slapped her hand hard over her face. "I'm sorry, I don't know what gets into me sometimes."

"That's all right. Tonight has been a strain."

"Yes." Cynthia sighed. "But a familiar one. I should not take it so." These words were reflexive, and her tone without true meaning.

"Have you remained close with your cousin?" asked Rosalind.

"No," said Cynthia. "When Mother did die, Father took it into his head to blame her. He decided that she should have offered to come and nurse Mother rather than simply agree to take us all away. Never mind that it was Mother who asked her to keep us." She rubbed her hands together restlessly. "But it was at Lyme that we became acquainted with Admiral and Mrs. Walsingham, and all their family. While we were there, he often remarked that he planned to retire, and take a house somewhere away from the coast. In fact, he joked about being like Ulysses—marching inland until he came to a place where no one had ever heard of the sea." She smiled fondly at this memory. "So, when the crisis came, and the horses had all been sold off, and father's man of business mentioned that we might put the house up for rent, I naturally thought of the admiral, and suggested he be written to. There." She smiled, but something strained and uncomfortable remained in her eye and her demeanor. "I did tell you it was a convoluted story."

"Only a little," said Rosalind. "You've said your father was reluctant to rent out the house. Did Mrs. Lynn play any part in convincing him?"

Cynthia laughed again. "Oh, yes! Elizabeth brought her into all our counsels, but this was another point where, I must say, she proved herself remarkably useful. She kept up a constant stream of talk about the delights of Bath—how many grand people stopped there, how one could not call oneself a true person of consequence unless one were known in Bath . . . she quite won him over."

Rosalind paused for a moment, and then said, "The admiral spoke of visiting the stables, and he accused your father of playing some game. Do you know what he meant?"

Cynthia shook her head. "I have no idea." Her gaze slipped to her writing desk.

Rosalind pretended to ignore this. "Whose idea was it to enter Kinsdale's Pride in the sweepstakes?"

"That came from Elizabeth. She and Clara kept up the management of the stables between them, although, of course, Father took the credit. However, once Beth proposed it, Mrs. Lynn took up the cause with enthusiasm."

Rosalind filed this fact away with the others she had gathered.

"If Elizabeth and Clara oversaw the stables, did they have anything to say when the head groom was fired?"

"Oh. You've heard about Nathanial Spence." Cynthia sighed. "He was a good man with horses. He looked after our stables diligently and tried to interest breeders in our thoroughbreds . . . but when the money really began to run out, to the point where the bailiffs were threatening to drag him into court, Father began to cast about for people to blame. Spence was one of the people he settled on."

"Is that why Mr. Spence was accused of poisoning your horses?"

"Oh, that." Cynthia twisted her hands. "You must understand, Miss Thorne, Father has always been a man of . . . obsessions. Ideas get planted in his head and they take very firm root. His dislike of the navy is only one such example. He saw that our studs were no longer in demand, and our brood mares no longer selling. He had also heard some story somewhere about a groom poisoning a family's stock out of spite, and he knew he had not paid Spence—or any of our staff—what he owed them, and these things got mixed together in his mind. And from the mixture rose the accusation."

"But there was nothing to it?"

"Good lord, no! If there had been, Elizabeth would have seen it immediately. Or Clara would. Father just makes pronouncements and curates his wardrobe." She stopped. "You don't think Spence has something to do with this?"

"I think that a man who has had his reputation damaged for no reason may try to get some of his own back. It may be he had something to do with making sure Sir Anthony found out about the admiral's nephew."

"Because it is very well known that Father will cut off his nose to spite his face," murmured Cynthia. "Yes, that could have happened. Putting the house up to let was one blow to Father's pride that he has never quite managed to rationalize away. It eats at him. Now that he has an excuse to assert himself, no matter what the cost, he will do it. And we will all suffer for it." These last words she spoke in a whisper.

"It may not come to that," said Rosalind. "Mrs. Lynn seems to have soothed his spirits."

"Yes." Cynthia's voice grew stronger. "How very strange I should yet again have a reason to feel grateful to that woman."

"Well, from what you and Clara have told me, she would also have an interest in matters remaining, as they are."

"Yes, there is that," agreed Cynthia grimly. "If our family goes into a full collapse, there will be no house at which she can entertain her many friends."

"How is the expense managed?"

"I don't know," admitted Cynthia. "I know she justifies it by saying these are men who should know my father, because they will be interested in our horses once Kinsdale's Pride wins the sweepstakes." Her hands twisted. "She's quite taken over the house. I've seen her turning away tradesmen with bills at the door, insisting they come back next week, when they will be paid in full. But I ask you, Miss Thorne, how could that be?" She spread her hands. "Even if Casselmaine is not driven away by this profligacy, she cannot assume he will be ready to pay all her bills without blinking."

"Is the frequency of the parties increasing?"

"We have as many as one a week now."

Rosalind nodded. "It is possible she is trying to hold as many as she can before the wedding. But I wonder—"

A knock on the door cut off her words. The door opened.

"Cynthia dear, I came to see—"

The woman who spoke saw Rosalind, and stopped in mid-sentence.

It was Mrs. Lynn.

CHAPTER 19

Mrs. Lynn

"I always look upon her as able to persuade a person to anything! I am afraid of her, as I have told you before, quite afraid of her, because she is so very clever . . ."

Jane Austen, *Persuasion*

"Why, Mrs. Rutherford, here you are!" cried Mrs. Lynn as she breezed into the room. "Mr. Rutherford was asking if I'd seen you."

Rosalind was quite certain this was a lie, but let that pass. "I came to see how Miss Cynthia was doing."

"Well, we were of the same mind." Mrs. Lynn laid her hand on Cynthia's shoulder and beamed tenderly down on her pale, angry face. "How are you, Cynthia? Can I send for anything?"

"You need not concern yourself with me," Cynthia croaked.

"But I do," said Mrs. Lynn earnestly. "As you are so dear to Sir Anthony, I don't see how I can help myself."

Cynthia responded with a cold glower. Mrs. Lynn sighed and threw up her hands.

Rosalind got to her feet. "If Mr. Rutherford is looking for

me, then I should return to the party. Mrs. Lynn, let us allow Cynthia her rest. I'm sure it will do her good."

The look Mrs. Lynn returned was quietly speculative. "Yes, yes, of course," she said. "Good night, dear." She planted a small kiss on Cynthia's forehead. Rosalind wondered if that gesture was meant to soothe Cynthia, or to convince Rosalind of Mrs. Lynn's tender feelings for the young woman.

When Mrs. Lynn straightened, she made a small, slightly mocking curtsy toward Rosalind.

"Mrs. Rutherford?" She indicated Rosalind should proceed her out the door.

Once Cynthia's door was closed behind them both, Mrs. Lynn caught up to Rosalind so that they walked side by side down the narrow, dim corridor.

"It was very good of you, Mrs. Rutherford, to come and keep Cynthia company. I try my best, but I confess the child tries my patience sorely. Poor thing. She is so jealous of her sister's engagement. She cannot help but try to draw attention to herself with her sighs and tears and woes. I suppose it is understandable. She was jilted so cruelly. You will have heard of it by now."

It was a blatant invitation to gossip. "No, I had not heard."

"Yes. So very sad. A young man met in passing. He flirted, probably out of boredom, and she, naive creature, took him seriously. Began to hint to the entire neighborhood that she was engaged. Then, of course, he left as lightly as he came, and she became a complete laughingstock. A rather shoddy tragedy, really."

And a very neat way of letting me know that Cynthia's word is not to be trusted.

"Then I am sorry for her," said Rosalind. "And it was good of you to take time to check on her. I know you are very busy managing your gathering downstairs."

Mrs. Lynn laughed her sparkling laugh. "Why, Mrs. Ruther-

ford!" she cried. "Are you accusing me of being a managing female?"

"Oh, never," said Rosalind lightly. "But one can see you
have taken the Kinsdale household well in hand. I truly admired the skill with which you diverted the gentlemen when
Admiral Walsingham made his unexpected appearance."

"Oh, that." Mrs. Lynn waved her words away. "It is only
that I have such a dislike of unpleasantness. Especially between
gentlemen. They are such children, really, and their tempers are
so easily spoiled."

Rosalind returned Mrs. Lynn's conspiratorial smile. "Still,
it is plain to me that this is a house and a family that very
much needs someone who can steer matters in the correct direction."

At these words, Mrs. Lynn's countenance shifted. The sparkle
and lightness she affected dimmed, replaced by something
sharper, and much colder.

"You are quite perceptive, Mrs. Rutherford," said Mrs. Lynn.
"I begin to wonder what else you have seen."

"What should I have seen?" replied Rosalind.

"Well, that depends entirely on who you really are," said
Mrs. Lynn.

It took all Rosalind's years of practice to hold her face still.

Mrs. Lynn smiled, as if she had just selected a winning
card for her hand. "Now, I shall make a confession." She
leaned forward and said in a stage whisper, "I followed you."

"Did you?" Rosalind considered the narrow stairs and the
straight hall she had traversed to get here. If Mrs. Lynn had
followed her, it had been at a distance.

"Elizabeth noticed you had gone upstairs, and I came to
see what you might be doing. I confess I may have listened a
moment at the door before I entered. But then, I am a wicked,
designing woman, am I not?" she paused. "And *you* are Miss
Rosalind Thorne."

Rosalind said nothing.

"What, no protestations? No insistence that you don't know what I mean?"

"Would it matter?" asked Rosalind.

"Not in the least," declared Mrs. Lynn.

"Then you will agree it is best that I save us both the trouble."

"You are very cool."

Rosalind made no answer to this.

Mrs. Lynn's eyes narrowed. "I shall, of course, have to tell Sir Anthony."

"Very well," replied Rosalind calmly. "Shall we go now?"

That surprised her. "Now?"

"Yes," said Rosalind. "If we are to lay our cards on the table, as the saying goes, this is a most apropos time and place, do you not agree?"

"You would choose to be humiliated in front of half of Bath society?"

"The half of Bath society represented downstairs is more likely to be amused by my presence than anything else," said Rosalind. "I do not fear for my reputation personally or professionally in this case. But, as I am sure you understand, I will have to tell Sir Anthony why I am here and who asked me to come."

She met Mrs. Lynn's gaze directly. That lady did not flinch, or look away. Neither did she offer any protestation of her own.

"I must admit, I expected more . . . dismay at having your veil ripped away."

"I expected to be recognized," Rosalind told her. "And I thought it would probably be sooner rather than later. Bath is a small world, and large swaths of London society pass through here."

"Yes. That they do."

There was another burst of laughter from below, and an indistinct shout. A muscle in Mrs. Lynn's cheek twitched.

She is worried what is happening in her absence. She expected to have the upper hand with me by now. Rosalind felt an unusual, but genuine, prickling of her pride.

"Since you recognize me, Mrs. Lynn, I expect you have some idea why Miss Clara has asked me to Bath."

"One of the things I most admire about the Kinsdale girls on the whole is that they are all quite direct." Mrs. Lynn meant this, Rosalind felt sure. "Clara has made it very clear she suspects me of being up to no good, as has Cynthia."

"What answer do you make to those suspicions? Or do you mean to suggest that it is Miss Cynthia's jealousy that drives her?"

A fresh burst of laughter erupted from below them. Mrs. Lynn glanced toward the stairs. She clearly wished to be back with her company. Rosalind did not move.

When Mrs. Lynn smiled again, it was a strangely wistful expression. "Clara Kinsdale is an intelligent and perceptive young lady. Which, I'm sure you will agree, is a surprise, given the family she comes from." Mrs. Lynn drummed her fingers for a moment on the stair railing. "In fact, I should not be surprised to learn that Clara and her fiancé paraded you before me in order to frighten me off as quickly as possible."

Rosalind said nothing.

"Yes," Mrs. Lynn went on thoughtfully. "A good choice of strategy. I am indeed frightened, and, given the circumstances, I fully intend to be off. As soon as matters can be arranged, in fact. You may, if you choose, tell Clara and Cynthia as much."

Rosalind felt her eyes widen. It took her a moment to find an answer to this declaration.

"How long do you think it will take you to arrange matters?"

Again, Mrs. Lynn gave her that arch, wistful smile. "Not very long. When you are a woman in my position, Miss Thorne,

you learn the value of being prepared to make an orderly retreat. Sir Anthony seemed an ideal mark for my needs—"

"Mark?"

"Match, I meant."

You did not.

"But now that his daughters have acted so decisively on
their suspicions"—here she nodded toward Rosalind—"I
would be a fool to believe that I could lodge snuggly or comfortably in the bosom of the family any longer, or that his
grace would be inclined to assist his father-in-law with any
additional request for money." She did not, Rosalind noticed, make any allusion to the gaming parties she had been
running from the Kindsales' home. "What I would ask, if
you would be so kind, is that you give me one more day to
make my excuses. Let the party play out. Then, tomorrow I
will let it be known I have received a letter from some relative. Perhaps my goddaughter?" she mused. "Yes, a goddaughter should answer nicely. She will be suffering from an
illness or some other sudden disaster, and beg me to come to
her. I will go, promising to return as soon as may be. Will
that suit?"

"Admirably," said Rosalind. "You understand that I plan
to stay in Bath at least a fortnight, and will remain in contact
with the Misses Kinsdale—"

"To make sure I am truly gone?" Mrs. Lynn interrupted.
"I would not expect anything less. But I also ask you to believe that I'm not such a fool as to try to return once I know
the jig is up."

Rosalind found she could well believe this.

"So," Mrs. Lynn went on briskly. "You may let Clara
know her engagement is in no further danger from my presence. Again, all I ask is that you do so quietly, and let me take
my leave. Both she and his grace will surely be able to see the
advantage of that. The last thing either of them will want is
more controversy."

"I will regard this conversation as a confidence," said Rosalind. "Unless a change of circumstances requires me to do otherwise."

"That is all I could hope for." Mrs. Lynn's smile turned coldly polite. "Now, I really must return to the party. Some of my friends can become a bit boisterous if there is not someone there to *manage* their high spirits." She picked up her skirts and breezed past Rosalind, taking herself down the stairs without looking back.

Rosalind, on the other hand, stayed where she was for a long moment, trying to understand what had really just happened.

CHAPTER 20

An Orderly Retreat

She hoped to be wise and reasonable in time; but alas! alas! she must confess to herself that she was not wise yet.

Jane Austen, *Persuasion*

When Rosalind at last descended the stairs, her plan was to find Clara and Devon. At first, she'd thought she should look for Adam. But after a moment, she realized that if she was seen in conversation with Clara and Devon, Adam would quickly come to them.

After a brief search of the rooms, Rosalind discovered Devon and Clara together in the corner, hemmed in by a pair of gentlemen. Rosalind could not make out any of the conversation, but she could tell from Devon's expression that he was having difficulty remaining polite. So, for that matter, was Clara.

Rosalind assumed a breezy air and stepped directly up to them. "Ah, there you are, your grace, Miss Clara. Oh!" She let her eyes widen as if she'd just noticed the other men. "I'm so sorry, I did not mean to interrupt."

The gentlemen looked at each other, clearly annoyed by

the intrusion, but Devon smiled. "Ah, Mrs. Rutherford. There you are! Miss Clara and I would be glad of a word. You will excuse us?" he added toward the gentlemen. The pair had no choice but to make their bows and withdraw.

"Thank you," murmured Devon fervently to Rosalind as soon as the pair was out of earshot.

"Yes, your timing is excellent," Clara added. "In another minute, I would have thrown them both out the window."

"I'm afraid I would have insisted you let me do that," said Devon.

"If you say it's not a job for a lady, I will have to remind you again who hauled you out of that ditch you entirely failed to jump at our picnic last May."

"I would never be so crude," said Devon rapidly. "But rank has to have *some* privileges."

Rosalind was prevented from inquiring about this eventful picnic by Adam's arrival.

"I apologize if I'm late," he said. "Were we throwing someone out the window?"

"Mrs. Rutherford has interrupted those plans," Devon told him. "Thus continuing her reputation as a force for all that is good and orderly in this world."

"But we can find them later, if necessary," added Clara. "Although, do make sure the windows are open. I shudder to think what the repairs might cost otherwise."

She and Devon shared a smile, and a fleeting touch of fingertips. Then, Clara turned to Rosalind.

"Have you discovered anything?"

"Not as much as I hoped," said Rosalind. "And I'm afraid I have been recognized."

"By Mrs. Lynn?" said Adam.

Rosalind nodded. "However, it appears to have served our purposes. She has agreed to leave."

"What!" Devon choked. "When?"

"Tomorrow," murmured Rosalind.

"As easy as that?" Adam breathed.

"So it appears," said Rosalind. "Mrs. Lynn is an experienced adventuress, and she knows she is in danger of being fully exposed. All she asks is that we allow her to leave quietly." She outlined the plan Mrs. Lynn had given her.

Clara closed her eyes and let out a long sigh. "Thank goodness."

Devon, however, was watching Rosalind carefully. "Do you advise that we cooperate with this plan?"

"I do," she said. "If for no other reason than it will put an end to these parties, and their ongoing expense and social disadvantage. It will also allow Miss Kinsdale and her sisters to gain more influence over their father and his decisions."

"Elizabeth will be furious when she finds out," said Clara.

"We will deal with that when the time comes," Devon told her. "But I don't like simply letting Mrs. Lynn go. Something feels . . . wrong."

"What else can we do?" asked Clara. "We do not know that she has done anything against the law. If she leaves and stays away—what more could we ask for?"

Devon was looking at Adam. Adam, on the other hand, was looking at the crowd. Across the room, Mrs. Lynn was passing from table to table. She paused frequently, speaking to this guest and that, usually laughing at the responses. When she reached Sir Anthony's table, she leaned close over his shoulder, looking at his cards. She said something to the gentlemen he played with, then something to him, and plucked a card from his hand and threw it on the table. A shout and a groan went up, and all the gentlemen folded their cards. Mrs. Lynn straightened and smiled, fluttering her fan as if she was applauding her own cleverness. Sir Anthony beamed, as if basking in his.

"Casselmaine, if you really want to bring her before the magistrates, there's evidence enough in this room," Adam said. "If I was still with Bow Street, that's what I'd say should be done." He paused, unusually hesitant. "But you've said you want to spare Miss Kinsdale and yourself the scandal. Having Mrs. Lynn, or Sir Anthony, arrested won't do that."

Rosalind caught his eye. It was not like Adam to recommend letting anyone leave, especially when they were likely to make more trouble wherever they went. But the look he returned told her to be patient. He was not saying all that he thought. Not yet.

Devon nodded absently. Clara touched his arm. He looked down at her, and his expression changed, softened and warmed. "You're right, you're right. It comes of being a magistrate as well as a duke. I always want to do *something*."

"You did," Clara told him. "You brought our friends here, and they have stopped the immediate harm to my father, and my family. As soon as Mrs. Lynn is gone, we will be able to start repairing the damage."

"Do you think she will keep her word?" asked Devon.

"I do," said Rosalind, and she found herself wondering at her own certainty.

"Then we will let her leave," said Devon finally. "Thank you. Both of you." He stopped and shook himself. "Well. We had planned to go to the refreshment room. Will you join us?"

Rosalind looked to Adam. "If you don't mind, I think we will take our leave." Adam was not saying something, and she very much wanted to hear what it might be.

"Of course. I'll have my carriage called. You can send it back when you're finished."

Clara took Rosalind's hand. "Thank you so much."

They said their farewells, and Devon beckoned one of the bored footmen over so that he could send for the carriage. He took Clara's arm then, and led her away.

"I'm very interested in how that conversation between you and Mrs. Lynn went," Adam said to her. "But are you sure you don't want to stay? There might be more to learn."

Rosalind surveyed the room—the raucous laughter, the

slap of the cards, the ladies whispering behind their fans and openly eyeing the men at the tables. She looked through the doorway to the refreshment room and Clara standing so close to Devon. She looked across the way to Elizabeth, who stood apart from it all, her attention fixed on Mrs. Lynn, her fan hanging limp and forgotten in her hand.

She saw Sir Anthony beaming as he surveyed his little party, clearly well-pleased with the scene unfolding around him.

"No," said Rosalind. "Unless you can give me a definite reason to do so, I have no wish to stay here."

CHAPTER 21

The Consequences of Idle Chatter

*All that sounded extravagant or irrational in the
progress of the reconciliation might have no
origin but in the language of the relators.*

Jane Austen, *Persuasion*

A dam let Rosalind keep her silence on the ride home. Rosalind was grateful for it. For one thing, the evening had turned rainy and so Laurel had decided that she did not wish to take her accustomed seat beside the driver. Although the maid dutifully busied herself with a bit of mending from her work basket, Rosalind was not prepared to have any sort of delicate conversation in front of her.

But more than that, Rosalind was not prepared to talk yet. Despite the fact that she appeared to have achieved all the ends Clara and Devon had hoped for, she found she was still unsettled and dissatisfied.

Is there something I missed? Should we have stayed longer, and asked more questions?

But there was no way to tell. At least, not yet.

Mrs. Leigh was the only one still awake when they returned to the Green Briar. She'd sat up in the common room so there'd be someone to greet them, and to light candles for them all to take upstairs. She also brought up a pot of tea at Rosalind's request.

Feeling tired and dull, Rosalind remained silent while Laurel helped her out of her evening gown and into her nightclothes.

"I'll take this to my room and get it brushed and tidied," said Laurel as she draped Rosalind's gown across her arm.

"Thank you, and that will be all for tonight."

Laurel was perfectly used to the various comings and goings in Rosalind's Orchard Street home, so she didn't bat an eye at this early dismissal. "Yes, miss."

Her maid carried the gown away, and Rosalind sat down with a sigh and began the long business of brushing out her hair.

After a time, she heard a soft footstep outside the door. She turned just in time to see Adam slip inside.

"I hoped you'd still be awake," he said, closing the door. "I had to be quick. I'm sure our landlady suspects me of something." Of course Mrs. Leigh knew their real names, and their real relation to each other, or rather, their lack of real relation.

"You should hint at her we are genuinely engaged," said Rosalind.

"I did, but I don't think she believes me."

"I'm sure Mrs. Kendricks told her."

"Perhaps. Or perhaps she thinks you're still in line for the duke."

Rosalind fell silent.

"I'm sorry. That sounded like a better joke when I said it to myself."

"Do you think I'm still in line for the duke?" asked Rosalind softly.

Adam bent down and took her face gently between his hands. The kiss was long and it was slow—as if there were no suspicious landlady, no anxious families, no worry over anything at all. There was only this moment of comfort, of intimate warmth, and the two of them together.

When breath finally demanded they part, Adam drew back, just a little, and smiled. "Do we need to talk about the party?" he asked, brushing her loosened hair back from her cheek.

Rosalind sighed and tilted her head, so she gently captured one of his hands between her cheek and shoulder. "I expect we'd better, before the details become . . . clouded. Come and sit down. I think there's still some tea in the pot, but it's quite cold."

Adam laughed. "I've spent more nights surviving on cold tea than I can count. It will be a great improvement to drink some while I'm warm and in good company." He kissed her again, then sat down in the chair by the room's small table. Rosalind moved to sit across from him and pour out the tea.

"So, what happened between you and Mrs. Lynn?" asked Adam. "And the Kinsdale sisters?"

Rosalind told him about Mrs. Lynn engaging her in conversation just long enough for Elizabeth to slip away from the party and then waiting in the garden to see Elizabeth come back in after meeting a man who never showed his face. She detailed her conversation with Elizabeth, and Elizabeth's story of having met Mrs. Lynn by disrupting a less-than-honest transaction over a horse. Then, she talked about Cynthia, and her worries about Admiral Walsingham being evicted from his tenancy of Kinsdale House. She told him how Mrs. Lynn disrupted that conversation as well, and then about the confidential talk she held with the widow in the upstairs corridor, which ended in Mrs. Lynn declaring she meant to retreat without fuss.

"Victory then," said Adam mildly.

"So it would seem."

"Are you wondering why it was so easy?"

"Yes," said Rosalind. "I am also wondering if somehow

Mrs. Lynn's original design in taking up with the Kinsdales has already been achieved."

"It's possible that it has, at least in part."

"What did you find out?"

Adam sighed and reached for the teapot to refill his cup. "I thought at first those guests of Mrs. Lynn's were just idle rich folk, come for an evening's heavy play. And some of them were. Perhaps most of them. But the more I looked about, the more I realized there were also a number of hardened, professional gamblers among them—men and women both. They'd been lured to the house on the promise of good pickings."

"Lured?"

Adam nodded. "I managed to have a little conversation with the men who were loaning out the money in return for the promissory notes. They may have mistaken me for one of their kind."

"I can't imagine how that might have happened," said Rosalind.

Adam shrugged. "People see what they expect to see. But it seems that the loans they make carry interest, and it further seems that Mrs. Lynn is paid a percentage of that interest, in consideration for her work in arranging these parties and bringing in the pigeons—"

Rosalind raised her brows. "Cant language from you, Mr. Harkness?"

"It is a highly economical means of expressing oneself," he answered, his tone filled with mock indignation.

Rosalind nodded solemnly and Adam grinned. "I was also able to talk with Sir Anthony a little. He seemed entirely ignorant of the matter. Either that, or he was supremely unconcerned." Adam frowned. "It's unusually difficult to tell which it is with that gentleman. But I suspect Mrs. Lynn is using some of her profits to keep his Bath creditors at bay, and that, combined with her expert flattery, keeps Sir Anthony complacent."

"Cynthia said that she had seen tradesmen coming to the door, and heard Mrs. Lynn telling them that if they come back next week, they would be paid in full."

"It would also explain why Mrs. Lynn has been so diligent in reinforcing Sir Anthony's faith in Kinsdale's Pride. If Sir Anthony is certain his fortunes will be restored after the race, he'll be able to convince himself that any money Mrs. Lynn lays out on his behalf is just a loan. This will soothe his pride and make it easier to convince himself that all is right."

"Yes." Rosalind swirled the remnants of the cold, bitter tea in her cup. "That is very possible."

"But you are not satisfied?"

"No. I keep wondering about what part Miss Smith back in London plays in all of this. Not to mention the horse," she added dryly. "Poor Kinsdale's Pride has been mentioned so often since we came to Bath, I am having difficulty believing she is an innocent bystander. And then there's the matter of the head groom."

"The groom?" said Adam. "Has he returned to the story?"

Rosalind nodded. "His name is Nathanial Spence. Cynthia told me he did good work for the Kinsdales, and that when he was dismissed, he had not been paid for some time. She also said that the accusation of him poisoning the horses for a rival breeder was entirely without foundation."

Adam considered this. "Was there any mention of him going to court to try to claim his wages?"

"It would be an incredible risk for him, wouldn't it? When there is this accusation that he was a poisoner hanging over his head?" It was unfortunately true that a man who possessed rank and land was likely to be believed over a man who worked for his living. Even if that man was such an object as Sir Anthony Kinsdale.

"Perhaps," said Adam. "But being a head groom is a skilled, and a potentially lucrative occupation. I would think he might at least try his chances, especially against someone known to be so delinquent with his creditors as Sir Anthony."

Rosalind frowned. "I wonder whether Mr. Spence was dismissed before or after Mrs. Lynn made her appearance. I should have asked that, and did not."

"It would be good to know," agreed Adam. "That would tell us if Spence is part of this, or if he is another victim of Mrs. Lynn's plans."

"Do you think there's a connection between Mrs. Lynn and the dismissal?"

"I don't know. It's possible that the only thing Mrs. Lynn is doing is skimming off proceeds from illegal gaming parties. On the other hand, some of the most elaborate frauds I've ever seen have involved horse racing."

Rosalind fell silent. "What is it?" asked Adam.

"The . . . meeting Elizabeth had in the garden, with the man from the stables. The one Mrs. Lynn tried to prevent me from seeing."

"Are you thinking Caleb might be Nathanial Spence?"

"I'm thinking that it might be possible. If we think that Mrs. Lynn, and Elizabeth, have both been playing a long game."

"We also have Elizabeth's story of meeting Mrs. Lynn around a scheme to sell an old horse to add to the disgraced groom," said Adam. "And poor Kinsdale's Pride being forced into a race that we have it on good authority she cannot win."

"Not to mention some professional gambling men who know more about that horse and the race than they are willing to tell." Rosalind frowned. "But it does not make sense. If Mrs. Lynn came to the Kinsdales because she already had a horse racing scheme in mind, a dedicated head groom might be a detriment to her plans. She would not assist in making sure a meeting between him and Elizabeth went off smoothly."

"Unless Mrs. Lynn, or Elizabeth, found Spence and enlisted him in the scheme."

"Or unless Elizabeth did not tell her who she was really meeting," suggested Rosalind.

"Or unless we were wrong, and this Caleb is not in fact Nathanial Spence." Adam drained his teacup. "I think that after I've spoken with the admiral, I had best get myself out to the Lansdown stables and talk to the men there."

"A very good idea," said Rosalind. "If I haven't heard from Alice tomorrow morning, I will write to let her know what has happened and say that she should step up efforts to find Miss Smith. After that, I'll call on the Kinsdales and make sure Mrs. Lynn is keeping her promise to leave." She paused. "I may also see if I can find out anything more about Elizabeth's meeting last night. It is more than we have been asked to do, but if there is a wider scheme unfolding around the Kinsdales, we need to understand what part, if any, Elizabeth is playing."

"I agree," said Adam. He also reached out and drew his fingertips lightly down her cheek. "But that is for daylight." He cupped her chin with his calloused hand. "What shall we do in the meantime?"

Rosalind met his gaze, and felt her heart begin to pound. "Blow out the candle."

It was sometime later that Rosalind awoke, fuzzy headed, and aching as much from exertion and thirst as from the awkwardness of being part of a couple sleeping in a bed meant for one person. Slowly, she realized what had woken her was a soft, insistent knocking on the door.

"Miss Thorne! Miss Thorne!" hissed the person on the other side.

"What is it?" Rosalind struggled out from under the blankets. Adam, clad only in his shirt and smalls, got to his feet with her. Rosalind opened the door.

On the other side was one of the Leighs' scullery maids. She held a lit candle in one hand and a folded note in the other.

"There's a messenger downstairs. He brought you this. He

says it is most urgent." The maid looked up and saw Adam behind Rosalind. Her jaw clamped shut.

Rosalind declined to worry about the maid's scruples. She took the note and peered at it in the flickering candlelight. Her name had been scrawled hastily across the front, but in the dim light, she did not recognize the hand.

Adam stood at her shoulder as Rosalind unfolded the paper. She read, and felt the blood drain from her cheeks.

Come at once. Sir Anthony is dead.
Devon

CHAPTER 22

The Scene

. . . and for a little while it was only an interchange of perplexity and terror.

Jane Austen, *Persuasion*

Adam knew what the letter said before he read the words over Rosalind's shoulder. He knew it from the way her body tensed and the color drained from her cheeks. Knew it from the way her expression became a perfect, blank mask meant to conceal any emotion at all.

"There's a carriage waiting," said the scullery maid uncertainly.

"We'll be downstairs in a few minutes," Adam told her.

"Yes, sir." The maid bobbed her curtsy and hurried down the stairs.

Adam met Rosalind's gaze. She nodded in answer to his wordless question. She was all right. Of course she was. A world in which Rosalind could not rally herself was almost unimaginable. Adam touched her shoulder and left to go get dressed in his regular clothes. The evening attire scattered about Rosalind's room now would be nothing but a hinderance.

Adam dressed by rote, his mind too full of questions—or rather one specific question—to take full note of what he did.

What the devil happened to Sir Anthony?

When Adam arrived downstairs, he found Leigh waiting for them in the common room. The man looked more alert than one might expect, but then a landlord would be used to being roused at all hours. He'd thought to light a branch of candles, and handed Adam a half pint of porter.

"Carriage is outside, sir."

"My thanks." Adam drank off the small beer. He fished some coins from his pocket and handed them to Leigh, along with a note he'd written in his room.

"This needs to be taken at once to the house of Mr. Peter Layng." Adam gave the direction. Layng was Bath's coroner. There was no telling if the Kinsdales had thought to alert him to Sir Anthony's sudden death.

It may have been an accident, after all, or perhaps his heart simply gave out.

But if that was the case, why would Casselmaine send for Rosalind and himself with such urgency?

Rosalind came down the stairs, pulling on her gloves as she did. "I've told Laurel she will not be needed."

Adam helped her into the waiting carriage and gave the driver the direction. The man was sober and awake, and clearly understood this was some extraordinary circumstance. He touched up the horses almost the moment the door was shut.

The dawn was just beginning to show itself. The streets were crowded with people on their way to their work, and with carts and wagons—not to mention flocks of geese and sheep—on their way to market. But the driver navigated the erratic traffic with a deft hand and the horses clearly knew their business, so they arrived at the Royal Circus in short order.

At the Kinsdales' house, the lamps had all been lit, and a young footman—who looked both bleary-eyed and badly shaken—let them in at once.

Casselmaine was already in the opulent foyer waiting for them.

"Rosalind, Harkness. Thank you for coming," he said. "I'm afraid we're going to need your . . . expertise."

"What's happened?" asked Rosalind.

Casselmaine glanced reflexively toward the stairs. "Sir Anthony was found in the garden. It looks as if he fell from the window in his room. It might have been an accident, but . . . well, Mrs. Lynn is gone."

"Gone?" repeated Adam.

Casselmaine nodded. "No one saw her leave, but Clara said they tried to rouse her after Sir Anthony was found. She didn't answer the shouts, and the door was locked. When the servants got in, they found the room empty, but there's signs she packed in a hurry."

"Where are Clara and her sisters?" asked Rosalind.

"In the amber salon," Casselmaine told them.

"I'll go to them. Mr. Harkness . . . ?"

Adam nodded and touched her hand. Rosalind hurried away down the corridor and he turned to Casselmaine.

"Where's Sir Anthony?"

"Laid out in his bedroom. Clara . . . she didn't want him left outside, but we agreed his rooms should not be otherwise disturbed before you'd had a chance to look at them."

That was unusual, and good luck. The first instinct of the servants, and the family, would be to tidy away any mess. This time, there might still be some useful sign to point them to what had happened.

"We've sent for the coroner, Mr. Layng," Adam told Casselmaine. "Will you wait here to meet him? The family will be badly distraught as it is." *And might object to such a man being in their house.* The *haut ton* frequently did. So did those who were responsible for the unexpected deaths the coroner investigated.

Casselmaine nodded. "Of course. And thank you, Harkness. The rooms you want are on the second floor, middle door on the left.

Adam raced up the stairs and down the central hallway. But when he reached his destination, he cursed softly. He could see a flickering light under the door.

Someone was already in Sir Anthony's rooms.

Adam pushed his way in without knocking. The fire had been lit, along with several branches of candles. An old man in shirtsleeves knelt on the floor, sponging carefully at the carpet.

Evidently the decision about not disturbing the rooms hadn't been communicated to the staff.

The old man looked up as Adam entered, and blinked.

"I'm sorry, sir," he croaked. "The scorch mark will simply not come out. The whole of it will have to be replaced."

"It's all right." Adam squatted down, bringing his eyes level with the other man. "What's your name, sir?"

"Thrush, sir," the old man replied. "Elias Thrush. I am, was, Sir Anthony's valet."

"Thrush, I'm Adam Harkness. His grace has asked me to see to things up here." Which was both true and entirely ambiguous. "You can leave the carpet for now. Come and sit down." Adam extended his hand to help the man up. He was shaking so badly that Adam kept hold of his arm as he crossed to the chair and lowered himself onto the embroidered cushion.

Fortunately, a decanter of port and two glasses waited on the round table beside the chair. Adam poured out a good measure of the wine and handed it to Thrush. The valet blinked again.

"That is Sir Anthony's private stock, sir," he said. "He would not—well, I suppose it doesn't matter, does it?"

"You need something to steady you. Go on," said Adam. Thrush didn't need any more urging. He drank off the dose.

"Thank you, sir." Thrush's color improved immediately,

and his voice has ceased its shaking. "I admit, late nights and . . . and sudden shocks are harder on me than they once were. I meant to retire years ago, but Sir Anthony so disliked change he would not hear of it. . . ." Thrush stopped, apparently deciding he had said too much.

"Can you tell me what happened?" Adam asked him.

"I wish that I could. My own room is just there—" He indicated one of the two connecting doors. "I was here when Sir Anthony came up from the evening's entertainments, of course. I had already laid out his night things and ordered his dressing table as he liked and was ready to help him to bed, all as usual. It was that *person* who brought him up to me," he added darkly.

Meaning Mrs. Lynn. Adam nodded encouragingly.

"She was laughing, I remember, and saying 'what fol-der-ol!' as he complained at her. Really, such behavior! She all but dropped him into my arms. 'You take good care of him now, Thrush,' she says. 'I must get back down before there's trouble.' And she breezes away before I can say anything else."

"What did you do then?"

"I settled Sir Anthony in his chair—this chair." Thrush caressed the arm sadly. "I meant to help him out of his things, but he'd spilled some wine on his coat and he was very upset about it. He insisted that I see to the stain immediately before it set. So, I took the coat down to the laundry." He moistened his lips. "I admit, once I'd hung the coat to dry, I sat down in the servants' hall. I only planned to be a moment. I was tired, sir." Thrush hung his head. "And I thought that if anything was urgent that Sir Anthony would ring. But . . . I fell asleep." He pressed his fingertips against his eyes. "God help me, I fell asleep in my chair, and when I woke, it was because Cook and the scullery maids had arrived and . . . and they found him, and were screaming." Thrush shuddered.

"Did you see him?"

Thrush turned his face away. "He had fallen onto the garden terrace," he said softly. "I told the footmen to take him upstairs, and lay him on the bed."

Adam allowed himself and Thrush a moment's silence. It was a hard thing to know that one might have saved a life, if only things had been a little different.

"Do you recall if the window was open when you came into the room?"

"It was," said Thrush. "I had assumed that Sir Anthony opened it for the air."

"Did you notice if he was the worse for drink?" asked Adam.

Thrush looked shocked. "Sir Anthony abhorred drunkenness. He never permitted himself to indulge too deeply. If he was at all careless last night, it was the fault of that *person*." Thrush's professional mask crumpled into an expression of profound distaste. "I said she'd be his ruin. I said, mark my words, she will finish him off, and the young misses with him! And I was right," he added with grim satisfaction. "God help us all, I was right."

Adam poured out another dose of port in acknowledgment of this prediction. Thrush nodded his thanks and tossed the drink back.

"What of the other servants?" Adam asked. "Did anyone else hear anything during the night?"

"No one's admitted to it, at least not in my hearing. Normally, there wouldn't *be* anyone, as I'm the only one who sleeps in. The expense, you understand . . ."

Adam nodded.

"Last night, though, there was more staff in the house than usual, because of the party, and it all had to be cleared away before the morning, but most of those who were meant to do the work were off well before dawn." Thrush's face wrinkled, as if he'd caught a bad smell. This told Adam what he thought of this recently hired staff. "Cook and the scullions, they were away as soon as they could be to get a bit of kip before the next day's work. So, no, I don't think anyone would have heard anything."

"Has anyone said they saw Mrs. Lynn leave?"

"Not to me. You might ask Keegan. He's in charge of the footmen. One of them might have seen it. But, as I've indicated, sir, they aren't a particularly *diligent* crew."

"Well, we'll have to try," said Adam. "Now, this scorch mark you were cleaning when I came in, I assume that was new?"

Mr. Thrush drew himself up. "I am *not* one of these hirelings. I would never have left such a mark unattended."

"My apologies." Adam gave a small bow. "I didn't mean to suggest you'd neglected your duties. I just wanted to be sure it wasn't there when you took Sir Anthony's coat away."

"It most certainly was not," said Thrush. "Imagine the outcry!"

Even having known Sir Anthony for such a short time, Adam found he could well imagine it. "Can you say what made it?"

Thrush opened his mouth, and closed it again. "I would guess that it came from a fallen candle. Perhaps that one." He nodded to the unlit candle in a silver holder that stood on the spindly-legged table beside the window.

Adam nodded. "Was anything else disturbed when you came in?"

Thrush's gaze darted about the room. "No, sir, I can't say that it was, nor is it now."

"And did you empty the pockets of Sir Anthony's coat when you took it away?"

"Yes, sir. His things are just there." Thrush gestured to the dressing table. There was a watch and a chain with an abundance of fobs and seals, and Sir Anthony's quizzing glass. There was also a purse and a pocketbook. Both of those proved to be entirely empty.

"What . . . what will happen now, sir?" asked Thrush.

"The family will decide things, of course" said Adam. "But for now, I hope you'll do me the favor of going down and telling the staff there will be some questions for them."

"Yes, sir. Not that any one of them's worth their salt, but I will tell them." Thrush stood. He moved stiffly, but more steadily than he had when Adam had first come in. "But the carpet—" The man stopped, and gave a hoarse, mirthless laugh. "I suppose that doesn't matter now either, does it?"

"No," agreed Adam. "I'll do what's necessary here. You go downstairs. Get yourself something to eat, if there's anything on the fire. I'll let you know if you're needed again."

"Thank you, sir." Thrush hesitated. "Sir . . . will there, that is, will I . . . ?"

"I'm sure no one will blame you for this," said Adam. "You only did what you were told."

"Yes, sir, thank you, sir." Relief was plain on Thrush's lined face. The valet took his leave and Adam turned his attention toward the room itself.

Sir Anthony favored jewel-toned velvets and silk brocades in his personal decorating. The furniture was the gilt and marble confectionary that had been in style during the previous generation. And, as Thrush had said, everything seemed to be where it belonged. When Adam had poured out Thrush's drink, he'd noted that the glasses were clean and dry, and the decanter full.

Adam went to the windows. There were two, and they ran from floor to ceiling, more like French doors than ordinary windows. He opened the first, noting that it pulled open rather than pushed. This was necessary, because outside, a wrought iron railing had been bolted to the side of the house. This was clearly an attempt to prevent the exact tragedy that seemed to have overcome Sir Anthony.

Adam looked down. By now, there was more than enough daylight to see the flagstone pied-à-terre below, and the dark stain there that no one had yet cleaned up. Adam frowned at it. He latched the window once again and turned back to the room. He squatted down beside the scorch mark, measuring the distance between the burn and the window. He touched the elaborately patterned carpet, feeling the dampness. The damp had spread well beyond that burned patch. Perhaps Thrush had cleaned up some soot and wax from the dropped candle before Adam got there.

Or was something else cleaned up?

Adam straightened. He crossed the room and opened the connecting door that Thrush said led to his room.

It was a single bare, windowless chamber. There was a narrow bed, a clothes press, a dressing table, and a single chair. The press contained two spare sets of clothes, and that was all. The table had one drawer, and in it was a shaving kit and a battered Bible.

Adam pushed the drawer shut. He left the sad little chamber, and then, steeling himself, he stepped into Sir Anthony's bedroom.

CHAPTER 23

Those Left Behind

*She had a great deal to listen to; all the particulars
of past sad scenes, all the minutiae of distress
upon distress, which in former conversations had
been merely hinted at, were dwelt on now with a
natural indulgence.*

Jane Austen, *Persuasion*

The Kinsdale sisters were in the same gold and amber salon where Rosalind and Adam had been received before dinner. It seemed a hundred years ago now. Rosalind might have expected to find the young women huddled together, trying to comfort one another. Instead, however, the sisters had spread themselves out as far as possible. Elizabeth stood at the window, arms folded. Cynthia hunched on a chair on the opposite side of the room in front of the empty hearth. Clara stood between them, clutching her handkerchief.

"Oh, m . . . Mrs. Rutherford!" Clara cried when Rosalind entered. "Thank you for coming!"

Rosalind met her as she crossed the room and took both her hands. "I am so, so sorry this has happened."

"What is she doing here?" demanded Elizabeth.

"Casselmaine thought she might be able to help," replied Clara.

"Help?" Elizabeth cried. "What could she possibly do? Father is dead. It was a stupid accident. We never should have taken this house. Never should have come here. Never—" She stopped and pressed her hand against her eyes.

"You all must be exhausted," said Rosalind. "Let me get you some tea, and something to eat."

Elizabeth barked out a laugh. "That would be lovely, thank you. And some biscuits. Perhaps some sandwiches?"

Rosalind blinked. "If you like. I'm sure . . ."

"The servants have left," Cynthia told her.

"Shortly after Father . . ." Clara stopped, swaying slightly on her feet. "Shortly after Father was found. It's just us now."

Cynthia giggled, the same high-pitched sound she'd made last night when she was talking about the admiral. Her sisters stared at her.

"I'm sorry," Cynthia whispered. "I don't know what's got into me."

"It's the shock," said Rosalind. "You must not mind it."

"What do you know of it?" demanded Elizabeth. "Why are you even still here? I told you to go!"

"Oh, no. Please," said Clara. "I'd much rather she stayed."

"Why?" snapped Elizabeth. "Because Casselmaine wants her here? Because with Father dead, we must obey him now?"

The force of Elizabeth's exclamation froze them all. To Rosalind's surprise, it was Cynthia who recovered first.

"Tell her, Clara," she said wearily.

"Tell me what?" demanded Elizabeth.

"She's Rosalind Thorne," said Cynthia.

"*What?*" shouted Elizabeth. "You *lied* to me? To *Father?*"

"We had to," said Clara. "You wouldn't listen to us when we tried to warn you about Mrs. Lynn."

"And given the way things have gone, can you say we were wrong to be suspicious?" asked Clara.

That stung badly, and Clara had meant it to. Elizabeth

looked away. Her chin trembled. It was obvious she was holding back her tears.

In the silence, a soft knocking sounded on the door. Every head turned. A moment later, Devon opened the door.

"The coroner's come," he told them. "He's upstairs with Mr. Harkness."

"Who invited him here?" demanded Elizabeth. "This was an accident!"

"And I'm sure he will say so," said Devon. "But the formalities have to be observed."

Elizabeth's glower said she did not agree, but neither did she make any additional objections.

"I know I am not welcome here," said Rosalind, softly. Devon clearly wanted to protest, but thankfully, he decided it would be better to hold his peace. "And I know that you are all suffering from multiple shocks, but I still may be able to help."

"Are you going to use your miraculous powers to find out what happened to our father?" growled Elizabeth.

"Father fell," said Cynthia. "He *fell.*"

Rosalind pretended not to have heard any of this. "With your permission, I can have some new staff brought in," she told them. "To help until you can arrange for your own people."

"How soon?" asked Clara.

"Immediately, I should think."

Clara crossed to her sister. "Elizabeth? Please. We cannot manage without staff."

Elizabeth looked away, clearly thinking furiously. But in the end she threw up her hands. "Very well. If she's going to be here, she may as well do something useful."

"Thank you, Miss Thorne," said Clara. "Whatever help you can find us will be most welcome."

"There's something else," Rosalind said.

"Lord!" cried Elizabeth. "What?"

"Admiral Walsingham is expecting Sir Anthony's man of business at ten o'clock this morning."

Cynthia clapped her hand over her mouth. "I forgot. How could I forget . . . ?"

"It's not your fault, Cynthia," said Devon. "How could you remember such a thing with everything that's happened?"

"We can send him a note," said Clara. "Someone—"

"I can go," said Devon.

"I can't ask—" began Clara.

"You're not. I'm offering," said Devon. "I can deliver whatever message Miss Thorne needs carried to make sure there's staff in the house, and then go straight on to the admiral."

"If we're lucky, he's left a card on the tray," said Rosalind. A writing desk waited in the corner of the salon. Rosalind found paper inside, and useable ink in the bottle. She quickly drafted and signed the message. "Thank you, Casselmaine."

"I'll walk out with you," Clara told him.

"And I will go see what may be done in the kitchen," said Rosalind. "With your permission?" she looked to Clara and her sisters.

Elizabeth deliberately looked away.

"Yes, thank you," said Cynthia. "That would be greatly appreciated."

Rosalind let Devon and Clara leave ahead of her. As much as she wanted to linger in the hallway to catch what they might say to each other, she did not. Such behavior would be too close to real eavesdropping for even Rosalind's lax standards.

Instead, she found the traditional green baize door that was the portal to the world of "belowstairs" and took herself through.

Belowstairs was a maze of rooms for work, storage, and even living. Generally, in a town house such as this, the female staff was lodged under the attics while the male staff slept in the basements.

Fortunately, one of the first rooms Rosalind found off the main corridor was the servants' hall. There, an ancient man whom Rosalind assumed was Sir Anthony's valet sat on a scarred bench with his head in his hands.

She cleared her throat. His head jerked up.

"I'm sorry, ma'am, erm, miss." He struggled to his feet. "I didn't see you there. . . ."

"I do apologize," said Rosalind. "I didn't mean to startle you. It's Thrush, isn't it?"

"Yes, miss. How can I help? I'm afraid . . . well, I'm afraid I'm all there is."

"Yes, and I hope we will be remedying that shortly. I have sent for some additional help. In the meantime, perhaps between us we can manage some tea and some food for upstairs? The Misses Kinsdale are very much in need of some sustenance." *As I suspect are you.*

"Yes, yes, of course, I should have thought. . . ."

Rosalind stopped him. "It has been a hard time for everyone. We can only do our best."

"Yes, miss." He agreed, with only a hint of dubiousness.

Thrush showed Rosalind through to the main kitchen. There, he checked the firebox of the great iron stove and discovered there were still some smoldering embers inside. While Thrush coaxed the fire back to life with kindling and coals, Rosalind investigated the pantry. The results were more heartening than she had dared hope. She found several loaves of bread in useable condition, along with a crock of reasonably fresh butter, and, much to her surprise, an excellent country ham.

Thrush pulled a face at her expression of surprise.

"Cook sometimes decided there were better uses for certain victuals than putting them on Sir Anthony's table."

This was much less surprising than the existence of the ham.

With the stove burning, and the kettle on to boil, Rosalind and Thrush set about making a considerable pile of ham and butter sandwiches. The valet tried to insist this was no task for a gentlewoman and that Rosalind should go back upstairs. Rosalind returned that the sooner the ladies were fed, the better able they would all be to face what was sure to be a difficult day.

"Well, I can't argue with that, miss, can I?" murmured Thrush.

"You could, but it would only delay matters," said Rosalind as she spread butter on another slice of bread. "So, perhaps we can note your objections, agree that this situation is most unusual, and get on with the task at hand?"

That earned her a ghost of a smile. "Yes, miss."

They finished the sandwiches in short order. Thrush even allowed her to carry the tray with the sandwich platter and tea things, so that he could remain in the servants' hall to greet the fresh staff that would (hopefully) be arriving shortly from the Green Briar.

"We are promoting you to butler, Thrush," she said.

He bowed solemnly. "I shall endeavor to give satisfaction, miss." He paused. "Miss, do you know . . . Sir Anthony's will . . . has there been any . . . word?"

Clearly he'd been promised an annuity or inheritance in return for so many years in service. Rosalind hoped that in this one thing Sir Anthony had kept his promise.

"Not yet," she said. "But I'm sure you will be notified as soon as the details are known."

"Thank you, miss."

The tray was heavy, the stairs were steep, and the upstairs corridor a long one. Rosalind made a quiet note to herself to increase her parlor staff's wages as soon as opportunity permitted.

Finally, she reached the salon. Taking a deep breath, Rosalind shouldered open the door.

". . . we do not know she had anything to do for Father's accident," Elizabeth was saying, her voice shaky, but insistent. "We don't know anything!"

"Then why has she run away?" asked Clara. Two spots of red colored her pale cheeks. "If Mrs. Lynn is such a harmless, charming innocent, why isn't she here, condoling with the rest of us?"

It was Cynthia who turned her head to see Rosalind. The other two noticed her standing there a heartbeat later, and closed their mouths.

Rosalind carried the tray forward as briskly as she could manage, and set it down on the tea table. "Shall I pour?" she asked them.

"I'll do it," said Elizabeth. She plopped herself down onto the sofa and began splashing tea into cups.

"If you do not mind, I'll take something up to Mr. Harkness."

"Yes, yes, please do," said Clara.

"Do you—" stammered Cynthia. "Do you know what will happen now? I mean, now that the coroner's been . . . ?"

"You'll be asked to give statements," said Rosalind. "As will I. So will Casselmaine, and all the servants."

"We are all of us suspected of wrongdoing now?" Elizabeth's words dripped acid. "Did we all conspire to kill Father?"

"No one is suspected," said Rosalind. "It's a matter of law. Sir Anthony's death was unexpected, therefore the coroner must determine whether to hold an inquest. To make that determination, all those who were nearby must say what they saw, or did not see."

The sisters looked at each other. The silent communication that passes between those who know each other well vibrated through the air between them.

There were times, Rosalind knew, when silence and time could serve better than any other form of persuasion. Now, she sensed, the Kinsdale sisters needed each other, and, even more than that, they needed to remember who they were to each other.

So, she took her plate of sandwiches and left them to-gether. When she came back, she would understand more of what had happened, and know better how to help them all.

Perhaps it would prove true that Sir Anthony's death was only a tragic accident, but somehow, Rosalind could not bring herself to believe it.

CHAPTER 24

The Mortal Remains

These convictions must unquestionably have their own pain, and severe was its kind . . .

Jane Austen, *Persuasion*

Sir Anthony's bedroom was dominated by a four-poster bed that had been stripped of its coverings. The shape of his corpse was visible beneath a plain white sheet. The ruined clothes had been laid on the press at the foot of the bed.

"Well, what have we here then?" said a man's voice behind him.

Adam turned and saw Peter Layng, the coroner for Bath, coming into the room. Layng was a plump, sallow-complexioned man with a mane of gray hair. His love of pipe smoking meant that the smell of tobacco hung about him everywhere he went. It kept out the smell of other things, he said.

"Harkness, isn't it?" said Mr. Layng as he stepped up to the bedside.

"Yes, sir."

"Sir David said he'd taken you on. After some trouble at Bow Street, or so I've been told."

Adam made no answer. Layng quirked a brow at him, and then shrugged.

"That's none of my business, of course. However, this poor bastard is." Layng folded the sheet back, exposing Sir Anthony's corpse.

Sir Anthony had not been dead long. The corpse had only just begun to stiffen. Layng was still able to turn the head as he leaned forward to squint at the wounds—because there were two. The most immediately obvious was the one that had stove in his forehead. But there was another, on the right side of the head, this one little more than a spongy depression. But not all head wounds had to bleed to be serious, Adam knew.

Layng grunted and peered under the dead man's linen vest, and then looked beneath the small clothes. He grunted again.

"Window in his sitting room was open when he was brought up?" Layng asked.

"That's what his valet said."

Layng went into the sitting room. He opened the window, just as Adam had done, and looked down to the pied-à-terre. He tapped the railing twice with his open palm.

"Well, that's clear enough."

"Is it?" asked Adam.

"I'm surprised you don't see it yourself," said Layng. "The man comes in, drunk. Sends his valet off to deal with his coat, but he's so unsteady on his pins, he staggers and falls. Hits his head on the table, probably here." He tapped the square table beside the window.

"The valet says he was not drunk," Adam told him.

Layng shrugged. "A loyal servitor talking to a stranger. I expect that story will change when it comes time to swear to it. Now, this table, the top's marble, in case you hadn't noticed. Deal a man a nasty blow if he came down on it wrong. So. Our fellow there falls, and knocks over the candle on the way down." Layng nodded toward the scorch mark. "He's stunned, or perhaps knocked out entirely. But eventually, he does get up. Only, now he's befuddled from the blow as well as the drink. He picks up the candle and puts it back in place, and means to head for the door, or his bedroom, but goes to the window instead." Layng shook his head. "Tragic, of course, but perfectly simple. What do you say, Harkness?"

"I don't know," Adam admitted. "That could be how it happened."

"Could be?" Layng snorted. "All right, out with it, man, what's bothering you?" asked Layng.

"I'm wondering about Mrs. Lynn," Adam told him.

"Who?"

"A friend of one of the daughters. She'd become much attached to Sir Anthony recently, and she was running what amounts to a casino from his house."

"Was she, b'gahd?" muttered Layng.

"Yes, sir, and she was staying here. But now she's gone missing."

"Damn," Layng muttered. "Well, that wants looking into, I suppose. Still, if we're lucky, that may turn out not to have anything to do with this business." He went to the washstand and frowned to find the basin and the jug empty. With a sigh, he picked up the towel and rubbed at his hands. "Hey ho, another fine night." Layng dropped the towel onto the basin's edge and knuckled his eyes. "Got statements from the servants yet?"

"Only the valet. The rest have scattered, and they were all newly hired as it is."

"Wonderful. All right. I'm going to leave this business to you, Harkness. As I was getting set to come here, I had word there's another death needs seeing to. Man shot in the street. Some robbery gone badly, I shouldn't wonder. Unless it was a quarrel over money and women." He went back into the sitting room to fetch his bag and his hat where he'd left them. Adam followed. "I know I can trust you to see things done properly here. Get the statements from whoever was in the house at the time as soon as you can find them, and bring them to my office. And you can tell Sir David I'll take care of your fee."

"Thank you, sir," said Adam. "And if I may? We'll want some constables to go around to the coaching inns and ask about any women traveling alone. I can give a description of Mrs. Lynn."

"Yes, I supposed we've no choice but to try to find the troublesome creature." Layng consulted his watch. "But you'll need to be quick. The first stage to London sets off at eight." He tucked the watch away and looked toward the boudoir, and the corpse.

"Poor sod," he muttered, and turned away.

Alone in that dim, silent, luxurious room, Adam found himself agreeing with this.

But the rest?

He looked at the square table by the window, and the candle in its heavy silver holder, and how it was just off center on the table. He could see the faint ring on the marble where it usually stood. He glowered at the silent room, and at the closed window.

Thrush had said nothing save that candle had been disturbed. Adam agreed. Everything was in order. But nothing was as it should be.

CHAPTER 25

A Planned Departure

*"She is a shrewd, intelligent, sensible woman.
Hers is a line for seeing human nature; and she
has a fund of good sense and observation . . ."*

Jane Austen, *Persuasion*

I might be getting too old for this, thought Sylvia.

Bath, for such a small city, slept only lightly and briefly. It was relatively easy for a woman in a drab dress, plain shawl, and equally plain bonnet to find places to linger without attracting too much notice—a tea stall, an alley gin shop, and, eventually, the early morning market, where she could lose herself among the dozens of other women setting up their booths and uncovering their barrows. If anyone had asked, she was quite prepared to tell them she was on her way to her work as cook and charwoman for a family that had just arrived, but no one did.

It had all seemed to be going so well, she sighed to herself. She'd seldom encountered a mark as willing as Sir Anthony Kinsdale. Indeed, she felt a great deal of sympathy for his poor daughters. She was even a little sad to know that they soon would look such incredible fools. She did sincerely hope Lord Casselmaine would take good care of them.

At the same time, she could not help but feel that if even one of them had showed a bit of backbone, the scheme would not be as easy as it was.

As it had been, she thought with a heavy sigh.

Now, as the sun rose, Sylvia made her unhurried way to the coaching inn. She knew to a nicety when the mail coach left for London. She intended to be just in time. Of course, she'd need a fresh name for the weigh bill. Mrs. Pole, she decided, was a suitably innocuous choice.

Once she reached London, she would pick up Sophia, and the two of them would take the money that they'd already made and fulfill their plans for a long holiday on the Continent. Wallace would shortly join them. From the coaching inn, she could send him a letter with an X cut into its seal. That was their mutual signal that it was time to up stakes. That it was not safe. That all was lost.

With these thoughts humming through her, Sylvia entered the inn's yard. It was filled with chickens and boys, both types of animal running to and fro on errands known only to them.

But as she looked up from dodging a cluster of birds, she stopped dead. The man who had charge of the coaches and their loading, one Mr. Cobb, was coming out of the inn. Mr. Cobb did not surprise her. What surprised her was that Mr. Cobb was deep in conversation with a second man whom she could not name, but whom she recognized as one of Bath's overly busy constables.

Fortunately, they hadn't yet seen her staring. Sylvia let herself fade back into the shade of the yard's sprawling chestnut tree, turning her head so that her bonnet's brim hid her face. She shook out her skirts, and strolled slowly back into the street, and did not pick up her pace until she had turned the corner.

Now what? The question drummed through her thoughts in time to her hurrying footsteps. *Now what?*

She could try to wait things out. There were any number

of rooming houses where no questions would be asked, even of a woman who arrived on the doorstep with just a portmanteau and a bit of ready money. But the constables might be keeping watch for days, and questioning any woman who showed up on her own to purchase a ticket. And in the meantime, there would be Miss Thorne and her man working who-knew-what-sorts of mischief.

She could hire a gig and drive herself to London. In general, Bath's constables were fools and a bit lazy, so they might not think of that possibility. But Miss Thorne's conduct thus far said she was not a fool. She'd send her man around to the liveries to ask questions. A woman traveling alone was always memorable.

I should have stayed with Elizabeth. I should have brazened it out.

Sylvia reached the high street. She made herself stop and take a deep breath. It was too late for regrets. Things were as they were. She must think.

They would be looking for a woman alone, so she would not be a woman alone. Simple as that. She picked a direction and started walking.

CHAPTER 26

The Evidence of What Did Not Happen

*There is a quickness of perception in some, a
nicety in the discernment of character, a natural
penetration, in short, which no experience in others can equal . . .*

Jane Austen, *Persuasion*

Rosalind found Adam on the second floor. He was staring
down the length of the central corridor, so lost in thought
that he did not seem to notice her until she was just next
to him.

"Will you eat something?" She held out the plate of sandwiches.

"If you will," he said, but he did not take his attention
away from the corridor.

So, they stood there like that—the pair of them munching
ham sandwiches and staring at nothing, each thinking their
own thoughts.

"How are the Kinsdales?" Adam asked finally.

"Angry," said Rosalind. "Frightened, and now that they
know who we are, suspicious of us both."

"I can't say I blame them for that."

"What have you learned?" she asked.

Adam sighed. He finished off the last bites of his sandwich and helped himself to another. "It does appear that Sir Anthony fell from his window, and Mrs. Lynn is indeed gone."

"What did the coroner say?"

"He says Sir Anthony probably fell twice—once against a table in his room, and then from the window. He's a competent man, but also content to take things at face value. I agree that Sir Anthony's head was struck twice, once in back and once in front. But exactly what happened?" Adam added softly, almost angrily. "I can't tell yet."

"You're thinking about Jasper Aimesworth," said Rosalind.

Adam nodded. Jasper Aimesworth had been a rash young man. He, like Sir Anthony, had been found after a fall—in that case, he'd fallen from the musician's gallery of Almack's ballroom—and it was assumed that fall had killed him.

It was the inquiry into Jasper's death that led to Rosalind meeting Adam.

"I admit, I was thinking about him, too," said Rosalind.

She was also thinking about last night's party, Sir Anthony sitting, drinking, and gaming with that crowd of men he barely knew, let alone understood.

"Did you find any money or notes with Sir Anthony?"

"No. And I did check. Thrush had emptied his coat pockets, so his purse and pocketbook were on his dressing table, but there was nothing in them."

"I strongly suspect Mrs. Lynn took the proceeds from the party when she left."

"That would seem likely. Thankfully, the coroner did agree we should send out some constables to the coaching inns, to see if we can catch Mrs. Lynn as she tries to leave Bath."

"But there has been no word?"

"Not yet." Adam finished the second sandwich. "I was

hoping you'd come look at Mrs. Lynn's room with me. You may be able to see something I would miss."

"Of course." She handed him the plate with the remaining sandwich, dusted her hands, and followed him down the corridor.

Mrs. Lynn's room was the first door on the right side of the hallway. Inside waited a pretty little boudoir, although one decorated with more pink satin and ruffles than Rosalind herself would have been comfortable with.

Rosalind took three steps into the room and paused. She looked about her, turning slowly to take in the whole of it.

The room was a disaster. The bed covers were askew. The wardrobe door hung open and its drawers had been pulled out. The dressing table was a sea of overturned bottles and boxes.

Inside the wardrobe, several gowns still hung on their hooks, but some were obviously missing. An abandoned bonnet lay in the bottom, and another was on its shelf, but there was no coat or pelisse. Nor did a cursory search turn up a bandbox or portmanteau, although a trunk waited in the closet.

Adam opened the clothes press at the foot of the bed. The clothes inside had been disarranged. The small clothes were gone. As were the stockings.

"Did she fly in haste, or was the room searched after she left?" asked Adam.

"I was wondering much the same." Rosalind crossed the room to the small jewel cabinet on the table. It was open, and its drawers emptied. She opened the dressing table drawer and found a mess of handkerchiefs and gloves.

"But there was no reason for Mrs. Lynn to fly, at least not when we parted company," Rosalind said. "She had a plan for a graceful—or at least organized—retreat and it seemed to me she had reasons to want to leave things in good order. However, it is possible that when she discovered the tragedy of Sir Anthony's death, she decided speed was more important."

"But there's a problem?" prompted Adam. "Another problem, I should say?"

Rosalind nodded. "Mrs. Lynn is a woman of experience. She had to know that if she fled in the middle of the night, it would raise more suspicions than if she stayed and pretended to be as shocked and grieved as the rest of the house."

"Or if she was the one who raised the alarm."

"Exactly."

Rosalind went back to the writing table. It had only one drawer, with paper and quills and a penknife, and sealing wax and all the other paraphernalia needed for writing letters and lists.

"There's no letters," murmured Rosalind. "Not here, not in any of the other drawers. If Mrs. Lynn had been staying here long enough to organize multiple card parties, she should have been receiving her post here as well."

Adam went to the hearth and picked up the poker. He squatted down and stirred the ashes. "No signs of any papers having been burned," he said. "At least, not recently." He straightened and put the poker back in its holder. "I'll ask that any letters that come for her today be set aside. Once there's someone to set them aside," he added ruefully.

Rosalind glowered at the room, willing it to give her some sign as to what truly happened. But the mess remained as it was, and no revelations occurred to her. She sighed at her own foolishness and turned back to Adam.

"You did not sound as if you agreed with the coroner's assessment that Sir Anthony fell because he was drunk," Rosalind said. "Why is that?"

"Let me show you."

Adam led Rosalind to Sir Anthony's luxurious sitting room with its silks and velvets. It was a bright morning outside, but the light seemed to enter tentatively, as if obstructed by the rich fabrics. Despite this, the black scorching on the carpet stood out at once.

"That"—Adam scuffed at the scorch mark with the toe of his boot—"is what bothers me. Mr. Layng thinks Sir Anthony fell and hit his head, here." Adam touched the edge of one of the marble-topped tables. "That he was dazed by the combination of the fall and the drink, or even rendered unconscious. That eventually, he got up and staggered away. He meant to ring for help, or go to the door, but instead opened the window, and fell out."

Rosalind considered this. She bent to examine the scorch mark, and then looked up at the silver candlestick on the table where Sir Anthony was thought to have hit his head. The candle had not yet been refreshed, and a shameful amount of wax dripped down the heavy silver holder.

"When did the candle fall?" she asked. "And how did it fall all the way over here?" She gestured toward the scorch mark. "Was Sir Anthony holding it when he fell?"

"But if he dropped it when he fell, when was it picked up again? And by whom?" Adam asked. "Thrush was already gone. He said he left Sir Anthony sitting in his chair. That burn goes almost right through to the floorboards. The fire would have spread quickly if it wasn't smothered within seconds of starting. If there was the potential for a fire, even a dazed, drunken man would shout for help, and if he's unconscious—"

"His clothing will catch along with the carpet and the room would be alight shortly afterward," finished Rosalind. "Was any of Sir Anthony's clothing scorched?"

"No. I checked after Layng left. And Thrush says if that scorch had been there when he was helping Sir Anthony out of his things, he would have seen it."

Given Sir Anthony's fastidious nature, Rosalind could well believe it.

"And then there's a final point," Adam went on. "Thrush

says Sir Anthony abhorred drunkenness, and never drank to excess."

"But Mr. Layng dismissed that?"

"As a show of loyalty from a faithful servant," replied Adam.

Rosalind sighed, and declined to comment. "So," she said slowly. "The candle fell, or was dropped. The carpet burned. Someone put out the fire before it could spread, and put the candle back. That someone was either Sir Anthony, or someone who came into his room after Thrush left."

"After Thrush left, but before Sir Anthony fell? And they themselves left without choosing to alert the house to the accident with the candle?" He left off the third possibility—that this person had caused Sir Anthony to fall.

"We need to speak with Clara and her sisters," said Rosalind.

"And Mrs. Lynn," said Adam.

When we find her, thought Rosalind, but there was no need for her to say as much out loud. She could tell Adam was thinking the same thing.

In that moment, they were interrupted by a scratching at the door, which opened a moment later.

"Ah, there you are, miss," said a familiar voice. "I thought it best we come look for you first."

"Mrs. Kendricks!" Rosalind cried delightedly. "I had not expected you to come yourself!"

Indeed, she had specifically not asked her former housekeeper to come and help. She had not wished to presume on their former connection, or to put any further strain on Mrs. Kendricks's decision to try to come to terms with Rosalind's choices.

"And, Laurel, thank you so much," Rosalind added belatedly. Her maid returned a prim, tolerant smile, but the light in her eyes told Rosalind she had not truly taken offense.

"And where else should I be, miss?" Mrs. Kendricks lifted

her chin. "Mrs. Leigh can assemble a group of likely girls, but not one of them has the kind of experience needed to take charge in such an emergency."

"Well, I will not deny I am glad to see you both," Rosalind told them earnestly. "Nothing's been done, the young ladies are in complete distress, and the house will have to be put into mourning as soon as may be. Have you met Thrush?"

"We have," said Laurel. "He was downstairs when we came in."

"Good. I expect he will know what's available and what must be ordered. If you can begin making some lists? And nothing's been cleaned or set to rights this morning. And there will be the matter of a luncheon. . . ."

"You may leave it all to me, miss," said Mrs. Kendricks, and Rosalind felt a surge of relief. "On one point, there may be a need for money, and I understand. . . ."

She didn't need to go any further. "Yes," agreed Rosalind. "You may have difficulty getting credit with any of the shops. I will ask Lord Casselmaine to draw out some funds so you can pay down something on account with any merchant you must deal with. I'm sure he will be glad to help." Rosalind paused, and lowered her voice. "I do not know how long you will be needed, and during that time there may be . . . questions to be asked, especially about the young ladies. If you do not want to be part of it . . ."

Mrs. Kendricks shook her head. "I knew what I was getting into when I offered to come. And I've made sure Laurel understands."

Laurel returned a cheeky grin. "As if I hadn't seen enough of what goes on back at Orchard Street."

"Thank you, Mrs. Kendricks, and thank you, Laurel." Rosalind gathered up her hems. "Now, I must go downstairs and join his grace and the Misses Kinsdales."

And the lord only knows what I will find when I do.

But before any of them could say anything more, they

heard the sound of a heavy door being thrown open. They blinked at one another, and then Adam turned and ran out into the corridor with Rosalind right behind him.

They met Devon coming up the stairs.

"I hoped you'd still be here," Devon gasped.

"What's happened?" cried Rosalind.

"Admiral Walsingham"—Devon drew in a deep breath—"has been shot. He's dead."

CHAPTER 27

Alone

All the overpowering, blinding, bewildering, first
effects of strong surprise were over with her.
Jane Austen, *Persuasion*

Wallace had taken a discreet set of rooms over the Venetian, a coffeehouse in the heart of Bath. When Sylvia reached its busy street, she was footsore and famished, but not so far gone that she didn't remember to be cautious.

Like all streets in the town, this one sported a population of loafers of various ages and types. Sylvia picked out a scrawny lad with a gleam in his eye that was either desperation or intelligence.

"Here." She slipped a penny into his hand. "And another when you come back. There's a man up the stairs of the coffeehouse, door number three. You tell him Miss Smith is waiting for him in the mews, and bring back his answer, all right?"

The penny vanished in a flash and the barefoot child was already pelting across the cobbles, dodging the morning crowds without once breaking stride.

Sylvia didn't wait. She took herself around to the mews behind the Venetian, and stationed herself so that she had a wall at her back and an alley immediately to her left. She could see Wallace's window from here, which meant she could also be seen. She was not, however, so close that her face could be easily made out, and the alley offered a quick retreat should she need it.

While she waited, Sylvia busied herself with examining her shawl, as if she'd caught it on something. After all, one never knew who might be watching.

She'd just rewrapped her shawl about her shoulders when her urchin came dashing around the corner.

"Said I was to give you this." He held up a—now much wrinkled and dirt smeared—letter, and held out his other hand for the penny.

Sylvia surrendered the coin, and the urchin surrendered the letter, and immediately took himself off.

Sylvia held her breath and turned the letter over. And saw at once the X cut across the seal.

She didn't bother to open it. There wouldn't be anything inside. The seal was the message. It meant: *Time to up stakes. It's not safe. All is lost.*

It meant she was alone after all.

Sylvia picked up her bag and started walking.

CHAPTER 28

The Death of an Admiral

". . . but I have never been satisfied. I have always wanted some other motive for his conduct than appeared."

Jane Austen, *Persuasion*

A dam did not wait for carriage or horse to take him from the Kinsdales' house to the City police station. He walked, almost ran, shoving his way through the morning crowds. The whole way, he cursed himself for not having asked any questions when Layng said there'd been a second death. Some part of him tried to insist that Bath was a lively city, and he'd had no reason to suspect that two deaths could possibly be related. Indeed, Rosalind would ever-so-gently laugh at him for his self-deprecation. But he felt it all the same.

"He was found in the small hours by another lodger at the private hotel where he stayed," Casselmaine had said. "It's a place much favored by sailors staying in Bath."

Casselmaine had had no other details. His only thought had been to get back to the Kinsdales before they could hear of the murder by some other means. Adam could not truly fault him for such a response, but he was immensely frustrated all the same.

When Adam had been an officer with Bow Street, he had spent a good amount of time in Bath. It was one of the watering places of the *haut ton*, and the royals, after all, which meant that every so often officers were sent in an attempt to clear out the worst of the pickpockets and cut purses.

Policing in Bath, like in London, was a patchwork affair. There were essentially three separate police forces—the Walcot police, the City police, and the Bathwick police. Each patch of ground was practically the personal fiefdom of the station's commissioner. Mr. Layng worked from the offices of the City police, Adam knew, and frequently held the inquests in the public house across the street.

Adam was so lost in his own thoughts and the flood of questions that he wasn't watching where he was going, and crashed into the large, Black man coming the other way.

Adam looked up, his mouth open to apologize, but froze dead.

"Goutier!" he cried.

"Harkness!"

The men clasped hands eagerly.

Sampson Goutier was the newest of Bow Street's tiny cadre of principle officers. He had, in fact, been promoted to replace Adam when Adam walked away from the office and the station. He was a towering Black man whose parents had come to London via the Caribbean and Paris. When Adam was still with Bow Street, they had worked together closely and the two had remained friends since.

"What brings you to Bath?" Adam asked.

Goutier laughed. "The races, what else would it be? Some of the royal dukes are planning to come for the week, and we're meant to have the pickpockets cleared out before they do. But what of you?" He slapped Adam's arm. "When's the wedding?"

"September, we think. You and Sal will come to the wedding breakfast?"

"Nothing could keep us away. Send word when the date is settled."

"How are things at the station?"

Goutier shook his head. "Mr. Townsend is . . . distracted, let's say. With the various outbursts of unrest around the country, he's becoming convinced that we are due for some sort of dangerous uprising in London. Between you and me, I'm concerned it's coloring his thinking."

Adam nodded. John Townsend was the head of the Bow Street Police Station. For the most part, he was a sound and experienced man, but he believed very firmly in established order, and distrusted those who questioned it. Especially those who might give public voice to their dissatisfaction. This tendency, and his willingness to ignore the law to enforce it, were among the reasons that Adam had resigned from Bow Street.

"But never mind that," Goutier was saying. "I'm on my way to meet Tauton. He'll be glad to see you, too." Sam Tauton was one of Bow Street's most senior officers. He was legendary for his memory for faces and his creative, and sometimes brutal, ways to deal with pickpockets. "Will you walk with me?"

"I need to speak with Layng," said Adam. "There's been a shooting."

"Walsingham. Yes. We've heard."

"What has he said?"

"Inquest is tomorrow, along with this other fellow—"

"Sir Anthony Kinsdale," supplied Adam.

Goutier narrowed his eyes. "You're not involved in that?"

"Up to my hips," answered Adam. "Miss Thorne as well."

"Well, well. But why ask after the admiral?"

"He was Sir Anthony's tenant. The admiral and his wife rented the Kinsdales' country house."

"Did they, b'ghad?" breathed Goutier. "Does Layng know that?"

"If he doesn't, I mean to tell him." Adam hesitated. "What's he said to you about the admiral?"

Goutier looked over his shoulder briefly. "He said it was likely an attempted robbery gone wrong. Probably some hooligan made the mistake of brandishing a pistol at a navy man, and it ended in tragedy. He's going to send an express rider to the widow, and he wants the body ready to go home with her before she arrives in Bath."

"Has he been to the man's lodgings? Talked to anyone?"

Goutier shrugged irritably. "He talked to the landlady at the hotel, and the fellow who all but tripped over him, but nothing more."

Adam let all this sink in. "Goutier, I need a favor, and it's got to be quick."

"What is it?"

"Can you get me a look at the admiral?" If Layng was in a hurry to have the matter tidied away, he might or might not be willing to give Adam the time he'd need to ask extra questions.

Goutier stared at him and then shook his head. "God's legs, man, you never let up."

Adam raised his brows and Goutier chuckled.

"All right. Body's in the station's cellar, but when you're done, you're meeting me and Tauton over at the King's Swan across the way and telling us the whole story."

"There's a bargain." Adam clasped Goutier's hand.

"Cellar door's off the alley," Goutier told him.

"I'm in your debt."

"Again." Goutier smiled.

"Again," agreed Adam.

Adam left his friend and strode out into the street. He kept his gait purposeful, but not hurrying. When he reached the corner he turned, and turned again, heading up the next street, until he got to the back of the station house. Adam trotted down the area stairs. The cellar door was closed. He pushed the handle experimentally, and it swung open reluctantly on rusted hinges.

Goutier had evidently already nicked down, unbolted the door, and nicked out again. Adam grinned and said a quick prayer of thanks to the fates for letting him run into his old friend.

Admiral Walsingham's corpse lay uncovered on a trestle table made from planks that had been laid across a pile of packing crates. His clothing was all askew, showing that Mr. Layng had indeed conducted some examination.

The light was dim. Adam didn't dare take the time to light one of the lanterns that stood nearby. But once his eyes adjusted, he was able to take in the details. A gun shot did abominable things to a man. From the sheer size of the wound, the person who fired the shot had been close. The shooter had either been lucky, or steady about his business, because the hole was in the exact center of the admiral's broad chest. The man would have been dead before his body fell.

But something's wrong.

Adam steeled himself, and looked more closely at the wound. He frowned. He searched the corpse for other wounds or bruises, but found none.

Adam found a piece of sacking and wiped his hands. Then, he left by the same door he'd entered through, circled the block once again, and walked back into the station through the narrow front entrance.

A constable directed Adam to a cramped office on the second floor. The windows had been thrown open to catch the morning air and Mr. Layng sat at his desk, writing in a great ledger.

"Ah, Harkness." Layng glanced up when Adam walked in. "Do you have those statements on the Kinsdale matter?"

"No, sir. But—"

"No, sir?" Layng cocked a skeptical eye at him. "Then you've found your missing lady?"

"Not yet, sir, but—"

"But what?" Layng made an impatient gesture with two fingers.

"I've come to ask about Admiral Walsingham."

"Eh?" Layng dropped his pen into the inkwell and rubbed his eyes. "Oh, yes. Bad business, that. Can see why you'd want to know. Well, fortunately it's nothing to do with Sir Anthony. Fellow was shot dead in an alley. Purse and pocketbook stolen. So, we've a hooligan out there someplace who'd better hope his fence doesn't peach on him, or he's for the gallows." Layng dipped his pen in the inkpot and made another note in his ledger.

"But there's some complications," said Adam. "The admiral was Sir Anthony's tenant, and Sir Anthony was planning to evict him and his wife."

"Poor fellow!" said Layng. "Come on business and got himself in the way of some fool with a pistol and no sense at all. Perhaps wherever he's gone he can gain some satisfaction in the fact that Sir Anthony's been foiled in his plan to displace the family." Layng chuckled at his own grim joke.

"Surely, we have to ask if their deaths are related."

"Why?" For the first time since Adam walked in, Layng looked directly at him. "Do you think your Mrs. Lynn pushed Sir Anthony out his window, and then went out and shot the admiral?"

"I don't know," said Adam. "But it may be."

Now Layng was staring at him. "It may be?" he echoed. "And I suppose it may also be that Walsingham crept into the house, knocked Sir Anthony on the head, and shoved him out the window, and then got himself shot on the way home from that particular murderous deed." He paused, waiting for Adam's answer with theatrical patience. "I don't suppose you have a witness that could speak to this possibility? One of the servants perhaps?"

"The servants have left the house," Adam told him. "They'd

not been paid and decided they wanted nothing more to do with the place, or the family."

"And the daughters? What do they say? Did they see or hear anything?"

"They witnessed the quarrel between Admiral Walsingham and Sir Anthony. As did I," said Adam. "As did Mrs. Lynn. And they heard the admiral accuse Sir Anthony of playing some game when it came to the horse races. Possibly, he thought Sir Anthony was cheating."

Layng sighed. "Harkness, I know your reputation. You're a good man. Sir David says it, and even old Townsend admits it, despite the fact that you tweaked his nose with your resignation. But I won't have any man come to me and start spinning stories when he's got no witness to back up what he says!"

"I've had no time to find witnesses yet," said Adam.

"Well, both inquests are tomorrow," said Layng. "Three o'clock sharp. Bring me your witnesses before then and we'll hear what they have to say."

Adam was hard pressed not to gape at him. Layng saw his surprise, and gave out another great, loud sigh.

"This isn't London, Mr. Harkness. Bath is a simpler place and things here tend to be exactly what they look like. Men get drunk and fall because they get drunk and fall. Other men make the mistake of being out late while wearing gold braid and gold buttons and find themselves waylaid by robbers. Just now, I have the sad duty of presiding over the inquest of a young fool who threw himself off a bridge because his lady love chose a rival over him, and I've got to talk the jury into death by misadventure rather than suicide so the church will agree to a decent burial and give his mother a bit of peace. So." Layng heaved himself to his feet and planted both hands on his desk. "Unless you find me a witness who will swear otherwise, your Sir Anthony died of a fall and the admiral died of a gunshot and that's all there is to it."

He met Adam's gaze and waited. There was nothing for Adam to do but bow and take his leave.

But his problem still remained. Adam had begun his career with the horse patrol. That patrol was specifically charged with clearing out the highwaymen that plagued the roads and pikes crisscrossing Britain. He'd seen what happened to men who failed to stand and deliver. They were shot. But they were shot from the front.

Admiral Walsingham had been shot from the back.

CHAPTER 29

Correspondents

She was obliged to recollect that her seeing the letter was a violation of the laws of honour, that no one ought to be judged or to be known by such testimonies, that no private correspondence could bear the eye of others . . .

Jane Austen, *Persuasion*

When Adam left, Rosalind and Devon found themselves alone at the top of the stairs. Rosalind pressed her hand against her mouth, holding back a mixture of sobs, shouted questions, and a dozen different exclamations, none of which were fit for company. Her mind was racing, but her thoughts did not seem to have any destination.

"We must go tell Clara and her sisters," said Devon. "They need to know what's happened."

"Yes," agreed Rosalind reluctantly. "Devon, will you go? I will join you in a moment."

"What is it? You've thought of something." His frown was an expression of uncertainty that verged on actual suspicion. Rosalind saw it, and a wave of exhaustion threatened to overwhelm her.

Rosalind pushed the feeling back and looked Devon directly in the eye. "Mrs. Lynn's letters have gone missing. She probably either destroyed them or took them with her, but I just realized where she may have left some behind. They might give us an idea of her plans, or the identity of her confederates. I want to look for them before the new staff tidy everything away."

She wanted to hold her breath. What she said to him was mostly true, but she needed him to believe all of it. Had he not been so distracted with the news of the admiral's death and his thoughts of what it would mean for Clara and her sisters, he might have questioned her more closely, but as it was, he simply nodded.

"Very well. Join us as soon as you can."

Devon hurried down the stairs, while Rosalind climbed up and rushed down the corridor. She did not worry about being seen. For this one moment, she knew where every person in the household was, and it was vital she conduct her search before that changed.

Because Mrs. Lynn's room contained no letters, but Elizabeth's might.

And not just from Mrs. Lynn.

Rosalind did pause as she reached the door to the sisters' sitting room and look over her shoulder, in case Devon had changed course and come after her. She did not believe he would easily forgive her if it looked like she was about to violate his fiancée's privacy.

Which I am.

Because it was not only Elizabeth's things Rosalind meant to search, if she had the chance.

But she was alone, and, thankfully, the door had not been locked. Rosalind slipped into the sitting room and closed the door softly behind her.

Under other circumstances, Rosalind would have been shocked at how untidy the room was—candles had burnt down in their holders; books were scattered across the tea table; shawls were tossed carelessly over the end of the sofa, with one crumpled in the middle of the floor. A quill lay forgotten on the writing table next to an open bottle of ink. The grate was heaped with ashes.

Three portable writing desks waited on the long table by the window. They were identical. Rosalind ground her teeth in frustration.

You might at least have thought to label them. . . .

She told herself she was being ridiculous and went to the first of the desks.

Its lid had been left unlocked, and she lifted it. Inside waited a good amount of blank paper, some untrimmed quills, a penknife, and some sealing wax, but nothing else.

Rosalind opened the second desk. Here, her luck was in. A half-written letter waited inside. It was splotched and scratched, and barely legible. Nonetheless, Rosalind made out:

> *My Dear Admiral Walsingham:*
> *~~You will~~ You must forgive Father. You must not do any rash thing. Only a little time is wanted. ~~I must ask~~ . . . I beg you for all the bonds of ~~love~~ ~~admiration~~ affection that are between ~~us~~ our families . . . wait, and the matter will blow over, I ~~promise~~ swear. . . .*

In her mind, Rosalind heard Cynthia's voice recounting their visit to their cousins, where they first met the admiral, her talk of warmth, of stability, of finally not feeling that she must walk on tiptoes. She also remembered her shutting a splotched and much-crossed-out letter into a writing desk so that Rosalind could not accidentally read it.

Then, she saw another letter in the bottom of the desk. This was written in a different hand. She read:

> *Dear Miss Kinsdale:*
> *I don't know if this will reach you in time, and I know you will be surprised to hear from me, but after*

some wrestling with my conscience, I felt I should warn
you that my brother, the admiral, has left for Bath, and
means to confront your father over his threat to end the
lease on Kinsdale House.

I am sorry to report this latest threat has greatly in-
censed Jack, and I cannot be sure his temper will have
cooled by the time he reaches you.

He is staying at his usual . . .

She got no further.

"Carefully, carefully now."

The words were spoken softly, but Rosalind jumped, startled. She quickly closed the writing desk and went at once to
the door. She paused long enough to take a deep breath and
rearrange her features into a mildly concerned mask.

Rosalind opened the sitting room door. As she did, she saw
Clara supporting Cynthia down the corridor, with Devon
close behind. Cynthia's face was a sickly shade of gray and
she leaned heavily on her sister's arm.

"I'm all right, I'm all right," Cynthia declared, even though
this was obviously untrue.

"What's happened?" cried Rosalind.

"She was overcome," said Clara before Cynthia could
speak. "It's been too much for her."

Rosalind pulled the door open further, so that Clara could
help her sister inside.

"I was stunned for a moment," muttered Cynthia.

"You fainted," said Clara. She lowered her sister onto the
sofa and went to ring the bell. "Oh! There's no one—"

"There is," Rosalind told her. "Some staff has arrived
from the Green Briar Inn."

"Thank goodness." Clara rang the bell. "We need to get
Cynthia to bed at once."

Cynthia looked ready to protest this, but was interrupted
by Laurel appearing at the door.

"Tea and brandy," ordered Clara. "And someone must make up the fire."

"Right away, miss," said Laurel.

Devon was hovering just outside the room, clearly unsure as to whether propriety allowed him to cross the threshold into the women's private apartments. Rosalind stepped out into the corridor, and drew the door partway shut.

"What happened?" she asked softly as they both stepped away from the door.

"I broke it to Clara and her sisters that the admiral had been shot, and Cynthia collapsed in a faint."

Rosalind thought about the letters she had seen in the writing desk, and bit her lip.

Devon, of course, noticed, and was about to question her, when a hidden door further down the hallway opened, and one of the Leigh cousins emerged, toting a heavy coal scuttle.

Rosalind signaled that Devon should wait for a moment and went over to the young woman. "I've a favor to ask," she breathed. "When you've cleaned the hearth, please make sure the ashes are set aside, not thrown on the dust heap."

The girl looked at her like she'd suddenly begun speaking Russian, but recovered quickly. "As you like, miss," she said, making it clear that if Rosalind wanted to engage in patently daft behaviors, it was no business of hers.

"What was that?" asked Devon when she returned to him.

Rosalind looked at him. *I'm sorry*, she thought. "I told her not to build the fire too high. Cynthia needs warmth, but she will not recover if she's being stifled."

Did he believe her? Rosalind found she couldn't tell. Guilt clouded her judgment, and she pushed it back with great difficulty. She didn't know if there was anything to find in that heap of ashes, or who it might belong to, and yet, Devon had already shown himself to be uncomfortable with her means of proceeding. She couldn't let his fastidiousness allow her to miss a chance at discovering the answers they both needed.

"Did you find the letters?" Devon asked.

"Not yet." But even as she said this, another thought struck her. "Where's Elizabeth?"

"We left her downstairs."

"I think I should go talk with her. It might be easier without her sisters."

"She won't welcome the attempt," Devon warned her.

"I know, but I need to try."

Devon nodded. "I'm going to Sir Anthony's bookroom. Elizabeth certainly won't welcome this interference either, but if there are ledgers, or records of any sort, we need to see them sooner rather than later."

For so many reasons. "An excellent thought."

"And I'll see if any of the banknotes from the card party last night have found their way to that room."

Shame at her deception curdled, but there was no time to talk more.

"Thank you," she said, and took herself to the stairs. Behind her she heard Devon knocking softly on Cynthia's door.

Downstairs, she made her way straight to the amber salon. But when she opened the door, she found the room entirely empty.

Rosalind stared at the salon for a moment, as if she thought she could compel some answer from it. Then, she turned and strode to the entrance hall.

A young man whose name she remembered was Duggin, was shrugging his shoulders uneasily in one of the overdecorated coats that were the Kinsdale livery. He looked up and saw her, and blushed bright red.

Rosalind pretended to ignore all this. "Did any of the young ladies go out while you were here?"

"Yes, miss." Duggin shifted his weight uncomfortably under his borrowed coat. "Just a minute or two ago. Miss Elizabeth Kinsdale, I think?"

"Did she say where she was going?"

"No, miss. Just said to tell anybody who asked that she needed some air and she'd be back soon. Oh!" He snapped the fingers on one hand and dug into the coat pocket with the other. "This came. The boy said he'd been told not to wait for an answer."

From Adam? Rosalind thought as she took the folded paper. But although her name was on it, she didn't recognize the hand.

There was no seal. Rosalind opened the note and read:

I am at the Green Briar. I beg you to help me.
S. Lynn

CHAPTER 30

What May Happen in Bath

"I had no more discoveries to make than you . . ."

Jane Austen, *Persuasion*

The King's Swan was a modest pub, filled with working men. The weather remained clear, so Goutier and Tauton had claimed a table in the yard. When Adam arrived, they had a pitcher and several pewter pint pots in front of them, along with the remains of some cold roast beef and bread.

"And now he comes." Tauton kicked out a stool he'd been keeping under the table. "Sit, Harkness, and tell us what's the to-do."

Adam sat and reached for the pitcher. Goutier pushed over a—presumably clean—pint pot so he could pour out some beer for himself.

While his former colleagues listened, Adam told them what had happened—how Clara Kinsdale had come to ask Rosalind's help in discovering the truth about Mrs. Sylvia Lynn, how Miss Smith had appeared so quickly afterward. He told them about the invitation to the home of Sir Anthony for an "evening of supper and cards with a few select friends." How Admiral Walsingham had arrived to object to Sir Anthony's plan to evict himself and his wife from the house they had leased. How the small card party had turned out to be anything but that. He detailed the presence of the faro bank and the money lenders, and the guests supplied by that same Mrs. Lynn.

He told them how Sir Anthony was found dead in his garden the next morning, and how word came that Admiral Walsingham also now lay dead in the cellars of the City police station.

Goutier leaned back against the yard's wooden fence and whistled. "And what's Layng got to say about all this?"

"I'll wager not much," put in Tauton. "Layng keeps his appointment as coroner by making sure any and all unpleasantness is found to have some simple answer and is tidied away as quick as may be."

"He's given me until tomorrow to find a witness," Adam told them. "What I've got instead is a houseful of servants who have scattered themselves to the four winds, and I'm not sure I could get all their names by next Lady Day, let alone before tomorrow afternoon. Then there's these two pleasant gents who were acting as moneylenders to that gaming crowd. God alone knows where they've got themselves to. Then there's the three good ladies who have lost their father. If the looks they've been giving to each other were any dirtier we'd have to send them out with the week's washing."

"Well, what a good thing you've got us to lend a hand," said Goutier. "And your Miss Thorne. We can leave the ladies and their dirty looks to her, I daresay."

"I'll start on the coffeehouses," said Tauton. "If there's anyone in this city willing to lend out half a crown, they'll know about it there."

"And I've a mind to take myself round to the stables," said Goutier. "Since you tell us there's some lads there who know a thing or three about the late Sir Anthony's business."

Despite himself, Adam felt a smile forming. "Aren't you both supposed to be clearing out Bath's pickpockets ahead of race week?"

"No place like a coffeehouse to find your most hardened members of the criminal classes," said Tauton with a perfectly straight face. "Almost as good as a gin shop."

"And I need to go out to the racecourse to get the lay of the land and see where our cutpurses are likely to be lurking on race day," said Goutier, his face as serious as Tauton's. "Otherwise how am I supposed to know where best to station our constables?"

"Well," said Adam, carefully matching his friend's gravity. "If you don't mind, Goutier, I'll come with you to the stables. I've an idea that it would be good to have a look at the famous Kinsdale's Pride and make sure the horse hasn't suffered the fate of the master."

Goutier procured them a couple of saddle horses from the City police, and he and Adam rode up the sloping road to Lansdown. When they got to the racecourse, they found a hive of activity. Workmen were everywhere, erecting the grandstands and setting up the posts that would mark the racecourse. Mingling with the workmen were dozens of gentlemen in their high hats and summer coats. And then there were the horses. These were not the sturdy, patient animals that filled the city streets pulling vans and cabs, or even the tough, canny, country animals Adam had learned to ride. These were tall, delicate creatures with gleaming hides and flowing manes and legs as slender as a deer's. They came in every color from the brightest white through shining copper to midnight black.

Several exercise yards had been marked off between the racecourse and the stables. Grooms and trainers and riders put the animals through their paces, or led them to and fro.

When Goutier stopped one of the grooms to ask about Kinsdale's Pride, the man rolled his eyes and called over his shoulder. "Foote! Another one for you and that bag of bones!"

"Pay him no mind, gents." A broad man swaggered up to them. His skin was deep brown, and his tightly curled hair had gone almost entirely gray. His hands were thick and calloused, and he'd rolled up his sleeves to expose his muscled forearms. He looked like he could have wrestled any man to the ground, including Goutier.

"Charlie Foote at your service." He bowed. "And Kinsdale's Pride is the finest animal on the turf today. You've a letter from Sir Anthony, I'll assume? Very particular he is about who comes to see Kinsdale's Pride when he's not about. Jealous lot around here. Threats have been made to try to keep her out of the race." He nodded seriously.

"We've no letter," Adam said. "Sir Anthony died last night."

Foote froze. "'S truth. What did for him?"

"Fell out a window," said Goutier.

If anything, Foote looked even more stunned. "Fell, is it? Last night? You sure?"

"I saw the body," said Adam.

Foote cursed, at length and with impressive originality. "Well, God rest him I'm sure," he concluded, finally. "Have you brought my money?"

"What money?" asked Goutier.

"What I'm owed for taking care of his horse!" cried Foote. "And all his guests, not to mention dealing with the madmen he sends my way!"

"Madmen?" said Adam.

"Just yesterday, fellow came up here, demanding to see Kinsdale's Pride and Sir Anthony and I don't know what all."

"Did he wear a naval coat?" asked Adam.

"That he did, sir," said Foote, much more stiffly. It was clearly sinking in that he probably was not going to get paid at all, and this was occupying much of his mind. "Tall fellow, not young anymore, yellow hair. Bellowed like he meant it to carry all the way to London."

Goutier and Adam exchanged a long look.

"Look, what about the pay I been promised?" interrupted Foote. "I've kept up my end this last fortnight, and I want what I'm owed."

"We'll do what we can," Goutier assured him. "But we need to know what happened here."

"Why?" Foote shot back.

"Because Sir Anthony might have been helped out that window," Goutier told him. "And this big bloke with the yellow hair and the naval coat might have had something to do with it."

"'S truth," muttered Foote again. "Look, I don't want trouble here."

"No trouble's coming," said Adam. "At least, not that I know of. But it would help if we could see the horse."

A dozen expressions flickered across Foote's face, but at last he turned and started trudging toward the long rows of wooden stables.

"Why so glum, Foote?" called one of the grooms they passed. "Somebody finally figure out you've got a hound in there rather than a horse?"

"Skinned rabbit, more like," quipped another.

Foote made a rude gesture toward the wits, but didn't break stride. Inside, the stables smelled strongly of warm horses and dry hay. Adam had seen whole families of laborers sleep in spaces smaller, and far meaner, than the horse boxes here. Most of the boxes were empty. Adam supposed the animals were out for their exercise. The last box, however, held a delicate dapple-gray mare. She was munching her hay with a distracted air, and barely seemed to notice Foote when he brought them up to the door.

Adam was not by any means an expert when it came to horses, but he had cared for them and rode frequently. This was not a horse he'd pick out for himself, and compared to the gleaming, spirited creatures out in the exercise yards, she looked like what she really needed was a quiet pasture and a good feed. She'd make a decent saddle horse for a child or a nervous rider, perhaps, but a racing horse? In a dead sprint, he'd probably be able to beat her himself.

It was easy to tell Goutier was thinking something similar.

"Finest animal on the turf?" Goutier cocked a brow toward Foote.

"Not her fault," said Foote stoutly. "Nor is it mine. I was told to talk her up to the gents who came with Sir Anthony or with a note from him. Was told I'd be paid handsome for my trouble after the sweepstakes." He gave them both a pointed look.

Adam ignored it. "Were there many lookers?" he asked.

Foote nodded. "All sorts. London gents mostly."

"London?" echoed Goutier.

"That's right. Steady stream of 'em. The sort that comes for the waters, and what have you." The set of his brow and the sly shift in tone spoke volumes about what that "what have you," might entail.

"Didn't you wonder what was going on?" asked Goutier curiously.

Foote shrugged. "I'd a bargain with Sir Anthony, and no one was asking me to hurt the poor creature. Believe me, there's some come here an' ask you to do something they wouldn't dare themselves, and think that you will for a pound note and a word on the sly."

"And you told the lookers what you told us?" said Goutier. "That Kinsdale's Pride was the finest animal on the turf?"

"That, and a bit extra, depending on how long they stood about."

"And they believed you?" asked Adam.

Foote laughed. "You'd be surprised what those London gents will believe. Not one in twenty of the men Kinsdale trotted up here knew a horse from a hole in the ground. All they wanted was odds and was she going to win by a nose or a length or what have you. Slipping me money on the sly for my predictions." He stopped. "Not that I made no promises," he added.

" 'Course not," said Goutier. "They asked, you answered, that's all."

"That's right," said Foote.

"Now what about the admiral?" asked Adam.

"Admiral?" echoed Foote. "Is that what the yellow-haired bloke is?"

"Was," said Goutier. "He's dead, too."

" 'S truth! He fall out a window as well?"

"Shot, I'm afraid," said Adam.

"God save us! Did they catch who did it?"

"That's what we're after," said Adam. "And they knew each other, the admiral and Sir Anthony."

Foote's jaw worked itself back and forth for a long moment. "Who's going to take charge of Pride now?"

"I imagine one of Sir Anthony's daughters," said Adam. "Did they ever come out here?"

"Not that I saw," said Foote. "There was the merry widow, but no daughters."

"Dark-haired lady, well-dressed, by name of Mrs. Lynn?"

"That's right. Knew more about horses than any of the chaps she brought with her."

He clearly had more to say, but some slight motion made Adam's gaze flicker toward the door. Habit made him look toward the ground. There, he saw a person's long shadow stretching out just past the threshold.

Someone was standing there, just out of sight. Standing and, more likely than not, listening.

Adam gently elbowed Goutier. Goutier followed his gaze and spotted the shadow at once. Foote realized something was up, and his words faltered. Adam motioned for the men to keep talking.

"So, what was it Sir Anthony promised you?" prompted Goutier.

"Wasn't him. Was the widow," Foote told him. "Says I'll be paid twenty-five pound, direct after the race, whether the horse won or not. Gave me a guinea on account and a promise for the rest."

Adam listened with half an ear, but his attention was fixed on the shadow. Moving slowly, he skirted the boxes, making sure to keep himself out of the light. Behind him, Goutier kept Foote talking. Foote detailed the promises he'd been given, the people he'd seen, because it was men and women both who'd traipsed up the hill to see the famous horse he said, and the sneers from the other grooms who couldn't fathom why Foote would take on such a job for any money.

Adam stopped on the near side of the open door. He beckoned to Foote to come stand behind him. The groom moved as quietly and carefully as Adam had. Adam looked to Goutier, and gestured toward the door. Goutier nodded his understanding, and strolled right out the door.

"All right, my man, what're—" he began.

He didn't get any further. The man, whoever he was, bolted like a startled rabbit. Goutier lunged for him and got hold of his coat collar, but the man let his knees buckle and Goutier, already off balance, stumbled and the man tore himself free and hared off down the slope.

Goutier spat and cursed. "Well, Harkness, if you wanted to know if the man was spying on us, you should have your answer now."

"Did you see him?" Adam asked Foote. "Know who he was?"

"Not as such," said Foote. "He's one of the ones who hang about, looking for a day's work. Made use of him, here and there, mucking out the stables and such. Caleb, I think he said his name was. Wonder what it was spooked him so badly?"

That, thought Adam, *was a very good question.*

CHAPTER 31

A Desperate Plea

"I had been grossly wrong, and must abide the consequences."

Jane Austen, *Persuasion*

"Oh! There you are, Mrs. Rutherford," said Mrs. Leigh as Rosalind walked into the common room at the Green Briar. "There's a woman up in your parlor. . . ."

"Yes, I know," Rosalind said. "I got the note she sent."

"I hope I did right," said Mrs. Leigh. "She didn't look entirely . . . your sort, but she said she was looking for Mrs. Rutherford and she did say that she'd dined with you last night."

"You did exactly right," Rosalind assured her. "I'll go up at once. Oh, she's likely hungry. Is there anything on the fire?" Rosalind had frequently observed that a meal and a cup of tea could do more to convince a person to speak the truth than the most detailed questioning ever could.

"I'll put something together," said the landlady. "You go up now and see to your visitor."

Rosalind obeyed.

The parlor door was closed when Rosalind reached it. She knocked softly to announce herself.

"It's open," came the reply.

Rosalind took a moment to compose herself, and pushed back the door.

Mrs. Lynn stood as Rosalind entered. She was, Rosalind saw at once, a very different person from the enchanting hostess who graced Sir Anthony's table. Her dress was drab. Her eyes were red, and had dark circles under them, but a bright snap remained in her gaze. She was indeed tired, Rosalind thought, and she was knocked out of her place, but she was in no way defeated.

"Thank you for agreeing to see me," Mrs. Lynn said. "I had no right to ask, or expect it, so I am grateful."

"I admit, I was surprised to hear from you." Rosalind closed the door. The parlor had one horsehair sofa, and she took a seat there. "You know, I'm sure, about Sir Anthony?"

A muscle spasmed in Mrs. Lynn's cheek. "Yes. May God rest him. You will not believe I mean that, Miss Thorne, but I do."

Rosalind waited to see if she would say anything more, or ask any question, but Mrs. Lynn remained silent.

"Do you know about Admiral Walsingham as well?" asked Rosalind.

"As well?" This time, Mrs. Lynn's brow furrowed. "What has happened to the admiral?"

"He was shot," said Rosalind bluntly. "He's dead."

Mrs. Lynn froze, rigid as a statue. Fear, cold and bright, sparked in her eyes.

"Have they caught the one who did it?"

"No."

Was that relief that relaxed her spine? Rosalind found she could not be sure.

"Well." Mrs. Lynn smoothed her plain skirts. Rosalind noted the speckles of mud around the hems. Wherever she had been since she left the Kinsdales, she had gone very much on foot.

"I am aware that circumstances have placed me in what might be termed a delicate position." Her tone held a hint of her habitual levity, but Rosalind found herself unable to smile. "Miss Thorne, I know you've helped other women accused of murder; I need you to help me. Once I am in court, once the magistrates hear who I am—what I am—they will send me to the gallows without a second thought."

This was almost certainly true. The law, and those who upheld it, tended to believe that a woman who was capable of one transgression must be equally capable of them all.

"I do not ask you to find out who committed these crimes." Mrs. Lynn's tone was flat and cold, as if she feared to let any emotion at all take hold just now. "That will take time I do not have. All I ask is that you find some way to convince the coroner that it could not have been me, because I swear to you that Sir Anthony was very much alive when I departed from the Kinsdales' home, and I have not seen the admiral since he left us yesterday evening."

Rosalind waited. She kept her gaze locked on Mrs. Lynn, but Mrs. Lynn did not waiver, nor did she offer to fill the silence that stretched out between them.

A knock on the door broke that silence, and a moment later, Mrs. Leigh shouldered her way into the room. The landlady carried a tray with a roasted fowl and crusty rolls. One of the serving men followed with yet another tray, this one holding ham salad, a dish of stewed fruit, as well as the pot of tea that was necessary for any repast at whatever time it might be served. Two boys came behind with dishes and glasses.

Mrs. Lynn directed them where to set all the things, and when they were finished, she beamed at Rosalind, glowered suspiciously at Mrs. Lynn, and urged the servers to hurry out and not lolligag. She paused only long enough to admonish "Mrs. Rutherford" that she should ring if anything more was wanted.

"I hope I have not wasted too much of your credit with your landlady," remarked Mrs. Lynn when the door closed.

"I'm sure she will recover herself. Please." Rosalind indicated the freshly laid table. "Do help yourself."

"Thank you."

Mrs. Lynn wasted no time on polite deference. She sat down on one of the rush-bottomed chairs and immediately helped herself to a substantial portion of everything. Rosalind joined her, and took a roll and some ham salad, more to be polite than from hunger. She did pour them both tea, and was glad to find it both hot and strong. With all that the day had brought so far, she very much needed the comfort.

She let Mrs. Lynn eat in peace for a moment. Then, she said, "I will need some answers before I agree to help you."

"Yes, of course." Mrs. Lynn was clearly not happy about this, but she was just as clearly resigned to it. "What do you need to know?"

"What is your given name?" said Rosalind.

"Well, I cannot fault you for beginning at the beginning. Very well. I was born under the name Sylvia Caroline Wallace."

"And who is Miss Sophia Smith?"

"Who did she tell you she was?" countered Mrs. Lynn.

"She said she was your natural daughter."

Mrs. Lynn smiled softly. "Although I'm sure it will surprise you, Miss Thorne, she is who she says she is. Sophia Smith is my daughter by Mr. Lewis Smith. We were . . . together until he died, which was when I took up with Mr. Lynn. I was nineteen at the time," she added.

Rosalind nodded. Those who lived by their wits were frequently forced to begin at a very early age, and women in such a life just as frequently had their children young. What was surprising was that she had not only kept the child, but had clearly been able to raise her, even though it might have been in an irregular manner. That spoke to not only wits, but determination.

"Tell me how you became acquainted with the Kinsdales," she said.

Mrs. Lynn's smile was weary, but this time it did reach her eyes. "You think you will catch me out, Miss Thorne, but I see your game. You've heard a story from Elizabeth. She's told you we met over the most absurd circumstance involving a fraudulent horse sale and a pair of ruined gloves."

Rosalind tipped her head to the side, silently acknowledging this was true.

"That was the story we agreed to," said Mrs. Lynn. "The truth is a bit less flattering to us both, I'm afraid."

Rosalind waited.

Mrs. Lynn helped herself to some additional salad. "You understand, I'm sure, Miss Thorne, that sometimes it is necessary to remove oneself from a locality for a while."

"A change of scene and society is frequently beneficial," said Rosalind, her tone carefully bland.

"Just so. Well, such a time had come to me, and after I left London by a somewhat circuitous route, I found myself in Cassell Village. I had no particular plan. I only wanted to rest quietly and recoop my energies. But during my stay, I heard some gossip about the Kinsdales, and their fading fortunes, and their horses."

Rosalind waited.

"Well, I confess, it appeared this might present an opportunity for me. My fortunes, like my spirits, were in need of refreshment. Therefore, I became determined to make the Kinsdales' acquaintance. It is a small village, and a chance soon came my way. I crossed paths with Miss Elizabeth Kinsdale while she was engaged in the thoroughly undignified occupation of begging a dealer in hay and feed to extend the family another week's credit."

Rosalind nodded.

"A crowd had gathered, and it was evident the dealer would remain unmoved, and likewise it was evident that the situation was desperate, or the lady would be making her case in the public street.

"So, I joined in the argument, on her side, of course. With two women standing there pleading, the crowd began to turn against the feed merchant. Eventually, grudgingly, he was induced to grant Miss Kinsdale the credit she asked for.

"She was in tears as I walked her away, and was more than willing to accept a handkerchief and a sympathetic ear. I bought her tea—with what was very nearly the last of my own funds, may I add—and she poured her heart out to me, as one sometimes does to a stranger. I suggested to her there might be ways to help her family. She declared that her father would never listen to her. That he was willfully blind, and wanted to pretend that all was the same as it had been when their mother was alive, because he could not bear to think that it was Lady Kinsdale, not he, who had been responsible for maintaining what there was of the family fortune."

Rosalind found she could readily believe this.

"I needed a place to stay. I needed some occupation and a fresh income. Elizabeth Kinsdale and her troubles could provide me a chance at both. So, I suggested to her that we join forces, and she agreed.

"That, Miss Thorne, is how I came to know the Kinsdales."

Rosalind nibbled another bit of her roll. It was a very plausible story. Her talks with Samuel Tauton and Sampson Goutier—not to mention Adam himself—along with her own experience told her how schemers and frauds tended to keep their eyes open for such "opportunities."

And her interactions with Elizabeth Kinsdale told Rosalind that Elizabeth might well have become convinced that she had been left with no choice but to accept the help of a clever, self-interested stranger.

"Was it you or Elizabeth who decided to build your plans around Kinsdale's Pride?"

Mrs. Lynn blinked, and then rolled her eyes. "Lord, Miss Thorne, what can you be thinking! Have you seen that poor animal? If it lives to see the starting post, I will be amazed. No. The horse is purely Sir Anthony's delusion. Elizabeth and I played along because that kept him complacent. While he could convince himself that the horse could win the sweepstakes, he could also convince himself that anything else that was done in the meantime was simply a means to an end."

Which was very close to what she and Adam had speculated.

"Did she ever talk to you about Nathanial Spence?"

"The head groom?" Mrs. Lynn took another roll. "Yes. When she was enumerating her father's shortcomings, she told me how he'd been fired. I always thought there was something more to it," she added. "But I haven't yet been able to find out what that might be."

This might even be true. "Who was it she went to meet in the garden the night of the party?"

Mrs. Lynn sighed. "A man from the stables called Caleb. Elizabeth thought, and I agreed, it would be prudent to have someone keeping a close eye on who came and went around Kinsdale's Pride. Given the admiral's . . . declaration about the games Sir Anthony might be playing, it seemed prudent to question him about what the admiral had seen or done at Lansdown and warn him to keep a closer eye out for that gentleman or his representatives." She paused. "So, we sent word and he came down to tell Elizabeth what he'd seen. I recognize that may not help either of our cases, but that is the truth."

But is that all of it? "Are Caleb and Nathanial Spence the same person?"

"Do you know, Miss Thorne, that had not occurred to me," answered Mrs. Lynn. "It may be. It was Elizabeth who selected him for our spy."

"Tell me what happened to you after we spoke at the Kinsdales'."

"I returned to the party," said Mrs. Lynn. "I intended to put an end to the evening as quickly as possible, and then get a few hours' sleep before I had to face the family and announce that I would be leaving. My plan was to play out the ruse I had outlined to you.

"Unfortunately, as sometimes happens at such affairs, some of the gentlemen were reluctant to leave. They had lost a great deal at faro and were inclined to believe that there was some jiggery-pokery with the box. Indeed, I was afraid it might actually come to blows, but his grace stepped in—with impressive directness, may I add—and when it was over, the disgruntled gentlemen were not entirely satisfied, but they did leave the house.

"Still, the incident was very unfortunate, all the moreso because Sir Anthony hates, hated, any form of unpleasantness. Once the gentlemen were turned out, he began to protest the situation most vociferously. I had a great deal to do to convince him to retire upstairs."

"Had he been drinking?"

"Not to the point of drunkenness. He abhorred the sight of a drunken man, and feared the loss of dignity and control in himself."

Which was what his valet said, and Mr. Layng had refused to believe. "I see."

"But he was very upset," Mrs. Lynn went on. "And his temper grew worse when he discovered there was a wine stain on his coat. I left him in Thrush's hands, trusting that he could deal with both his master's stain and his mood."

"And then?"

Mrs. Lynn did not answer immediately. She pushed the remains of her salad about with her fork and stared at them, as if she might divine some additional truth from the arrangement of the bits of ham and celery.

"I returned to my own room. I thought I should give Sir Anthony some time to calm down, and take a moment to refresh my appearance. Then, I would go back to him and soothe any remaining temper.

"But when I got to my room I found a note had been left there for me." She paused again. "My friends, the gentlemen who were assisting those who might need to arrange some extra funds in order to continue to play—"

The moneylenders.

"One of them had left a note of warning. The argument was not finished, they told me. There was a chance that it might recommence, and that blame would be attached to me. I was already worried, Miss Thorne, and, frankly, your appearance had stretched my nerves thinner than I care to admit. I decided discretion was the better part of valor, and I packed my bags and I took myself down the servants' stair and I left."

"Do you have the note?" asked Rosalind.

Mrs. Lynn smiled. "I burnt it. As I said, Miss Thorne, I decided discretion was the better part."

Which was prudent, but it was also convenient.

"You were not afraid to be out at that time of night?"

Now, Mrs. Lynn's smile turned positively condescending. "I have been abroad at all hours, Miss Thorne. I know how to take care of myself.

"I intended to wait for the morning and then purchase a ticket for the London stage as soon as the coaching inn opened for business. However, my plans were spoiled by the presence of not one but several constables. I managed to overhear them say that they were looking for a woman trav-

eling alone and that she might be using the name of Mrs. Lynn."
She stopped. "From this, I intuited that something bad had
happened. I assumed it was something to do with the gentlemen at the party." She stopped again, and swallowed. "I was
stunned to discover that Sir Anthony had died."

This last was true, Rosalind felt sure of it. Mrs. Lynn was
a skilled liar, and Rosalind was certain that what she was
being told now was far from the whole truth. However, in
this moment Mrs. Lynn was pale and grave. Her eyes had
gone distant, reliving some moment that she had not named.

It was a long moment before Mrs. Lynn was able to drag
her attention back to the present, and to Rosalind. "I was . . .
slower to recover than I might have otherwise been," she
said. "But when my wits were fully my own again, I realized
I was in deeper trouble than I had ever been, and that my op-
tions were exceedingly limited. That was when I resolved to
come to you."

Rosalind carefully regarded the woman in front of her. She
was much more composed now, and her color was better. She
also seemed more at ease. Still, this Mrs. Lynn remained a
very different person from the one she'd met with the Kinsdales. All the brittle gaiety had vanished. In its place was a
determined practicality that struck a cord with Rosalind. She
understood that feeling, or at least she thought she did.

But can I trust it? Was this practicality as much a ruse as
the gaiety had been? Rosalind found she didn't know.

There came a knock on the parlor door. Rosalind rose and
went to answer and found Mrs. Leigh standing there, her
face hard as stone.

"I'd have a word with you, ma'am, if you please," she said
stiffly.

Rosalind stepped at once into the corridor and closed the
door behind herself. "What is it, Mrs. Leigh?"

"Miss Thorne, you are dear to my sister, and for that I'm

willing to allow some irregularities, but this is a *respectable* house, and I mean to keep it so!"

A cold tide of worry washed over Rosalind. "Mrs. Leigh, please tell me what's happened?"

"The sheriff is downstairs demanding I let him in. He says he's a warrant for your Mrs. Lynn on a charge of murder!"

CHAPTER 32

—A Sworn Statement

"I cannot produce written proof again, but I can give as authentic oral testimony as you can desire, of what he is now wanting, and what he is now doing."

Jane Austen, *Persuasion*

I need a favor.

Asking for help tended to leave Adam more than a little chagrined. Rosalind teased him (gently) for his pride, and he returned the favor. But it was also true that having to ask for yet more help from Goutier reminded him of all that he'd left behind when he'd walked away from Bow Street. For the most part, Adam did not let this worry him, but there were times when he missed the aura of authority that smoothed the way when he had an outrageous request.

"If you can, I need you to talk to Layng about postponing the inquest," Adam had said to Goutier. "Tell him you want a chance to talk to Townsend about what's going on here."

"And say it has to be ahead of the races?" Goutier had suggested. "That if there's something crooked going on, we'll want it all cleared up before the sweepstakes?"

"Exactly."

"All right," Goutier had agreed. "Let's see what can be done."

But in the end, it proved to be for naught.

"Ah, Harkness," Layng hailed him as he and Goutier walked into his office. The room was low-ceilinged, window-less, and bare. There was a crooked shelf full of books and ledgers, and a few wooden pegs for coats and hats. The fur-nishings were limited to a pair of wooden chairs and a bat-tered desk where Layng sat. He had evidently had a guest here recently, because there was a teapot that was almost as battered as the desk, and two used cups.

"Thank you for bringing him here, Mr. Goutier," said Layng. "I'm afraid I must make an apology."

This drew Adam up short. "For what, sir?"

Layng pushed a stack of neatly written out papers across the desk. "I've just spent the last two hours taking a state-ment from one Miss Elizabeth Kinsdale. She swears that it was Mrs. Sylvia Lynn who pushed Sir Anthony out his window."

Adam did not often find himself flummoxed. It took an ef-fort to keep his jaw from hanging open. *Elizabeth* Kinsdale had turned on Mrs. Lynn? Elizabeth, who had been the one to bring Mrs. Lynn into the family, who had been supporting that lady's plans for her family, and been supported by her.

My God. Could it be true? Could Mrs. Lynn have been the other person in the room when Sir Anthony died?

Goutier whistled, one long, low note. "Miss Kinsdale saw it then?"

"As good as." Layng folded his hands across his stomach.

Adam picked up the papers. His throat had gone unusu-ally dry. He read silently:

I, Elizabeth Anne Kinsdale, daughter of Sir Anthony Kins-dale, baronet, residing at number 3, Royal Circus, do hearby swear and affirm the following:

There followed a paragraph about how Elizabeth had come (innocently and guilelessly) to introduce Mrs. Lynn to her family.

. . . believing at the time she was a true and honest friend . . .

After this, came the description of how Mrs. Lynn and Sir Anthony grew gradually more attached to each other.

. . . at the time, (Adam read) *I was delighted, and cherished the hope that my dear friend might also become my stepmother. . . .*

There followed descriptions of the card parties, and the long nights that Sir Anthony and Mrs. Lynn, and by extension Sir Anthony's daughters, spent in increasingly dubious company;

. . . what had begun as fairly ordinary amusements quickly degenerated . . .

Elizabeth went on to fault herself for not listening to her sisters' growing concerns.

. . . so confident was I in my friend that I carelessly disregarded the earnest pleadings of those closest to me . . .

Adam skimmed these descriptions and lamentations. With each word, he felt his jaw tightening, and his suspicions sharpening.

At last he came to the description of the card party:

That night, that terrible night, the party proceeded as had become usual. Mrs. Lynn was at her gay and glittering best. But this time, perhaps because of my sister Clara's impending engagement, or perhaps because his natural good sense had at last begun to reassert itself, my father was not inclined to be amused by the riotous proceedings. He began to complain that such a gathering was no credit to a gentleman's house. . . .

Adam remembered Sir Anthony standing with his chest puffed out as the guests swirled around him. He remembered the man smiling his small, superior smile as they offered him flattery and thanks for allowing them to be part of such a distinguished company.

What he did not remember was any sign of discontent. *So why does Miss Kinsdale say there was?*

Adam read on:

I mentioned the seeming change in our father's manner to my sister Cynthia and she confided to me that Father had several times that evening said he intended to separate himself from Mrs. Lynn.

Adam stopped. He read that segment of the text again. And a third time. Satisfied he had not mistaken what it said, he moved on.

At last, Father had had enough. He ordered Mrs. Lynn to send her guests home. This she did slowly, and with great reluctance. Overwhelmed as I was by my sister's confidence, and the flood of emotion that it occasioned in me, I decided to retire to bed at once. But I could not sleep. I lay awake, trying to calm my warring emotions. I both welcomed Father's decision and dreaded it, because I could not deny my responsibility for bringing Mrs. Lynn into our house.

Eventually, I heard the sound of voices engaged in a loud argument. These voices belonged to my father and Mrs. Lynn. I could not be mistaken, as I knew both voices intimately. I had, however, never heard them raised in such animosity. I could not make out the words, but the tone was very clear.

Then, I heard a sharp, wordless cry and a sound like furniture being overturned. I leapt from my bed and pulled on my wrap and hurried to knock on my father's door.

The door was opened by Mrs. Lynn, but only a little. I could not see into the room.

I asked if anything was the matter. She told me that my father had discovered a wine stain on his coat. My father was unusually particular about his clothing and appearance, so it was easy for me to believe that this discovery had made him shout. She assured me that she had rung for his valet and said I should return to bed.

I am deeply ashamed to say that I obeyed her. Yes, I had

begun to doubt her sincerity, but how could I have realized that she could lie in such a cold-blooded fashion?

But when morning came, and the tragedy of my father's death, and the ignominy of her flight were discovered, I understood what I had heard. Once the shock of that realization faded, I determined I should tell my story to the coroner.

Written by my own hand,
Elizabeth Kinsdale

Adam passed the papers to Goutier so he could read them.

"And so, I admit it, Harkness." Layng spread his hands. "I was wrong and you were right. You said it was likely not as simple as it seemed, and I should have listened. But no harm done. I've been to the sheriff and the warrant has been issued, and the woman is now in custody."

Adam felt himself go still. "Where was she found?"

"The Green Briar Inn," said Layng. "Evidently she'd gone there to hide until she could find some way to get herself out of Bath. We'll be holding her over at the King's Swan until the inquest is finished, and then I don't know what we'll do with her." Layng sighed and scratched his head, hard. "We've no jail for female prisoners here. Probably have to hold her at my house, which the wife will not like but—"

Adam found he wasn't listening. Mrs. Lynn was found at the Green Briar? She must have been looking for Rosalind.

Why?

Which was only one question of many questions bubbling up in him. At the moment, it was probably the least consequential.

Because Elizabeth Kinsdale had sworn to a statement full of lies and omissions—starting with her declaration of her father's discontent with Mrs. Lynn, and moving on to whom she'd spoken to about it.

Elizabeth swore she spoke with her sister Cynthia. She said Cynthia had talked of being confided to by their father "several times" that evening. But Cynthia was not at the party. She had been exiled in disgrace. Adam had been keeping as close an eye on the gathering as he was able, as had Rosalind. He did not see the youngest Miss Kinsdale, and if Rosalind had seen her, she would have said.

And yet, when Elizabeth wrote out this statement, she must have been confident that Cynthia would confirm the story, if she was asked.

Why would Elizabeth believe that Cynthia would lie for her but Clara would not?

Especially when it was Cynthia, as well as Clara, who decided to bring Rosalind to Bath.

But the most important question was why had Elizabeth decided to turn on her friend? And in such a decided manner? Could she have really seen what she declared? It was possible. Were the lies about the party simply an attempt to preserve her father's reputation, and by extension the family's?

Or perhaps she feared that if she didn't speak first, Mrs. Lynn would tell some story about her that she wanted kept quiet?

But there were no answers to any of these questions, or the dozens of others that gathered in Adam's uneasy mind. At least, not here.

"Well, it seems clear enough," said Goutier. It was only because Adam knew him so well that he understood that Goutier meant the exact opposite. "You'll forgive me, Mr. Layng, but given Sir Anthony's rank, and the fact that Admiral Walsingham was his tenant, it might be advisable to postpone the inquest for a day, to see if there's something more to come from all this." He laid the pages of Miss Kinsdale's statement back down on the desk.

But Layng shook his head. "My only concern is determining whether Sir Anthony's death was murder, and we have a statement that says it was. And as the admiral did not shoot himself, a verdict of person or persons unknown will cover that. The magistrates can sort out whether Mrs. Lynn had a hand in that business as well. No need for us to delay the inquest."

"Unless Miss Kinsdale lied," said Goutier.

Layng's expression became one of long-suffering patience. "If Miss Kinsdale lied, that is also for the courts to determine. She swore the oath, and she gave her statement. My job is to see that the statement is heard by the jury. My answer to you, Mr. Goutier, is the same as it was to Mr. Harkness. If you think there's something amiss, bring me the witness. I promise their words will be entered into evidence with the jury on the same basis as Miss Kinsdale's."

He did not point out that if the inquest found against Mrs. Lynn, the magistrates would be most likely to follow suit. Because given the circumstances, it was the easy conclusion and the obvious one, and because Elizabeth Kinsdale and her sisters were the daughters of a baronet, while Mrs. Lynn was a Bath widow up to her hips in cheating the local gentlemen out of their money.

And because Elizabeth Kinsdale was lying.

CHAPTER 33

Arrested

It did not surprise, but it grieved . . .

Jane Austen, *Persuasion*

When Rosalind stepped back into the parlor, she found Mrs. Lynn standing by the window. She had lifted the curtain just a little and was staring down into the yard.

"You heard," said Rosalind.

A mirthless smile flickered across Mrs. Lynn's features. "Eavesdropping is another of my bad habits, I'm afraid."

"I did not know this was going to happen."

Mrs. Lynn looked directly at her. For the first time, Rosalind thought she might be seeing the real woman underneath the many facades. She was tired, but clearheaded. Her eyes were sharp and the intelligence behind them unsparing.

Rosalind, much to her own surprise, felt her throat tighten from Mrs. Lynn's pointed scrutiny.

"No, I don't think you did know," said Mrs. Lynn at last. "But I should have."

"The sheriff will not be prepared to wait for long," said Rosalind.

Mrs. Lynn's gaze flickered toward the door.

"Don't," said Rosalind urgently. "It is bad enough you decided to leave in the middle of the night. If you try to run now, you will be hunted, and will very likely be caught. As it is, there will be little sympathy for you with the courts or the public, given the nature of the crime. If there is a chase, you will be even more sensationalized, and by the time you do reach the Magistrates' Court you will have lost all your chances. If you are cooperative and humble, there remains the possibility you will save your own life."

At the words "cooperative and humble," Mrs. Lynn's mirthless smile returned.

"Then you do believe me?" she asked.

"I don't know," Rosalind admitted. "But I believe there are some questions that should be answered."

"Will you help me?"

Rosalind hesitated. A thousand different thoughts and feelings surged through her, but she had no time to resolve any of them.

"If I can," she said. It was the closest she had to an honest answer.

"Well," said Mrs. Lynn. "That's all I can expect, and probably more than I deserve." She batted fruitlessly at her skirts and then reclaimed her bonnet and gloves, and picked up her portmanteau. "How convenient it is that I'm already packed. Shall we go?"

Mrs. Lynn's formal arrest proved a remarkably swift and efficient affair. When she and Rosalind came downstairs, Mrs. Leigh took them to the mews that ran between the inn and the stables. A clearly bored and much bewhiskered driver slouched on the box of a closed carriage. A raw-boned man with a long, horsey face and an equally bored demeanor slouched against its side.

Rosalind recognized this man as the sheriff by his staff of office, which he rested casually against his shoulder.

As they approached him, he straightened, and dropped one broad hand on Mrs. Lynn's shoulder.

"Mrs. Sylvia Lynn, I hearby arrest you in the king's name," he intoned. "And do charge you with the willful murder of Sir Anthony Thomas Whittiker Kinsdale, baronet."

"I am innocent," she told him calmly.

"Doubt that," he replied with equal calm. "But it's not my concern. In you get." He opened the door to the closed carriage and let her climb inside.

Rosalind stood, silently enraged at her uselessness. Surely there must be something she could do, some assurance or understanding she could give.

But there was nothing. She watched the driver touch up his horses and set them walking almost daintily down the narrow alley. They took the corner carefully and without scraping the side of the carriage against any wall, and then disappeared from sight.

Rosalind's mind was an unaccustomed blank as she returned to the inn's common room. She was aware that Mrs. Leigh watched her with a mix of indignation and pity, but she found she did not have the energy to stop and speak with her.

I will apologize later. And explain.

She climbed the stairs to the parlor and closed the door. She sat down and—because she could not think what else to do—she poured herself a cup of tea. She sat there for a long time, not drinking, just holding the cup, staring at the curtained window and trying to organize her churning thoughts.

It was then she noticed that a letter had been propped up on the mantelpiece. She set her cup aside and went to get it. She recognized the hand at once as belonging to Sanderson Faulks.

Her heart leapt into her throat. Rosalind quickly broke the seal and opened the letter.

My dear Miss Thorne: (she read)

Sanderson had beautiful handwriting, although, perhaps he was overfond of curls and flourishes.

> *I am writing on behalf of your many London friends. We are all very pleased to tell you that through the diligence of Mr. Littlefield and Miss McGowan (both of whom send their fondest greetings), we were able to locate that young lady who called on you so unexpectedly the other day.*
>
> *You will not be surprised to learn that she is not the schoolgirl she represented herself as. Indeed, Miss McGowan was able to trace her to the gaming club, Barron's. There she proved to be very familiar not only with the roulette wheel, but several of the gentlemen who were playing.*
>
> *A conversation with a friend (who is himself a habitué of Barron's) revealed that our adventurous miss is one of that company of fair ladies who are allowed entry to the club in order to encourage the gentlemen to drink more, play more, and generally spend as freely as possible. He also said that she was reported to be operating in her own line of business, quite apart from the interests of the club owners.*
>
> *It would seem that once the young lady has made herself fully agreeable to a gentleman, he is then induced to take what we may assume is a fatherly interest in her affairs. She will tell him of some venture she has encountered, and beg him to look it over for her and advise her as to whether it is sound enough for her to risk investing her tiny savings. This the gentleman does—again I refer to that fatherly concern—and in the end, he generally bolsters her "investment" with some amount of his own.*
>
> *I will not insult your intelligence—or that of Mr. Hark-*

ness, with whom you are surely sharing this letter—by suggesting that anything happens with this money other than that it vanishes entirely.

My friend says that her current scheme is related to horse racing, and either the purchase of, or investment in, a thoroughbred who is guaranteed to win its race. I cannot believe that this is all there is to the tale, however . . .

Rosalind got no further. The parlor door opened, and Adam entered, his expression grim.

"Mrs. Lynn has been arrested," he told her.

"I know," Rosalind said. "She was here, and I watched it happen."

Adam kissed her brow and dropped himself onto the rush-bottomed chair that Mrs. Lynn had recently vacated.

"What did she want here?"

"My help. She says she did not kill Sir Anthony."

"Did she present any proof? And may I?" He gestured toward the remains of the meal.

"Of course," said Rosalind. "And she had nothing substantive."

As Adam loaded his plate with some of the remaining food, Rosalind fixed his cup of tea and set it in front of him.

"Mrs. Lynn did freely admit that she had no proof as to her assertion," Rosalind told him. "Nor did she know who might have committed what she is nonetheless certain was a murder. She claims she does not care who did it, only that it be proved that she could *not* have done it."

Adam stared down at his plate as if suddenly dissatisfied with all his choices. "That may be difficult."

"What's happened?"

"Elizabeth Kinsdale has thrown her friend to the wolves." He pulled his memorandum book from his coat pocket and laid it on the table. "She's made a sworn statement with the coroner. I was able to copy down the salient points. What do you have there?" He pointed his knife at Rosalind's letter.

"It's from Sanderson. Miss Smith has been found." She held out the letter to him. "It seems our initial assessment was correct. She is not a schoolgirl. But my real surprise is that Mrs. Lynn has acknowledged the young woman as her natural daughter. Of course, it may be they simply agreed on the story beforehand."

Adam read Sanderson's letter between bites of roll and ham salad. At the same time, Rosalind—who had become perfectly accustomed to Adam's minute shorthand—looked over his notes.

Adam gave a low whistle. "Well, if nothing else, now we know what Mrs. Lynn and her friends were up to."

"Do we?" Rosalind raised her brows.

Adam nodded. "There's a very old cheat in racing. And a relatively simple one. A horse is entered in a race. It's a broken down creature that's got no business running the length of the paddock, let alone two full miles. Of course, no one bets on that animal. Instead, bets are laid on a favorite, or at least on an animal with a better chance. With each bet laid on a different horse, the odds against the broken down animal increase.

"But at some point, usually just before the horses are brought to the post, the broken down animal is diverted and a lookalike is put in its place. Only this new animal can actually run.

"This lookalike horse enters the race and, ideally, wins, and the few people who knew to bet on it collect a tidy sum."

Rosalind frowned. "I will admit that racing cheats are not my particular area of expertise, but even I know that the more people who bet on a horse, the lower the share of winnings for each person. Miss Smith is supposed to be rounding up a great many 'investors.'"

"And she's succeeded, or Mrs. Lynn has," said Adam. "I

went up to Lansdown and met a groom there named Charlie Foote. He said there'd been a steady stream of what he termed 'London gents' up to look at Kinsdale's Pride. He further indicated he was of the opinion that not one of them knew a horse from a hole in the ground."

"I don't understand it," admitted Rosalind. "If Mrs. Lynn and company were engaged in this lookalike scheme, why would they want *more* people to bet on their horse?"

"I suspect that Miss Smith's gentlemen, and not a few of the people at Mrs. Lynn's parties, have been told a fairy story," replied Adam. "My guess is that the punters are being told that the money was being collected to use in the lookalike scheme. They are also told that Mrs. Lynn and her confederates will hold on to the money until the last minute, so that their extremely large bet will not change the odds being offered. That way, when the race was run, and the sure loser becomes the surprise winner, the betting gentlemen would stand to collect the largest possible sum."

Rosalind considered this. "I assume no one is told just how many other gentlemen are in on the scheme?"

"And they are all sworn to secrecy about its existence," said Adam.

"But if that's the story, what is—or was—really going to happen?" But as soon as Rosalind said it, she knew. Sanderson had told them in the letter. "Good lord. They were going to take the money and disappear."

Adam nodded. "Probably while the race was still being run. The best part, from their point of view, would be that when the scheme was discovered, not one of the men they'd robbed would be able to complain to the race's officials, or to anyone else, because if they did, they would have to admit they'd been planning to profit off a cheat."

Rosalind opened her mouth. She closed it again. She felt very glad she was sitting down, because her head felt light.

"In its way, it's rather brilliant," she said.

"Yes," agreed Adam blandly. "In its way."

"And it may explain the true nature of the friendship between Elizabeth and Mrs. Lynn."

"You think Elizabeth Kinsdale was part of this?"

"If not at first, then she became part of it," said Rosalind. "Mrs. Lynn told me that the man Elizabeth met in the garden was from the Lansdown stables. She said Elizabeth was paying him to keep an eye on who was coming and going around Kinsdale's Pride."

"His name wasn't Caleb by any chance?"

"It was. Did you meet him at the stables?"

"He was eavesdropping when Goutier and I talked with Foote."

"Mrs. Lynn said that they'd sent word for him to come down to hear about what had happened when Admiral Walsingham was at the stables. I did not have a chance to learn any more than that," she added, seeing his inquiring look. "She was arrested too soon for me to finish."

"Did Mrs. Lynn say whether this Caleb might be our disgraced groom Nathanial Spence?"

"She said she didn't know," Rosalind told him. "I find I do not believe her."

"I find I cannot blame you." Adam pushed his plate away. "What I don't understand is why bring Elizabeth into the scheme, but not Clara or Cynthia? We know they can't have been involved, or they would not have wanted us here."

"I don't know." Rosalind took a roll from the basket and tore it in half. "Something clearly drew Mrs. Lynn to Elizabeth as a confederate." She tore the roll again. "But what induced Elizabeth to lie? Because she did lie." She tapped a finger against Adam's notebook.

"Blatantly," agreed Adam.

"But she must have a reason to believe that Cynthia will support her lie." Rosalind tore off another bit of roll. "Cynthia, but not Clara, who truly was at the party."

"Perhaps she was concerned that Clara would tell Cassel-maine."

"Perhaps. But there's something else. One of the Kinsdale girls had received a letter from the admiral's brother, warning that the admiral was on his way. She'd been trying to write an apology, but the draft I saw wasn't finished, and she'd been very upset while she was writing. She might even have been crying."

"One of them?"

Rosalind nodded, obscurely ashamed. "I believe it was Cynthia. She concealed a poorly written letter when I spoke with her at the party, but the truth is, I am not sure. There were three writing desks, and nothing inside with her name on it."

"We know that she was very worried about the loss of income," said Adam.

"And perhaps the loss of something else," said Rosalind. "Cynthia told me that she and her sisters met the Walsingham family while they were staying with a cousin in Lyme. She spoke of that time with great warmth and affection, and whoever wrote that apology letter, she wrote, and then crossed out, mention of the bonds of love between them."

"You're thinking of this boy that so infuriated Sir Anthony," said Adam.

Rosalind nodded.

"Do you think Cynthia had relations with the admiral?"

"I think it's very possible. The warning letter from the brother said he'd wrestled with his conscience before writing."

"The admiral was married," said Adam. "Layng has sent a letter to his wife."

"So, a letter came warning one of the Kinsdale sisters about the admiral's anger. Sir Anthony was going to evict the admiral after learning of the existence of a child. Mrs. Lynn heard Walsingham rage about knowing what game Sir Anthony was playing."

"The admiral visited the stables, and Caleb would have seen him. And now the admiral is dead."

"And when Cynthia heard about the admiral's death, she was overcome," said Rosalind. "Which was not something that happened when she learned her father died. At least, not that anyone said."

"It's Sir Anthony's death that confuses me," said Adam. "In order to succeed, the whole of the lookalike scheme *needs* Sir Anthony. He owns the horse. He hosts the parties that help bring in the local gamblers. He provided a facade for Mrs. Lynn and her confederates to hide behind, and . . ."

"And he was the one who would be blamed when they vanish," said Rosalind.

"Exactly."

A new, and unexpected idea sprang into Rosalind's thoughts. "Adam, what if he was already blamed?"

"I don't understand."

"Mrs. Lynn said there was an altercation at the party, or there nearly was," Rosalind said. "She told me it was because someone thought the faro box was rigged. But what if it was because someone found out about the lookalike scheme and confronted Sir Anthony? What if they were demanding their money back?"

"And snuck back into the house afterward to reinforce their demands?" Adam's expression turned sour. "It's possible, but it wouldn't be my first thought. And yet this damn thing has so many moving parts I can't say it's impossible." His voice dropped to a growl. "We need more time, and we don't have it."

"When is the inquest?"

"Tomorrow. Three o'clock. Layng says if I want to bring any new witnesses, I need to find them before then."

"He will not delay?"

"Not for my asking, or Goutier's."

"Mr. Goutier is here?" asked Rosalind, surprised.

Adam nodded. "And Sam Tauton. Bow Street sent them both to help keep order during the races. Goutier went out to Lansdown with me. Oh, and sends his heartiest congratulations on our upcoming marriage."

Rosalind smiled softly. "I hope he and Mrs. Goutier will be able to attend the wedding breakfast."

"They are planning on it."

"Well, at least we are not without allies." Rosalind looked down at the heap of crumbs she had made of her roll. "I wonder—" She stopped.

"What?" prompted Adam.

Rosalind was very tempted to say "nothing," but instead she took a deep breath. "Mr. Layng will not yield to a request from you, or from Bow Street, but perhaps he could be induced to listen to the Duke of Casselmaine."

Adam was silent for a long moment. "Would Casselmaine agree?" he asked finally.

"If I ask him."

Adam regarded her quietly. "He won't like it."

"No," she agreed. "Nor will he like me any better for asking it of him. But what choice do we have? Whatever her other crimes may be, we cannot allow Mrs. Lynn to hang for the thing she did not do."

CHAPTER 34

A Charitable Call

. . . but internally her heart revelled in angry plea-sure, in pleased contempt . . .

Jane Austen, *Persuasion*

"Are you going out then, miss?" asked Laurel.

Elizabeth paused, caught in the act of pulling on the black gloves she had finally found after several minutes scrabbling through her dressing table.

"Yes," she said. She hoped she sounded brisk rather than angry, or frightened. "I find I very much need some fresh air. Will you tell Clara if she asks?" She picked up her rather battered and out of date black poke bonnet from the chair where she'd left it. "Help me with this, would you?"

"Certainly, miss." Laurel came forward at once to straighten the bonnet and tie the black grosgrain ribbon. "Only—"

Elizabeth sighed sharply. "What is it?"

"It looks to be turning rainy, miss. You don't want to risk a cold."

"No. I won't be long, I promise."

Seeing that there was no dissuading her, the maid turned practical. "Well, then, you'll want your half boots, I daresay. And an umbrella."

Although she wanted to scream at the delay, Elizabeth realized she had no choice but to submit to her maid's ministrations. Going out at this hour was strange enough. To show signs of undue hurry would draw even more attention to herself.

Elizabeth realized she'd gotten careless. Since they'd come to Bath, she'd been used to a staff that simply didn't care what the family did. They stuck to their own work, or at least that part of their work they chose to do.

She had not fully appreciated how much easier it had made the entire situation.

Because now Cook wanted to know why she needed bread and cheese from the pantry. Mrs. Kendricks, who should have been thoroughly absorbed by the business of helping Thrush put the house into mourning, seemed to be everywhere she was not wanted, especially when Elizabeth was going into rooms that were not hers. And now Laurel insisted on knowing the details of her outing so that she could be properly attired, and did miss intend to be back for supper?

Worse, as Laurel handed Elizabeth the umbrella, she surely noticed the basket with its gingham cover.

"Is it a charitable call, miss?" Laurel asked.

Brazen it out. Remind yourself you're doing nothing wrong.

The irony was that this very sound advice had come from Mrs. Lynn.

"A sick friend," replied Elizabeth. "And yes, I will be back for supper."

Elizabeth felt her mouth tighten as she hurried out the front door and plunged into the busyness of Bath. She wanted to be fully out of sight of the house before she tried to hail a cab.

No one wants to lie to their family, continued Mrs. Lynn's voice from memory. *But sometimes our families leave us no choice.*

Elizabeth remembered what a relief it had been to hear

that said out loud. She'd tried so hard for so long to be the good daughter—to be the prop and support their father needed once Mother died. She'd worked every day to keep him safe from himself, as Mother had begged them all to do. But then she watched as first Cynthia, and then Clara, began to turn from Mother's memory and the duty they owed her, and each other. Her sisters didn't think twice about leaving her with the mess that was Father and his rudderless pride while they chased their own dreams. They insisted she keep all their secrets—that she help them gain what *they* most wanted—but neither of them would lift a finger to help her.

She'd poured out all this, and much more, to Mrs. Lynn within a few days of meeting her. Why? Elizabeth found she couldn't remember. But she did remember Mrs. Lynn pressing the handkerchief into her hand.

Well, my dear, she'd said. *I'm here now, and I think perhaps you and I might be able to help each other.*

But she hadn't meant it. Sylvia Lynn was as bad as Clara and Cynthia with her smiles and her sympathy and her lies. She meant only to help herself.

Well, my dear, it's now time for me to help myself. The thought burned through Elizabeth like a swallow of illicit brandy.

She alighted from her hired cab while she was still a street over from the King's Swan. She put up her umbrella and walked quickly, dodging puddles and pedestrians. It was high summer, but the low clouds had brought evening on early. Despite her gloves and stout boots, Elizabeth shivered.

The pub was crowded. No one paid any attention to the unaccompanied woman who came into the common room from the side entrance. The constable who was sitting on a stool at the bottom of the stairs only looked up at her once she came to stand directly in front of him.

"I've a few things for Mrs. Lynn," Elizabeth told him, indicating her basket.

"And who are you?" His voice was nasal, and hostile. Clearly, he resented the interruption.

"Bessie," she answered. Another day, she never would have been believable as a serving woman of any sort, but mourning had come to her rescue. The black dress she wore now was relentlessly plain, and several years behind the fashion, as were her black shawl and bonnet. "I know her from back home."

The trick to a good lie, Mrs. Lynn always said, was to avoid specifics as long as possible. *Let them fill in the gaps on their own.*

The constable lifted the cloth on her basket and gave the contents a cursory rummage. Elizabeth prayed she looked bored. The truth was that her heart was hammering and she felt certain he would send her away.

And what do I tell Nathanial then?

But the constable just straightened up, and sighed. "All right. Come along."

Elizabeth followed the lanky man up the stairs and waited while he turned the key in the first door on the left.

Mrs. Lynn rose to her feet as they entered. She saw Elizabeth, but the only sign of recognition she gave was to widen her eyes ever so slightly.

"And here's Bessie for you, Mrs. Lynn." Elizabeth bustled forward in what she hoped was a decent imitation of an efficient maid servant. "Poor thing! I've brought you a few necessaries." She held up the basket and the portmanteau.

"Oh, how very good of you, Bessie!" exclaimed Mrs. Lynn. "I am very much in need of fresh linen." She paused, and looked at the constable. "Would you excuse us a minute, please, Constable?"

"All right, but don't take all day over it."

The constable went out and closed the door. Elizabeth tried not to wince as she heard the key turning in the lock.

The room was narrow and cramped. The ceiling sloped so

sharply that it would be impossible to stand up at the far end. A narrow bed and a chair were the only furnishings. There was no window.

"I cannot tell you how glad I am you're here." Mrs. Lynn grasped Elizabeth's hands eagerly. Elizabeth tried not to flinch. "What did you tell your sisters about where you had gone?"

"I didn't tell them. I haven't long." She slipped the basket off her arm and held it out.

"Well, that's for the best." Mrs. Lynn took the basket she offered and set it on the bed. "Tell me," she said, without turning around. "How are matters . . . outside?"

"Very bad, I'm afraid," Elizabeth said. "What have you been told about how you came to be arrested?"

It can't have been much or you would not be so happy to see me now.

"I have been assuming it was because I was a fool and ran when I should have stayed put." Mrs. Lynn sat down on the bed. "Is there more?"

"There is. The coroner has a sworn statement that you were heard arguing with Father in his room just before he fell to his death."

Mrs. Lynn had been about to reach into the basket. Now she lowered her hands and rested them both on its braided handle. "I see. And who swore to this?"

"I did," said Elizabeth.

"Ah."

She had hoped for a stronger reaction. She had wanted Mrs. Lynn to turn pale, to sway a bit on her feet. To show some sign, *any* sign, that she understood Elizabeth now had the upper hand between them.

This cool acceptance stabbed hard at what little confidence she had left.

"But it's not just my word," Elizabeth told her. "Cynthia is prepared to confirm my story in every particular."

Now Mrs. Lynn did turn pale. She did not sway on her feet, but her pretty hands clenched around the basket's handle.

"So," she said, and there was just the tiniest tremble in her voice. "The pair of you have decided to hang me."

"Not quite yet," said Elizabeth. "I can still retract my statement. I can say I was mistaken and Cynthia can swear to that just as easily."

"How very accommodating of her." Mrs. Lynn looked down at her fists where they curled around the basket handle. She loosened them. She turned, and Elizabeth saw the effort it took for her to raise her eyes.

"May I ask what will convince *you* to convince *her* to testify that you were mistaken?"

It was a tiny victory, but there was pleasure in it. There was also the uneasy awareness that it was a very tainted victory indeed.

Brazen it out.

"Where's the money?" asked Elizabeth.

"Ah," said Mrs. Lynn again. "I thought that might be it."

"It is . . ."

Now Mrs. Lynn was staring at her. "*That's* what this is about? That was part of the plan. You know that was part of the plan."

"That was *our* plan. *Your* plan was to leave one step ahead of us, with your Mr. Wallace and all the money we've been collecting these past months."

"Who told you that?" demanded Mrs. Lynn.

"It's enough that I know it," Elizabeth shot back. "And it's enough for you to know that if you don't want to die, you'll tell me where the money is. When I have recovered it, I'll retract my statement. There will be no witness against you and you will be set free."

"And how do I know you'll do as you say?"

"You'll have to trust me."

"No, I think I will not."

"You'll be hanged, you and your confederates," Elizabeth reminded her. "Or transported, if you're very lucky."

Mrs. Lynn threw back her head and laughed. She sat there,

locked in a room awaiting the inquest and her trial, and she laughed.

"Oh, my dear! You will need to do better than this."

Elizabeth drew back. For one moment, she wondered if Mrs. Lynn was becoming hysterical. But in the next breath, she realized that would have been preferable, because now she saw that Mrs. Lynn truly was laughing at her—laughing her bright, brilliant laugh, as if they sat at the dinner table and she had made some particularly clever remark, rather than just explained a plan to condemn her to death.

"Oh dear." Mrs. Lynn gasped and dabbed at her eyes. "You must excuse me. It has been a trying day." She cleared her throat. "Because we have been friends, I will offer you some advice, Elizabeth. Before you make threats, you should always consider carefully what you will do when those threats do not succeed. And you should be very conscious of what those threats might expose you to."

Understanding settled slowly into Elizabeth's mind. "You are planning to inform against me now."

"It crossed my mind," replied Mrs. Lynn.

"It will do you no good. I am respectable, you are not."

"We are both women, my dear." Her smile was bright, and so very, very condescending. "Your reputation tarnishes just as easily as mine."

Elizabeth got to her feet. "Clearly it was a mistake for me to come here."

"Clearly."

"If you change your mind . . ."

"I will not," replied Mrs. Lynn. She sounded exactly as she did in the salon—cheerful, cool, and utterly unperturbed by anything.

It was too much. Fury and shame burned in Elizabeth, but she could not look at that unruffled countenance. She whisked around and banged on the door.

"Think over what I said," she hissed.

"Oh, I shall, believe me," replied Mrs. Lynn. "Thank you for the basket. Bessie," she added.

The key scraped in the lock, and the door opened. Elizabeth pushed past the constable. She felt Mrs. Lynn's gaze on her the entire time, even when she descended the stairs.

It was still raining outside and Elizabeth realized she'd left her umbrella behind, but she could not stand the thought of going back for it. Instead, she turned up the collar of her coat and ran across the cobbles.

She did not look back to see Laurel, with her market basket on her arm and her own umbrella in her hand, slip out of the pub and hurry after her.

CHAPTER 35

The Price for Buying Time

*. . . she had been eloquent on a point in which her
own conduct would ill bear examination . . .*

Jane Austen, *Persuasion*

It was late. Bath's streets were full of pleasure seekers. As impatient as she felt, Rosalind agreed with Adam that it would be easier for them to navigate the town on foot than to wait for a carriage and be caught in the snarled traffic.

The long day and near-sleepless night dragged hard against Rosalind's limbs, but she made herself keep moving. They had very little time as it was, and she was not at all certain Devon would agree to the outrageous favor she intended to ask.

They might have left at least a little sooner, but Rosalind wanted to make sure her letter to Alice was included with the final post. It contained a full accounting of all that had happened to them thus far, and all that they knew regarding the events swirling around the Kinsdale family, and even some of what was confidently suspected.

In the end, she had sealed three full sheets covered front and back into the packet, and had to remind herself several times that she and Alice were both well past the days when they would have had to count their pennies before deciding whether they could stand the expense of receiving such a voluminous letter.

On the way to the Royal Circus, Adam and Rosalind agreed that Rosalind would present herself at the front door, while Adam went around to the side.

"That way you can talk with the scullery maid," Rosalind said. "I asked her to hold the ashes from when she cleaned out the grate in the sisters' sitting room. Someone had been burning papers."

"Excellent," said Adam. "And besides that, I want to talk with Thrush again. I need to get the names of any of the others who may have come back looking for their pay. There may be fresh details to be had from them."

Once they reached the Royal Circus, Adam and Rosalind paused and faced each other. They were in public, so a kiss between them was out of the question. Rosalind extended her hand, and Adam bowed over it, his gaze meeting hers. Such a moment, where she could look into his eyes, would always cause her heart to swell, no matter what else might be happening.

But this particular moment was short lived. She must turn away, and she must walk up the broad, shallow steps to the Kinsdales' door, and try to decide what on earth she would say to Devon.

In the end, it was Devon who spoke first.

"I thought you might come back," he said as she was shown into the bookroom.

Like the rest of the house, this room was a study in extravagance—all vibrant color and thick carpets. However, the shelves that another man might have filled with books were here filled with prints, sketches, and engravings. All of them showed horses. Rosalind assumed these were representatives of the Kinsdale bloodline.

So many portraits of horses, but none of his wife, or his daughters.

Devon was sitting at a great mahogany desk and he looked thoroughly harried. His cravat had been loosened and his hair rumpled like he had been running his hands through it. The piles of papers stacked all around him made Rosalind think of a boy building a fortress. A tray with the remains of what had probably been his supper had been shoved to one side to make more room for no less than three broad ledgers, all of which Devon had opened in front of him.

"You've heard about Mrs. Lynn, of course?" He got up and pulled one of the room's two armchairs around to the side of the desk, and then dropped back into his own chair. "Please, sit down."

"Yes, I have heard." Rosalind took the chair. She also gestured at the account books. "How bad is it?"

"Bad enough," muttered Devon. "But the real problem is what's not here." Rosalind raised her brows and Devon sighed. "I've just talked with one Mr. Florian Oswald. He was Sir Anthony's solicitor, and he says Sir Anthony died without a will."

Rosalind felt the blood drain from her cheeks.

Devon ran his hand through his hair. "*That* of course means most of the land will go to the nearest male relative along with the title, or the lot of it will go back to the Crown. And we don't know who that relative might be."

Rosalind's heart banged once against her ribs, hard.

"There's some cousins in Ireland," Devon went on. "But they'd have to be traced and that might take years. And what *isn't* entailed is so encumbered, it's going to take at least as long to sort it all out. Oswald seems like a professional man, but he's been working to keep Sir Anthony's head above water for years now, and he freely admits it's been heavy going." Devon glowered at the books in front of him. "Clara and her sisters will be lucky to see anything at all."

As Rosalind listened to this assessment, she felt several pieces of the puzzle that was the Kinsdales and all their many tragedies slip together. The picture it made was not one she wanted to see.

"I'm sorry to hear it," she said softly.

"I hate this feeling that all my help is just making matters worse," said Devon. "Even if I'm just the messenger."

"I do sympathize."

His expression turned assessing. "Yes, I imagine you do."

Movement caught her eye through the study's open door. Clara stood on the threshold, twisting her hands together.

Devon was on his feet at once, crossing to her, taking her hand, drawing her into the study, and closing the door behind them.

"Miss Thorne, you must forgive me," said Clara. "I've only just heard that you arrived."

"I'm the one who should be asking your forgiveness," Rosalind said as Devon ushered his fiancée to the room's remaining chair. "It is hardly polite visiting hours."

"Are you all right, Clara?" Devon asked her. "You look exhausted."

"I am, a little," Clara confessed. "I just wanted . . . I cannot thank you enough, Miss Thorne for sending us Mrs. Kendricks. She has taken the whole house in hand."

Rosalind allowed herself a smile. "I knew that she would. She kept house for me and my family for many years."

Clara smiled in answer, but her expression was only polite. "I imagine Casselmaine has told you our latest discovery? About the estate?"

"Yes," said Rosalind. "And I am sorry to hear it."

"And I suppose you have also heard about Mrs. Lynn . . . and Elizabeth?"

"That was why I came, in fact," Rosalind told them both.

"How is Elizabeth?" Devon asked Clara.

"Terribly agitated. I'm afraid we may need to send for someone, but I don't know who." Clara twisted her hands again. "Father always chose his medical men more for fashion than efficacy."

Which came as no surprise to Rosalind. "May I suggest Mr. Howland in the Market Lane?" she said. "He comes highly recommended."

"Thank you. In truth I don't know what we would have done without you these past days." Clara blinked back her tears. Devon seized her hand at once, and pressed it gently.

"I'm all right," she told him, and tried to smile again. She almost managed it.

"I have assured Clara that very little will be required of Elizabeth tomorrow at the inquest," Devon said to Rosalind, very clearly hoping she would confirm this.

Rosalind nodded. "Yes. She should only be asked to swear that the statement is hers, and that it is true." *The trouble lies in the fact that we know it is not true.*

"I am sorry for Elizabeth," said Clara. "She truly did believe that Mrs. Lynn was her friend. Elizabeth was very close to our mother, you see. They shared that great love of horses. In fact, it could be a chore to get them to talk about anything *except* horses. So, when it all fell apart, Elizabeth lost her best friend, and then watched her life's passion sold away for a pittance. It would be enough to break the strongest of hearts."

"She must be very angry," ventured Rosalind. "To find herself so betrayed."

"Yes. She's trying to hide it, but she is furious."

"Clara," said Rosalind. "I must ask you something."

Clara, as a matter of reflex, glanced at Devon. "What is it?"

"Is Elizabeth angry enough that she might seek revenge against Mrs. Lynn?"

"What . . . what do you mean?"

Rosalind said nothing. Clara pressed a hand against her throat.

"Miss Thorne, you cannot mean you think Elizabeth lied in her statement to the coroner?"

Devon's frown was a warning. It took all Rosalind's strength to ignore it, and him. "I do not know," she said. "There are questions raised within her statement about other matters. It makes me afraid."

"What questions?" demanded Clara. "What possible questions could there be? Elizabeth heard Mrs. Lynn and Father arguing. She saw the woman in father's room . . ."

"Miss Thorne—" began Devon.

"Elizabeth says that your father had been considering separating from Mrs. Lynn," said Rosalind.

Clara drew back. "She said that?"

Rosalind nodded. "The statement was very plain."

"You've read it?" asked Devon, and Rosalind felt the suspicion in the question like a blow.

"Mr. Harkness has," Rosalind told them. "He is assisting the coroner and Bow Street with the inquiry into both deaths." This was stretching the truth, but not so much as to distort it beyond recognition. That distinction, however, did nothing to ease Rosalind's realization that she had begun to mislead both Devon and Clara, and that she was not going to stop.

They were looking at each other now. Clara sat mute, but her gaze betrayed her silent pleading for some way that this conversation was not leading to yet more heartbreak. Devon was equally bewildered, and quickly becoming angry. Except, of course, he could not let himself be angry—not at

Clara, not at her sisters, not at the circumstances—because that anger would accomplish nothing at all.

Rosalind watched him squash his own feelings, and her heart went out to them both.

"It may be that she mis-remembered," said Devon, gently. "We sometimes assign to memory things we wish to be true."

"Yes," agreed Rosalind. "I've seen it many times. But what worries me is that when a person is being questioned in front of a coroner, or the magistrates, and they are caught in a moment of . . . confusion, it rarely goes well for the witness." She paused just a moment to let Clara absorb this. "If Elizabeth spoke in anger, if she swore to what she wished was true rather than what she knew, it could jeopardize the entire inquiry against Mrs. Lynn."

It was true. All of it. But Rosalind was still left with a growing consciousness of her own guilt. She had steered conversations in this manner before, but it had generally been with strangers, or with persons she understood to be lying. She had never faced a friend—two friends—and worked so hard to lead them down her chosen path.

She was playing them both false and she was sure this must show in her countenance and that Devon would see it instantly.

But Devon wasn't looking at her. He was looking at Clara.

"Elizabeth cannot be exposed to censure or ridicule now," Clara said. "It would do lasting harm. I feel sure of it. And Cynthia . . . Cynthia cannot bear another shock. She is nearly crushed under all that has already happened."

Rosalind swallowed her guilt in one great lump. When she was sure she could control her voice, she said, "Mr. Harkness asked the coroner to delay the inquest, just for a day or two so that more facts can be determined, and to minimize the chance that any of the findings will be . . . misinterpreted at the trial."

"Is there really a chance of that?" asked Clara.

"Mrs. Lynn has been engaged in a series of schemes," said Rosalind. "We cannot assume she is friendless and helpless. We know, in fact, that she has collaborators in London. It may well be that during the course of her career there she has gained some influence with powerful men."

"You're talking about the potential for extortion," said Devon.

"Or something very like it," agreed Rosalind. "Her influence, if it exists, might be used to garner aid for her trial. Our proofs, and our witnesses must be strong, from the first stage to the last."

Clara turned pale, and Rosalind felt her heart sink further yet.

Someone was knocking at the door.

"Come," called Devon curtly. The door opened. It was Adam.

"I apologize for the intrusion," he said. "But I've made a discovery that you should hear, Casselmaine."

"Yes, yes, come in." Devon ran his hand through his hair again, as if he thought he could find some remaining bit of patience there. "What is it?"

Adam did come in, and he closed the door behind himself. He glanced toward Rosalind and she silently returned her thanks for his interruption.

"I was speaking with Thrush," said Adam. "When we finished, the new footman, Duggin, came to ask if he should talk to his cousin who is apprenticed to a locksmith about the scullery door."

"The scullery?" echoed Clara.

Adam nodded. "According to Thrush, the lock on that door has been broken for some time. No one on the staff was told to do anything about it, so no one did. It means that anyone could have come or gone through that door at any time during the party, and none the wiser."

Clara and Devon stared at each other. Rosalind watched this new development sink in and settle with them both. It mixed with what she'd already said, and raised new fears, and new understanding.

"It is probably nothing," Adam went on. "But it is the kind of detail that can turn a simple matter into a complex one if it is raised during a trial."

"Especially when it becomes known that there was an allegation of cheating during the card party," added Rosalind.

Devon went dead white. "Who . . ." Rosalind opened her mouth, but he held up his hand. "Never mind, it doesn't matter. Damn." He spat the curse through clenched teeth. "Apologies," he added to Clara. She waved it away.

Rosalind said nothing. Accusations of cheating at cards could lead to duels, and similar lethal behaviors, and everyone knew it. Combined with an open door . . . many conclusions might be drawn by a jury.

"Did Layng grant your request for more time?" Devon asked Adam.

"No," said Adam. "And he says he will not, unless I can produce reliable witnesses, which I cannot promise I'll be able to find in time."

"To say Elizabeth is lying," breathed Clara.

"Or to prove that she is telling the truth," said Rosalind. "We don't know now which it will be. We do know Elizabeth is angry and that she has been through great loss. Her judgment may not be as clear as it would be under other circumstances."

"Do you want me to speak to Layng?" Devon asked Clara. "I might be able to buy Harkness and Miss Thorne, and Elizabeth, additional time."

Clara did not answer. Instead, she walked over to one of

the shelves and picked up a framed etching. "Morning's Pride," she said. "She was Kinsdale's Pride's dam. Mother was up all night with the stable hands while she was being born. Papa bemoaned her unladylike behavior and she just laughed and said he'd be glad of it when he saw all the new foals we'd breed off her."

"Clara—" said Devon.

"No, no, don't," she said. "It must be done. I see that. Elizabeth will be even more furious, but I think she will understand, eventually."

She wrapped her arms around herself. Devon saw and started to his feet. He crossed to her, but stopped halfway.

Rosalind turned immediately to Adam. "I should go speak with Mrs. Kendricks."

"I'll go with you," Adam offered. "I have some questions for her as well."

They did not flee, precisely, but they did remove themselves from the bookroom with considerable dispatch. Adam closed the door behind them, firmly.

"I hope I shall not have to engage in that sort of conversation again for a very long time," murmured Rosalind as they walked down the corridor toward the entrance hall.

Adam brushed his fingers against the back of her hand in understanding.

"You overheard the conversation, I assume?" Rosalind asked when they were safely out of earshot of the bookroom.

"That was why I came in when I did." Adam had far fewer scruples than she did when it came to eavesdropping.

"Is it true then, about the scullery door?"

"It is, and it complicates matters, but there's more."

"What is it?"

They had reached the entrance hall, and the door to belowstairs. Adam glanced sharply about to make sure there was no one to hear. Even so, he stepped close to her.

"I already spoke with Mrs. Kendricks," he breathed. "She had a message from Laurel."

Rosalind felt her brows rise.

"It seems Elizabeth went out earlier today, and Laurel followed her. She went to the King's Swan, and she spoke with Mrs. Lynn."

CHAPTER 36

The Bonds of Sisterhood

*She was accordingly more guarded, and more
cool, than she had been . . .*

Jane Austen, *Persuasion*

Devon wanted to stay the night. Clara very much wanted to let him. With Devon, she could be weak. If she needed to spend the whole night sobbing on his shoulder, he would never speak a word of admonishment. He'd just hold her close until she was finished.

Had they still been on the cusp of their engagement, she might have yielded to both their desires. But the fact was that Father's death meant they could not make any formal announcement for at least another six months. Even then, they'd risk accusations of unseemly haste. And if it became known that Devon had spent the night under her roof before that time, the gossips would make all manner of guesses as to why the haste was needed.

Clara wondered what Devon would say if she suggested they climb into a carriage and ride for the Scottish border. She strongly suspected he'd drive them himself.

But she would not do that, of course. No. She would stay

put and make sure that the world saw that all the Kinsdale daughters properly mourned their ridiculous, profligate, elegant, astonishing father. That they would present the correct face to the world, no matter what it cost.

Devon, being Devon, understood all of this, even when she was barely able to say any of it. He had kissed her before he left, kissed her like it was the first time—when they were hidden in the walnut grove, when she turned to see him looking at her like he was seeing the future open up in front of him and it was beautiful.

The memory of that moment still made her shiver with warmth and need, and she suspected it always would.

And what have I given him? Clara thought sourly as she climbed the stairs. *He's laid his life and his heart at my feet, and what am I returning?*

Clara ruthlessly shoved this thought away. *Devon stays because he loves me. I have hidden nothing from him. He has already seen all of us. He grew up knowing who we were, the way we grew up knowing him, and his brother. He already knows the worst and he accepts it. He is strong enough, experienced enough, to understand me. Understand all of us.*

I can trust him.

I will trust him, and I will not weaken in this.

She had reached the door to the apartments she shared with Elizabeth and Cynthia. She took a deep breath and forced herself to adopt an expression of calm. Only when she felt sure she had succeeded did she open the door.

All the sitting room lamps had been lit, and the golden light rendered the place almost cheerful. Cynthia sat at her writing desk, sorting through a pile of condolence cards she had promised to answer. Elizabeth stood at the window, looking out over the darkened garden. She had her face turned mostly away, but even so, Clara could see her cheeks were flushed.

Is it embarrassment or anger?

Cynthia's face was also unusually pink and her eyes glimmered in the lamplight.

So. They'd been arguing. Cynthia, at least, had been crying.

Clara decided she would ignore these facts. *For now.*

She made herself sweep past her sisters and head for the boudoir, then sit down at her dressing table.

"Do you know, I was thinking we should have Mrs. Kendricks pack away Mrs. Lynn's things," she said as she began removing her earbobs. "She will need them sent on to her, eventually, after all, and when they are cleared away, one of us can take the room. We are so crowded in here."

"What does his grace say?" asked Elizabeth from her post by the window. "You'd best make sure it is in line with his wishes."

"Elizabeth, please," sighed Cynthia. "Let it be."

But Elizabeth, clearly, was not interested in letting anything be. Looking in her mirror, Clara saw her sister stalk over to stand in the doorway.

"What were you two talking about so long?" Elizabeth's question sounded like yet another taunt. "What portion of our future were you and he deciding this time?"

Clara found her patience had run entirely dry. She twisted around on her stool. "Since you ask, we were discussing the fact that Father left no will."

There was a clattering sound. Cynthia had dropped something. Now she ran to stand in the doorway beside Elizabeth. Stand, and stare.

"Yes, believe it," said Clara coldly, even though neither one of them had spoken. "Our father—who could not stand to acknowledge the fact that his hair had gone gray—refused to consider the idea that he might die. So, he has left the entire estate in disarray. Which means, as I understand it, the creditors will have first grab at anything that isn't part of the entail." She stood, fists clenched, emotions coming close to choking off her breath.

"So, Elizabeth, I suggest that you be a little nicer about Casselmaine," she said. "Because as soon as our Irish cousins can be traced, we could all very well find ourselves out in the hedgerows."

Cynthia was trembling. Elizabeth wrapped an arm around her shoulders. "Stop it! You're upsetting her!"

"She should be upset!" shouted Clara. "We all should! And you should be helping, not making things even worse!"

"I—" began Elizabeth.

The last of Clara's patience snapped.

"You!" she cried. "We would not *be* in the middle of this disaster—Father dead, the admiral dead—if you had not brought that woman into our family!"

Elizabeth flushed scarlet. "I would not have had to bring her if you had been in the least willing to remember the loyalty you owed us, *and* our mother!"

"I said I'd marry Devon to *save* us!"

"You said you'd marry him to rule over us!"

"Stop it, both of you!" shouted Cynthia.

Silence fell so abruptly, Clara found her ears ringing. She couldn't think. She couldn't breathe. She sat down gracelessly on her stool, both hands pressed against her stomach.

Elizabeth turned away and stalked off into the sitting room. Clara could see her by the hearth, staring at the empty grate.

Cynthia came into the boudoir and dropped onto the bed, plainly as exhausted and heartsick as Clara.

"It's no good, Clara," she said, and the defeat in her voice pierced Clara's heart. "What's done is done, and whatever Elizabeth's part in it, it was Father who let himself be so deluded. Anyway, it's over tomorrow. Mrs. Lynn will be taken away for trial, and she will hang, and that will be an end to it, or as near as an end can be."

"Only it won't," said Clara.

"What?" croaked Elizabeth.

"Casselmaine is going to ask for the inquest to be delayed."

"*What?*" Cynthia's hand clenched around a fistful of counterpane. "Why would he?"

"It seems there are some questions about Elizabeth's statement." Clara was answering Cynthia, but she kept her face turned to Elizabeth. Talking between rooms was unseemly. Father would have admonished them for it, but she did not want Elizabeth to miss a single word. "It seems that in her sworn statement Elizabeth said Father was thinking of separating from Mrs. Lynn. It also seems she said he was quite discontent and ordered that the party be broken up early. The problem is that I, and a dozen others, heard Mrs. Lynn tell *him* it was time to end the evening." Clara turned her gaze back to her younger sister, who perched on the edge of her bed, her fists knotting up bunches of the covers. "It also seems she said she spoke to you, Cynthia, at the party. But we all know you were in this room the entire time."

"Who told you that?" demanded Elizabeth.

"Miss Thorne told me, and Mr. Harkness confirmed it."

Elizabeth snorted. "And you believe them?"

"Yes, I do," answered Clara. "Especially since what you were *really* doing was sneaking about and meeting strange men in the garden!"

Elizabeth's mouth snapped shut.

"Yes, I saw you," said Clara. "And I saw Mrs. Lynn keep Miss Thorne from following you out. I've said nothing because you're my sister and I love you, but I don' t know how much longer I can protect us! You have to stop! Whatever it is, you have to stop!"

Tears sprang into her eyes and Clara wiped uselessly at them. She yanked out the central drawer of her vanity and began hunting for a handkerchief.

"I told the truth," said Elizabeth behind her. "Cynthia will bear me out."

Clara found a handkerchief. It was an old one. The linen had been washed so many times, she could have read a novel through it. She pressed it against her eyes.

She noticed that Cynthia had not yet said anything. So did Elizabeth.

"Cynthia?" Elizabeth prompted, worry plain in her voice.

Cynthia looked away.

"Oh, yes, pretend you can't hear me," sneered Elizabeth. "Pretend you didn't bring this trouble on yourself when you agreed to bring the oh-so-helpful Miss Thorne to plague us all!"

"You may yet have reason to be grateful to Miss Thorne," Clara told her. "She has managed to trace some London collaborators of Mrs. Lynn's. She may be able to use these additional days to blacken that woman's character to the point where the coroner and the magistrates will overlook whatever lies you have convinced Cynthia to swear to."

She sat there, meeting her sister's outraged stare, and not flinching, not even blinking.

Slowly, Elizabeth withered. She blinked and fumbled at her sleeve. At last, she pulled out her handkerchief and wiped her eyes. She turned and strode out of Clara's field of view.

Clara got to her feet and followed. Elizabeth had turned to the window. She stood, framed by the deepening darkness on the other side of the glass. She was breathing light and quick, trying to dissolve the sobs so clearly knotting inside her.

Clara wanted to say something to soothe her pain, but she could not for the life of her think what that might be.

At last, Elizabeth's breathing eased. She turned away from the window and faced Clara.

"Very well," she said. "You may tell his grace I agree entirely with the decision to delay the inquest, if that will help anything. Indeed, I find upon reflection that I welcome it, because in the end I know it will be proved that I have—that *we* have—done the right thing."

Cynthia was behind her. Clara could feel her there.

"Have you?" she asked. "Both of you?"

"Yes," said Cynthia. "And yes, I will swear it."

"Then," said Clara, "there is nothing else for us to do."

CHAPTER 37

Some Convenient Arrangement

*". . . and from that moment, I have no doubt, had
a double motive in his visits there. But there was
another, and an earlier, which I will now explain."*

Jane Austen, *Persuasion*

Before they left the Kinsdales' house, Duggin found Adam
and presented him with a burlap sack. "Your ashes, sir,"
he said. His tone was dubious. Clearly, even for one who had
seen all manner of behaviors on the part of the "quality," this
one was beyond the pale.

Adam offered no explanation. He just thanked the young
man and slung the sack casually over his shoulder.

Outside, the night remained mild. Light shone gently from
the windows around them. The only sounds were distant—a
carriage's rattle, a random shout. They walked down the
steps to the cobbles.

"I thought it best we conduct our search where we couldn't
be interrupted," he said in answer to the question she hadn't
asked.

"I thought it might be something of the kind." Rosalind

meant to sound amused, but was aware she only sounded distant.

"Tired?" Adam asked her.

"A little," Rosalind confessed. "And yet I find I am not ready to sleep."

"Neither am I. Shall we walk a ways?"

"Gladly." But even as she said this, Rosalind looked back over her shoulder. The draperies on Kinsdale House were tightly closed, as if the house was determined to shut itself away from the rest of world.

Or shield itself?

She turned again, and saw Adam offering her his free arm. She took it gratefully and let him lead her around the curve of the Circus and out to the high street.

Whenever Rosalind found herself in the middle of some complex matter, she walked. The exercise allowed her to breathe and settle her mind. Adam had maintained a similar habit during all his time as an officer in London. Now, they walked together frequently, enjoying the quiet companionship as much as the time to think.

Church bells sounded the hour of ten. Bath remained busy. Its streets filled with carriages and its walks full of young men, and not a few young women, in search of their next amusement. With Adam on her arm, the general run of roustabouts and ruffians would not trouble Rosalind, so she could let her attention drift back to all that had happened in the past two days.

Has it only been two days? That idea alone was enough to start her tired head aching.

Rosalind set this aside. It would do no good. "Do you really believe someone entered the house through the scullery last night?" she asked.

"I really believe I don't know," replied Adam, and she heard the combination of weariness and frustration under his words. "Schemes, especially the big ones, can turn ugly in a hurry, and I'm afraid honor among thieves is something that mostly exists in the minds of novelists."

"I'll warn Alice."

A tiny smile flickered across Adam's face. "The question is, why would someone take the risk? And why choose Sir Anthony for their victim?"

"If someone did not know the whole story, it would be easy to assume it was Sir Anthony who was in charge of the scheme," suggested Rosalind. "And he was the host at the party."

"Or, if someone wanted to utterly ruin Mrs. Lynn and her whole cohort, this would be the way to do it."

Rosalind was silent for a long moment. Could someone be driven to the point where they were willing to take one life to destroy another? If she was being completely objective, she knew it was possible.

"If that is the case," she said slowly, "it does not need to have been someone from outside the house."

"No," agreed Adam. "It does not."

The Green Briar was brightly lit when they arrived. Patrons filled the courtyard and the common rooms. Laughter and snatches of song rose up through the fog of tobacco smoke.

Despite the crowd, Rosalind and Adam easily picked out two familiar faces.

"Goutier! Tauton!" Adam hailed the Bow Street men.

"There you are!" cried Mr. Goutier as he and Tauton shouldered their way through the crowd to come stand in front of them. "We were just about to send out a search party! Miss Thorne, delighted to see you again." Both men bowed and Rosalind returned a solemn curtsy. Then, Mr. Goutier turned to Adam.

"Where on earth have you been?"

"With the Kinsdales, and Lord Casselmaine," Adam told them. "Come up and we'll give you the full story."

"Gladly," said Mr. Tauton. "I've breathed enough smoke today to last me a month or more."

The window of the private parlor had been closed against the night air, and Rosalind was inclined to leave it, so as to dampen at least some of the noise from the common room and the yard. She'd spoken with one of the serving men, so shortly after Adam and their guests had hung up their hats and she'd removed her bonnet and gloves, a waiter arrived with a pitcher of beer and tankards, as well as bread and cheese and an apple tart and a pot of tea.

"Please do help yourself, Mr. Goutier, Mr. Tauton," Rosalind said, falling at once into the role of hostess.

When they'd all filled their plates, acquired their drinks, and ranged themselves about the room, Mr. Tauton pointed his fork at Adam.

"Now then, Harkness, what did you find?" he demanded around a mouthful of apple tart and cheese.

"We found that the lock on the scullery door at the Kinsdales' house has been broken for some time," said Adam. "Meaning anybody who wanted to get into or out of that house at any point would have a way to do it."

"We also found that Sir Anthony died without a will," said Rosalind. "And no known male heirs."

Mr. Goutier raised his eyes to heaven, praying for patience. Mr. Tauton took a long swallow of beer.

"Any sign of what Sir Anthony was up to before that?" Mr. Tauton asked.

"I doubt he was up to anything more than keeping up appearances," said Adam. "But there was certainly plenty more than that going on around him."

"I take it you're referring to the famous Mrs. Lynn," said Mr. Goutier.

Adam nodded. "It's looking like she was organizing a racing scheme that I can only describe as sprawling, and she's probably getting help from at least one of the Kinsdale daughters."

That was enough to make both men forget their food, and their drink. The officers leaned forward. Adam carefully outlined the "lookalike scheme," to them. He talked about how the card parties were used to pay the bills and find the marks, and how Miss Smith and her entrée into London's gaming clubs shunted yet more money into the scheme.

When Adam finished, Mr. Tauton slouched backward. "Well, I'll be . . . jiggered," he said, apparently remembering Rosalind's presence at the last minute. "I thought I'd heard it all, but this one . . ." He shook his head. "I don't mind telling you, Harkness, this may be the biggest fraud I've ever come across."

"It does fit with what Foote was telling us at the stables," said Mr. Goutier. "That no one was to be allowed near the horse without special permission. He, or she, would be trying to make the pigeons feel like they were being let in on a secret."

"It's almost a pity how it's all turned out." Mr. Tauton poured himself some more beer, and topped off Mr. Goutier's tankard for good measure.

"Did you find something?" Adam asked.

"Well now." Mr. Tauton took a swallow of beer. "I don't know if your man has had time to tell you, Miss Thorne, but this morning we decided I should take myself round to the coffeehouses, see if I could maybe follow those obliging chaps from your card party who were helping those who had run short to some extra cash."

"Were you successful?" she asked.

"Eventually. Knowing something of Bath and its habits, I decided our best chances to hear that sort of news would be either the Silk Road or the Venetian. The Silk Road proved a disappointment, on our business anyway. But I did hear about some goods going up for sale that might have escaped the notice of the customhouse." Mr. Tauton chuckled softly. "So, maybe not a complete waste of time, at that.

"However, when I got to the Venetian, it turned out my

luck was in." Mr. Tauton folded his hands across his stomach, clearly relishing his narrative. "I come into the common room just in time to find two rather down at the heels gentlemen arguing with a big, bald fellow whom I take to be the landlord, on account of his apron, you see." He tapped the side of his nose, and smiled at his little joke. "Well, I listen for a bit, and what I hear is that the two gents want to get into a room. The problem is, the room's not theirs."

Rosalind felt her brows arch. Mr. Tauton nodded solemnly.

"Now, that is not the landlord's problem. *His* problem is that the person the rooms belong to has scarpered, without payment, and he wants his money. If they won't pay what's owed, he says, he won't let them, or anyone else, near the room.

"The gents hold fast. They tell him that the money they'd need to pay that rent is inside the room." Tauton spread his hands. "This is what we in the trade call 'an impasse.'"

"Who did the rooms belong to?" asked Adam.

"Some bloke named Wallace."

"Wallace?" exclaimed Rosalind. "When I spoke to Mrs. Lynn, she told me her maiden name was Wallace."

"Did she now?" Mr. Tauton whistled.

"I wonder. . . ." Rosalind turned to Adam. "At the beginning of all this, Miss Smith said sometimes her mother's man of business came to her school—"

"And that he might also have been her uncle." Adam considered. "But the part about her being in school was a lie."

"It is now, but that might not always have been the case," put in Rosalind. "She was trained in parlor manners somewhere. And it would make sense that her mother would send a trusted family member to keep an eye on her."

"And it most definitely would not be the first time a whole family made theft and fraud their business," said Mr. Goutier.

Rosalind found she did not like the way her mind turned at once to Clara and her sisters.

"Well," Mr. Tauton went on. "The pair of gents in the Venetian was telling the landlord that they were partners with this Wallace. They said he hadn't been able to hand over what they were owed direct after business was concluded, as was their custom. Instead, he'd left it in his room and all they wanted was leave to go in and get it, and then they'd gladly settle his bill.

"This all sounds very interesting to me, so I step up and beg their pardon for the interruption and ask the gents if they happened to be at the Kinsdales' last night.

"Now, I expected they might turn a bit missish—begging your pardon, Miss Thorne—at this, but didn't expect they'd look scared to death. I thought they might both take to their heels then and there. So, I quick tells them it's Wallace I'm looking for, and that I owed him money.

"And just like that, I'm a very popular fellow." Mr. Tauton puffed out his chest. "And the pair, whose names, by the by, were given as Crocker and Vest, a thing you may not be surprised to learn," he added to Adam.

"That's the pair from the Kinsdales' card party," he confirmed.

"Messrs. Crocker and Vest, as well as Mine Host, are all most anxious to explain once again how Wallace has up and vanished without paying them, so any money I meant to give *him* should rightly go to *them*. The landlord is insistent, in fact, that he has the greater claim because Mr. Wallace owes him a good two months' worth of room and board.

"Now, I agree with them that this Wallace is a wrong 'un. Clearly, I say, he's been holding out on all concerned. But I represent to them that a better understanding of just what's happened is needed. So, I stand everyone to drinks and I get Messrs. Crocker and Vest to tell me all about their business dealings with Mr. Wallace."

"We know that Crocker and Vest have been lending money in Bath for several years," said Adam.

"That's right." Mr. Tauton nodded. "And they'd done business with this Wallace before. But some months ago he comes to them with a new proposition. Said that a lady and gent were going to be giving a series of faro parties and they could have exclusive right to make out loans to the punters that showed up and wanted to play deep. The price of admission would be a cut of the profits, and intelligence."

"Intelligence?" echoed Rosalind.

Mr. Tauton nodded again. "Crocker and Vest were to pass on their professional assessments of the punters. Wallace wanted to know which gents, and ladies (as there were some of those), might be ripe for hearing about additional . . . investments."

Adam opened his mouth, but Tauton held up his hand. "Before you ask, I did inquire as to the nature of these investments, but they said they'd never been told, and they hadn't asked, not after the first night, when they realized they were onto a very good thing indeed."

"But now we know," said Mr. Goutier. "It was the lookalike scheme."

"So it would seem," said Mr. Tauton. "I expect that once Crocker and Vest had identified the likeliest pigeons, either Wallace or Mrs. Lynn paid a call on them, and sold them on some aspect or the other of the scheme you describe."

"And all this time, Miss Smith is doing the same in London," murmured Rosalind. "Good Lord."

"My thought exactly, miss," said Mr. Tauton. Rosalind suspected his actual thoughts were not ones that could be repeated in polite company.

"Well, I expressed admiration to the gents for this neat arrangement with Mr. Wallace and asked what had gone wrong," Mr. Tauton went on. "Vest, he tells me that they'd arrived in the wee hours of the morning to turn over their takings and make their report, all as usual. Mr. Wallace invites them into his rooms, and they share a friendly drink before sitting down to business. There's no sign that anything is wrong.

"But just as they're getting ready to open the cash boxes—

as Vest described it—this wild-eyed madman runs into the room, screaming about how they're all scoundrels and he'll cut every man Jack of 'em to ribbons. And, said Mr. Vest, he had a sword to do it with."

"A *sword*?" cried Rosalind.

"That's what Vest said," Mr. Tauton told them. "And Crocker agreed. What it may really have been, I've no notion, but it frightened all of them, and while Wallace was attempting to tell the invader that whatever had happened it had nothing to do with them, and the man they wanted was Sir Anthony Kinsdale. Crocker and Vest in the meantime were doing their best to get themselves out the window. Which they did eventually succeed in doing." Mr. Tauton chuckled again, clearly imagining what a sight that must have been.

"I don't know what to think," breathed Rosalind. "Is it possible Sir Anthony's death was caused by one of the card players after all?"

"Did your Messrs. Crocker and Vest know Sir Anthony was dead?" Adam asked Mr. Tauton.

"I'd say not, or I'd never have got so much out of them. Neither of them acted like men who understood every word they spoke was building a case to arrest them on suspicion of at least one murder."

At this, Mr. Goutier just shook his head.

"What are you thinking, Goutier?" asked Adam.

"'S truth, Harkness, I'm thinking that some one of these people has been profoundly unlucky."

CHAPTER 38

Intimate Secrets

"If there is anything in my story which you know to be either false or improbable, stop me."

Jane Austen, *Persuasion*

"Unlucky?" echoed Adam. "Why's that, Goutier?"

But Mr. Goutier didn't answer. Instead he got to his feet and went to the window. He looked down on the courtyard for a time, clearly putting his thoughts in order. Every person in the room understood the need for such a moment, and waited patiently for him to speak.

"After we talked to the coroner, and found out about Miss Kinsdale's statement, I decided it would be worthwhile to learn more about the admiral's death, if anything could be learned. No matter what Layng thought about the matter, I couldn't help but believe that the two deaths must be linked."

"No one here's going to say otherwise," said Adam.

Goutier gave a soft chuckle. "Thought not. Well. I took myself down to the admiral's lodgings. Landlady there is a captain's widow—spent years at sea herself. She knew Admiral Walsingham well and had nothing but praise for him.

Wept very real tears as she told me how she'd heard nothing out of the ordinary that night until she was awakened by the gunshot right outside her doors." Mr. Goutier shook his head. "She'd no doubt what it was, either, having heard gunshots more than once during her own travels."

"Poor woman," breathed Rosalind. The men all murmured their agreement.

Mr. Goutier leaned against the windowsill and folded his arms. "Well, after what she told me, I thought to go over the ground where the admiral died, maybe speak with some of the other guests. The landlady approves of the plan, and offers to help smooth the way with any guest who might be reluctant to speak with me. But just as I'm leaving her sitting room, I'm accosted by a whole crowd of seamen, all of them demanding to know my name and my business.

"I told them I'm from Bow Street, and they got properly angry then." Somewhat to Rosalind's surprise, he smiled at the memory. "They demanded to know what I meant to do about Walsingham's death and let me know in no uncertain terms that if the fellow that had shot him was allowed to slip free, the Royal Navy would be taking matters into its own hands."

Any trace of good humor Mr. Goutier might have shown now faded away. Rosalind felt a chill pass over her at the thought of how close Bath had come to experiencing a riot.

"There I am, starting to think I might have to fight my way out of this," Mr. Goutier was saying. "When a new man elbows his way through the crowd. He's a little fellow—comes barely up to my shoulder—and wiry, with bulging blue eyes and a crooked nose. Not very imposing, all things considered, but clearly these sailors hold him in some high esteem, because when he tells them to calm themselves and that he'll find out what's what, they listen. And, what's better from my point of view, they take themselves off. Although they do make sure this new man knows they're not going far, in case they might be needed.

"The man introduces himself as Captain Marbury. He says he'd sailed with Walsingham many times and that they were close friends. He had, he said, already arranged things with Mrs. Walsingham so that he would be the one to accompany the admiral's body home after the inquest, which would spare her the journey. He went on to say he was anxious to help in any other way he could, especially if it would allow him to bring more definite news back to Mrs. Walsingham.

"Well, naturally, I tell him he's the very man I want to meet. We go up to his rooms and there he tells me that he has retired from the sea and resides in Bath permanently. He says that just yesterday, Walsingham arrived in town in a state of extreme agitation. Marbury'd had no advance warning that Walsingham was planning to visit Bath, and in fact, the admiral asked if he could share Marbury's rooms, all the hotels being full up for the races. Marbury agreed at once, and asked what had caused his friend to come to Bath in such a hurry. But Walsingham only promised to tell him later, and left as quickly as he came.

"Marbury said he was due to dine with some other friends and go to the concert afterward, which he did. When he came home, Walsingham wasn't in the room. He was concerned, but not overly so, believing the admiral well able to handle himself in any situation. He swore he had no idea that anything might be truly wrong until he heard the shots, and the shouts. And he cursed himself as roundly as his landlady had herself for not taking more care."

"Well, I told the captain at least some of what I knew. As soon as I mentioned the Kinsdales, he turned angry. He cursed again and said he was not surprised that Walsingham's business involved that family. Indeed, he said, if I hadn't arrived when I did, he'd fully intended to call on them himself and ask them what they might know about the admiral's death."

"Did he know about Sir Anthony?" Rosalind asked.

"He did, and that made it all the worse as far as he was

concerned," said Mr. Goutier. "It seems Captain Marbury had made it his business to keep an ear out for gossip regarding the Kinsdales since they came to Bath. That, in fact, Walsingham had asked him to pay attention to how the family did, particularly the daughters."

Rosalind felt her eyes widen. Mr. Tauton wiped his hand over his mouth, probably to cover some impolite exclamation. Adam just leaned forward.

"Did Marbury say why Walsingham asked him to keep an eye on the Kinsdales?" Adam asked.

"Apparently Walsingham and his wife had become acquainted with the girls when they were staying in Lyme and the Walsinghams thought the daughters might eventually need some kind of help. It seems that tales of Sir Anthony's . . . excesses had apparently reached them via mutual acquaintances."

Rosalind expelled a long breath. From Mr. Goutier's description, the relationship between the Kinsdale sisters and the Walsinghams was much more than simply landlord and tenant. She thought again of the letters she'd seen, and of all her previous suspicions of a love affair between Cynthia and the admiral.

What if I was wrong? What if the situation is even more complex?

"Did you ask him about the Walshinghams' nephew?" asked Rosalind. "The child that Sir Anthony was saying was the reason to end the lease?"

"I did," said Mr. Goutier. "Marbury told me that was a tragic story, but an everyday one. Walsingham's brother— who was also a navy man—had fallen in love. He'd wanted to make an honorable offer, but the young lady's family didn't approve. So, they wed in secret and he sailed off with every intention of making his fortune and coming back awash in prize money to claim his bride. But his ship went down with all hands, and the young bride was left with a baby on the way and no husband to point to.

"So, the admiral and Mrs. Walsingham offer to adopt their nephew, them having no children of their own. They promised to raise him until the time might come when his mother could acknowledge him."

Rosalind felt her throat tighten. "Did he say who the mother was?"

"If he knew, he wasn't going to name her to me."

"But they—Walsingham's brother and this young lady— they did marry?" Rosalind pressed. "He was certain of it?"

"He seemed to be."

But Rosalind wasn't really listening anymore. She leapt from her chair, strode to the hearth, and snatched up the sack of ashes Adam had brought from the Kinsdales' house. She felt the inquiring glances from Mr. Goutier and Mr. Tauton, but she ignored them. Carefully, she upended the bag, spreading the ashes out across the hearthstones.

When she was satisfied the bag was empty, she tossed it aside and knelt, like Polly Flinders in the children's rhyme, playing among the cinders. Carefully, she began sifting the ashes with her hands.

Adam knelt with her. "Definitely someone burning papers," he said, drawing out some fragments of foolscap. "Letters?"

Rosalind didn't answer. *There must be something, there must be. Please, let there be something. . . .*

Something like rough string snagged at her fingertips. Rosalind brushed aside some remaining cinders and lifted it out of the pile as gently as she could. "Oh, good heavens."

"What is it?" asked Mr. Goutier.

"It" was a chain, or the remains of one. It was tarnished black from heat and ash, as was the ring on its end. But it was not a whole ring, Rosalind saw. It was only one half, with the fine chain threaded through a piercing in the metal.

A love token. The sort exchanged when a couple expected to be parted for a very long time.

Rosalind held it up to Adam and he knew at once what he was seeing.

"But does it belong to Cynthia? Or Elizabeth?"

Rosalind stared at the ring. She moistened her lips. She did not want to speak the next words, but she had to.

"Or Clara?"

CHAPTER 39

Distressing Possibilities

. . . the allusions to former practices and pursuits,
suggested suspicions not favourable of what he
had been.

Jane Austen, *Persuasion*

The silence that fell was so thick Rosalind found she could not think clearly for the sheer weight of it.

It isn't true.

She should say something, she knew. Everyone was waiting for her to be the one to break this silence that she herself had brought down. But how could she? How could she even be thinking that this ring, this affair, and this *child*, could belong to Devon's fiancée?

It cannot be true. It may be Cynthia, or Elizabeth, but it is not Clara.

But she couldn't make herself say it. She couldn't make herself say anything. Instead, she dropped the token and its chain into Adam's cupped palm and left the room.

It is not true! I will not have to tell Devon he's fallen in love with someone who would lie to him about such a thing.

Rosalind pushed open the door to her own room and

crossed to the washstand. She poured water from the pitcher into the basin, noted the black smears her fingers left behind, and promised herself she would wipe them clean. She found the cake of yellow soap, and slowly, methodically, began to wash her hands.

He may know. She bit her lip. *He may have decided that it was too personal a matter to relate to me. Indeed, Clara may have asked him not to tell me.*

There are two other sisters. It was Cynthia who was writing to the admiral.

Clara did not kill him.

Devon did not kill him, and he did not kill Sir Anthony because he was so angry for his fiancée, for her reputation, for her child. I need to stop thinking that.

But the letter from the admiral's brother had been addressed to "Miss Kinsdale." Which Miss Kinsdale? She'd allowed herself to believe it must be Cynthia, because Cynthia had been so overcome by the admiral's visit. But the splotched reply she had found had no signature. She had no way of knowing which sister had actually penned it.

No. Clara did not do this. I will not permit *that to be true.* Rosalind bared her teeth to the gray water in the basin.

She heard the door open. She heard Adam's soft step on the floor. She knew every sound he made and did not have to look to know it was him. She reached for the clean white towel that hung from the edge of the stand and wiped her hands dry.

Adam was directly behind her now. He rested his hands on her shoulders. He said nothing, made no attempt to turn her toward him. He waited until she put the towel down, until she turned to rest her brow against his shoulder. Only then did he fold her into his strong embrace.

"I don't even know why I'm so upset," she said.

"Because you don't want to break Casselmaine's heart," Adam replied evenly. "Or your own."

"He loves her," whispered Rosalind. "He would do anything for her."

"Yes, and she loves him, and she would also do anything."

Because they both knew that love could make someone just as desperate as hatred.

Someone was knocking on the door. Adam let go of her and went to answer. Rosalind turned back to the washstand and busied herself with using the towel to wipe down the smudges she'd left on the pitcher. Behind her Adam opened the door. The man on the other side replied a note had come. Rosalind dabbed at her eyes with a clean portion of the towel. Adam closed the door.

Rosalind folded the towel. She should turn around now. She should ask who the note had come from.

Except, to her shame, she was not sure she wanted to know.

She heard the rustle of paper being unfolded.

"Some good news," said Adam quietly. "Casselmaine writes he was able to corner Layng and convince him to delay the inquest for two days. Apparently, he put it to Mr. Layng that with persons of all sorts filling the streets for the races and the broken lock on the scullery door, there was currently no way to be certain Sir Anthony didn't die during the course of an attempted robbery."

Given what they had just learned from Mr. Tauton and Mr. Goutier, this seemed a much stronger possibility than it had just a few hours before.

Rosalind drew in a deep breath and turned. "That is very good news, especially . . . especially in the light of all we have just learned."

"I expect Layng will look back and find he has saved himself quite the headache." Adam folded the note and tucked it into his coat pocket. "Rosalind, you are exhausted. Permit me the privilege as your future husband to say you should go to bed. I'll finish things with Goutier and Tauton and be back when they've gone."

Rosalind wanted to protest that she was perfectly well, but the look in Adam's eye told her he wouldn't believe it, no matter what she said. Worse, she knew he was right.

She nodded. "Thank you."

He kissed her. "I'll find one of Leigh's girls to come play lady's maid."

She nodded again. He left her there. Slowly, Rosalind sank onto one of the room's rush-bottomed chairs. She lifted back the curtain, and stared out the corner of the window, seeing her reflection, and the darkness, and very little beyond. But she stayed that way until the maid came.

Because she could not think what else to do.

Rosalind was not certain she'd be able to sleep. But the moment Adam slipped into bed beside her, the safety and the warmth of his presence banished all other feeling. She could let go. She could sleep. And she did.

There was a noise.

Rosalind's mind swam slowly up from a thick fen of dreams.

There was a noise and it wouldn't stop and she was very angry about it.

Slowly, she realized someone was pounding on the door—loudly, urgently.

Her eyes flew open. Adam rolled over, muttering curses through his teeth. Rosalind scrambled to her feet, looked for her wrapper, and failed to find it.

"Miss Thorne?" It was Mrs. Leigh. "Miss Thorne!"

Rosalind abandoned thought of her wrapper, hurried to the door, and cracked it open.

"Beg pardon," said Mrs. Leigh breathlessly. "You're needed at once. You and Mr. Harkness. There's a carriage in the yard. Driver says he's been sent from Lansdown to fetch you both. Says he's from Lord Casselmaine and Miss Clara Kinsdale."

Rosalind felt her heart plummet.

"What's happened?"

"It's about that horse, Kinsdale's Pride, miss," said Mrs. Leigh. "She's been stolen."

CHAPTER 40

Theft

*It was a dreadful picture of ingratitude and inhu-
manity . . . no flagrant open crime could have
been worse.*

Jane Austen, *Persuasion*

As soon as Rosalind and Adam were dressed, they raced
downstairs to the common room. Mr. Leigh stood at the
bar beside his wife. Both straightened as she and Adam
reached them.

"Leigh, I need a message sent to Sampson Goutier," Adam
said. "You can ask for his direction at the City police station.
Tell him what you told us, and say he and Sam Tauton
should meet us up at Lansdown as fast as they can get there."

"I'll go myself, sir." Leigh pocketed the coins and strode
away, bellowing, "Davey! Saddle the bay! Davey!"

"If anyone comes asking, you may tell them where we've
gone," Rosalind told Mrs. Leigh. "But nothing more."

"As you say, miss." Mrs. Leigh curtsied. "I hope all comes
out right."

Oh, so do I. But Rosalind said nothing, she just followed
Adam to the coach-and-four that waited in the yard.

Adam waved for the driver to keep his seat. He helped her inside himself and shut the door behind them. Seeing Rosalind was settled, he banged on the roof, signaling the driver they were ready. The man touched up the horses and eased them into the early morning traffic.

"Why would anyone steal a horse that was going to go missing anyway?" asked Rosalind. "Is this the switch we've been expecting?"

"It can't be," said Adam, more to the world outside the window than to her. "A lookalike scheme depends on no one knowing that anything has happened to the original horse. If Pride has gone missing, it can only mean that things are falling apart."

Yes. Surely, two murders would strain the best-laid plans. "Do you think the principals in the scheme are hoping to cover their tracks?"

"Possibly," said Adam.

"Once we've talked to Devon and Clara, we should go back to the Kinsdales and talk with Laurel and Mrs. Kendricks," Rosalind told him. "I want to know where Elizabeth has been this morning."

"If she's still there," muttered Adam.

"Yes," said Rosalind. "If she is."

Something in her tone turned him toward her. "Do you want to go there now? I can drop you off and go ahead to Lansdown on my own."

Rosalind considered this, but then shook her head. "No, I want to talk with Clara first."

Adam was silent. Rosalind sighed.

"You want to ask if I still suspect Clara of . . . participating in this mess?"

"Do you?"

"I suspect her of loving her sisters as much as she loves Devon, while also being very angry at both of them," said Rosalind. "I think it's very possible she might have spirited the horse away to keep Elizabeth from getting herself into even worse trouble."

Adam nodded thoughtfully. "That wouldn't be a bad idea, as such. If Kinsdale's Pride vanishes because she's been stolen, rather than just because Clara and Casselmaine want her out of the running, Elizabeth can't try to argue them out of it."

"Neither could Cynthia, if she's involved."

They both fell silent then, each of them wrapped up in their own thoughts. Rosalind turned the pieces of what they had learned over in her mind. She fit them together and pulled them apart again, trying, and failing, to find the picture that was true. A single glance at Adam told her he was occupied in the same manner. Neither of them could stop worrying at the problem, but neither was ready to speak any more about it. Not yet.

They'd left Bath now, and turned onto the road leading up to Lansdown. The coach rocked badly and listed to one side, but the driver did not slow down. Rosalind pressed both hands against the seat to try to keep herself steady. Adam raised his hand, probably to knock on the roof and tell the driver to have a care.

Then, all at once, the driver shouted. They heard hoofbeats and a scream. Their carriage lurched, and swerved and bounced. Adam grabbed Rosalind and they both slammed against the door as the vehicle teetered badly, and for one wild instant, Rosalind felt sure they must be overturned. But they came to a rest upright, although at a precarious angle.

Adam held on to Rosalind's shoulders as she pushed herself away from the door. His gaze met hers and she nodded. She was all right, and so was he.

Adam let down the window glass and worked the door handle. After a small amount of struggle, the door opened. He climbed out and helped Rosalind down behind him. Now she could see they were just on the edge of the ditch. A few inches further, and the coach would have been on its side.

"Madman!" The driver was already among the horses, catching hold of the reins and working to keep them from tangling themselves in the harness. "Came tearing down the hill!" He waved one arm. "I had to swerve, sir, or we'd've been hit."

"No harm taken," said Adam. "I can help with the horses."

"Yes, sir. If you can just hold of the off lead here. . . ."

Adam hurried around to take control of the horse's head, just as the horse threatened to rear up. Rosalind watched, her heart in her mouth, her attention entirely on Adam and the driver.

She never felt the blow.

CHAPTER 41

The Missing

He was gone; he had disappeared . . .

Jane Austen, *Persuasion*

"Ah, Mr. Goutier!" Charlie Foote hailed Goutier and Tauton as soon as they reached the stable yard.

"Something's off," he muttered to Tauton, and Tauton nodded. They both knew that if Kinsdale's Pride was stolen, the man in charge of her would not be so cheerful.

"Was waiting on you," Foote told them both. "Got a message. Now where the devil . . ."

Foote started patting his pockets, and, if Goutier was honest, it looked like this was going to be a long business. He folded his arms, as if that would hold back his straining patience. Tauton just rolled his eyes.

"Ah, here!" Foote finally dug two fingers into his waistcoat pocket and extracted a twist of paper. He held it out to Goutier. "Next time, tell your man not to be so stingy with his writing materials, yeah?"

"I'll pass it along," said Goutier gravely as he took the note.

Foote had reason for complaint. The paper was little more

than a scrap, and now it was a grimy, wrinkled scrap from having survived its term in the stableman's pocket.

"Let me know if you need anything else," he said, and loped off to return to his own work.

"Who's it from?" asked Tauton as soon as Foote was out of earshot.

Goutier squinted at the smeared writing. "Harkness," he reported. "Says there was trouble on the road. Business with the horse was a distraction. Longer letter waiting for us back at the Green Briar."

Tauton made a throttled sound. "Can't keep anything simple, can he?"

"Not since I've known him." Goutier tucked the note into his own pocket, and found himself staring hard at the stables, as if he thought he could see through the walls.

"Oh, now you're getting one of those looks," Tauton muttered.

"What looks?"

"Like our esteemed Mr. Harkness gets when he's had one too many thoughts in that head of his. Come on, man, out with it." Tauton made a *come hither* gesture with two fingers. "What's wrong?"

"I was just thinking we'd better check on Kinsdale's Pride anyway," Goutier told him. "I'd hate to find out this note was the distraction, and it's meant to pull us out of here."

Tauton huffed. "As it happens, I was thinking much the same thing. And we might have a word with Foote as to the details of the situation." He bowed and gestured elaborately. "After you, Mr. Goutier!"

"Is that for me, Duggin?" asked Miss Cynthia.

The young footman stood uncertainly on the threshold of the sitting room. He stared at the pile of dresses heaped on the sofa as if it might rise up and bite him. Laurel hid a smile.

She would tease him mercilessly about how he had faltered when faced with that mountain of delicate femininity.

Laurel and Miss Cynthia were alone in the sisters' rooms. Right after breakfast, Miss Clara had gone to call on Lord Casselmaine. Laurel suspected she wanted the chance to talk about money without being overheard by the rest of the household. The eldest Miss Kinsdale had left shortly afterward, without saying where she was going, or when she intended to return. Laurel determined she would make sure Mrs. Kendricks knew that as soon as she could get away.

Although that might be awhile. Laurel and Miss Cynthia were engaged in the tedious process of sorting through her wardrobe to help convert it to full mourning. They needed to determine which dresses could be sent away to be dyed, or otherwise suitably altered, and which needed to simply be packed away, and how much new stuff would have to be ordered. Laurel already had a pile of gloves and stockings to mend, not to mention the slippers she had been handed with the rather limp directive of "see if anything can be done with these."

"Well?" Miss Cynthia was saying impatiently to Duggin. Laurel prepared to fade into the background, but she kept her ears wide open.

Duggin looked uncertain. "No, miss, that is . . . the note's for Laurel. It's just come from the Green Briar, sent from Miss Thorne. They said it was urgent."

"Well, you'd best take it, hadn't you?" said Miss Cynthia. Her voice was flat, but her disapproval was plain.

She had some reason to be snippy about it, Laurel supposed. By the normal rules, any message for one of the staff would have been left in the servants' hall. Not that Laurel had ever received many written messages. In fact, she'd only learned to read a year ago, thanks to Miss McGowan and her copybooks.

"Thank you, miss. Sorry, miss," Laurel murmured as she took the note. The look Duggin gave her said "better you than me," and the footman made a hasty retreat. Laurel felt a twist of envy as he vanished. She did not at all like the way Miss Cynthia was watching her.

Laurel made herself ignore her employer and unfolded the paper. Slowly, carefully, she spelled out the words, keeping her lips pressed firmly together so that Miss Cynthia would not see her murmuring to herself.

"Well?" asked Miss Cynthia impatiently. "What does Miss Thorne say? Or is it private?"

Miss McGowan would have urged her to say it was private. Miss McGowan was very much one for standing on one's rights, even if one was "just" a servant. And Laurel found she very much did not want to tell Miss Cynthia about it. She had done her best to be sympathetic toward the young woman. After all, she'd been through such lot in such a very short time. But, if Laurel was honest with herself, Miss Cynthia's abrupt shifts of temper about every small thing were becoming increasingly difficult to deal with.

Laurel swallowed all this. The last thing she needed was Miss Cynthia angry at her. If she was ordered out of the room, it would hinder her real job, which was keeping as close an eye on all the sisters as possible.

Or, at least that had been her job.

"Miss Thorne says she's been called back to London," Laurel said. "It's to do with this business with Mrs. Lynn. She asks to have her things packed and for me to follow on as soon as may be." She lowered the paper. "I'm sorry, miss. . . ."

"No, no," said Miss Cynthia at once. "You'd best go immediately. This can all wait." She gestured to the dresses draped over the sofa.

"Yes, miss. Thank you, miss." Laurel made her curtsy, genuinely grateful that Miss Cynthia had decided not to make a fuss. She hurried out to the corridor, and down the servants' stair.

She found Mrs. Kendricks ensconced in the butler's pantry with Thrush and Cook. A whole array of bills and notebooks had been spread out on the table between them.

Laurel paused in the doorway and cleared her throat. "A word, please, Mrs. Kendricks?"

Mrs. Kendricks frowned up at her. But when she saw the urgency of Laurel's expression, she excused herself at once from the household conference and stepped out into the corridor.

"This is come from Miss Thorne." Laurel handed her the note. Mrs. Kendricks opened it, and her frown deepened. "I should leave at once and—"

"You should do no such thing," snapped Mrs. Kendricks.

"But, Miss Thorne—"

Laurel got no further. "Miss Thorne never wrote this," Mrs. Kendricks declared. "I know her hand. Besides, she would never send such a careless letter, even if her house was on fire. There's no mention of how you are to travel, and no instruction for Leigh, and not a single word of how anybody is to be paid for their trouble. She would *never* forget such details."

Laurel felt the blood drain from her cheeks. "What do we do?"

Mrs. Kendricks glowered at the wall, clearly thinking furiously. "You carry on here," she said. "But you keep your ears and eyes open wide, you understand?"

"Yes, ma'am." The fact of the matter was that Mrs. Kendricks spoke so sharply that Laurel probably would have said yes to almost anything.

"*And* you tell that Duggin, and Thrush as well, that if anyone comes looking for Miss Thorne or Mr. Harkness that they're over at the Green Briar getting ready to go back to London. Is that understood?"

"Yes, ma'am," said Laurel again. "What will you do?"

"I am going to fetch Lord Casselmaine," said Mrs. Kendricks. "And pray that we are not too late. Because something has gone badly wrong."

CHAPTER 42

Rallying

*"We must be decided, and without the loss of an-
other minute. Every minute is valuable."*

Jane Austen, *Persuasion*

"Gentlemen," said the Green Briar's landlord. "What
can I do for you?"

Goutier and Tauton had made good time getting back to
the inn. It had taken only a few moments to see that Kinsdale's Pride was still in her roomy box at the stables. When
they questioned Foote about the note, and told him what had
brought them to the stables, he'd been righteously indignant
that *anyone* would think he'd have permitted a theft on his
watch.

Foote might have a sharper's instincts and a horse dealer's
smile, but he also had his pride, and Goutier and Tauton had
years of experience seeing through a vast array of fabrications. Whatever was going on, Foote had no part in it. So,
they believed him when he said that neither Harkness nor
Miss Thorne had actually been out to Lansdown that morning. Likewise, they accepted his promise that if they did arrive, Foote himself would tell them all that had happened.

"Because I think we've had enough of notes," Tauton had growled, and Goutier agreed.

They'd ridden fast on the way back. Goutier felt worry nipping hard at his heels the whole way. He hoped against hope that they'd find Miss Thorne and Harkness together in the inn; hoped they would have some story to tell; hoped they would be ready to lay out all the answers to this maddening pile of riddles.

But now, he and Tauton stood in the public room and the landlord was eyeing at them like they'd come to rob the place.

"We're looking for Adam Harkness," said Tauton.

The landlord—Leigh—didn't even blink. "I've no one here by that name."

Goutier wanted to roar to the man that he knew them full well, that they'd been in this room just the night before, that he must have *seen* them going upstairs last night with Harkness and Miss Thorne.

Tauton laid a warning hand on Goutier's arm.

"He's traveling under the name of Rutherford," said Tauton to Leigh. "Accompanied by Mrs. Rutherford."

Leigh's eyes narrowed. "And what business would you gents have with the Rutherfords?"

We've no time for this! Frustration made Goutier grind his teeth, but he forced himself to speak evenly. "My name's Sampson Goutier, and this is Samuel Tauton. Now, I've no proof to give, but we're from Bow Street. You can ask after us over at the City police station, or the coroner's office, if you want. We're friends of Harkness, and Miss Thorne, and helping them both on this business with the Kinsdales and the admiral, and something's gone wrong."

"Maybe they left us some message?" prompted Tauton.

The landlord considered all this for an infuriating length of time. But at last, he nodded. "Aye. Message came. For a Mr. Goutier." He reached under the bar and handed Goutier a folded paper.

"It came?" said Tauton. "Who delivered it? Harkness wasn't here himself?"

Leigh shook his head. "Haven't seen either of them since this morning. Carriage called for them, saying a horse had been stolen out at Lansdown and that Lord Casselmaine and Miss Kinsdale needed them both up there."

Goutier felt a cold clench in his guts as worry tightened into a knot of genuine fear.

This new message was written on another scrap. It was much tidier this time. Goutier recognized the paper as a leaf from Harkness's notebook. The pencil writing was smeared, but the words were still legible. Tauton leaned over his shoulder to read with him:

> *Lynn's confederates fled to London. Following after with Miss Thorne. Get on road as soon as possible.*
> *A.H.*

"Damn," muttered Tauton.

"Who was it who gave this to you?" Goutier asked Leigh. "Was it the same man that drove the carriage?"

"Nah, nah. This fellow came in on horseback. Thought I recognized him from the crowd of stablemen that come down to drink of a Sunday, but wouldn't like to swear to it."

"Black fella like me?" *Because if it was Foote who stood there like butter wouldn't melt in his mouth, I am going back up there and giving him the thrashing of his life. . . .*

"Nah," said the landlord. "White fella, long, horsey face. Scarred hands, like he'd been a boxer. Didn't give no name."

"All right," said Goutier. "Thanks for your help." He laid some coins down on the bar. "A drink for yourself and your good lady."

"Very kind of you, sir." Leigh swept the coins into his palm.

Goutier and Tauton both headed into the inn's yard to get out of earshot.

"I don't like this," Goutier said.

"Neither do I." Tauton stuck his thumbs into his waist-coat pockets. "It's got a strong smell of wild goose chase about it."

"That it does," Goutier agreed. "Which raises the question, what do we do now?"

They were not given much chance to consider the question. Just then, an open carriage clattered up to the inn's doors. Before you could say "knife," Leigh had nipped out into the yard to take the horses' heads so the driver could jump down.

But the man in the driving cape and low-crowned hat was no servant. This was Lord Casselmaine, looking tousled and grim. Goutier saw then that one of the two women in the carriage was Mrs. Kendricks, who used to keep house for Rosalind Thorne.

The duke recognized the two Bow Street officers immediately.

"Goutier!" he cried. "Tauton. Are they here?"

No need to ask who "they" were. "No," Goutier told him. "Nor have they been since this morning."

The duke helped Mrs. Kendricks down, and also a young woman—a lady by her dress, and one of the Kinsdales by her hair and eyes.

"Something's gone wrong," Lord Casselmaine said to them all. "Someone tried to convince Mrs. Kendricks that Rosalind and Harkness were on their way back to London."

"Same word was left here," said Tauton.

"By whom?" demanded Lord Casselmaine, but Tauton shook his head.

"No name given. Fellow with a horse face and scarred hands."

Mrs. Kendricks swayed on her feet. The young lady grabbed her elbow. "We need to go inside."

"Yes, yes, of course." Leigh bustled forward, and took Mrs. Kendricks's arm. "You come along now, Mariah."

"I'm all right," protested Mrs. Kendricks. No one paid her any mind. Leigh took them all into the ladies' parlor. His wife appeared as if from nowhere, carrying a tray that held a full decanter and several glasses. Mrs. Kendricks took one of the glasses, looked at it, and pulled a face, but she also downed the measure of brandy as if it was medicine. Her color returned almost immediately.

Goutier drank his own measure, and decided now was not the time to inquire where or how the landlord had come across a bottle of brandy of this quality.

"Now, down to business." Tauton rested his elbows on the table. "Do we know where Miss Thorne and Harkness were last seen?"

"Here," said Mrs. Leigh, who having delivered the brandy stayed at her husband's side. "They arrived last night and went to their rooms. A driver with a coach-and-four came early this morning. Said he came from you, your grace, and Miss Clara Kinsdale."

Casselmaine and Miss Kinsdale stared blankly.

Mrs. Leigh plowed ahead; her tone, Goutier noticed, was both defensive and dismayed. "He said that the horse everyone's been in such an uproar over, Kinsdale's Pride, had been stolen. His instructions were to take Mr. Harkness and Miss Thorne up to Lansdown as soon as ever they were ready."

"Was anyone else in the carriage?" asked Tauton.

"I'd say no," said Mr. Leigh. "But I didn't look close."

"And this driver, could you describe him?" put in Goutier.

Mrs. Leigh shook her head. "He'd his hat pulled low and his face muffled. But he'd clearly been driving fast and it was a damp morning, so I didn't think anything of that."

"I knew this would happen one day," breathed Mrs. Kendricks. "I knew it. I warned her. She wouldn't *listen*."

"It will be all right, Mariah," murmured Mrs. Leigh. The look the landlady turned on Goutier, Tauton, and Casselmaine then said it had damned well better be. "What are you going to do?"

The three men looked at each other uneasily.

"We should divide our efforts," began Casselmaine.

"That'll be best," agreed Goutier. "I'll head back up the road to Lansdown, see if there's some sign of mischief I've missed, or if I can find someone who might have seen something. One thing we can be certain of is that neither Miss Thorne nor Harkness would be taken quietly."

Tauton snorted. "That'd be the truth. I'll get over to the City police station and tell Layng what's happened. Then, I want to have a word with Mrs. Lynn. Might be she can be convinced to name her confederates, especially as it seems clear they've left her to swing. I've been wanting a look at her anyway." Tauton's memory for faces was the stuff of Bow Street legend. They said he could remember a pickpocket he'd seen once ten or more years ago. Tauton never contradicted those stories.

Casselmaine nodded. "Excellent. Goutier, I'll catch you up as soon as I can. I want to send word to London and our friends there. They should be warned about what's happened. Or, if it happens we're wrong, and Harkness and Rosalind really have gone back to town, they should know to send back word quick as may be."

"We're not wrong," said Goutier flatly. "I wish to God we were."

"I know." Casselmaine's tone was grim. His blue eyes filled with memories, and none of them—if Goutier was any judge—were any good. "Miss Kinsdale, Mrs. Kendricks, will you go back to the Kinsdales?"

"No," said Miss Kinsdale immediately. "I'm staying with you."

"Clara—" began Casselmaine.

She didn't let him finish. "If there's a trail to be followed, or messages to be carried, you'll need someone else who can help, and that person may need to be a fast rider. If you can say there's anyone here who is my equal on horseback, I'll go home now."

No one answered. And Casselmaine nodded, even though it was clear he was not happy. "All right. Mrs. Kendricks, can you at least go back to the house? We'll need someone to keep an eye on matters there."

"Yes, sir."

"I'll roust the boy and drive her myself," said Mr. Leigh.

"You can take my carriage," said Casselmaine. "And we'll need the hire of two good saddle horses."

"Whatever your grace needs," replied Leigh smartly.

The problem was what they really needed was something none of them could supply right now—the answer to one simple question.

Were Adam Harkness and Rosalind Thorne even still alive?

CHAPTER 43

An Extremely Rude Awakening

"I lived in perpetual fright at that time, and had all manner of imaginary complaints from not knowing what to do with myself . . ."

Jane Austen, *Persuasion*

"Rosalind."

Her head hurt—threads of pain seemed to have been woven into her skull, and they were all squeezing at once.

"I know, dearest, I know, but you must wake up."

Adam.

"Look at me, Rosalind."

He was afraid. He was insistent. How could she refuse him? Rosalind opened her eyes.

Adam was leaning over her. He held a candle high. The light made her wince.

"Where are we?" she croaked.

Adam didn't answer. Instead, he gathered her into a one-armed embrace and held her like that for a long time.

At last, he let her go. It was only then Rosalind realized they were both sitting on a dusty floor. Adam put his hand under her chin, bringing the candle close and peering anxiously at her eyes.

"How is your head?" he asked. "Does it hurt?"

"Some, yes." The words rasped against her throat. Her mouth was dry and her tongue felt leathery. Rosalind swallowed, and swallowed again.

"No blurred vision? Are you seeing double?"

"No. I don't think so." She moved his hand away from her chin, but squeezed it gratefully. She wanted to see past him. She wanted to understand what was happening. "Where are we?"

Adam sat back on his haunches. "I don't know. I only came to myself a bit ago. I suspect that the blows we took were assisted by laudanum, or something similar."

Now that her eyes had adapted and her mind had stopped spinning so rapidly, Rosalind could see fresh bruises around Adam's neck. A surge of anger burned through her and she was glad of it, because somehow it also lessened the pain in her head.

"Someone tried to strangle you."

"And nearly succeeded." Adam rubbed the dark spots ruefully. "I heard you cry out, and I turned, and the blackguard came at me from behind. I twisted 'round and grappled with him, but he got his hands round my throat."

Rosalind found she was having difficulty breathing. She could not think about Adam being overpowered. Adam being hurt. Adam being dead.

I will not think about this. I have enough to think about.

"They've taken my clasp knife," Adam was saying. "And my notebook, and my watch."

"I'm sorry." That watch had belonged to Adam's father and he held it dear. It was a small matter at such a time, but it was one she could actually wrap her thoughts around.

He shrugged irritably. "At the moment, I'd rather have the knife back."

"As would I, I must admit," she said. "Will you help me stand?"

Adam stood carefully, so as not to extinguish the candle. He reached out his free hand. Rosalind grasped it and pulled herself to her feet. The effort blurred her vision, but Rosalind gritted her teeth and, although she swayed briefly, she found she was able to quickly steady herself.

Now she could see better, not that there was much to see. They were alone in a small, narrow room. A low door waited at one end of the room and a shuttered window at the other. The air smelled of damp, and dust. Filthy whitewash covered the rough walls. There was no ceiling, only roof beams and timbers. Cobwebs filled the corners and trailed ghostly streamers down the walls. The rustling from the shadows said that the mice, and perhaps the rats, were active overhead.

Rosalind decided this was something else she did not need to think about, and instead went to the door. Adam carried the candle to the little window at the opposite end of the room.

"Locked." Rosalind rattled the doorknob. It turned freely, but the door wouldn't budge. She bent down and ran her fingers across the wood. "From the looks of it, there was a hasp lock here, but it's been removed."

"This has been nailed shut." Adam straightened up and glared at the window. "And recently. If we needed any more proof that our abduction was planned in advance, we have it now."

Footsteps thumped on the other side of the door—the unmistakable sound of people trudging up a set of stairs. Rosalind retreated to Adam's side and he pushed the candle toward her. Rosalind took it and backed away, sheltering the flame. Adam faced the door, and flexed his hands.

There was a jingle of keys and the sound of metal scraping against metal. A moment later, the door opened and Elizabeth Kinsdale walked in, followed closely by a man Rosalind did not know. He had a long, hard face and thick hands.

One of those hands clutched a wicked looking knife.

CHAPTER 44

A Most Informative Discussion

How was the truth to reach him? How, in all the peculiar disadvantages of their respective situations, would he ever learn of her real sentiments?

Jane Austen, *Persuasion*

Do you want help?

Layng's question still rang in Tauton's ears as he heaved himself up the stairs at the King's Swan.

Tauton had left the Green Briar and gone straight to the City police station, and Layng's office. The man himself was out, presiding over a separate inquest, which left Tauton with nothing to do but pace in angry circles until he returned.

"What's happened?" Layng had closed the door immediately.

"What hasn't?" Tauton answered grimly, and then went on to tell him how Harkness and Miss Thorne had gone missing, and how it looked fair to have been some one of Mrs. Lynn's confederates who managed the disappearance.

Do you want help?

Layng hadn't asked this immediately, of course. First,

there'd been a great deal of cursing and then some other questions as the coroner tried to extract as many details as Tauton had. These were frustratingly few, which led to more cursing.

I can call up a dozen constables, and the militia if we want them. Search the countryside hereabouts. Not that many places they could be hiding. . . .

Whatever happened next, it would all rest on the answer Tauton had given to the coroner, and Tauton would never be able to forget that.

Because he'd stood silently for a moment, listening to the inner voices that came from nigh on thirty years of walking London's streets and seeing all sorts of schemes, great and small.

"Best not," Tauton had said. "We don't want to panic them. They're already for the drop, and they know it, so what's two more bodies in the ledger?" Even now he was amazed at how coldly he'd spoken those words. "We find where they're at first, and organize the raid afterward."

And Layng had agreed. So, there'd be no constables searching the countryside.

And so if Harkness and Miss Thorne weren't found in time, it was his fault.

Well then, you'll just have to make sure they are found, won't you? Tauton curled his hand into a tight fist and banged the side against the prisoner's door.

"Come!" called a lady's voice from the other side.

Tauton pulled out the key given to him by the constable at the foot of the stairs and unlocked the door.

The room on the other side was plain but clean. The woman was well-dressed and her hair neatly styled. She sat on the bed, her attention seemingly occupied by reweaving a bit of the basket in her hands. She did not look up until he'd shut the door again.

But when she did, Tauton recognized her at once.

"Well, well. Hullo, Sylvia."

"Do I know you, sir?" she asked coldly.

"As it happens, you do. Samuel Tauton."

Mrs. Lynn froze in place. Tauton lowered his bulk carefully onto the stool beside the door.

"You'll forgive me, I'm sure," he said. "Knees just ain't what they used to be. How do you do, Mrs. Westerford?"

"Lynn," she said. "My name is Mrs. Lynn. And I'm afraid if we ever knew each other—Mr. . . . Tauton, did you say?—I have forgotten."

"Well, I'm not surprised." He grinned. "You were rather busy the last time we met. Let me see, that would be seven years ago now. At Newmarket, it was. You'd just talked a gent into laying good money on a bad horse, and picked his pocket afterward."

Nice little double game it had been, too. He smiled at the memory, the way a craftsman might smile at fine workmanship. Tauton had always suspected she'd been working with the bookmaker, but couldn't prove anything. Now he found himself wondering if that bookmaker hadn't been this fellow Wallace.

"Had a little girl with you, then," he said. "Pretty quick on the dip she was, too. What's happened to her?"

She didn't answer that, not that he really expected her to. Instead, she gave him another cold, imperious stare.

"What do you hope to accomplish by this slander, sir? Or are you simply in the habit of humiliating helpless women for sport?"

"You may believe me, Mrs. Westerford . . . sorry, Mrs. Lynn, I've got no interest in humiliating anybody. But some friends of mine have gone missing, and I'm trying to find them."

"Friends of yours?" She snorted, as if the idea of Tauton having friends at all was too ridiculous to be contemplated.

"Miss Thorne and Mr. Harkness," said Tauton.

And just like that, Mrs. Lynn's mask shattered. Her face

went dead white and she clutched at the basket in her lap like it was the only thing keeping her from falling over.

"They're missing?" she croaked.

Tauton nodded gravely. "Since this morning. We were supposed to meet at Lansdown, but they never arrived. You may imagine we're all deeply concerned, especially since there's already a pair of deaths connected with you and the Kinsdales." He leaned forward, planting his elbows on his knees. "I was hoping you might be able to shed some light on their possible whereabouts."

"What light could I shed? I've been here the entire time. I've had no visitors, no notes—"

"Ah, now," he stopped her. "That's not *entirely* true, and we both know it."

She was considering lying. He could see it. But she saw the gleam in his eyes, and changed her mind.

"Oh, that," she said. "Yes. Well, that was not really a visitor. It was more in the nature of an opportunity for Elizabeth Kinsdale to point and laugh."

Tauton considered the woman in front of him for a long time. She was remarkably poised, all things considered, but she was tired, and not a little afraid. At the same time, he could sense her anger simmering just underneath the surface of all that confidence. He'd seen this combination before in other prisoners. Mostly they were the ones whose partners had hung them out to dry.

"Well, would you say maybe she's the one we should be talking to?"

She knew what he was suggesting. He could read it in her eyes. He'd just offered her the opportunity to turn on her confederates. Odds were she'd laugh in his face. But Tauton waited, and Mrs. Lynn did not laugh. But neither did she answer.

So, Tauton shrugged and got to his feet. "Well, perhaps I'd best take my leave. I don't seem to be helping here. Good

luck to you, Mrs. Lynn. I'm glad to see you're putting a brave
face on things."

She let him unlock the door and pull it halfway open before she spoke.

"It was all a mistake," she said. "I knew it from the beginning, or nearly the beginning."

Tauton closed the door and turned to face her again. Her
jaw had hardened from fear and anger. Tauton waited. He
wasn't as famous for it as Harkness, but he could be very patient when need arose. It was a hard thing to inform on your
confederates, and a dangerous one. As urgent as matters were,
he could still grant her a moment to reconcile herself to the
idea.

"It was, as I have told you, Elizabeth Kinsdale who came
to see me," said Mrs. Lynn. "This entire mess was her doing.
Hers, and that man of hers."

"What man?" he barked.

"His name is Nathanial Spence. He served her family as
head groom. Until, that is, she and he made the age-old mistake of falling in love."

I might have known. Tauton settled carefully back onto
the creaking stool. "Go on."

"Ordinarily, I never would have taken up with such a pair,
but I was very low at the time and a bit desperate. She was
able to name a mutual acquaintance whom I trusted, and she
begged me for help."

"Begged you for help?" echoed Tauton.

"I know, how very strange." Mrs. Lynn's smile was filled
with bitter irony. "What's worse is that was what did me in.
It made me curious. What help could I be to this young
lady?" She fussed with the basket's loose reeds again. "But
then she told me her name—Elizabeth Kinsdale. Sir Anthony
was very much the talk of his neighborhood at that time, and
if he wasn't dead now he'd have expired on the spot to know
what sort of talk it was. The butt of every joke. They were

actually selling prints that caricatured him in the post office." She paused. "I don't suppose he recognized himself," she murmured. "A more willfully blind man I never knew."

"But his daughter found you—"

Mrs. Lynn shook herself. "Yes. She said she'd heard about me from her man Nathanial Spence. She told me that she and Nathanial wanted to elope, but that they needed money. She told me about their plan to run a horse swap at the village fair, and that if I helped them, I would be cut in for a substantial share.

"Well, what could I say to that?" Mrs. Lynn's attitude of innocence and incredulity was truly impressive. "I asked her some questions, and it was clear neither she nor her man had any experience, and I thought, well, here is the answer to all my prayers. A young woman in need of my particular expertise with a line on a game just waiting to be played. I agreed to help, with conditions, of course."

"Of course," said Tauton blandly.

"And so, I set to work on the girl."

"And her father?"

Mrs. Lynn smiled. "Oh no, that came rather later. First, I had to tutor the precious Miss Kinsdale as to how such a game is actually played, and how long it takes before one starts turning a profit. She was very impatient, and very angry. She wanted to run away with her man, yes, but more than that, she wanted to leave her father and her family flat-footed.

"But, despite this, she proved to be a good student and it was not too long before I was introduced to the rest of the family as her new bosom-beau, and matters proceeded very smoothly from there."

"What was the plan?"

"As I said, it was to be a swap. Mr. Spence had found a horse that could very well pass for Kinsdale's Pride. He demonstrated to my satisfaction that he possessed the skills to train a potential winner. We used the card parties—I assume your Mr. Harkness has told you about the card parties?" Tauton nodded and she continued. "We used the money raised there to pay for the care and feeding of the animal. If the scheme was to work, we had to be able to show at least *some* of the pigeons that our doppelgänger existed, and we needed her in good enough shape that it was plausible she could win the sweepstakes. That, unfortunately, was a somewhat costly proposition."

"So, it wasn't true that you were taking your share off the top?"

Mrs. Lynn didn't answer. Again.

"It all worked exceedingly well, for a time," she told him. "The rich patrons came to the parties. I had my people look them over and pick out the likeliest. Elizabeth would contrive to run into one or two at some innocuous spot. She'd feed them the story about the switch. If they insisted, she would arrange to show them the doppelgänger. Her man kept one eye on the horse at Lansdown, and another on our doppelgänger, and we were—if you will excuse the expression—raking it in."

Tauton could not help but notice that not once during this whole story had Mrs. Lynn mentioned her brother, Wallace, or her daughter, Miss Smith.

Well, well, blood's thicker after all.

"What was the plan if the doppelgänger lost?" he asked.

She smiled sweetly. "Oh, my dear Mr. Tauton, you cannot think we were actually going to run the race! That was the part of the plan that Elizabeth seemed to relish the most. We were all to disappear with the money the night before the race and leave her father, and Lord Casselmaine and both sisters, to take all the blame."

"What went wrong?"

Mrs. Lynn smiled sadly. "Mr. Tauton, do you know what is the most unfortunate truth about persons in my profession?"

Tauton could think of several answers, but understood none of them were wanted just now. "What is that, Mrs. Lynn?"

"We are always convinced we are the smartest people in any room. It may seem like a contradiction, but this can make us very easy to fool." She sighed, and for a moment Tauton was certain he saw real regret weighing down her lively features. "I didn't realize what Elizabeth's true plan was. I didn't understand that I was being set into place as a scapegoat so she could murder her father."

Tauton waited.

"That was their true plan from the beginning, you see. Elizabeth pushed her father out that window and blamed me." She faced Tauton fully and met his gaze. Tauton could read her intentions as easily as if she were an actress playing her part on the stage. Mrs. Lynn wanted to be seen and heard fully. She needed to be believed, and she understood this was her very last chance. "If you want to catch who killed Sir Anthony Kinsdale, you need to find his oldest daughter."

CHAPTER 45

To Understand the Full Situation

*"I am afraid you must have suffered from the
shock, and the more from its not overpowering
you at the time."*

Jane Austen, *Persuasion*

The knife must have been eight inches long, perhaps even ten. The blade curved like a wicked smile. It was the sort of instrument used at slaughtering time to dispatch pigs and sheep.

It could, in fact, have been mistaken for a short sword, thought Rosalind idly. Especially if one was already occupied with trying to climb out a window.

Though it took every ounce of strength she had, Rosalind calmly and deliberately lifted her eyes away from the knife blade and looked instead at Elizabeth Kinsdale. Elizabeth's manner, Rosalind noted, appeared calm and her person neatly arranged. She was plainly and practically dressed in stout boots and a simple forest-green dress with a high collar. She appeared stern and she was plainly angry, but she was not in the least afraid.

She is part of this thing. She has helped plan this thing.

The man beside Elizabeth was tall. His long face showed all the signs of days spent out in every sort of weather. The sun had bleached his hair bright gold and it made a dramatic contrast to his rich brown eyes. He held the long, curved slaughtering knife with a familiarity that sent a chill up Rosalind's spine. He did not once let his gaze flicker from her, or Adam. He did kick the door shut behind him.

"I'm glad to see you both awake," said Elizabeth. She slipped the basket she was carrying off her arm and held it out to Adam. "If you're planning on knocking me down, Mr. Spence has said he will kill you both, so please, do not try."

Adam gave Spence a long, measuring look.

"You take your dinner basket like a good boy," Spence said. His voice was low, and as steady as the hand that held the knife. "I'll kill your lady friend first, so help me, I will."

Somehow, it was this that made Rosalind find her voice. "Miss Kinsdale," said Rosalind. "What are you doing?"

"What I must, thanks to you." Elizabeth's voice was as steady as Mr. Spence's. She heard his threats, had repeated them to add her own emphasis, and she did not flinch in the least at doing so. Anger blazed through Rosalind. How dare either of them decide that their needs were more important than others' lives? How dare they lay hands on her? On *Adam*?

But Rosalind also felt a wave of sorrow wash through her. How trapped must these two feel to resort to this whole, desperate scheme?

The contradiction roiled her empty, uneasy stomach.

"If you'd let this matter rest when you were asked," said Elizabeth. "If you'd been able to keep your grubbing hands out of our affairs for just two more days, my father would be alive, Sylvia would be free, and *none* of this would be happening."

"And Admiral Walsingham?" Rosalind asked. "What about him?"

Mr. Spence's gaze jerked abruptly toward her. It was all Rosalind could do not to cringe away. Gathering her nerve, she made herself step forward and take the basket in her free hand, so Adam should not be encumbered if opportunities arose. He was holding himself very still, but she knew in his mind he was measuring distances. He was assessing Spence—his build, his position in the room, how he stood, how he held the knife. She did not need to watch his face to know this. It was simply what Adam would do.

"If you will just wait patiently," said Elizabeth. "This will all be over very shortly. We will be gone, and I will send the letter I've written to Clara explaining everything, and letting her know where you can be found."

"I'm sure you mean that," said Rosalind. "But—"

"Let's go, Beth," said Spence softly. "We've a lot to do."

"Yes, of course." Elizabeth opened the door. Spence backed away, putting himself between her retreating back and Adam. He nodded toward Rosalind and held up the knife. Adam's jaw tightened, but he did not move.

The door closed. Once again, they heard the sound of the key in the lock.

Rosalind let out a long breath.

"Did you know we'd see her?" asked Adam.

Rosalind shook her head. "I knew she was more than just Mrs. Lynn's dupe, but I was not sure how much more. I must assume, however, that Mr. Spence is the groom Sir Anthony so badly maligned."

"He's also Caleb, the inquisitive groom from the Lansdown stables."

"And the Kinsdales' back garden," added Rosalind.

"Are they lovers, do you think?"

"They are in love at the very least," said Rosalind. "And have been for quite some time."

"Perhaps the ring from the ashes was Elizabeth's."

"It is possible." Rosalind felt suddenly, terribly weary, and some of her dizziness was returning, but she steeled herself against it. She would not give in. Not now. Not while Adam could see. "Elizabeth helped oversee the Kinsdales' horses with her mother. She and Mr. Spence would have been together a great deal. And if Sir Anthony suspected that a common stable hand was laying hands on his daughter—"

Adam nodded. "That nonsense about poison might have been to cover over the fact that his daughter was caught in an affair of the heart?"

Rosalind sighed. "I should have suspected before. I should have—"

Adam laid his hand on her shoulder. "Don't," he said softly. "This is not your fault."

"No, of course, you're right." She attempted a smile. That didn't work, but she did manage a somewhat lighter tone. "Besides, we have more important matters to consider." She held up the basket.

Adam took the candle so that Rosalind could pull the cloth off the basket. Underneath, she found a cottage loaf and a wheel of fresh cheese. A small crock proved to be filled with potted meat. There was a crockery jug as well. Adam handed back the candle, pulled the cork, gave the contents a sniff, and took a careful sip.

"Small beer," he said.

"Well, we are not to starve, at least," said Rosalind. "Or languish in the dark." There were four candles in the bottom of the basket, although their captors had not seen fit to supply them with a flint. They would have to be very careful with their light.

The room was entirely unfurnished, so Rosalind set the basket down and gathered her skirts. Adam felt in his pockets and came up with a handkerchief that he used to solemnly dust off a portion of the floor. She looked at him. He bowed, his face entirely serious. Rosalind raised her hand, which he took, and helped her to sit down on the battered floorboards.

Adam uncorked the jug again and passed it to her so she could drink.

"Thank you." She raised it. "Your very good health sir."

It was a strange meal. Adam tore chunks of bread from the loaf, which they each dipped into the potted meat. The cheese they would save for later. They passed the jug back and forth between them like field hands. Despite everything, Rosalind felt grateful for the food. It eased the aches and the dizziness, and restored her equilibrium. Indeed, by the time they packed all the things away again, she was feeling almost herself again.

She also couldn't help but note that the candle had already burned halfway down. Rosalind met Adam's gaze. He didn't say anything, and neither did she. They both knew. The four candles they had been given would not last for long, especially since they were obligated to keep one burning to light the next from. Unless their captors could be induced to bring them more, any escape attempt needed to be made before their last candle burned away and left them in the dark.

Adam stood and went to the window again. A half knothole made a gap between two of the boards. He put his eye to it.

"Daylight still," he remarked. "Meadow around us, maybe some trees. So, we're in the countryside somewhere. Can't see much beyond that." He spoke in a whisper. Rosalind nodded, understanding. It was possible that someone was standing guard on the other side of the door.

"I gather we do not believe in this promise that we will be released shortly." Rosalind kept her tone light, but inside her heart shrank painfully.

"No," breathed Adam. "Having come this far, I don't think our lovers are going to risk leaving any witnesses behind."

"In that case, we should not linger unnecessarily." Rosalind got herself to her feet. She spoke easily, as if she feared they would be late to tea. She did not let herself inquire into how much fear she was keeping at bay, or how long she could manage it. "Do you have any ideas?"

"We're clearly at the top of whatever house this is, so the window would not be my first choice. Let's see what other chance we've got."

He took the candle from her. Then, moving carefully so as not to cause the boards to creak, he slipped up to the door, and squinted at the rusted hinges. He scrabbled his fingertips against the top hinge and managed to pull one of its pins out, just a little. He sucked a breath through his teeth, and Rosalind saw his eyes flash with satisfaction.

He settled the pin quietly back into place and retreated to the far side of the room. Rosalind followed, and stood so close she could feel his warmth against her skin.

"As I hoped. The pins are loose," he whispered. "We can pull them out, and that will allow us to take the door down without having to deal with the lock. But we'll need to wait until full dark," he told her. "And we'll have to get through the house without alerting our guards. What I don't know is what kind of watch our jailers have set. If there's more men here than we've seen yet—"

"I think I can find out," said Rosalind.

Adam bowed, and gestured for her to proceed. Rosalind curtsied in response. Then she returned to the front of the dingy room. There, she took a deep breath, ran to the door, and screamed at the top of her lungs.

CHAPTER 46

Fresh Employment

*. . . she was extremely glad to be employed, and
desired nothing in return but to be unobserved.*

Jane Austen, *Persuasion*

Normally, one's first day of work in a new house involved meeting the rest of the staff, settling into one's room, and being shown one's duties by the housekeeper.

"No time for that, I'm afraid, my girl," Miss Smith's cook told Amelia. "We need you to hop right to it. Now, no grumbling. It's the mistress's at home day, so we'll need the front hall tidy and you're going to be receiving the visitors."

After that came a lot of instructions about where to take the hats and walking sticks, to make sure to admit no one without a card, no matter how many flowers they brought, and above all, to spread the gentlemen out as they were waiting.

"Put one in the blue room, one in the bookroom, one in the salon," Cook puffed. "Put one in the garden if it comes to that. Just promise 'em she'll be down soon and get yourself out of there."

"And the ladies?" asked Amelia innocently.

"Bless me," said Cook. "If a lady comes to call, show them right up. Miss'll want to see such a rare bird."

So it was that Amelia found herself in the town house's foyer, straightening the flower arrangements and making sure that the table for hats—as well as the stand for umbrellas and sticks—was sheltered by the carved screen, so that no gentleman might know that others had proceeded him.

Wonder what Mrs. Black would have to say about all this? Miss Thorne's sister, now Mrs. Black, had had a colorful career, to say the least, and like Miss Smith, she'd kept her own establishment for quite some time. *I should ask her how she arranged things. Might come in handy to—*

The door banged open. Amelia jumped and spun about in time to see a pink-faced gentleman in a black coat bolt across the entrance hall. He thrust his dripping umbrella at her. It was pure reflex that made her grab for it. Not that he looked. He just ran up the stairs.

"Sophia! Sophia!"

Well.

This was too much to miss. Amelia tossed the umbrella toward the waiting stand and charged up the stairs after the intruder.

"Sir!" she bleated weakly. "Sir!"

As she expected—indeed hoped—he paid her no attention at all.

"Sophia!"

He was puffing badly by the time he reached the second floor. Micheals—Miss Smith's formidable lady's maid—stood in the corridor, her arms akimbo as if she might need to be ready to repel boarders. As Amelia reached the top of the stairs, Miss Smith herself was coming out of her boudoir, tying the sash on her wrapper.

"Uncle!" she cried. "What is it?"

"Trouble, I'm afraid, my dear," he wheezed. Exertion had

changed his complexion from pink to scarlet. "I've just come from your mother. We need to be on our way. How soon can you be packed?"

"Come from Mother?" echoed Miss Smith. "Why isn't she with you? I thought—"

"Not here, my girl." The man grabbed her elbow, steered her back into the boudoir, and shut the door.

Amelia stared at Micheals. Micheals stared at the door, her mouth compressed into a thin line.

"Miss Smith is not at home to visitors today," she announced.

"Yes, ma'am," said Amelia.

"Well?" demanded Micheals in a tone that meant "why are you still here?"

"Sorry, ma'am." Amelia bobbed a quick curtsy and hurried back down the stairs. When she reached the foyer, she hesitated. Then, she peeked out one of the sidelights. A plain carriage—probably hired—stood in the street. The driver was off the box, checking the harness and patting the horses. All signs that he thought he was leaving in the next few minutes.

Amelia bit her lip, thinking fast. Then, she whisked around and trotted down the servants' stairs to the kitchen.

"What was all that ruckus?" demanded Cook from her post at the kitchen counter where she was busy spreading butter on brown bread to make refreshments for the expected visitors.

"Miss Smith's uncle's arrived," said Amelia. "Micheals said no other callers today."

"Lord! What am I supposed to do with all these sandwiches!"

"I expect the gentleman will be very hungry. I'm to go out and speak to his driver." She nicked out the kitchen door before Cook could ask what about.

Amelia ran up the area stairs and nipped across the street as quick as she could. She also noted that a lanky man in laborer's clothes was strolling up the walk. He touched the brim of his cap to her, and walked straight past.

Amelia ignored him and instead went up to the driver. "Gentleman asked me to bring in his box," she said.

She wasn't exactly sure what she thought she'd find, or if she'd find anything at all, but she couldn't think of any better excuse to talk to the driver. He was a round man with a double chin and canny eyes. But he took in her neat maid's kit and made no protest, just opened the carriage door and pulled out two metal boxes.

Two cash boxes, in point of fact.

"Ta," said Amelia. "I'll take them."

"All right," said the driver. "And you might let Mr. Wallace know that if we're off for Dover today, we're going to need at least two changes of horses, and that's not counting the change before we leave town. These are run almost ragged, and I'm not injuring any animals just because he doesn't want to wait another hour."

"I'll tell him," agreed Amelia, and took herself briskly toward the area stairs.

A glance over her shoulder showed that the driver had gone back to his horses. Instead of heading down the stairs, Amelia ducked down the walk between the houses and emerged into the kitchen garden.

Where George, in his workman's dress, was waiting for her, behind the shed, and out of sight of the kitchen window.

"What's the to-do?" he asked as Amelia dropped the boxes in front of him.

"Miss Smith's uncle arrived out of the blue. He's getting her packed. Driver says they're to leave for Dover." *And doubtless for the Continent as soon as could be arranged after that.*

George swore, and tried the box latches. "Locked." He reached in his pocket and came up with a clasp knife. "Keep watch."

Amelia peered out around the shed, watching for signs of movement in any of the windows that overlooked the garden.

A few frantic heartbeats later, she heard a click, and then heard George whistle. Amelia turned, and saw him staring at the open box, and then saw the piles of bank notes and coins.

"I think we'd better get word to Mrs. Black," said George. "It seems to me something's gone wrong in Bath."

CHAPTER 47

In Captivity

". . . he had promised this and he had promised that . . ."

Jane Austen, *Persuasion*

Rosalind beat frantically against the locked door.
"Help!" she screamed. "Someone! Anyone! Please! Please!"
She hammered her fists against the chipped planks and sobbed.
"Please!"

"Hey!" shouted Adam helpfully. "Hey there!"

"Help me!" wailed Rosalind. She gestured to Adam and pursed her lips. He understood the signal, and blew out the candle, plunging the room into darkness.

Rosalind flattened both hands against the door, making a great show of pressing herself desperately against it. And she listened.

There. Footsteps down below. One step. No voices, though, at least none that she could hear.

One, two, three . . . Rosalind counted off the seconds steadily. . . . *Ten . . . eleven . . .*

The footsteps moved from floorboards to the stairs. . . . *Twenty-one,* Rosalind counted, *twenty-two, twenty-three . . .*

Now the steps sounded against the boards right outside their door. Rosalind sobbed several times, for effect. This was answered by the ragged scrape of the lock opening. Rosalind jumped back. The door swung inward.

It was Mr. Spence. He had his knife out, and held low, and pointed directly at Rosalind.

"I, I'm sorry," Rosalind gasped, and backed away slowly. She wiped at her face as if brushing away tears. "The candle went out. I do not . . . I don't like the dark," she whispered. For good measure, she gulped and wiped at her cheeks again.

Spence gaped at her. Then he burst out laughing and tucked the knife into his belt. Rosalind felt her cheeks burn.

"And this is the fearsome Miss Thorne they've all been so scared of!" Spence shoved his hand in his pocket and brought out a tinder box. "Well, you bring the candle here, missy. You—" He glowered at Adam. "You stay well back!"

Adam retreated to the far wall. Rosalind came forward doing her best to look timid, and perhaps even grateful, although she suspected she mostly looked like she was about to be sick. She held out the candle in its holder, and let her hand shake a little to put the seal on the performance.

Spence snorted.

"There's no need to keep on with this, Spence," said Adam.

"Sad to say, there is." Spence plied flint and steel over the candle's wick. "We've gone too far to do aught else. Would have thought you'd've noticed that, Harkness. You've a reputation as a clever man." At last, the wick caught and the candle's flame blossomed.

"You know you've already been cheated out of most of your take on this," said Adam.

"Aye," he answered flatly.

"So why keep your neck in the noose?"

"'Cuz I got no choice. That money's gone, and if we don't do something, it ain't comin' back. Now," he tucked the box away. "As Miss Kinsdale is otherwise occupied, you and me is going to have a little chat." He rested his right hand lightly on the knife's hilt and looked right through Rosalind as if she no longer mattered.

"Usually, I'm a patient man, Harkness," he said. "I'll allow that circumstances is bad, and a lady is entitled to a fuss. Once." He tapped his index finger once against the knife. "Next time, I'm taking your lady friend away with me, and you can just sit and wonder what may be happening to her. Any trouble after that, and I'm killing her, or maybe I'm killing you. We'll have to see. So, you can risk both your necks by making trouble, or you can sit quiet and wait and let this all be over soon. You understand me?" Now Spence looked at her, and his eyes were cold. But as Rosalind met his gaze, she saw fear there as well.

"Yes," she whispered. "Yes, I do."

"Good then."

He left them, and locked the door.

Rosalind drew herself up and glared at the door. A series of entirely shocking phrases and assessments paraded through her mind.

"So," remarked Adam. "We are left with a door that opens inward, we have our hands free, and with our warders anywhere from thirty seconds to a minute away, and down at least one flight of stairs. I think I should be offended they think so little of my reputation."

"I believe I'm the one who should be offended," said Rosalind crisply. "You will notice he did not once suggest I might be capable of leading our escape."

"Yes, I did notice and will be offended on your behalf, as soon as there's an opportunity."

"What should we do?"

"We should wait until dark," said Adam. "And in the meantime, we should be very careful with that candle."

CHAPTER 48

The Limits of Loyalty

... one half of her should not be always so much
wiser than the other half, or always suspecting the
other of being worse than it was.

Jane Austen, *Persuasion*

The trip up the Lansdown road had proved fruitless. There were some scrapes and tracks about a mile from the race-course that suggested a carriage might have gone off the road there, but there was nothing that they could follow, or draw any definite conclusions from. Devon was beside himself. Mr. Goutier was furious, it seemed, with the whole of the world.

And I? Clara asked herself. *What am I?*

Clara found she didn't even know.

She had expected to find that Mrs. Lynn was a gold digger. She had expected to find that the woman's family connections were inferior and her stories were false. She had thought she would lay that at her father's feet. With Cynthia's help, she also would be able to whisper it into the ears of those Father esteemed and who could convince him as to the truth of matters if (when) he would not listen to his daughters.

She had expected Mrs. Lynn would gather up her things and leave. Sometime after that, she would marry Devon and that would be the happy ending for her, as well as for her family.

But now Father was dead, and Admiral Walsingham was dead, and Miss Thorne and Mr. Harkness had vanished, Cynthia had retreated into herself, and Elizabeth . . . what was Elizabeth even doing?

Clara was afraid to find out.

She discovered Cynthia in the room that was called the library. It was, like the rest of the house, hung with silks and filled with art objects. But rather than being a place to house a collection of books, this room was reserved for curiosities. There were a dozen different tables and cabinets, all stuffed with curios and artifacts said to be from far distant lands and times. But Clara had found a key and opened one to examine a brooch that the label said had belonged to Queen Boudicca. However, a quick inspection—and a polish with a towel—had showed it to be nothing but glass and tin.

Still, the room had good light and it was generally quiet. Clara could understand why Cynthia had brought her writing desk down from their crowded sitting room. The day had turned oppressive, and at least down here the open windows seemed able to bring in some sort of breeze.

"Have you seen Elizabeth?" Clara asked her sister.

Mourning did not flatter any of them, but on Cynthia it looked particularly poor. The unrelieved black turned her complexion sickly. Laurel had been making a supreme effort with all their hair, but Cynthia's curls had already started to frizz.

"She's gone to Miss Summerscale," said Cynthia without looking up from her writing.

"*Now?*" cried Clara.

"Have mercy, Clara," murmured Cynthia. "She's lost more in this than either of us."

Clara felt herself gape at her sister.

"Cynthia, what's happened to you?"

"What do you mean?" But she spoke to her desk, and the half-completed page, not to Clara. She dipped her pen, wiped the nib on the blotter, and added a few more words to her missive.

"I mean it was you who sounded the first warnings about Mrs. Lynn and her influence over Elizabeth, even before we knew she'd gotten her hooks into father!" Clara strode around to stand in front of the table. She jerked the pen out of her sister's hand and dropped it into the inkwell, scattering black droplets across the marquetry. "It was you who first had the idea to ask Miss Thorne to come help us. Now, when Elizabeth had turned around and begun to lie about what she's seen, you take *her* side, as if she's nothing but a victim in all this!"

A light sparked in Cynthia's eyes, and Clara found herself strangely glad to see it. It was better than the dull, dead look that her sister had worn since yesterday.

"That's because she is a victim. We are all of us victims of this family, and we should hold together because of that, not pull ourselves apart!"

"We have also all made our choices—Elizabeth as well as you and I—and she has chosen to *lie* about how Father died."

"She isn't lying." Cynthia's voice was low, as if she did not dare to raise it. Clara could feel the emotion thrumming through her, but could not tell if it was fear or anger.

"She *is*," Clara cried. "And you're supporting her in her lie. *Why*, Cynthia?"

"She's only done what she had to and so have I," said Cynthia flatly. This was Cynthia at her most intractable—all displays of temper were wiped away now, and there was nothing left but the bare stone of her determination. "I'm sorry if you don't like it, but it is already done."

I do not accept that. I do not accept this. "Miss Thorne has gone missing, Cynthia."

Cynthia's brow furrowed. "What do you mean?"

"I mean Miss Thorne has gone missing," repeated Clara. "So has Mr. Harkness. They were lured away from their inn with a message telling them that Kinsdale's Pride had been stolen. But the man at the stables says they never arrived there, and no one has seen them since."

Cynthia swallowed. She swallowed again. She reached out to the letter she'd been working on, and turned it over, so that now only the blank side showed. Clara watched, her heart sinking under the weight of her fear, and her anger.

"It must be some of Mrs. Lynn's confederates," said Cynthia. "There was a scheme, you said—"

I have no time for this nonsense! "Where's Elizabeth gone, Cynthia?"

"I told you." Cynthia retrieved her pen from the inkwell. "She's gone to Miss Summerscale." She wiped the nib carefully. "That is the only answer I have."

Frustration robbed Clara of all speech. She slammed both hands on the table, rattling the desk and the inkwell, but making no change at all in her sister's expression. Clara was afraid she might actually scream. She turned on her heel instead, and strode out of the library.

The door swung shut behind her. Clara stopped dead in her tracks, uncertain where to go next, or what to do.

What can I do? She pressed her hands against her face. *What can I do?*

"Miss?"

Clara looked up. Mrs. Kendricks stood in front of her.

"Is there anything I can do, miss?" asked the housekeeper.

Staring into her anxious eyes, Clara felt an idea blossom inside her. At that same time, she felt her heart break.

"Mrs. Kendricks, I need you to get my sister out of the library."

"Miss?" she frowned.

"Please, do not ask. Just manage it."

"Yes, miss."

The library doors were flanked by a pair of large urns. They were purported to have come from the Summer Palace in Saint Petersburg. Clara suspected they were from the same Somersetshire shop that sold the counterfeit brooch.

They were, however, exactly what was needed now. Clara could stand behind one, and watch who came and went from the library, without being easily seen herself. She waited, shifting her weight impatiently, until she saw Mrs. Kendricks and Laurel come bustling up the corridor. Mrs. Kendricks scratched at the library door, waited for a moment, and then she and Laurel disappeared inside.

Please, please, please, Clara prayed. *Please. I'm sorry. I know I shouldn't be deceiving her, even now, but please. . . .*

The library door opened again. Clara shrank back deeper into her hiding place. Laurel came out, followed by an exceedingly annoyed-looking Cynthia. And then, a heartbeat later, came Mrs. Kendricks.

She carried a letter in her hand.

Clara sucked in a breath. Mrs. Kendricks must have heard, because she stopped, and she stood, watching, as Laurel and Cynthia vanished up the nearest set of stairs.

Then, she turned. Clara stepped out from her little nook.

"Did Cynthia give you that?" she asked.

"She asked for it to be taken by hand to a Miss Summerscale."

Clara's heart skipped a beat. "I wouldn't ask—"

"And if it was normal circumstances, I would never agree," replied Mrs. Kendricks stiffly. She glanced over her shoulder and then handed Clara the letter.

Clara ducked back into the library with Mrs. Kendricks behind her. The housekeeper needed no urging to keep her eyes on the door. Without hesitation, Clara broke open her sister's seal. Her eyes skimmed past the direction and the greeting to the body of the letter:

Be ready (she read). *Clara is coming and probably his nibs with her. Remember story of elopement.*
E. is counting on us both.

CHAPTER 49

After Nightfall

*" . . . but as long as we could be together, nothing
ever ailed me, and I never met with the smallest
inconvenience."*

Rosalind had not expected being abducted to prove such
a dull affair.

In novels it was always terribly thrilling and tended to involve ruined abbeys, mad monks, and the imminent risk of
losing one's virtue. Somehow, there was always a white nightdress involved, and a moonlit flight on bare feet.

Their captors, however, had so far neglected to take her
half boots, or provide a nightdress. The man to whom she
had lost the vast majority of her virtue was sitting on the
floor beside her with one arm draped around her shoulders.
They speculated about whether their friends had missed them
yet. They talked about Adam's brother, who might soon become senior clerk at the warehouse where he was employed,
and about what his mother had planned to make for their
upcoming wedding breakfast. They talked about improve-
ments that might be made to the house on Orchard Street
and the fact that Sir David had promised to raise Adam's

wages upon his marriage, and whether that meant they might be able to add to their staff, and perhaps even employ Mr. Goutier or Mr. Tauton on occasion to assist with various inquiries where their experience could prove useful.

They talked as if the door in front of them were open and they might walk through it at any time. As if the day were sunny and they were on their wedding trip. Because to do anything else was to invite panic and anger and blame, and they did not have the luxury of indulging in such feelings.

They paced across the floor, trying to find all the boards that might squeak and give them away. It was a strange, childish game and Rosalind was surprised to find herself smiling once or twice.

At some point it began to rain. The roof proved to be in want of repair. Rivulets ran down the filthy walls, and individual drops plunked onto the floor. The mice rustled and squeaked, and Rosalind wished desperately for a glass to shelter the candle.

They dozed in turns, with one person staying awake to mind their precious light. Rosalind felt sure she could not possibly sleep, but Adam insisted she try.

"You'll do no good if you're tired, or if you have a dizzy spell when you need to be clearheaded," he said.

To her surprise, Rosalind did eventually manage at least a short nap. Adam, enviably, was asleep and snoring the minute he closed his eyes. Later he told her it was a skill he'd learned in his time with the horse patrol.

"You had to be able to sleep anywhere, at any time, because you never knew when you were going to be up all night hunting a highwayman."

At last, their tiny knothole showed that it was fully dark. Rosalind touched Adam's shoulder. He came awake as quickly as he'd fallen asleep.

They had one candle left.

"It's been quiet downstairs," she said.

Adam nodded. He got to his feet. He went to the door. Rosalind set the candle on the floor out of the way, and then set her back against the door. Adam nodded.

Adam's careful fingers got a grip on the first pin and drew it out. The door sagged gently against Rosalind's shoulders. The boards creaked. They both froze, but there was no sound below. Adam put the pin in his coat pocket and reached to find his grip on the second.

We'll have one chance, Adam had said while they were waiting for darkness. Rosalind knew he was right. There would be no way to conceal what they had done, and nowhere to retreat or to hide if their plan went wrong. Their only chance was to move quickly.

Adam found the second pin and eased it out of the hinge. The door hitched against Rosalind's shoulders. She pressed it back, trying to hold it level so it would not weigh too much on the last pin and cause it to jam in place.

Still no sound came from below. Rosalind bit her lip. Adam rubbed his fingertips, squatted down, and scrabbled at the third pin. He twisted and he pulled. It drew out slowly. The whole weight of the door leaned itself against Rosalind's back.

Adam quickly pocketed the third pin. He grasped the door, taking the weight and allowing Rosalind to slip sideways. He peered into the gap between the door and the frame, and nodded to her. So far, the way was clear.

Rosalind blew the candle out.

Darkness dropped at once, impenetrable and absolute. Rosalind squeezed her eyes shut, hard, willing them to adjust. She felt rather than saw Adam moving the door. She stepped backward, just remembering to pull her hems out of the way so she didn't stumble.

She opened her eyes and found she could now differentiate between the shadows, which was better than feeling she'd been struck blind. She could make out Adam as a silhouette in motion against the deeper darkness. He folded the door backward so it leaned against the wall. The latch—now the only thing holding the door to its frame—strained and creaked. Rosalind's heart leapt into her throat. But there was still no sound from below.

Should that worry us? she wondered, but she did not want to take the risk of asking the question out loud. She tried to tell herself the sound of the rain would drown out the sound of movement, but she could not make herself believe it.

Adam found her hand with his. He leaned in close enough that his lips brushed her ear. "I'll go first. Keep moving, no matter what. Our only goal is to get out of here."

She pressed his fingers, signaling she understood. He pulled away and she followed him out the open door and down the stairs.

She tried to move smoothly, to keep plowing forward as instructed, but it was hard. The boards creaked underfoot. The rain drummed relentlessly overhead and the wind whistled under the eaves. The whole house seemed to sigh with the effort of having to keep standing another night.

They reached the bottom of the stairs. Rosalind could smell smoke and the remains of cooked cabbage. A fire had been lit, it told her. Supper had been made. Someone had been here recently.

Where are they now?

She knew Adam was thinking that as well. Dark as it was, she could see the tension in his movements. It was not possible their jailers had left them alone. And yet this house, whatever and wherever it might be, seemed empty.

Perhaps we were lucky. But Rosalind knew better than to put faith in that.

She laid her hand on Adam's shoulder, turning him toward the cabbage smell. Whatever sort of house this might be, the kitchen could be counted on to have a door to the outside. Adam touched her hand briefly, letting her know he understood. He glided like a ghost down the narrow corridor until they reached the kitchen.

The darkness here was not quite as deep as in the stairwell and the corridor. There was a tiny window, but that only showed them slick fingers of rain streaking down thick glass. What little light there was came from the faint glow of embers that had been carefully banked under a bed of ashes.

Someone had taken care of the fire. Someone meant to come back. But where had they gone?

Adam was lifting a patch of shadow from the dark expanse of the wall. It took Rosalind a moment to realize it was a cloak. She bundled herself into it, and then she grabbed the tinder box off the hearth's mantel and passed it to him along with several splinters from the can waiting there. There was a lamp as well. She tucked it under her cloak. Wherever they went, they'd need to see the way, and a lamp would burn more reliably than a candle in this rain.

Her heart was hammering, keeping time with the rain and the one thought occupying her mind:

Where are they? Where are they? Where are they?

Adam turned toward her. She had a glimpse of his eyes, and the hard line of his jaw. He was reminding her they needed to keep moving. She nodded. He pulled the door open and they plunged out into the rain.

It was as if someone had upended a bucket overhead. Rosalind gasped and would have drawn back, but Adam was already clutching her hand and dragging her forward. Awkwardly because she had to keep hold of the pilfered lamp, she grabbed her hems. She hiked them as high as she could so she would not trip as they splashed and stumbled their way across a stony yard toward a sprawl of shadow Rosalind guessed to be an outbuilding.

Despite the rain, the faint smell of horses reached her. *It's the stables*. Of course. There was no knowing where they were or how far they had been taken from Bath, or anywhere else. If they were to make good their escape, they would need horses.

They would deal with the fact that Rosalind could not ride when that became necessary. Perhaps there would be a wagon, or even the coach that had brought them here.

Adam shoved the stable door open and dragged them both inside. Rosalind felt like she was a drowning sailor suddenly cast onto a dry shore.

A horse—startled and clearly annoyed—whickered angrily and stomped and shifted in its box.

"Eas—" began Adam. But he got no further.

Light exploded around them. Reflex clamped Rosalind's eyes shut.

"Well," said a woman. "Nathanial was right."

Rosalind's eyes flew open. There, in front of them, with a lantern in one hand and a black cloth in the other, stood Elizabeth Kinsdale.

CHAPTER 50

Miss Summerscale's Predicament

. . . it did not surprise her, therefore, that Lady Russell should see nothing suspicious or inconsistent, nothing to require more motives than appeared . . .

Jane Austen, *Persuasion*

A s a girl, Clara had enjoyed dramas. She had constantly pestered her sisters and her mother to help act out plays she had written. She'd even read some to the horses, when none of her family could be persuaded to listen.

That girl would have enjoyed this moment, marching into a drawing room like Queen Elizabeth on her way to face down the Spanish Armada with a duke at her side and officers at her back.

The Clara of now—who had seen rather too much drama for comfort—simply hoped it would all work. And that she would not be sick or faint in front of Devon.

Olivia Summerscale and her family came to Bath every year so that her mother could take the waters and her father could attend the races. They always took the same house—a modest residence right in the middle of town. Mr. Summer-

scale liked the bustle, and Mrs. Summerscale liked the proximity to the baths.

The footman balked at admitting them until Devon presented his card. Then, they were shown into the neat little
parlor with its blue walls and comfortable furnishings. The
lamps had all been lit, rendering the room cozy, despite the
driving rain outside. Mr. Goutier and Mr. Tauton moved to
stand on either side of the windows, where, Clara could not
help but notice, they would be able to watch both doors to
the room.

Olivia herself appeared a few moments later. "Miss Kinsdale! Your grace! This is . . . unexpected."

"We do realize that, Miss Summerscale, and I apologize
for the intrusion," said Clara, because she must say something.

"Not at all!" said Olivia. "It is I who must apologize for
not being ready to receive. I was not expecting anyone at this
hour." Olivia clearly took note of the two officers, but as
they had not been introduced, she could not properly remark
on them.

"We're looking for Elizabeth," Clara told her.

"Elizabeth?" Olivia didn't even blink. She did, however,
let her gaze stray once more to Mr. Tauton and Mr. Goutier.
"I'm sorry, she is not here."

"Where is she?" asked Devon.

Olivia's pause was brief. Clara found herself wondering
what lie she would tell.

"Well on the way to Gretna Green by now, I should expect," she said at last.

Clara made no answer. Olivia, apparently assuming that
Clara had been stunned into silence, touched her hand sympathetically.

"I understand this is a shock, and I am sorry for that,"
Olivia said. "But I very much hope you will be able to come to

terms with it. Elizabeth has eloped with Nathanial Spence," she declared. "And yes, they had my help to do it."

She waited, very visibly steeling herself against whatever outraged display they might choose to make.

Clara looked to Devon. Devon nodded.

"I understand that is what you were asked to say, Olivia," Clara said. "But I need to know where she really is."

Olivia's mouth opened, but no sound came out. Quickly she assumed an attitude of outrage. "Are you suggesting that I have lied to you?"

A fresh wave of exhaustion overtook Clara. She gestured to Devon. He had already pulled the letter she'd intercepted from Cynthia out of his coat pocket. Now, he handed it to Olivia.

Olivia looked at him, and at Clara, and at the officers. She opened the letter and read.

"You had no business with this," she snapped. "It was private!"

Clara's patience snapped. "Olivia, that is not the point! Do you know where Elizabeth is or not?"

"You should be ashamed of yourself." Olivia drew herself up, very much on her dignity. "You should understand that Elizabeth is only doing this because she had no other choice."

There were times when something in Devon's presentation of himself shifted; when, suddenly, he was no longer Devon Winterbourne, who danced badly, rode beautifully, was happy to sit up all night with a dog while she whelped, and would be tenderly amazed by all the puppies. Instead, he was Lord Casselmaine, head of one of the oldest houses in England, who addressed Parliament, dined with the king, and was absolutely done with this nonsense in front of him.

"Listen to me, Miss Summerscale," he said evenly. "This isn't about love, or even family anymore. It's about murder. Sir Anthony was murdered. Admiral Walsingham was murdered. The man who is responsible for at least one of these deaths may be with Elizabeth now. The longer she stays with him, the more danger she is in of being put up on the gallows beside him." He paused, and then added, "And you, Miss Summerscale, are in danger of making yourself into their accomplice."

This, finally, seemed to reach Olivia. Her bluster wavered, and her face turned pale.

"You are trying to frighten me."

"I am trying to make you understand the reality of your position," said Devon. "You should also know that these men"—he nodded toward Mr. Goutier and Mr. Tauton—"are officers of Bow Street and if you persist in sheltering Nathanial Spence any further, they will take you in charge."

Mr. Tauton and Mr. Goutier did not move. They did not need to. Their presence was enough. Tears sprang into Olivia's eyes, and she raised a trembling hand to her mouth.

Clara's heart went out to her. This was not what Olivia had bargained for. She thought she was helping a friend to a rather ordinary escape, not taking the risk of becoming tangled in an investigation into two deaths.

Clara watched the other woman set her jaw. Her heart stopped. She couldn't breathe.

She cannot refuse to answer. She cannot.

"I don't know for certain," Olivia whispered.

Clara's relief was so intense that it drained the last of her strength from her. Darkness swam at the edges of her vision and for a moment, she was afraid she would faint.

Olivia swallowed. "But Elizabeth told me once that Mr. Spence's cousin had given him the use of a cottage. Mr. Spence was to look after the place while the cousin went out to Canada to see if he could make a start there. It was his way of helping after Mr. Spence lost his place with Sir Anthony."

"Where is this cottage?" demanded Devon.

Miss Summerscale's hands trembled. "Haven't I said enough?"

"No, Olivia," said Clara. "You know you have not."

"She is my friend," Olivia pleaded. "She begged my confidence. She didn't know. . . ." She gulped back tears. "I didn't know."

Clara made herself step closer, made herself take both of Olivia's hands. "I understand," she said. "But now you do know, and you must help us to help her."

"Yes." Olivia wiped at her nose. Devon held out his handkerchief, because it was the natural thing for him to do. Olivia stared at the square of linen for a moment, and then took it.

"It's close," she said, wiping her eyes and her nose. "Just off the road to Cold Ashton, about three miles or so from Lansdown, I think," she said. "Now please, I'd like you to go."

But they were already gone.

CHAPTER 51

The Consequences of Failure

. . . and all that remained was to marshal themselves . . .

Jane Austen, *Persuasion*

Rosalind froze where she stood. From the corner of her eye, she saw Adam raise his hands.

"One move toward her," grated Spence from behind Rosalind, "and I'll shoot you both dead, so help me I will."

Now, Rosalind raised her own hands, although more awkwardly, because she was still cradling the unlit lamp.

Adam turned, and Rosalind turned with him.

Spence stood between them and the stable door. He still had his knife, but it was sheathed at his belt. In his hands, he held a shotgun, and it was pointed straight at Adam.

"What is the matter with you two?" demanded Elizabeth, storming forward to stand beside Spence. "I told you! All you had to do was wait quietly. God in heaven!" She shook her head. "I'm sorry, Nathanial. I thought they'd be rational. What should we do now?"

"What we said," answered Spence. "Separate them. Let them understand that the other will be safe only as long as they behave themselves." He set the gun's stock against his shoulder. "You take her. I'll take care of Mr. Harkness, here."

For one wild minute, Rosalind wanted to beg. *Please, please, don't hurt him. We'll do anything you say, just don't hurt him. . . .*

But Adam was not begging, nor trembling. Adam was not even blinking. He had gone absolutely still, his attention entirely fixed on Spence, and the gun. Rosalind shoved all her fear behind her. She would not cower. Not here, not now. Whatever came next, she would not do that.

Elizabeth moved to the wall and pulled down a leather strap from among the harnesses, bridles, and other equine accoutrement hanging there. Rosalind could not tell which bit of tack it was, and this left her feeling absurdly frustrated.

Elizabeth moved to stand in front of Rosalind and seemed to take her full measure for the first time.

"What's under there?" She set the lantern down and dug underneath Rosalind's cloak and found the lamp she'd held in the crook of her elbow. She held it up. "Oh, excellent. I was afraid I might have to lead you around in the dark, and I know you do not like that." She set the lamp down beside the lantern. "Now, give me your wrists."

The presence of Spence and his shotgun made any thought of resistance impossible, so Rosalind did as she was told. Elizabeth wrapped the strap twice around Rosalind's wrists and cinched it tight.

"There." Elizabeth stepped back, as if admiring her handiwork. "I'll put her in the stillroom," she said to Spence.

"Good idea," he grunted.

Elizabeth lit the lamp, lifted it up, and took hold of the long end of Rosalind's strap in her free hand. "Come along, Miss Thorne."

Rosalind looked toward Adam. He met her gaze, although

his face remained as still as the rest of him. But Rosalind read all the feeling in his eyes. And knew he saw hers.

They would find each other again. No matter what.

Spence kept the gun pointed at Adam while Elizabeth led Rosalind back out into the pouring rain. Raindrops hissed against the lamp's glass housing and the flame guttered as the drops touched the wick. They crossed the cobbled yard, splashing straight through the many puddles, until they came to a low building

"Hold that." Elizabeth thrust the lamp into Rosalind's hands and moved to unbar a door. For a wild moment, Rosalind thought about running into the dark. But which way would she go, and what would happen to Adam? Even if she dared to risk flight, she would surely be caught, and with her hands bound like this, she could hardly fight off Elizabeth, let alone Spence and his shotgun.

Rosalind ground her teeth together in frustration.

Elizabeth had the door open. She took the lamp from Rosalind's hands and ushered them both inside. The flickering lamplight showed Rosalind the blocky remains of an ancient brick stove, some dusty shelves, and a single cracked bottle that had been left behind as a last testament to the cordials and syrups that had once been brewed here.

The stillroom had one window, high up over the stove. It was more of a vent, really, with a wooden screen over it instead of glass.

"Sit there." Elizabeth gestured to the corner. There was no furniture. Rosalind sat on the floor, an awkward business with her hands tied as they were. "Put your legs out straight."

Once more, Rosalind did as she was told. What choice did she have?

Elizabeth shoved Rosalind's skirts aside and produced another leather strap. This she wrapped around Rosalind's ankles.

"What is it you still hope to accomplish, Elizabeth?" Rosalind asked her as she worked. "You cannot possibly manage your substitution scheme now."

"Poor Pride," Elizabeth murmured. "Do you know, the only reason we even still have her is that no one would buy her from us? But no." She sighed and sat back on her heels. "You're right. We cannot enter that race, not that we'd ever planned to."

"Then what—"

"I rather think it's none of your business." Elizabeth stood and dusted off her hands. "But, if you must know, Spence has informed Mrs. Lynn's confederates that if they don't want to be implicated in my father's murder, and maybe the admiral's as well, they'll hand over the money she stole from us."

"She stole from you?" said Rosalind.

"She robbed us," Elizabeth spat. "At least, she was planning to. She meant to slip away ahead of our agreed upon time, with all the money. What a pretty pair of fools we must have looked to her!"

"And that's why you've turned on her?"

"She deserves it," Elizabeth sneered. "And much more. She is the reason my father is dead and that we are any of us in this mess. Including you and your man out there." She jerked her chin toward the door.

"You know that it was Mr. Spence who killed Admiral Walsingham," said Rosalind softly.

Elizabeth bit her lip. She was sorry, but once again, she was not surprised.

"That was my fault," she said. "I should never have told Nathanial about the admiral bursting in on us as he did. But I was afraid. Walsingham said he'd been to the stables. He'd guessed the plan, or I thought he had. If he told people . . ." she didn't finish that. "Nathanial never wanted to kill him."

"And your father?"

"Nathanial had nothing to do with his death." Her answer was quick, her voice certain. Rosalind found she was inclined to believe it.

"Was it you, then?" Rosalind asked.

"I have nothing more to say to you."

"All I ask is that you tell me why you are still here. If you were planning to escape, why not just go—"

"We need the money," said Elizabeth bluntly. "Canada is a long way from here, and starting a new life does not come cheap. You and Mr. Harkness cannot be allowed to interfere while we're waiting for Mrs. Lynn's people to bring us what we are owed. When we have the money in hand, we will leave and you will be released, as I promised."

"I do not think her confederates will agree to pay you."

Elizabeth lifted her chin. "Her confederates are a set of cowardly moneylenders. They will do as they are told."

"Her confederates," said Rosalind, "are her brother and her daughter."

"*What?*" cried Elizabeth.

Rosalind arched her brows in mock surprise. "You did not know? Mr. Wallace, who dealt with the moneylenders at the card parties, is Mrs. Lynn's brother. And her daughter was working in London to bring yet more gamblers."

"Of course," said Elizabeth. "She told me all about it."

But she was lying. Here, at last, Rosalind saw she had a chance. If Elizabeth could be convinced matters were not under as much control as she thought—if she understood there was more to this than she knew—her confidence might be shaken, she might be ready to change her mind about the risks she and Spence were running.

"Mr. Wallace has already left Bath," said Rosalind. "I expect he has gone to fetch the daughter, and to fly with her. Neither he nor Mrs. Lynn would allow the young woman to be entangled in an affair that has become a hanging offense."

"Then Mrs. Lynn will hang in her daughter's place," said Elizabeth coldly. "This Wallace must know that."

Rosalind met Elizabeth's gaze. "I expect she has accepted this."

Elizabeth snorted. "You give her far too much credit."

"Do I?" asked Rosalind. "Will you bet your future on that? Your life? Think, Elizabeth. How much have you and your sisters done for each other, *and* your father, even after he had driven you all to ruin? A parent will do as much for a child."

Elizabeth looked toward the door. Her mouth moved, shaping silent words. Rosalind held her breath.

Elizabeth took up the lamp and walked out the door without looking back.

Having gotten a look at the attic room, and what had happened to the door, Spence decided to take Adam down to the root cellar.

He made Adam carry the lantern, so he could follow behind with the gun pointed right at Adam's back. The lantern's unsteady light showed the cellar's rough, earthen walls and hard-packed floors. There were some wooden shelves littered with sacks and boxes, along with some coils of cord of the sort that would be useful for hanging washing and binding sacks. Some rakes and shovels leaned in the corner.

"Stop there," Spence ordered him, and Adam stopped.

"Don't you move."

Adam didn't move. He thought about it. He could swing the lantern, blind Spence for a moment, make him drop the gun. . . .

But it was already too late. Spence had braced the gun against his hip, and grabbed up one of the coiled lengths of cord.

"Lie down, on your back, keep that lantern up."

Again, Adam did as he was told. He laid flat on his back and held his arms straight up, the lantern balanced on his cupped palms. It was a smart decision, he thought idly. It would be very hard for him to launch any kind of attack from this angle.

Spence leaned the gun against the wall, and laid the knife on the floor, where he could get to it well before Adam.

He wrapped the cord tight around Adam's wrists, making the light judder.

"You can still get yourself out of this, Spence."

"Too late for that." Spence yanked his knot tight and then sliced the cord off with his knife.

"Because you killed Admiral Walsingham?" asked Adam.

Spence didn't answer, which was answer enough. "We never wanted any of this," he said through gritted teeth as he set about trussing up Adam's legs with the rest of the cord. "We wanted to get married. That's all." He drew the knot so tight Adam winced, and the lantern in his hands wobbled again. "We didn't even plan to stay and embarrass her family. We planned to go to Canada, buy a bit of land, raise a new line of horses there. All we needed was the money."

Adam said nothing, just let the man talk. He kept his attention on the gun against the wall, and on the shelves, and all the tools arrayed around them.

"At first we thought we could get some money out of her father," Spence was saying. "Elizabeth was sure she could talk him around, or maybe fake an engagement with some indebted titled fool so he'd have to offer up a dowery of some kind. The fool would take a share and disappear before the wedding, and we'd run away with the rest.

"But then we found out there was no money. None." He sheathed the knife, and stood, lifting the lantern off Adam's palms. "That blind fool who called himself her father was living on his credit, and whatever could be scraped together on the quarter day. We couldn't even rob him," he spat again. "So, we decided that we'd have to try something else."

"Was that why she killed him?" Adam asked.

"She didn't kill him."

"Who did?"

"I wish to God I knew." Spence took up his gun. "I'd beat their fool head in with my bare fists."

CHAPTER 52

The Plan

*"You can imagine what an artful man would do;
and with this guide, perhaps, may recollect what
you have seen him do."*

Jane Austen, *Persuasion*

Devon was familiar with his own anger. He knew the rush and the burn of it. Knew the way it tightened his sinews and sharpened his vision, even as it dulled all sense of right and wrong. The way it demanded action and would not be denied.

But not like this. Never like this. Anger had never burned so strong in his blood and in his brain; never made him want to howl like a madman and tear down walls like he did now. All because Clara was sitting beside him in the carriage, cold and quiet, putting up a mask to hide how badly her heart was breaking. Clara was looking out at the rain spattering against the carriage windows because if she looked at him, she would begin to cry, and she would not permit herself to do such a thing in front of strangers.

And she wanted to cry. She wanted to rage, like he did. He could see it in her. He had seen her rage over incompetence, unkindness, and sheer, stupid stubbornness. He understood down to his bones what she felt because her sister and this Mr. Spence had decided that they would rather try to get what they needed by theft than by asking for help.

And now they had stolen not just money but lives, and persons. Rosalind. His first love, whom he now loved as the sister he'd never had. Harkness. The man she loved, whom he respected, and called friend.

Spence should be glad he is not here. He should be glad I cannot order Tauton and Goutier to hold him down while I finish matters.

This was not like him, and he knew it, but he was not himself. This anger left no room for Devon Winterbourne to exist.

"What can we do now?" Devon asked the officers sitting knee to knee with him and Clara.

"We can't go out there in this filthy weather," said Tauton. His voice was flat and final. He was angry, too, as was Goutier. Good. He was not alone in this burning, black place. He had allies here.

"But even when it clears, then what?" Goutier asked, frustration plain in his voice. "Do we call in Layng's constables and the militia? Risk a standoff? We don't know who this Spence has out there with him, and we don't know what he's capable of."

No one seemed to have an answer for that. The rain drummed on the carriage roof, muffling even the sounds of the horses' hooves.

"We don't know Spence," whispered Clara. "But we do know Elizabeth."

The men waited. Devon forced his way past his own anger, so that he could be present, because she needed him now. Not his fury. *Him.*

"Elizabeth is practical," Clara said. "And she is stubborn. She believes there is a solution for every problem, and she will try them all before she gives up." She swallowed. He willed her to be strong. "If she did this for money, then we should offer her money."

"Miss Kinsdale, are you saying that we should offer a ransom?" asked Tauton. "And then what?"

Clara's mouth moved. Probably, Devon was the only one who was close enough to see the words her lips shaped. *Let them go.*

But that was not what she said out loud. "Devon and I can go to this cottage. We can bring money, we can promise"—she faltered—"we can promise they will be allowed to go free. But we have men in place to follow them once they do leave."

Devon looked to Goutier and Tauton. They were ignoring him, and looking instead at each other.

"It's a start," said Goutier. "Might offer us a chance."

"I'm assuming, your grace can lay hands on the ready?" asked Tauton gruffly.

"I can," Devon told them. "We can set out just as soon as the weather clears."

"Then that's what we'll do," said Goutier. "We'll just have to hope that until then Harkness and Miss Thorne have all their usual luck."

CHAPTER 53

In Separate Rooms

. . . she felt a moment's regret. But they should meet again. He would look for her, he would find her out before the evening were over . . .

Jane Austen, *Persuasion*

When Elizabeth left her alone in the darkened stillroom, the first thing Rosalind did was to stand up.

With her hands and feet bound as they were, the process was slow, tremendously undignified, and involved several false starts. But at last, by a combination of pressing her back against the wall, digging her heels against the edge of a crooked flagstone, and sheer determination, she did manage to inch, wriggle, and will herself into a standing position.

She felt weak as water. The strap had begun to bite into her wrists, but worse than that was the cold. The rain had soaked through her cloak to her dress, and that—along with the cold from the stones she'd been sitting on—had stolen all the warmth from her body. Even just standing with her back pressed against the wall, she was shaking so badly she was sure that she was going to fall over again.

For a moment, she had considered doing as she'd been

told. Just staying still. Just waiting for someone to come set her free. But in the middle of this moment of weakness, memory had surfaced. It was Adam's voice, soft and serious.

Having come this far, I don't think our lovers are going to risk leaving any witnesses behind.

The thought caused her to sob, a final indignity. At the same time, a burst of anger surged through her. It gave her the strength she needed. Rosalind tightened all the muscles in her abdomen, and forced herself to take a tiny step away from the wall. There was a shelf up above the carcass of the brick stove. She remembered that. On that shelf, there had been a bottle. It gleamed in her mind's eye. That bottle was her chance.

Because she and Adam were witness to all that Elizabeth and Nathanial had done. Because if they were brought to court, it was Rosalind and Adam's testimony that would hang them both.

But there was something more than this. Rosalind knew that wherever they had taken him, Adam was looking for a way out. The least she could do was be ready to meet him when he found it.

Rosalind tightened her stomach, swallowed her fear, and moved herself another inch forward.

When Adam was a boy, he'd spent a long stretch of time on a country estate. There, he'd made friends with a man named Joshua. Joshua took care of the gardens at the local vicarage. What made that remarkable was that Joshua was stone blind.

He was the only gardener the vicar employed, and yet the gardens were beautiful. Adam had followed the man about like a puppy, trying to understand how he could even take two steps forward, let alone tend such a variety of plantings.

Joshua could have chased him away. Doubtlessly, the man faced enough ignorant or pitying inquiries without having to deal with a boy's crass questions. But he didn't. He let Adam stay, made Adam help, and he talked.

"The secret is to make friends with the dark," he said. "Dark's my ally. Keeps me sharp, keeps the distractions away. Lets my hands, my ears, my nose, my *mind*"—he'd tapped his forehead—"do the needful work."

Later, when Adam joined the horse patrol, he remembered Joshua's words. It was following that advice that gained him such a reputation that the newspapers dubbed him "Watchdog Harkness."

Adam remembered those words, that practice, now. The darkness was his friend. The darkness would let him work. If he let it, it would help get him and Rosalind out of here.

So Adam held himself still. He kept his eyes open, letting them focus and find any light there might be. He listened. He heard the rustle and scratch of the mice and the rats, but nothing else.

Adam sat up. It wasn't easy. It would have been even harder if Spence had thought to tie his hands behind him. He hadn't, however, and Adam was grateful for that small mercy.

Once he was on his bottom, Adam wriggled, and twisted, and shoved, until he got himself onto his knees. From there, he was able to lever himself to his feet.

Adam paused, waiting for his breathing to slow and his senses to orient themselves. He let his mind's eye open.

There were shelves around him, he remembered. It was a root cellar, and it stored all manner of things that might become useful in the future. He had seen boxes and sacks—old and dusty and probably mostly empty. There were those shovels, and the rakes, however. That might be useful.

And there was something else. Adam's brow furrowed. A crock? No. It was a pouch. It had stuck in his mind, colliding oddly with the memory of discovering the attic window had been nailed shut. Why, of all the detritus he'd seen, was he remembering that?

Trust that instinct. He told himself. *Find the thing.*

For one heartbeat, Adam thought of the danger—of stumbling, of falling again, of losing his way in the dark and this whole desperate escape attempt dissolving into farce. He thought of Spence's threat to kill Rosalind. He would do it. He would hurt her. Would spill her blood across the ground and in doing so bring the world to an end.

If he lay back down, he might save her life, save his whole world.

But he remembered her sitting in the dusty attic, as poised as if she were in her parlor, turning to him and calmly inquiring.

"I gather we do not believe in this promise that we will be released shortly?"

I gather we do not believe in this promise that we will be released when they have accomplished their . . . task?

And he remembered his answer.

No. Having come this far, I don't think our lovers are going to risk leaving any witnesses behind.

But beyond all that, he knew, like he knew his own heartbeat, that Rosalind away in the old stillroom, wherever it might be, was already looking for a way out. And he knew she was counting on him to do the same.

Adam moved.

Traversing the width of the stillroom might well have been the hardest thing Rosalind had ever done. She hopped and tiptoed and shuffled. She gasped and cried and screamed through her teeth in frustration. She nearly fell half a dozen times. She cursed her skirts, mourned her lost dignity, and tried to imagine how this business would unfold in one of Alice's novels.

Alice, she thought, would have managed to provide her heroine with both a white nightdress, and a knife.

Well, we will just have to make do. She set her jaw and managed another hop.

The rain had let up. The world outside the window was still mostly dark, but the false dawn had turned the room pale gray. She was grimly certain that daylight would bring either Elizabeth or Spence back to check on her.

At last, breathless and shaking, she reached the old stove. She ran her hands over the bricks, and found a crack where the mortar had begun to crumble. It was not big, but it might serve her purposes.

On the narrow shelf overhead waited the one lonely bottle, forgotten by everyone but the spiders who had used it as a support around which to build their webs.

The skin on Rosalind's fingertips crawled with revulsion as she reached through those webs to grab the bottle and bring it down. She did not let herself think, or hesitate. She turned the bottle so she held its neck. Then, she turned her head away, and squeezed her eyes shut, and brought the bottle crashing down against the bricks.

Glass shattered. Shards scattered across the bricks and the floor. Rosalind laid the bottle neck carefully down on the edge of the stove, and awkwardly bent to pick up the largest of the broken shards. The wicked edge sliced through her finger. She hoped the blood would not interfere with her grip.

Working as carefully as she could, she used the shard's corner to pick away at the crack in the mortar she had found before. Slowly, she enlarged it, until she could jam the shard into the gap until it protruded from between the bricks like a wicked fang.

Rosalind rested the edge of the leather strap that bound her wrists against the edge of the glass shard. She prayed her makeshift knife would hold steady; prayed it would not break; prayed she would not cut herself too badly; prayed she could make this work.

Slowly, carefully, she began to saw.

CHAPTER 54

The Gamble

. . . here was that elasticity of mind, that disposition to be comforted, that power of turning readily from evil to good, and of finding employment which carried her out of herself, which was from nature alone.

Jane Austen, *Persuasion*

As Rosalind had guessed, Elizabeth came to check on her shortly after dawn. Rosalind watched from her place behind the door as Elizabeth paused on the stillroom's threshold, surprised by the broken glass scattered on the flagstones. Did she see the blood as well? Rosalind wondered.

It does not matter.

Rosalind slammed the door shut.

Elizabeth jumped and spun. Now she saw Rosalind between her and the door, and saw the neck of the broken bottle that Rosalind clutched in one bloodied hand.

"Sit down, Elizabeth." Rosalind raised the jagged bottle neck as if it were a knife. "With your back against the wall, if you please."

Elizabeth had kindly thought to bring a basket that Rosalind presumed contained something for breakfast. She had not, however, thought to bring a weapon of any sort.

Had not expected Rosalind to now be standing between her and the stillroom's only readily accessible exit.

"You won't—" Elizabeth began.

"Do not doubt for a moment that I will."

Rosalind watched impassively while Elizabeth gauged the distance between them, and then looked for a long moment at Rosalind's eyes.

It was entirely possible that Elizabeth's experience with horses had taught her how to understand when she was confronted by a being who was truly dangerous. Because she took a deep breath, and did as she was told.

Once Elizabeth was seated, Rosalind backed out the door, and closed it. Her arms shook as she lifted the bar and set it in place. That would not buy her as much time as she would like. It would not take Elizabeth long to scrabble up onto the stove and break open the grating. Perhaps that window was too small for her to wriggle through, but perhaps it was not. Rosalind needed to find Adam at once and—

That was when she heard a man scream.

By the time he heard someone coming down the stairs, Adam's feet were numb and his hands ached. The sound that reached him was the heavy clomp of boots, so this was most likely Spence, come to check on him, fetch him out, or kill him.

He steeled himself, willed his cold, stiff frame to do as he required.

Rosalind is expecting you, he reminded himself.

He'd found the leather pouch that had caught in his mind. It was on the second shelf that he'd carefully run his bound hands over. The minute his fingertips reached inside it, he understood why memory had held onto it for him, and why he'd thought of the window upstairs. It was a workman's pouch. It had lain beside a small, light hammer, and it was filled with nails.

Unfortunately, the hammer's shaft was broken, so it was of little use as a weapon. But the nails had given him an idea.

Now, the cellar door opened. Adam held his breath.

Spence raised his lantern, and his knife. He looked at the cellar floor, and saw Adam was not there.

Adam did not give him time to see anything else. He flung himself forward. The weight of his body knocked Spence to the floor, and onto the heap of nails Adam had poured out there.

Spence screamed and rolled and scrabbled, thrown into a panic by the sudden pain as nails bit into his hands and arms. Adam rolled to the side and up onto his knees. He raised his fists, one of which held the head from the broken hammer, and slammed them down on Spence's skull.

The blow landed. Spence fell still.

The light from the open door showed Adam where the knife had fallen. As quickly as he could, Adam inched his way forward and grabbed it up in his bound hands. He let himself fall back onto his buttocks and flipped the blade around.

He had just set the edge of the blade against the rope binding his ankles when the cellar door flew open. A silhouette in skirts charged down the stairs.

It was Rosalind. It was Rosalind wielding a broken bottle like a doxy in a tavern brawl, her hair streaming down around her shoulders.

He had never seen anything so beautiful in all his life.

"Adam!" She bent over him.

"Careful!" He waved toward the scattered nails, and the fallen man.

Rosalind stared at Spence's unconscious form, and then at Adam. Adam shrugged, and held the knife out to her. They'd swap stories later.

Rosalind tossed her broken bottle away and took the knife from his hands. She sliced the cords that bound his hands and feet. Adam gave a great, gusting sigh mixed with relief and pain as the hot blood rushed back into his fingers and toes.

Rosalind handed the knife toward him. He reached for it, and froze.

"You're hurt," he said thickly, looking at her bloodied fingers.

"We'll worry about it later," Rosalind informed him. "We need to get out of here. If Elizabeth hasn't already escaped the stillroom, she will soon." She looked down at Spence, who had not moved at all since she'd come flying down the cellar steps.

"Is he—"

Adam rolled Spence over and put his hand against the man's mouth.

"No," he said as he straightened up. "But he's going to be in a foul mood when he wakes up. I'll go to the stables and deal with the horses. You go inside the house and see if you can find the guns."

They barred the cellar door and stumbled up the stairs into the gray dawn. Adam staggered toward the stables. Rosalind did her best to prod her reluctant feet into something approaching a run to the cottage's kitchen door. There, as she hoped, she found the two guns—not to mention a powder horn, ramrod, and ammunition pouch lying on the kitchen's plank table. Evidently, Mr. Spence had been cleaning and priming the weapons last night.

She slung the pouch and horn over her shoulder and grabbed up the long arm and the pistol. She pushed the door open and stumbled across the yard. But as she reached the stables, she saw the stone horse trough, filled to overflowing from last night's rain.

An idea occurred to her.

*   *   *

"Where are the guns?" asked Adam as Rosalind ducked empty-handed through the stable door.

"In the horse trough," Rosalind told him. "Along with the powder horn and ammunition pouch."

Adam raised his brows.

"I didn't think we'd have time to shoot anyone while we were escaping," she said.

"Reasonable," he replied. "The truth is, it would have been difficult to carry them. We will be on horseback, I'm afraid, and there's only one horse."

Rosalind felt her throat clamp shut. "But . . . we came here in a coach-and-four!"

"Which, I expect, has been returned to their rightful owner, whoever that might be. All we have left is Doppelgänger." He finished cinching up the stirrups.

"Doppelgänger?" Rosalind echoed.

"The lookalike for Kinsdale's Pride." Adam patted the animal's side. "Doppelgänger."

Rosalind looked at the gray horse. The horse looked back and rolled its eye until the white showed.

Rosalind looked at Adam.

"It's not a sidesaddle," he said as he gave the girth one last tug. "You'll have to be astride."

"I don't think that's the part we need to worry about," said Rosalind.

"Truthfully, neither do I," Adam admitted. "But she's all we've got. Take hold of the pommel, put your left foot in the stirrup, and hold your breath."

Rosalind did as instructed. Adam grabbed her by the waist and lifted her up. Skirts, fear, and inexperience made her clumsy, but after a moment's exclaiming and scrabbling, Rosalind found herself in the saddle, with Adam behind her.

Doppelgänger whickered and stamped, clearly displeased with this turn of events. Adam gathered the reins. Had Rosalind had the leisure to admit it, she would have found the press of his arms and his chest against her quite thrilling.

She could have done very well without the horse.

The horse stamped again. She also backed and tried to turn, making it known that she could have done very well without Rosalind.

"Settle, settle," said Adam to them both. "We are doing this whether you like it or not."

Rosalind gripped the entirely inadequate nub of the pommel and closed her eyes. Adam leaned forward, bending them both low over the horse's neck. He kicked. The horse screamed high and hard, and bolted forward, like it meant to leave them behind.

Rosalind had been afraid in her life before, but not like this. The jolting, thundering ride through the watery dawn, her whole frame shaken beyond endurance, no control over herself, her speed, her balance, her breath. The horse veered and shifted and Adam cursed and shouted and Rosalind locked in the middle, her mind spinning so she could not even pray. She kept her eyes screwed shut, but fear would have blinded her anyway.

Did she hear hoofbeats behind them? Shouts? She didn't know. She couldn't even make herself open her eyes. She felt Adam bending them both even lower, heard him yelling, felt him slap the reins against the animal's neck, felt the fresh, outraged burst of speed.

Then, just as suddenly, Adam reined them all back. The horse wickered in its fury, weaved sideways, and finally spun in a tight circle and—finally, blessedly—came to a halt.

There were voices. Rosalind felt she should know them. Adam was gone from behind her, leaving her alone on the trembling, shifting horse.

"Come on, now," said Adam softly. "You can let go, Rosalind."

Rosalind was not certain she could, but she did crack her eyelids open.

And in front of her saw Devon on the driver's box of a light gig, with Clara Kinsdale beside him. In the next moment, she realized they must have been coming up this narrow lane as she and Adam were barreling in the opposite direction.

She also realized they were gaping at her.

Then, she realized there *were* hoofbeats behind them and shouting. Because there were two more horses coming up the lane from the direction she and Adam had fled. Panic and fury rose up together. She twisted around in the saddle, making the horse dance dangerously.

If they think to take us back . . .

But in the next moment, she saw that their pursuers were none other than Mr. Tauton and Mr. Goutier.

Relief loosened her grip on the saddle's pommel, and Adam was obliged to catch her about the waist and swing her down from the saddle before she toppled to the ground.

"What on earth are you all doing here!" she cried as Adam set her onto her feet. At least, she meant to cry. The words came out more as a croak.

"We were coming to rescue you," said Devon.

"We'd brought a ransom," added Clara.

"We rather thought you might need some help dealing with your captors," added Mr. Goutier, bringing his black horse to a halt besides Doppelgänger.

Mr. Tauton just threw back his head and howled with laughter.

"Should have known!" he bellowed. "God in heaven, we should have known you'd be gone before we could get here!"

Rosalind felt herself smiling. But the relief, on top of all that had happened already, was too much. She felt her knees beginning to buckle.

"I . . . I think I may need to sit down."

There followed a somewhat confused period where Clara, Devon, and Adam all surrounded Rosalind and boosted her into the gig. Clara climbed in beside her, glared at the men, and immediately pulled out a reticule that proved to contain an inordinate number of clean handkerchiefs, and bottles of both violet water and spirits of alcohol. From somewhere else a flask was produced that proved to contain strong tea laced with brandy.

In that moment, Rosalind found herself liking Clara Kinsdale a great deal.

While Clara cleaned and bound her injured hands, Adam was explaining to Devon where they had been and what had happened. In return, Devon was telling Adam that they were only a few miles from Bath, while Mr. Goutier and Mr. Harkness explained that they had been watching the cottage from the nearby woods, ready to follow Elizabeth Kinsdale and Nathanial Spence.

"Imagine our surprise when you two come bursting out of the stables like the devil himself is behind you! Almost fell off my horse!" cried Mr. Tauton.

"We need to get back at once," Adam told them. "Elizabeth Kinsdale and Nathanial Spence are still back there, and if they haven't . . ."

"No need," said Mr. Goutier. "We brought a couple of Bath constables with us. That pair will be in custody by now."

Clara went as pale as Rosalind felt. Rosalind covered her suddenly cold hand with her bandaged one.

"I'm sorry," Rosalind said.

Clara pressed her lips together and shook her head. "I'm just glad it's finally over. It . . ." She swallowed. "It is over, isn't it?"

"Almost," Rosalind told her. "There's just one more thing that needs doing."

CHAPTER 55

The Exact Circumstances

"Hear the truth, therefore, now, while you are un-prejudiced."

Jane Austen, *Persuasion*

Adam wanted her to rest. Clara insisted she at least eat something. Mr. Tauton and Mr. Goutier thought it would be prudent if she first gave her statement, and then took extra constables with her on her errand.

In the end, Rosalind agreed to stop at the Green Briar long enough to change her clothing and have Laurel and Mrs. Leigh between them clean and bandage her hands, and also find a pair of gloves large enough to fit over the fresh dressing. As a concession to her lingering weakness, she agreed to let Adam drive her to the Kinsdales' house on his way to the City police station where he meant to reconvene with Devon, Mr. Goutier, Mr. Tauton, and Mr. Layng.

She begged Clara to stay with Devon, and somewhat to her surprise, Clara agreed.

"I want to hear the whole story before I speak with Elizabeth," she'd said. "Or Cynthia."

So, when Rosalind climbed out of the carriage in front of the Kinsdales' house, she was quite alone.

"I will only ask once," said Adam as he helped her down. "Do you want me to stay?"

Rosalind took a deep breath. "Mrs. Kendricks is here, and the staff is all her people. She will take care of anything that comes up."

Adam smiled his tiny, beautiful, crooked smile. "Probably better than either of us could."

"Probably so." Rosalind paused and looked into his eyes, seeing that he was whole and well, if a little battered and pale. "Will you be all right?"

"As long as I know that you will be," he told her. "I'll be back to fetch you in an hour. Will that be time enough?"

"I think so."

He kissed her gloved and bandaged hands. Rosalind stayed where she was and watched while he climbed, a little more stiffly than was his wont, up onto the box and touched up the horses. It was only when he had rounded the curve of the Circus and rounded the corner into the next street that she turned and walked up the steps to the front door.

Duggin let her in. Mrs. Kendricks exclaimed over her, and embraced her and cried a little with her, a thing they would both resolutely deny happened when stories were told later.

"I trust Miss Cynthia is here?" Rosalind asked her.

"She hasn't left her room," said Mrs. Kendricks. "We've been watching closely."

Rosalind pressed her friend's hands and turned to face the stairs. She took a deep breath and put her hand on the railing, when movement caught her eye. She looked up. Cynthia stood at the top of the stairs looking down at her.

"I expect you wish to talk with me," said Cynthia.

"I do," said Rosalind.

"Well, do come up then." With that, she turned and began climbing back toward the family rooms.

When Rosalind reached what had been the sisters' private rooms, she found Cynthia sitting at the writing table by the window. The drapes had been pulled open to allow the daylight in. Cynthia was looking down on the narrow garden, and the crowd of statues and the empty pied-à-terre. She looked, Rosalind thought, exhausted, grim, and entirely alone.

Rosalind reached into her sleeve and pulled out a handkerchief. She took out the broken ring on its ruined chain and laid them on the table.

Cynthia looked down. She blinked.

"May I take it that Elizabeth has been found?"

"Yes. And Nathanial Spence with her."

"I see."

Rosalind waited to see if Cynthia would say anything else. Her head hurt, her hands hurt. Her legs were protesting at having to keep holding her upright. She was now very much regretting that she had not stopped for anything more than a slice of bread and cheese. She found she did not want to continue this conversation, that for one of the few times in her life, she really did not want to know anything more. She wanted to leave this room, walk down the stairs and out the door, and have nothing else to do with this house, this family, these lives and these deaths.

But, of course, she could not do that.

"Why did you agree to lie for Elizabeth?" Rosalind asked.

Cynthia bit her lip.

"Because of bad luck," she said finally. "Because there has been nothing but bad luck for me, and my son, and my poor lost Jack from the beginning."

"Was Jack your husband?"

Cynthia started, but then covered her mouth, holding back another of her mirthless laughs. "Johnathan Walsingham, but everyone called him Jack." She laid her hand on top of the broken, begrimed ring. "He was the admiral's youngest brother. The boy at Kinsdale House who so alarmed my father is our son."

"Why did you choose to marry in secret?" asked Rosalind. "Did your father not approve of the match?"

Cynthia shook her head. "He did not, for so many reasons, all of them ridiculous, except possibly for the fact that Jack had no money of his own." She bowed her head. "But Jack said he would quickly remedy that. He said as long as I was his, he could do anything."

Rosalind nodded.

"We married in Lyme," Cynthia went on. "Jack swore his brother to secrecy, took half my wedding ring and our marriage certificates as both proof and love token, and sailed away. He was sure—we were sure—he would come back with a fortune in prize money. But he didn't." Her voice dropped to a whisper. "He didn't come back at all."

"I'm sorry," said Rosalind.

"Yes." Cynthia's fingers curled slowly around her ruined wedding ring. "So am I. I think I shall never stop being sorry." Her eyes were bright with the tears she would not permit to fall. "When I got the news that his ship had gone down, I knew I was with child. I broke the news to his family. They offered to take me in, and dare my family's opinion. I should have accepted." For the first time, anger sharpened her tone. "But I was afraid and a fool and grieving and I could not think straight. I thought I'd wait until Clara was safely married to make a clean breast of my scandals. So, I bore my son in secret, and I gave him to his aunt and uncle to raise, and I came back home as if nothing had happened." She looked toward the windows. "For three years, I pretended nothing at all had happened."

"Until you arranged for the admiral to let Kinsdale House."

Cynthia's smile was bitter. "Clara took rather longer to make up her mind than anyone expected, and up until this very year, I was not sure what she'd eventually decide. I thought with the admiral at Kinsdale House, I'd be able to manage to see my son more frequently. If I could just bide my time, I'd be able to explain to Lord Casselmaine that there was a legitimate male heir to the Kinsdale estate. His grace is a rational man. He would understand the way of it, and not fight the thing."

"Unlike your father," said Rosalind. There it was, the real reason she had kept such a secret for so long. She knew Sir Anthony's vanity, and his desperation. She feared her father would turn on her and attempt to brand her son a bastard, and that he might just succeed.

This realization led to another. "Did Elizabeth find out about your son?"

"Elizabeth had found my copy of the birth certificate," she said. "And my marriage certificate. I don't know how long she'd known about them, but, after our father died she came to me and she informed me she had them both." Cynthia looked down at her fist. "She said she'd burn both papers if I did not help her. I was to confirm the statement she swore out to the coroner, or she would make the world believe that my son was illegitimate."

Which would mean he could not inherit the Kinsdale estate, even as encumbered as it was. Rosalind waited, curious to see if Cynthia would say the rest.

Cynthia met Rosalind's gaze, but what she saw there, Rosalind could not guess. Whatever it might have been, it was Cynthia who spoke next.

"And, yes, she also said that she would confess to the world that it was not Mrs. Lynn she heard arguing with my father."

"It was you," said Rosalind.

"Yes." Cynthia rubbed her eyes with her free hand. "After the admiral came to the house, after he showed himself to be at the very end of his patience—I was afraid of what he'd do next. He might break his vow to Jack and tell everyone about my marriage, and about . . . whatever else it was he knew. I realized then that matters had gone too far. That my cowardice, my obedience to my father . . . everything, it had clouded all my better judgment. The Walsinghams had been so patient, and cared so much for my son. . . . So, I decided I would be brave." The ghost of a smile crossed her feet. "The truth was, I knew that everything was falling apart as it was, so I thought I couldn't do any more damage by confronting my father.

"And so I did," Cynthia said. "I watched as Mrs. Lynn deposited him in his room. I watched Thrush leave, carrying his coat, and I went in. He was very surprised to see me. He was even more surprised when I told him I was done with silence and secrets. I told him about my marriage and my son and that I was done protecting him, or anyone else in our family."

"What did he say?" asked Rosalind.

Cynthia's expression hardened. "He raised his quizzing glass and he looked at me through it." Each word was sharp as glass and just as clear. "He sneered and he drawled and he described what he thought he saw in front of him. I was . . . well, I will not repeat it. But I ask you to imagine what it's like, Miss Thorne, to hear your father turn on you with such disdain. To hear him bleat about his injuries and how all his daughters showed was ingratitude when we should have given him everything . . .

"My temper shattered. I screamed at him. I don't even remember what I said. But he turned his back on me and said that I should leave his house. Now, at once, with only the clothes I stood up in." She stopped. She drew in a short, sharp breath. "I lost my mind, I think. I picked up a candlestick, and I swung it at him."

Rosalind waited.

"I meant to kill him," said Cynthia. "I'm sure that I did. I hit him in the head, and he toppled over and lay still, and . . ." She shook her head hard. "I don't remember much after that. I remember stamping out the candle flame because the carpet had caught. I remember being back in the hallway. I remember waking in my bed, although I was sure I had not been asleep. I remember the sounds of screaming.

"I remember Elizabeth coming back in and telling me that father was dead and that she knew it was my fault. She knew about my marriage and had helped herself to my proof, and would hold on to it, 'for safekeeping,' she said."

Cynthia stopped, and it was a long moment before she could go on.

"It was only afterward I found out that the admiral was dead," she breathed. "Only then I fully realized that if the greater world found out about my son . . . that they, that his grace, and Clara, and . . . everyone, would think I'd killed him because he was going to expose my secret. Was perhaps going to say that the marriage was a sham and that my son was illegitimate."

"So you agreed to say it was Mrs. Lynn," said Rosalind.

Cynthia didn't bother to answer. "What will happen now?"

Rosalind drew herself up. She laid her hand over Cynthia's fist, curled so tightly around her ring and the memory of her love.

"Now," she said. "We will see that the truth is told."

"And after that?" she whispered.

Rosalind pressed her hand. "After that, we will all find ways to heal."

CHAPTER 56

Endings, Which Are Also Beginnings

Who can be in doubt of what followed?

Jane Austen, *Persuasion*

The trial in the matter of the death of Admiral Robert Walsingham was a brief and straightforward affair. The only man suspected in the affair, Nathanial Spence, confessed and let himself be taken quietly away. The woman for whom he risked all was not beside him. Elizabeth Kinsdale had died of fever while in custody and was buried beside her father in the village churchyard, with all her family in attendance. It was speculated in some circles that her death was what finally removed Mr. Spence's desire to resist his fate.

The matter of the death of Sir Anthony Kinsdale never came before the magistrates. The coroner's jury, upon hearing the full circumstances as related by Mr. Adam Harkness, Mr. Sampson Goutier, Mr. Samuel Tauton, and Devon Winterbourne, Lord Casselmaine, and further sworn to by Miss Rosalind Thorne and Miss Cynthia Kinsdale, and her sister, Miss Clara Kinsdale, ruled the matter death by misadventure.

In an entirely separate matter, a certain Miss Smith and Mr. Wallace were taken up by the constables as they attempted to board a ferry at Dover. A letter of thanks was later sent to

Mr. Sanderson Faulks and another to Mrs. Charlotte Black from Bow Street.

Miss Alice Littlefield afterward denied this incident was in any way the inspiration for her highly popular adventure novel. No one believed her.

Cynthia Kinsdale returned to her family's home and there lived quietly, acting as trustee and guardian for her young son, Johnathan, who would inherit the estate and the title when he came of age. Any potential contest or irregularity over the matters was quickly settled when the vicar of the Church of St. Brendan's on the Shore proved perfectly ready to swear that he had indeed married Miss Kinsdale to Captain Johnathan "Jack" Walsingham five years before.

Clara Kinsdale and Lord Casselmaine were married in a quiet, private ceremony, and left at once on their honeymoon trip to the Continent.

When September arrived, Rosalind and Adam were married quietly at her parish church. The Reverend Mr. Button expressed his deep satisfaction with the event, and intoned the words of the service with a level of feeling that rendered the ceremoney all the more meaningful. Not that Rosalind followed much of it. To her embarrassment, her mind kept drifting away from the sacred admonitions and to the fact of Adam beside her, warm and whole and real.

Adam bowed his head as they knelt together, but his smile never quite left his face.

The wedding breakfast was held at the Harkness family home. Adam's mother insisted that it should be so, and Rosalind was not about to start married life by arguing with her new mother-in-law. The weather remained fine and the family took over the common yard between the houses. They festooned it with flowers and set up a dozen trestle tables. The entire neighborhood feasted on the efforts of Adam's mother and sisters, and Sampson Goutier and Sam Tauton rolled in barrels of ale, supported by the Harkness brothers and brothers-in-law.

A far more decorous meal was held at Orchard Street. Organized by Sanderson Faulks and presided over by Alice and George Littlefield, it was attended by select members of the *haut ton*. The next day, the whole affair was described in glowing terms in the major papers as an excellent match, uniting two of London's hidden treasures into a harmonious whole that would be sure to grace society's homes for years to come.

Alice denied that she had dictated the words personally. No one believed this, either.